I. A. F Stewart lives in Leeds, Yorkshire, with her husband and their large collection of movie memorabilia. She studied art and design at Wakefield College, specialising in fashion photography and illustration, but writing has always been her true passion. She has been creating stories since she learned to write. *The Quiet Place* is her first book.

To my mother, Elizabeth, who taught me to work hard and dream a little, and Glenn, my partner in everything, who taught me to dream hard and work a little.

I. A. F. Stewart

THE QUIET PLACE

AUSTIN MACAULEY PUBLISHERS™

LONDON ∗ CAMBRIDGE ∗ NEW YORK ∗ SHARJAH

A CIP catalogue record for this title is available from the British Library.

ISBN 9781398404915 (Paperback)
ISBN 9781398404922 (ePub-e book)

www.austinmacauley.com

First Published (2021)
Austin Macauley Publishers Ltd
25 Canada Square
Canary Wharf
London
E14 5LQ

Being my first novel and written largely from my imagination and life experience, my acknowledgements are not a comprehensive list of professionals, rather a more personal tribute to all those who have supported and believed in me, even when I didn't believe in myself. While I slogged away at my story, cocooned in a bubble of my own making, these individuals kept me going through the highs and lows. A huge thanks to them personally, and all my other family and friends I didn't have space to name individually.

Firstly, thank you to Austin Macauley publishers who gave me a chance, and without whom this wouldn't have been possible. Your faith in me – a first-time author – and, of course, your funding has allowed my dream to become reality.

I have a select group of friends who are the most supportive and amazing friends a person could wish for. Thank you especially to Rachel and Robyn, who gave me the kick I needed to stop talking about it and get it done. If it wasn't for you, my story would still be imprisoned in my mind rather than on these pages. To Rachel especially, for listening to me stress and rant about my story since it first entered my head ten years ago. You're one in a million, girl.

Amy, you have motivated me at every turn and believed in me wholeheartedly. I'll never forget it. Jodi, thank you for being the official first reader! Your patience during my rants, your excitable nature and your kind words meant more to me than you know.

Now, for my family, both blood and by marriage. You truly are the most diverse, interesting and special group of people. Your stories and lives have both shaped me and inspired me.

To the Stewarts – especially Mick and Lesley, who have consistently and completely maintained faith in me, thank you for everything.

To my mum, Liz, and her husband, Michael, I don't know what I'd do without you. You are always a grounding force and rational voice when I lose my head and my reason floats away.

To my dad, Stuart, who introduced me to so many fantastic authors, bands, films and artists. It is from you that I inherited my vivid imagination and love of all things creative, dark and weird.

Most importantly, thank you to my husband Glenn, who has put up with my moods (both the incredibly high and the incredibly low), supported my every decision and motivated me every step of the way. You're my inspiration, my life raft, my everything. My very own quiet place.

Chapter One

Let me tell you a story. My story is not that of your average person and yet, it is one that most people will be able to relate to. It's the story of me and my life, the people I've met, the things I've done and the places I've been. I've experienced terrible, crushing lows and glorious, intoxicating highs, suffered through loss and been reunited with people I never thought I'd see again and I've struggled, at times, to understand myself and my place in this world. Sound familiar?

Life, for everyone on this planet, is a balance between good and bad, happiness and sadness, beginnings and endings. What makes my story unique is my, let's call them, abilities. Ever since I was a child, I've been able to see another world within our own. At first, I believed this other world was in my head; a delusion or hallucination that my mind had created, possibly as some kind of defence mechanism or safe place to retreat to. Now, I know it *is* real and it is as much a part of me and my history as anything else.

First, let's start at the beginning.

I am Sara Black. My childhood was pretty standard for a British family— picnics in the park, weekend trips to the seaside, getting dragged around boring supermarkets, bedtime stories, stiff school uniforms, packed lunches, paddling in the sea, sunny days in November and unexpected downpours in the summer— except that I was raised by my mother's two sisters instead of my parents.

My father was a sergeant in the British Army, killed in action before I was born. My mother was a creative, artistic type; a free spirit, or some crap like that, who, after my father's death, took off and left me with my aunts.

My aunts gave me their family name instead of my father's out of no disrespect to his memory; they just wanted me to feel a sense of belonging as I knew nothing of my father's family.

My childhood was happy. We had our problems and hills to climb, like all families do, but we also had a lot of love for one another in our own unique ways. I can say this now with hindsight of course, but as a child, you view the world differently. Everything appears black and white—it's only as adults that we start to see the greys.

I started life as a cripplingly shy, quiet, sensitive soul, who loved being creative and hiding away from the outside world in my bedroom, imagining my own stories and worlds.

I didn't like other children; I spent all my time with adults and that was the way I liked it. When I was thrown amongst those of the same age as me, I felt lost. Some may say being an only child would explain some of that.

I never met my father and had very little memory of my mother; therefore, I could only see them through the eyes of those who had known them. All I surmised of my mum was that she was weak and couldn't handle responsibility. She carried me for nine months, popped me out and then disappeared. Where? I didn't know and I didn't really want to know, so I didn't ask; not for a long while anyway.

I lived with my aunt Lyanna. She poured her heart and soul into my upbringing and tried her best to help me feel like I wasn't missing out on anything. She gave up her career and social life and worked a café job, which she hated (she never explicitly said this to me, but I knew that she did), to provide for us both. She never complained though, not to me in any case.

My second aunt, Serafina, also provided for me in her own way and helped Lyanna out when she wasn't too busy, but somehow, I always felt like she begrudged the whole situation. I never felt close to her in those early years, not like I did with Lyanna, who had effectively become my mother.

Aunt Lyanna was the youngest of the three Black sisters and took on the youngest sibling stereotype: wild, free and a little spoiled. She was always the centre of attention and her parents fussed over her, which she loved.

Before I came along, she was a questionable, untrustworthy character. When *anything* bad happened—no matter how big or small—she was nowhere to be found. She was consumed by her own vanity and sense of self-worth. She never cared for anybody but herself.

The truth is that she did care really, she just didn't know how to show it. She was sheltered and pandered to as a child, showered with affection yet nothing was ever expected of her in return. Lyanna could be selfish and nasty and she thrived on drama; however, she was usually the sole creator of any drama in her life.

One of her favourite things to do was wind Serafina up. Serafina had a stick up her arse and wanted to ruin Lyanna's fun…well, that was how she saw it anyway. When Lyanna started dating boys in high school, Serafina would endeavour to embarrass her. She would ask question after question. Who is he? Have they slept together? Did she have any self-respect?

My mother, Evelien, was much more like Lyanna than Serafina; always up for going out and having a good time. Serafina was entirely different from her sisters. Her idea of fun was staying at home, surrounded by 'boring' books while her sisters tore up the town.

Lyanna and Evelien were pretty much inseparable during their teenage years and Lyanna believed it would always be that way. It was, until Evelien met the love of her life—my father, Mark Bannerman. The youngest sister found that hard to deal with. It was a betrayal to her, dramatic and selfish as she was. She felt like she'd lost her sister, her best friend.

Lyanna hated that my dad was a 'regular' guy who wanted to do 'normal' things. He was a loser in her eyes, who had turned up and showed her party partner what real life was like. Who wanted a traditional life? A life consisting of work and staying in and responsibilities? Lyanna now felt that it was her against the world.

So, she went off the rails for a time, fell out with both of her sisters and jumped from idiot guy to idiot guy, leeching friend to leeching friend. She was never careful or responsible; life was a whirlwind of parties, hangers-on and stupid decisions.

Then, I was born. Lyanna was so close to destroying her life but I brought her back from the brink of destruction. I was a small, soft light, shining through the fog. She told me I was the most beautiful sight she had ever seen. I saved her life and gave it meaning.

When my mother left us, it was down to my aunts to look after me, to raise me and give me the best life they could. They did eventually make up, though they didn't always see eye to eye. They tried to make it work for me.

Lyanna finally took some responsibility and she felt love, true love. Nobody and nothing else mattered in the world except that little girl—me.

When my nana and grandpa died, it was left to Serafina to look after her two younger siblings. They were some trouble, those two. When they were younger, she had loved that mischievousness and spirit, it had warmed her heart but as Lyanna got older, she had tried to push it too far. She became cruel and selfish, like there was a huge void in her life that she was desperate to fill. That void, of course, was her mum and dad and all the affection they had showered her with, which was now displaced. Lyanna resented Serafina for trying to help her and provide for them. Her rebellion was her way of saying 'you can never replace them'. That hurt Serafina profoundly.

Serafina was studying to become a librarian, following her dream and creating a happy life for herself but parallel to that, she was working all the hours she could to give her two sisters a safe and comfortable living environment.

Serafina never got the chance to grow up. She was a child and then an adult; there was nothing in-between. Even towards the end of her parents' lives, she was really the only one in the family with a sensible head on her shoulders. She was always the older, responsible sister and was never treated like a princess like the other two. Her parents put too much pressure on her and once they were gone, she had taken it upon herself to become her sisters' guardian, rather than letting them fall through the cracks of the system.

The sisters continued to live together even after Lyanna and Evelien came of age but Serafina never quite shook off her role as their guardian. She never wanted to be branded the 'boring' one, but her studies and her future meant so much to her. She could always see the bigger picture.

Things got rough for Serafina a few years later. Five years into her relationship with Jack Radcliffe—a man she had been in a relationship with since she was a teenager—he beat her so bad that her sisters didn't recognise her. Serafina was aware of his darker side—he had always had a fiery temper—but this had come as a total shock to her. To rub salt in the wound, she found out around the same time that he had been having an affair.

My mother was spending all her time with my father at this point and was hardly ever around, so Lyanna was the only person Serafina could really turn to, but she didn't want to know. She thought Serafina was weak and foolish, especially after she took Jack back. So, Serafina just got on with it all alone and eventually, things started to look up for her. Jack didn't make any more "mistakes", not that she was aware of anyway, and she landed a job at the local library once she finished her degree. She was finally content and proud of her simple life.

Then, my mum had me and disappeared off the face of the earth. Lyanna was desperate to raise me alone but Serafina felt that she couldn't be trusted with that level of responsibility, so they set about raising me together. Jack couldn't handle all the attention I was taking away from him, so he left her. All Serafina had left was her work (which luckily, she loved), a sister she could barely stand the sight of and somebody else's child to take care of. She tried as hard as she could not to take her bitterness out on me but there were times when I couldn't help but feel I had ruined her life. I didn't. She has since assured me of that, but when I was younger, believing that caused a whole load of issues.

I love both of my aunts immeasurably but in totally different ways. They are two extremely unique women who I am forever grateful to. They each contributed to who I am as a person. They laid the foundations upon which I was able to build my life; they were unstable, abstruse foundations, but foundations, nonetheless. What more can you ask of two people who had their lives upheaved because of the actions of a confused, angry woman who didn't know how to react to the situation she had found herself in?

Looking back, I can now see that you can never really see or understand the whole story. You can never truly judge someone's actions because everything is affected by everything else; everyone's paths are intertwined and stories connected, all orbiting one another and altering each other's fates. Every action has a consequence and it's our job as people, family members, friends, partners and members of society to deal with these consequences and help each other in the best way that we can.

This is the story of my life, but a life is not a life without the people around you helping you learn and grow and forge connections. We are all supporting characters in each other's stories.

There is no moral to this tale. It is not a how-to (or how-not-to) guide. It is just me and my quest for a quiet mind; a place where I can be myself, where I can feel comfortable with my past and present without the demons sitting on my back. A place where everyone hopes to get to in life: the quiet place.

Chapter Two

It was a fresh, warm, sunny day at the end of April. I was woken by the sound of birdsong drifting through my open window—the night had been humid—and the glow of daylight bouncing off my bedroom walls.

I opened the curtains and looked out over the golden fields and woodland behind our cul-de-sac. I squinted my eyes as the early morning sunlight highlighted my lime-green bedroom walls (yes, lime green, I don't know what possessed me) and my various Winnie the Pooh and Disney posters.

I had one of those loft beds—a bunk bed with a space below for my desk and beanbag chair. There was a small wardrobe in the corner of my room, upon which sat most of my teddies (the ones I could bear to sleep without) and next to it, a box full of Barbies and Polly Pockets. I loved my tall bed, my fortress. I felt as safe as could be up there, where there were no dark spaces beneath for the monsters to hide in.

The smell of burning toast wafting up from downstairs enticed me out of my comfy pit. I threw on my Piglet dressing gown and matching slippers, descended the ladder at the edge of my bed and trudged down the stairs, still encased within the thick fog of sleep-brain.

Serafina was sat at the end of the kitchen island reading a magazine, her dark, frizzy hair in a wild tangle around her studious face. Lyanna was buttering toast and turned to greet me with a glowing smile upon her face.

'Good morning, gummy bear.' She smiled brightly, kissing me on the head and smoothing down my knotted hair. The nickname 'gummy bear' was gifted to me as when I smiled, my top lip lifted high enough to reveal almost all my top gums. It still does, in fact.

'Hi,' I replied, as cheerily as I could, still half-asleep.

'Hey kid,' Serafina croaked in her husky voice, the result of her morning coffee and cigarette. I always found it strange that Serafina would disappear outside for five minutes at a time, coming back smelling odd—like a barbeque, only less tasty.

I sat and ate my two slices of toast—one pale and slightly squidgy, the other black around the edges. I was perched on a high stool, swinging my legs back and forth, scrunching my toes up to try and stop my slippers from flying off.

Lyanna sat herself down opposite me and asked me what I wanted to do that day. I looked through the patio doors on to our spring garden coming into bloom and decided right then that I wanted to go somewhere outdoors.

'Well, how about we go to Peake Lake?' Serafina suggested, tearing her eyes away from the article she was reading and perching her reading glasses on her head.

'What's there?' I questioned, slightly dubious, as I was with anywhere new.

'Well, there's lots of trees and wildlife and flowers, places for a picnic and some pubs and cafés down the road. And, of course, there's the lake itself. We could go for a paddle?'

I mulled it over in my head briefly and decided I'd like that. 'Yeah,' I nodded.

Lyanna clapped her hands together. 'Right, let's get you ready then!'

I picked out my own outfit, as usual, deciding on lilac shorts, a white t-shirt with a smiling rainbow on the front and a pair of silver trainers, plus a pair of navy socks. Lyanna told me they didn't match my outfit, but I didn't care as they were really comfy.

I tied my hair up in 'Mickey Mouse' buns, as I liked to call them, with tiny rainbow-coloured scrunchies. I thought I looked brilliant. The car rides on day trips were always one of my favourite parts of the day: the anticipation of getting to your destination, the selection of Jelly Babies, Opal Fruits and Drumstick lollies to munch on and the comfort of watching the pretty scenery flash by the window.

I looked ahead and saw the mid-morning sunbeams streaking through the windscreen, illuminating Lyanna's peroxide blonde hair and creating the illusion that her head was a bright, fluffy cloud. 'Are you okay back there?' she asked.

'Yep!' I replied, with a mouth full of sticky lolly. My teeth were glued together so it sounded like 'Gah!'

We reached our destination late morning and pulled into the carpark; the sound of gravel crunching beneath the tyres forever etched in my memory. I jumped out of the car when Serafina opened the door and instantly felt the small stones through the foamy soles of my trainers.

She rubbed sunscreen all over my face, arms and legs, slap-dash, leaving me with a scrunched-up face and globs of white cream smeared all over me. I rubbed it in so that I looked less like an ice-cream.

That day is one of my favourite memories from my childhood, but it was also a day when I realised that I was growing up, no matter how much I didn't want to. I noticed things I never had before, having always seen the world through the rainbow-tinted glasses of an innocent child.

We walked through seemingly endless woodland and I marvelled at how the beams of sunlight pierced through the branches overhead. We ate 99s and I revelled in the taste of the creamy vanilla ice cream coupled with the crunchy chocolate flake. We said polite hellos to other families, and I listened to the sound of other children screeching. I thought that I either wished I was like them or that they would shut up so I could hear the quiet. I walked along between Lyanna and Serafina, holding a hand each, and every now and then, they would swing me up into the air, making my tummy shoot up into my mouth.

The lake itself made me gawp. To me, it was positively the biggest, prettiest and scariest thing I'd ever seen. Families dotted the shore with their picnic blankets spread out and their rucksacks brimming with snacks, baby wipes and spare socks. The sharp shingle tried to bar our way to the water, but it gradually dispersed as we walked closer, allowing us right up to the water's edge.

The surface of the lake sparkled with sun-drops and the azure water kissed the shore lazily. Some part of me however couldn't help but wonder what lay beyond the shore in the depths of the lake. Could there be a Loch Ness monster (or something like it) hidden in those depths? The thought both terrified and excited me in equal measure.

We set up camp in a sandy alcove overlooked by pine trees and Lyanna took off my clothes to reveal the tankini I was wearing beneath. The sun was at its highest point in the sky; the temperature must have been over 25 degrees Celsius (hot for England) so she forced a silly hat down over my head to protect me.

I paddled and splashed in the water with my aunts for what seemed like hours. Lyanna stayed in with me the whole time, but Serafina kept retreating to our spot in the shade of the trees to write something down in her scruffy notepad, or to read a few pages of the door-wedge book she carried around with her.

It was getting towards evening and time for home. On the way back to the car, I took more notice of the people around us—families with two children or more throwing sticks to their dogs or running after each other, fathers carrying their daughters or sons on their shoulders and mothers brushing the grit out of their children's hair. For the first time, maybe, I realised that I had no male figure in my life. I had no father and also no mother, yet I didn't feel anything, no negative emotions whatsoever. I looked up at Lyanna and Serafina, who were chatting away obliviously, and felt content.

Back at the car, Lyanna rubbed me down with a towel and brushed the dirt off my feet, which tickled and made me giggle. I clumsily got changed back into my clothes and slumped down in the backseat, my limbs aching and my eyelids heavy. I waved goodbye to Peake Lake with a relieved yet sad heart.

We stopped off at a cosy, country pub on the way home. I devoured a plateful of chips smothered in ketchup and a small wedge of Serafina's cheeseburger while Lyanna tucked into an enormous plate of battered fish and chips. I never liked fish as a child as it tasted too fishy.

We arrived home as the sun was dipping below the horizon. While I took a bath to wash off all the dirt I'd accumulated, Lyanna prepared my packed lunch for school the next day.

My favourite songs to listen to in the bath were Madonna's *Lucky Star* and Ozzy Osbourne's *No More Tears*, an influence from each of my aunts. It always made me chuckle that "no more tears" was also written on the side of my shampoo bottle. I sang along to the music and blew soap bubbles up into the air without a care in the world.

I went downstairs feeling soothed and sleepy, once again wrapped up in my comfy dressing gown. I remember clearly the smell and sound of Lyanna ironing my school uniform. She didn't notice as I padded barefoot past the kitchen. I poked my head around the door of the living room and watched Serafina curled up in her large, shabby, leather armchair, reading that door-wedge book of hers, her glasses slowly sliding down her nose and her hair even more of a bird's nest than it had been that morning before we'd left the house. I wondered if she ever brushed it and if not, why I had to brush mine.

Lyanna placed her hand on my shoulder, making me jump. 'What are you doing down here?' she asked.

Serafina looked up, for the first time noticing me stood in the doorway. 'I just came down to say I'm ready for bed,' I replied.

Serafina sat forwards, sliding her glasses back up on to her head, pushing the wilderness of hair away from her face and setting her book heavily down on the coffee table. She leant over to kiss me on the cheek and gave me a light squeeze.

Over her shoulder, I spied the title of the book she was reading: *Lord of the Rings*. I thought that sounded like a cool story and I briefly imagined what kind of tales lay within those pages. 'Goodnight Sara,' she bid me, before turning back to her reading.

Lyanna took me up to bed to tuck me in. 'Do you want a story tonight?' she asked.

I glanced down to the pile of books beneath my bed. 'No, thanks,' I told her.

'Okay. It's been a long day, hasn't it?' She laid beside me for a short while, stroking my hair, soothing me to sleep while I dreamt of the Lord of the Rings, who he may be and what kind of adventures he went on. I awoke maybe an hour later to the sound of raised voices downstairs. I crept down the stairs and rested my face between the spindles of the bannister to listen.

Serafina and Lyanna were arguing, again. 'Why would we tell her about them?' Lyanna shouted.

'Don't you think she should know? Didn't you see the way she was looking at those families today?' Serafina yelled back.

'Why would we tell her when she's never asked? You never know what kind of Pandora's Box you'd be opening by bringing it all up when we don't even know what she's thinking!'

'Exactly! She needs a Pandora's Box opening. She barely even speaks more than one word at a time!'

'So? She's a quiet kid. So what?'

They were arguing over my parents, over me. 'No, Lyanna! She's odd. Everyone comments on it.'

'She's not odd!' Lyanna screamed defensively. 'And even if she was, who cares? Our whole family is odd. It's the way we are.'

'I just feel like she needs to open up about this stuff. It's not normal to not show any interest in her absent parents.'

'You're just being grouchy because we distracted you from your precious literature.'

'Oh, don't start that. I've had a great day. So what if I wanted to read a little?'

'Well, you never act like you want to be around us and now you're sticking your nose in and making huge decisions about talking to her about her parents.' There was a pause. 'Why are you even here, Serafina?'

Serafina sighed heavily. 'You just want her all to yourself so you can say that you raised her, that you came through. That's all this has ever been, some selfish ego-trip.'

'I love that girl! You can't handle it, can you? You always want to be the sensible one, the responsible one, and you can't handle that I've turned my life around and now have someone more important in my life than you!'

The arguing went on like this for some time. I'd heard enough so quietly took myself back to bed.

I thought that everything was my fault. Was I abnormal? Did people really think I was weird? Why hadn't I asked about my parents? I guess I'd never really thought about it. I'd never felt like I was missing anything from my life. Why were they so angry at each other? Was I the cause? It felt like a punch to the stomach.

I cried myself to sleep that night, confused and lonely. It was the first time that I saw the world for what it really was: harsh and deceiving. What I thought had been a lovely day out, to them was something entirely different. I vowed that night to stop seeing the world through those rainbow-tinted glasses and start opening my eyes to what was really going on.

Of course, kids are pretty resilient and tend to bounce back, so a few days later, I'd pretty much forgotten all about that night, but it did change me. I picked up on things that weren't said: a frosty atmosphere in the room when they were together, cutting sideways glances and snappy comments.

Everyone has that pivotal moment in their childhood when they start to see the world differently and understand things in a truer, deeper sense. Yet, we still don't see the grey area; everything remains black and white, bad or good. Becoming aware of the adult world yet not being mature enough to understand it is a recipe for disaster.

Chapter Three

I remember the first time I visited the "Other Place" as clearly as if it were yesterday. It's still one of my most vivid childhood memories, yet it also feels like a dream.

I was nine or ten years old—it wasn't long after that day out at Peake Lake— and I was watching television in the living room while Lyanna and Serafina were arguing in the kitchen. They'd been arguing a lot lately, though I tried to block out the subject of their animosity.

I couldn't bear to hear them tearing each other apart any longer, so I decided to escape outside into the garden. I left the TV on to disguise my departure, hoping they would think I was still engrossed in *Pete's Dragon*, oblivious to their conflict. I snuck out of the patio doors as quietly as I could, closing them carefully behind me.

Our garden was large, green and, in some places, overgrown. The square of garden closest to the house was neatly tended; a freshly cut patch of lawn surrounded by pebbles and potted plants with a few brightly coloured flower beds. At the bottom of the lawn stood a line of bushes and trees, expertly placed to conceal what lay beyond.

I looked back over my shoulder to check that I hadn't been noticed—I hadn't—then continued on my path to the hidden part of the garden. My heart loved that wild, untamed slice of nature that laid just metres away from my home. It felt magical, mysterious, like an adventure waiting to happen.

That day, there was a low and lazy sun. A fine mist hung in the air and the early morning dew collated on the plants having not yet evaporated. Insects buzzed around my head and pale rays of light pierced through the canopy of leaves overhead. The air felt fresh and cool, sending a chill creeping over my bare arms and face.

I sat for a few moments, enjoying the quiet, looking up at the trees, trying not to think about what was really going on inside my head. As a child, you don't worry, not like adults do, because you don't quite understand what there is to worry about, but you have a keen sense that something's not quite right, that things might change and not for the better, yet you can't comprehend exactly what that might entail.

The friction between my aunts made me uneasy and all kinds of emotions—uncertainty, fear, sadness, anger—swelled up inside of me. Right then, however, I was trying not to dwell on all that; I was in search of a moment of calm and solitude. Little did I know, I would spend the rest of my life in search of those moments.

I heard the sound of twigs breaking underfoot and braced myself for a shout of 'Sara! Where are you?' but that call never came. I looked up to locate the source of the noise and saw a figure standing in the shade of the tallest tree.

I was startled and a little frightened, confused as to who they may be and what their purpose might have been for being in my garden. I couldn't fathom another way they could have entered, except for the way that I had come, which now lay behind me. They couldn't have entered without passing me by, could they?

I didn't say anything, I just stared unreservedly. The figure was cloaked in black, their face obscured, but as they stepped out of the shadows, I saw that it was a beautiful woman and she was smiling at me warmly.

'Hello,' she greeted me, with a soothing, angelic voice.

'Hello,' I replied, breaking eye contact to look down at my feet, kicking the bark and mud nervously. I felt unsettled, certain that this person could not be trusted, but for some reason I felt the urge to look back up at her, so I did.

She was closer now, watching me intensely. I fancied that I could hear her musical voice inside my head. She turned and walked away; against all my natural instincts, I followed. She glided gracefully towards the end of my garden. Somewhere deep inside my mind, I knew I should turn back to the house, but I just couldn't bring my legs to carry me back. I felt I was no longer in control of my body and yet, I didn't feel wholly bothered by this.

We reached what should have been the edge of the garden, where there should have been a tall fence bordering the neighbour's garden, but instead, beyond the wild shrubbery, I could see the glow of sunlight across an open space.

The woman pushed through the greenery and I followed willingly, not for one moment stopping to wonder where the fence had gone. As I pushed through the dense thicket, I felt a change in the air; a wave of peace and warmth rippled through my body.

If I close my eyes, I can picture clearly the scene that greeted me as I left the boundary of my garden. A lush golden field fell away before my feet, as far as my eyes could see. The landscape shimmered in the glorious sunlight, the breeze rippled through the wheat, the glittering bugs darted to and fro.

In the centre of my view stood the lady, her dark form in contrast to the radiant backdrop. She let her hood fall to her shoulders, revealing flaming, auburn hair embroidered with flowers. Next, she removed her cloak and I gaped in awe as she unfurled her iridescent wings. She turned to look at me, exposing her pointed ears and her dainty, turned-up nose. I didn't comprehend what I was looking at in that moment, but now I know that I was seeing a faerie for the first time.

I followed her for what felt like hours through that field; the wheat brushing against my bare legs and the sun beating down on my shoulders. We never spoke a word out loud, but in my head, we communicated ceaselessly in a language that I had never heard before and could not remember after. I can't recall what it was that we spoke of, but I do know that she saw into my soul. She asked me questions that nobody had ever asked me before, and I answered truths I never knew I held. I was entranced.

We reached a deep, dark forest. She continued, but I stopped, for the first time realising the situation I was in. She beckoned me forwards, but I refused to go. I knew then that if I followed her into that forest, I would never return to my real life and that was too much for a young girl to get her head around. To never see my aunts again, to never sleep in my comfortable bed with my stuffed friends, to never go back to school (as much as I disliked it)—it was all too final. I decided it was time to go home.

And, with that, she was gone. She didn't walk away or disappear like a magician's trick; her image shivered like a mirage in the heat of the desert, became translucent, then vanished into the ether.

A word resonated around me, of the lady's language, not English. It hung in the air that I breathed, whispered through the trees and reverberated through my mind. It had not been spoken out loud, but it had come to me somehow. I didn't know the translation, but I felt its meaning in my bones—home.

I walked back in the direction we had come in a daze. My limbs were tired and weary, and my mind struggled to make sense of what had happened to me.

As soon as I crossed the boundary of my garden, my mind cleared and I was suffused with a new energy. I ran the rest of the way back to the house to find my aunts still arguing. My heart sank at the sound of their raised voices. Had they been so engrossed in their quarrel that they hadn't noticed I'd been gone for the whole day?

I poked my head around the kitchen door, hoping for a scolding, some kind of acknowledgement of my presence, but neither of them showed any sign of noticing me. I didn't say a word though; my attention was caught by the clock on the facing wall. The time read 11 am. How could it still be morning?

I went back to the patio doors and looked outside. The sun was still shining from the same spot it had been when I'd left the house, taunting me in its stillness.

I looked out over the garden and my eyes were drawn to the shade of wilderness at the end of the lawn. I never for one moment doubted that where I'd been was real. Some might say that I'd fallen asleep and dreamt it all; one of those dreams that occur during a short, deep sleep, that defy time and logic, seemingly lasting longer than the sleep itself, but I knew in my heart it wasn't that.

I stood looking at the garden a while longer, feeling a sense of euphoria, a feeling I'd never felt before in my short life. Serafina came in some time later and broke my trance. She placed a hand on my shoulder. 'It's a lovely day, isn't it?' she asked.

I nodded in agreement. 'I'm sorry if you heard any of that. It's just silly, adult bickering; it doesn't mean anything. Nothing we ever say or do will ever affect you, okay?'

I smiled to myself at the absurdity of that proclamation as it affected me so greatly but replied that I understood anyway. She rubbed my back comfortingly and told me they were making lunch, before stalking back into the kitchen.

It may have been a trick of the light, or my hopeful mind, but before I turned to follow my aunt, I could have sworn that I saw a figure watching me from between the trees.

Chapter Four

My aunts were really the only companions I had as a child. I didn't have any 'proper' friends as I didn't understand how to interact with other children. I liked my own company and didn't feel any need to make friends. That was, until Myla walked into my life.

It was the final year of primary school; a period when you know everything is going to start changing and you're trying to figure out how you feel about the coming transition. It was the first day back after the summer holidays and I was armed with new exercise books and a new Harry Potter backpack, with new uncomfortable shoes forced onto my unwilling feet. Everything was shiny and different, but the place and people were exactly the same. Once my teacher began speaking, everything felt familiar, except that I was writing with new stationery.

The head teacher knocked on the classroom door. She entered at a nod of my teacher's head, pushing an unwilling, golden-haired girl ahead of her. The girl was rake-thin and tiny with a pale complexion, a freckled nose and a halo of scruffy, light hair hanging bedraggled around her shoulders. She looked sad, uncertain, maybe a little defiant, but her eyes shone brightly, full of mischief and humour.

I noticed the sneakers she wore with her uniform first and her Harry Potter bag that matched my own. Right then, I fell in love with that girl. She was the coolest, prettiest, most interesting-looking girl I had ever seen. Most kids my own age were 'vanilla' clones, but she was unique and shone out like a shining star. I looked at the faces of the children around me and thought that they must be thinking the same, judging by their expressions.

The head teacher—her name escapes me—introduced her as Myla Raeburn. She had moved to Yorkshire from Northumberland and we were told to make her feel welcome, but I could tell some of the other girls in the class had other plans.

Myla took the only free seat in the room, next to the annoying, smelly boy I couldn't stand, and for the first time, I was jealous of him. He didn't even speak to her; I would have.

My opinion of Myla changed constantly over the next week or so. Sometimes I'd find myself staring at her, imagining what kind of interesting, cultured life she led away from that classroom, and then on other occasions I found myself disliking her. She both fascinated and bristled me in equal measure.

The way she spoke to my classmates gave me the impression that she thought she was better than us, better than our city, like she felt that she didn't belong there. She was precocious—a child trying to be an adult. It angered me because that wasn't how she was supposed to be or how I'd envisioned her in my head. She was supposed to be cool and aloof, but kind and interesting and warm. How we hold our idols to such high standards!

I found myself trying to catch her attention. I'd speak up in class (which wasn't like me at all) in an attempt to show her how intelligent I was, make witty jokes whenever she was in earshot and wore my uniform differently to prove to her that I wasn't like all the other clones. She didn't appear to notice my experimental attempts at style, and I got told off for not wearing my school uniform in the correct manner.

Myla thought I was a show-off, a fraud, which I suppose I was. She hated people who tried too hard. Even at such a young age, she could see straight through my act. I don't think it entered her mind that I was trying to impress her, she just assumed that I was always like that.

It's funny how we try to change ourselves in an effort to make ourselves more appealing to those we admire, but instead we end up repelling them, becoming a second-rate version of someone else instead of embracing our own unique, exceptional selves.

*****

One day, I was sat on the hill that bordered our playground, picking daisies and negligently giving myself grass cuts, when I heard a commotion behind me. I turned to see a group of girls pushing Myla around and trying to snatch her backpack.

I don't know why I did it—it could have been another effort to impress her, or maybe I would have done the same for anyone else. I wouldn't know because this was the first time I'd ever encountered physical bullying.

I stormed over to the group and demanded to know what they were doing. They didn't hear me, or pretended not to, and carried on harassing Myla. I said, 'Hey! Stop that!'

I waded in amongst them and grabbed Myla's bag, urging her to come with me. I think I shocked those kids: little, quiet Sara who never said a word to anyone, appearing out of nowhere and calling them out on their nasty behaviour.

Myla followed me, but she seemed less than impressed. 'Why did you do that?' she snapped, snatching her bag back from me.

I was stunned at her reaction and mumbled that I didn't know why I'd done it. 'Well, I can handle myself, thank you.' She slumped down on the cusp of the hill, her face creased in frustration and maybe a little embarrassment.

I stood and stared at her back, bewildered, then took a seat beside her. 'You just looked like you needed help, that's all,' I said sulkily.

Myla sighed and shrugged. 'Sorry,' I added insincerely.

Neither of us spoke for a while, just sat and watched the cars driving by on the road below. 'I'm sorry,' she admitted at length. 'I didn't mean to snap at you. I just hate this place—I want to go home.'

'What's wrong with Moraine?' I questioned. Moraine, my hometown, was a beautiful city in the heart of North Yorkshire. It wasn't a built-up, modern city; it felt more like a large, homely village. I loved my home and it got my back up to hear her dismiss it so easily. It never occurred to me that I would feel the same way if I was ever forced to leave my home.

'It's stupid and boring, and the people are different.'

'Different how?'

'They just seem dumb.'

The hairs on my arms prickled and I had to swallow my defensive words to prevent any conflict. Instead, I said, 'Yeah, they are pretty dumb.'

Myla chuckled and I felt the tension between us ease instantly. I saw something in her then, a vulnerability and similarity to myself. I saw that she was putting on a front as much as I was.

I realised in that moment that I wanted to make her laugh and comfort her, then maybe, one day, she'd think of me and Moraine as home. Maybe one day, she wouldn't want to leave us.

After that day, she warmed to me and eventually we became firm friends. We went through our final year of primary school together, we sat our SATs together, worried about high school together and took up new hobbies, like swimming on a Saturday morning. When we found out that we would both be attending the same high school, we were elated and had a sleepover at my house to celebrate.

Over the six-week holidays before high school, we spent almost every minute together. We went camping, for walks with my aunts and enjoyed unlimited sleepovers at my house, stuffing our faces with pizza and ice-cream and watching Disney films.

My favourite memory of that summer was a particular camping trip; we hiked all the way up what we presumed was a mountain (I've been back since, it's just a steep hill) and when we got to the top, ready for the magnificent view and a rest, the heavens opened. The four of us got completely, utterly drenched and had to immediately turn back, making the long trek back down with the rain bouncing off the ground into our faces.

We took shelter inside a pub and dried ourselves in front of a roaring fire. My aunts got tiddly on wine, while Myla and I played snakes and ladders and ate nachos. It was the most fun I'd ever had and I could tell that Myla felt settled and happy around us. I did wonder, on a few occasions, why we never did anything with her parents, but I wasn't complaining as I got to spend all my time with my three favourite people.

That summer was the last time that life was simple and I'll never forget it for as long as I live. Once the innocence and transparency of childhood is lost, it is lost forever.

Chapter Five

There was a reason for Myla's confident attitude: her upbringing. She told me that she was glad she was raised the way she was as it had made her tough, but I felt like she missed out on so much. I like to think that once she met me and became a part of my family, it allowed her, for once, to just be a kid.

Don't get me wrong, she had a privileged upbringing in a beautiful, grand home in the heart of Northumberland. She never wanted for anything material, but what she had in goods and *things*, she lacked in affection and human connection.

Her father, John, was an English teacher and her mother, Rose, was a talented, sought-after graphic designer. Their work lives were hectic and of course, that seeped into their home life. They always managed to make time for each other—nights out at the theatre and charity galas—but rarely for Myla.

Myla was effectively brought up by her nanny Joanna. Myla loved Joanna dearly and it had grieved her to leave her behind in Northumberland when they moved to Moraine, but she was no replacement for her real parents. She long expected that she had been an accident, an unwanted surprise, and they did nothing to quell those fears. Sometimes, Myla would go a whole week without seeing hide nor hair of her parents.

When I first became friends with Myla, one thing I noticed about her was how much she disliked being touched. My aunts would shower me with kisses, hugs and tickles, so physical intimacy never felt strange to me, but there were occasions when I'd try to link arms with Myla when we were walking, or hug her when I was excited about something, and she would pretty much shove me away, like I repelled her.

It baffled me that her parents never hugged her or congratulated her or even read her bedtime stories. It sounds like a sob story, I know, but I don't think it bothered Myla as much as it bothered me. It may have made her different to your average eleven-year-old, but she didn't care. She felt strong and smart and she always strived to be excellent at everything, not as a cry for attention, but because that was what was expected of her, by her parents and herself. Whenever she got an award at school or a good score on a test, she didn't get a present or even a pat on the back—she got a nod of respect. She learned early on that people should always try their hardest; it wasn't an achievement but the way you should be. I never understood any of this as a young girl, but now, as an adult, I know it helped equip her for adulthood. It's hard during the transition to adulthood when everyone stops stroking your ego, but Myla never had to adjust to that.

With less time spent at supermarkets, shopping centres and family parties—all the things kids hate getting dragged along to—Myla had more time for her education and not just her school education but her personal education as well. She was one of the smartest children I knew and that was because she spent all her time reading and drawing. My God, could she draw! Even back then, she created some truly stunning illustrations, advanced beyond her years. We fit perfectly together because I loved to write and she would illustrate my work. Together, we had the whole package.

Like me, Myla didn't have many friends, and definitely no close friends. We were two loners, destined to be alone together. Nonetheless, when her parents had broken the news that they were moving to Moraine, she had been outraged. They lived in a picturesque, inspiring place; a place where she was comfortable with the local people and the other school kids. She knew her village inside out and to leave it all behind seemed too huge a change to adjust to. She would have to start from scratch. Her parents reasoned that it was the perfect time to make the change—before she started high school. Regardless of her scruples, she was forced into moving as her father had been offered professor of languages at our university.

The first time she laid eyes on Moraine was through the car window on the way to their new home. She was livid; they'd moved her to a knock-off version of her paradise. They'd uprooted her from her home only to bring her somewhere pretty much the same, but less magical. The house too was like a poor mimic of their beautiful home in Northumberland. She'd been duped. She had been handed the sword of a king, only to have it snatched away and replaced with an unimpressive replica.

The first few nights in their new home, Myla had felt lost amongst the shadows. The house was a skeleton: empty, cold and devoid of life. She forced herself to unpack her things in her bedroom, which eased her homesickness slightly, but still, it felt like taking a photograph of someone you love to a foreign country—comforting but not the same as the real thing. If anything, it made her miss home more. She would sit for hours, staring out of the window, trying to adjust to the new view, and reminiscing about their old house. Now it was left far behind, bare and lifeless. It was a wholly melancholy experience.

It took her a while to scout the lay of the land: the main city centre full of craft shops, bakeries and quaint eateries, the canal that wound its way alongside the main street, the gothic cathedral imposing over the cobbled, tree-lined streets and the throngs of weekend tourists with their tan-lines and giant cameras. I brought Moraine to life for her. It became three-dimensional once I showed her the armoury shop hidden away off the main street, the library, the haunted cemetery and the best part: the hill on the outskirts of the city, which looked down on the entire valley. On a clear day, you could spot Moraine Manor nestled within the great, wide greenery, overgrown and decaying, but still an eerily charming sight.

Her resilience convinced her to go with the flow; she was there now, for the foreseeable future, so it was up to her to make the most of it. I know she would say now, as I do, that her move to Moraine was the best thing that ever happened to either of us.

Chapter Six

The first day of high school was the most terrifying day of my entire life up to that point. Lyanna dropped me off at the school alone as Serafina was snowed under at work. I had planned to meet Myla at the gates but she was nowhere to be seen, so Lyanna insisted on walking me in. I didn't care, at all, how uncool I may have seemed to the other kids right then, but I never wanted Lyanna to leave.

We reached the main hall and my stomach felt like it was both in my mouth and trying to escape out of my butt. Lyanna looked heartbroken as she waved me goodbye, while I was ushered into a seat at the back of the hall by one of the teachers.

The children around me were talking loudly to each other, laughing, obviously already acquainted. I picked at my fingernails and sweated through my stiff uniform, trying to stop the tears from spilling out. I had never felt so utterly alone as I did in that moment.

Then, I heard a sweet voice behind me. Myla sat herself down next to me as my tears escaped in a flood. I wiped them away quickly, a wave of relief rippling through me. She could see I was visibly nervous, so she gave me a comforting hug—a rare thing—and told me not to worry because she felt the same.

Why is there such a gaping canyon between primary school and high school? Why is there no middle ground? Primary school is a small, safe bubble: one class for every year, everybody knows everybody else, one teacher for all the subjects, a place where nobody cares about style, cliques or the opposite sex. High school, on the other hand, was a vast, intimidating place, where all the kids were immature yet trying to be grown up. Everybody cared what you were wearing, who you were friends with and how many people you'd kissed. It was utterly alien to us. We spent most of that first day wandering around with our mouths agape, trying to remain unnoticed.

Like with everything, you adapt and overcome, and very soon the little safe haven of primary school was a distant memory. I loved my exercise books—one for every subject—and I spent hours decorating them with sticky-back plastic, failing miserably at smoothing all the air bubbles out. I got a new pencil case, new lunchbox, new satchel, new everything, and I revelled in the smell of fresh paper—blank pages promising knowledge and inspiration. Yes, I was a geek. I'd always loved learning and had never been made to feel bad about it, until I started high school.

Myla and I stuck fast. Luckily, we were in the same classes and hadn't gotten separated or it may have been a completely different time for us. We never really integrated into a group; we liked it being just the two of us. We had no need for other friends as we felt we had everything we needed in each other, plus everyone else irritated us. Nobody understood our sense of humour or conversation topics, and we didn't understand theirs.

I thought that the other kids' clothes were strange, like nothing I'd ever seen anyone of my own age wearing. Where had all these children come from? How did they know what they were *supposed* to wear and act like? I felt totally unprepared, like I'd been hiding for the past year, oblivious to the fashion and lifestyle trends. The truth was, I had just been too busy all summer being a kid instead of worrying about becoming a grown-up.

It appeared that my trousers were too short, my tie was too long and my shoes were too clunky, but I was perfectly happy being comfortable. I didn't understand the tight trousers the other girls wore, or the way the boys left their top button undone and let their ties hang low.

I was very lucky that I seemed to be born with an innate sense of self—not giving a damn what anybody else thought of me and always doing things just to please myself. I was also very lucky to have found the only other kid my age, it seemed, who had also been born that way. When the other children laughed at us, we just laughed straight back. The joke was on them; we knew we had the better deal. It was our little secret. We were wise beyond our years.

The first year of high school is just an adjustment phase; still living inside a child's mind and body, but starting to branch out, gain independence, figure out your place in the world. As high school goes on, everything you think you know, everything you believe in, is tainted and warped by society. High school is the place where dreams are both imagined and crushed in the same breath. In that first year, school life wasn't so bad. We settled into the rhythm, revelled in the new workload and enjoyed just being ourselves, before the weight of teenage pressures started to bear down on us.

We were outcasts, sure, and we were teased, but we didn't care. Our friendship was still young and every day was an adventure. A brand-new world had opened up to us and we really felt like we could go anywhere and do anything. We were focussed on our goals: becoming a best-selling author and illustrator duo. It never crossed our minds, not once, that we would ever be anything but 'us' or do anything but what we dreamed of. We were resolved in who we were, where we were going and who we were going to be.

The second year wasn't so clear-cut. The work became increasingly difficult and the kids got meaner, so, before long, our resolve of the first year started to crumble. Hormones sky-rocketed and life wasn't so joyous anymore. We were tired, moody and self-obsessed—the curse of the teenage girl.

I used my diary to escape. I wrote all my feelings down as a way of releasing all my pent-up emotion. At the time, I thought I was writing Shakespearean prose, but when I re-read my entries later in life, I realised how frivolous my thoughts and concerns were. Every little thing that happened to me on a day-to-day basis felt like the end of the fucking world. And, may I just ask, how changeable is a teenager's mind? I would hate someone one week and love them the next and vice-versa. To be a teenager is to feel deep and think shallow.

Everything became a question: am I normal? Do I want to be normal? Why am I different? Am I doing this right? What do people really think of me? Do I care? Am I sad? Am I happy? Do I know anything?

Thank the gods Myla and I had each other to bounce these questions off, though we didn't really come up with any answers. I would say that you don't find answers until you leave your teens behind, but I don't think that's entirely true.

During the second year, I waded knee-deep into my fantasy writing. I had my every-day diary for documenting thoughts and events, then for my birthday that year, I was gifted a beautiful, leather journal with a tree embossed into the front cover and crisp parchment paper sewn into the binding. It was the most attractive thing I'd ever owned. This became my storybook; it deserved nothing less. Serafina always gave me the best gifts.

As a child, my favourite film was *Snow White and the Seven Dwarfs*. I can't explain why, but something about that story captivated my imagination. It was a true, quintessential fairy tale, possessing that dream-like quality that allowed you to get lost in another world—a world full of magic and princes, witches and beautiful creatures.

For my tenth birthday, Serafina had given me a charming, illustrated book of fairy tales and of course, my favourite story in there was Snow White, but there was another story bound within those golden-edged, crisp pages that enchanted me: Snow White and Rose Red. This story captivated me more so than the original, though I was not sure why. Maybe because it was a story of two girls, like Myla and me? Or maybe, for some other reason that hasn't occurred to me. Whatever the reason, I pored over the delicate, somewhat wistful illustration of the two sisters and read and re-read their story again and again until I could recite it from memory.

It's funny, the stories that stick with us from childhood. I found that book a few years back, in a box of my belongings up in Lyanna's loft. When I opened it, the pages creaked and the dust puffed up into a cloud. I flicked to the exact page where that illustration still resided without having to consult the contents page. I was overcome with nostalgia, transported back in time.

When I turned thirteen, Serafina bought me another book: a gothic, hardback book of the Grimm Brothers' fairy tales. Being older, my taste somewhat transformed by the arrival of teenage hormones, I obsessively lapped up every word. Their twisted tales struck a chord with me; not everything is as it appears. What is beautiful on the outside can be rotten within, and those who appear kind and gracious can be hiding the darkest secrets of all. Antithetically, those who appear hideous can shine with the warmest light from within.

Part of me still loved the purity and innocence of the original fairy tales as they allowed me to stay cocooned within a bubble of in-corruption and yet, as I grew, my mind became drawn more by the darkness; not only for its wildness and the thrills it gave me, but because it was realistic. Life is not all joy and happy endings, it is double-edged, perilous and intoxicating, just like the Grimm tales.

That year was the year that I read the *Lord of the Rings*, finally—Serafina lent me her copy. The first film had been released just before I began reading, but I refused to watch it until I had read the book. It's safe to say that I didn't get to see that film for quite a while.

That book was pivotal in my life. With all the doubts and uncertainty that come in that stage of life, I'd started to doubt my talents as a writer. My well of inspiration was drying up and Tolkien opened my eyes to all the possibilities of my imagination. I was an atheist, but I followed Tolkien's work like a religion, going on to read the *Unfinished Tales* and the *Silmarillion*, and anything else he'd written that I could get my hands on. He was the hero of my teenage years; whenever life dealt me a blow, I always turned back to Middle Earth to take me away from harsh realities.

Escapism, to me, is one of the most important things in life. Some people take a holiday, play sports, watch a film or take up arts and crafts. My escapism was reading and writing fantasy, and it saved my life in so many ways. How could anyone make it through this life without escaping reality once in a while?

Chapter Seven

I loathe bullying; it's so cruel and pointless. Just thinking about it fills me with anger. If I could tell 'teenage me' anything, it would be not to listen to the bullies and keep my head down and persevere because, one day, it would all be meaningless. One day, their wounding words would blow away on the wind and the hurt they caused would turn to ash.

I was one of the lucky ones; I was strong and most of what they said went in one ear and out the other. After high school, I never gave those bullies a second thought, but others took those malicious words to heart and carried them with them like a heavy stone for many years afterwards. Those nasty kids affected their victims' adult lives and yet, the bullies themselves probably never thought of us again.

I know the bullies were just children too, and usually children with issues of their own—there's two sides to every story—but I can't help but wonder how someone can be so oblivious to the pain they are causing another human being, someone who thinks and feels just like they do. Or, even worse, to not be oblivious to it but revel in it, get some kind of twisted enjoyment out of it. That, I can't understand. To break someone's spirit, to make someone feel bad about the traits that make them unique, is just so unspeakably cruel and perverse.

Unfortunately, the memories of bullying and all that entailed are the most vivid memories I have of high school—not the friendships I made, the end-of-school prom, the hard work I put in—but that feeling of dread that loomed over me most mornings, causing me to fake sickness or skip class, or that sinking feeling in my stomach when I walked in to a classroom and saw that *they* were there. The feeling of weakness and shame, vulnerability and fear, which followed me everywhere I went.

A lot of people, once they're an adult dealing with bills and work and responsibilities, say that they wish they could go back to high school, when life was so much simpler. Not me; life truly started for me once that period of my life was over. The minute I left that place, and even now all these years later, I couldn't be paid enough to go back there. The thought of it makes my stomach squirm.

I feel protective over my teenage self, like I'm my own parent. I feel for her—lost and angry and upset. I wish I could travel back in time to offer my young self some comfort, to share with her what I know now and help guide her in some way. She feels separate to me, not my younger self but a different entity altogether. This is probably because I'm such a different person now. Remembering times from my childhood and teenage years isn't like a memory, but like reading a story of someone else's life. My naivety, the bad choices I made, the things I did when I didn't worry about, or even consider, the consequences. But that is the gift, and the curse, of youth—to do and not to think, to act on impulse and pay for it later, to think everything will just turn out alright and never really think about the needs of others. Most of us were guilty of self-absorption at some point in our teenage lives, I'm sure. What differed was the extent to which we let that take over our reasonable, maturing side. Past that line is where the bullies stood, waiting to gift you with another miserable day.

The bullying started with small, juvenile things, like kicking the backs of our feet so that we'd trip up, pulling our hair when we walked past or shouting embarrassing lies about us, but the instances soon escalated, becoming malicious and more frequent.

My bullies were a group of 'popular' kids. I have no idea why they were labelled 'popular'. Sure, they were a large group, but nobody liked them really. I sometimes wonder if they even liked themselves.

Alex and Chloe were the worst of the bunch: nasty, maybe even sociopathic. Their words could cut like shards of glass and they always knew the most sensitive spot to hit someone on.

I still don't understand why they made a beeline for us. We kept to ourselves, never did anything to provoke them and I can't say that we were particularly 'unique'-looking, though we probably weren't the coolest. Maybe it was because we couldn't be provoked easily? We tried to ignore them as best we could, but sociopaths love a challenge.

I was fourteen and hadn't ever kissed a boy, when they spread a rumour that I'd had sex with a guy. On a school trip, Josh in the year above showed interest in me. We had a few brief, slightly awkward conversations, then exchanged phone numbers.

At first, he sent me sweet messages, asking when we were going to meet up and what kind of things I enjoyed doing, but then his texts became increasingly crude and erratic. I found out through a friend of a friend that he was a huge pothead who'd had sex with quite a few girls from our year. I stopped replying to his messages and that was the end of that, but he must have told other people that something quite different had happened between us. Chloe and Alex started that rumour and he did nothing to dampen it, which made me wonder how many people he had really slept with.

It didn't bother me what people thought because I knew the truth. It became mine and Myla's inside joke. I vehemently denied going anywhere near him, but I wasn't angry. He was just a stupid, immature boy. I actually found the whole thing pretty hilarious at first, and I was proud to be a virgin at fourteen years old.

I didn't care what they thought of me—I was comfortable enough with myself to take what they said with a pinch of salt—but as time went on, I began to dread school more and more and their actions started to wear me down.

At the end of year nine, I heard, in the middle of a history quiz, a group of boys talking about me. It was an individual quiz, so everyone was quietly working on their own paper, except for those obnoxious boys sniggering at the back. I didn't hear the whole conversation as I was concentrating on the questions, but I heard one part quite clearly and I'm sure the whole class did too. That was probably their intention.

Alex, in all his marvellous cruelty, proclaimed loudly, 'I'd fuck her, but I'd have to put a bag over her head so I couldn't see *that* face.' For a moment after, the silence was deafening. I felt every hair on my body stand on end and a great, deep, nauseating heat rushed from my stomach all the way up to my head. I ran out of the classroom with fire burning in my cheeks and tears stinging my eyes.

I sat down on a bench outside in the courtyard and tried to control my breathing. I felt upset, deeply embarrassed and completely worthless. I couldn't believe that everyone in the class had heard him say such an awful, personal thing about me; I felt violated. It hurt that they'd denounced me like that and stripped me so naked in front of a crowd of my peers. Then, the hurt gave way to anger.

Myla followed me outside moments later with the teacher's consent. She sat by my side but didn't put an arm around me; she knew I needed my space. 'They've been sent to the office,' she confirmed. 'Mr Osbourne is fuming with them.'

I gulped, unable to get any words out.

'Don't listen to them, they're fucking brain-dead. They don't know what they're talking about.'

I sat forwards, my hands gripping the edge of the bench, the skin on my knuckles stretched white across the bones. 'I don't care what they think of me, Myla, you know I don't,' I half-choked, half-sobbed through gritted teeth. 'It's just, it's just…' my voice became high-pitched and squeaky, '…how dare they!' I exhaled in disbelief. 'Who are they to judge whether I'm fuckable or not? Why do they get a say in who I have sex with?' I raged. 'I wouldn't want to have sex with him—he's an arsehole! I'd need a bag over my head so that I couldn't see him!' I let a little laugh escape at that. I hadn't meant it as a joke; it was true, but it tickled me nonetheless and the tension in my body eased somewhat. I hated him and that group with all my being. The thought of being intimate with any of them made my skin crawl. Even being across the classroom from them was too close for comfort.

Myla laughed too. 'I know, Sara. That's teenage boys for you though. They can't see past their own egos. They'll do or say anything to get a laugh and impress their mates.'

I hoped the class hadn't thought I'd run out because I was offended. I mean, I can't deny that I did contemplate how hideous I must have been for a moment, but I'd run out because I was so full of rage, and if I'd stuck around, I could have easily punched their sweaty, spotty, evil little faces into pulp.

I still felt humiliated and angry, but I held my head up high and went back to class to finish my quiz. I won.

*****

One morning, on my way to school, Myla texted me to let me know that she was staying at home with a sickness bug, and I knew right then that it was going to be a bad day.

I made it through to the last class of the day. I had math with Mr Powell—which was always hellish in itself—and I could feel *their* gazes searing into the back of my head. I actually felt a few things hit the back of my head at one point: little pieces of rolled-up paper. They were annoying, but nothing more than a swarm of flies buzzing around my head.

There was a boy I fancied at the time—Danny—and after the bell rang for the end of the day, I went to my locker to retrieve my coat and found him stood there, leaning near *my* locker. I took out my jacket and briefly glanced over at him. He must have sensed my presence, as he looked up and actually smiled at me! My heart melted. It wasn't just an acknowledgement, it was a full beam, 'pleased to see you' smile. But then, my heart's light extinguished like a dying bonfire when I heard Chloe and one of her friends laughing behind me. I turned back to my locker, locking it hastily with the intention of a speedy exit before Danny could see me blush.

Those bitches chose that moment to shout, at the top of their lungs, that I had nits. It was a stupid, childish remark but I still felt my cheeks turn from warmly flushed to boiling lobster. I must have been feeling a bit feisty that day, or maybe it was just the after-effects of being humiliated in front of my crush, but I sniggered mockingly in response to their jibe and said, 'Good one.' Their expressions turned to thunder at my unexpected retaliation and that's when I knew I'd made a mistake.

I was fifteen by this point and I knew I should have been sticking up for myself anyway, but I've always hated confrontation. Seeing my aunts arguing when I was younger and Jack laying into Serafina on a few occasions had given me an aversion to any kind of violence. So why did I choose to respond on that occasion? Especially when Myla wasn't there to have my back.

They grabbed a handful of my hair, yanked me backwards and smashed my head into my locker. In my shocked stupor, the only thought in my head was that I was glad Danny had left and hadn't seen that. I felt a prickling on my forehead and warm liquid trickled down my nose. At first, I just stood there, dazed and disorientated, unable to speak or react. In all the years they'd bullied me, they'd never physically hurt me. All it had taken was a small, knee-jerk reaction to provoke it.

The girls ran off, knowing full well they'd crossed a line. A couple of kids looked concerned and genuinely asked me if I was okay, while some others pointed and laughed. The foggy haze wore off and I felt the sudden urge to run.

I didn't get the bus home that day; I legged it until I was out of breath and as far away from the school as I could get.

There was a long country lane that wound its way down the hill to my street. At the top of the hill was a bridge over the motorway. I stopped there to catch my breath and calm myself down. I leant up against the railing and looked down at the road below.

There were no cars on the country lane, as was normal as it was a quiet road, and the humid weather was preparing to make way for a thunderstorm. There was something that struck me as unusual about the scene, but I couldn't put my finger on what it was at first. Once my breathing returned to normal and I could hear clearly again, I realised what it was: the motorway was closed. There were no cars whatsoever on a road that was usually jammed with traffic. There was no sound of tyres on tarmac or honking horns, just deathly silence.

The thunder and lightning began and the air suddenly buzzed with electricity. In between rumbles, the silence was stifling. I stood, looking out over the deserted motorway, listening to the storm as it moved out, until I felt the first spots of rain on my face.

Standing there, overlooking the abandoned road, with no civilisation visible for miles, I felt like I was in a post-apocalyptic dream. It was the end of the world, or I wished it was. Then, a car sped past, splashing me head to toe with puddle water, and ruined the illusion. My head began to throb and I was brought back down to earth with a crash. I trudged home, letting the raindrops mingle with my tears.

Chapter Eight

I visited the 'Other Place' many times during my teenage years. I named it the Other Place as I could think of no other way to describe it; it was somewhere here, yet not here, on this earth but not of this earth. Somewhere incongruous, disconcerting and unexplainable. I visited it both in my mind and physically, usually when I was trying to get away from something in the real world, whatever that is. Sometimes, I would seek out the Other Place and other times, it would creep up on me and spirit me away.

I saw full apparitions, like I'd fallen into the pages of a fantasy saga, and other times the transformation of my surroundings would be subtle; a gradual feeling within me that I was somewhere else, somewhere where things didn't make any sense and all the sense in the world.

After that very first time in my garden when I'd met the faerie, the instances I visited were just as peaceful, even joyous, but as I journeyed my way through adolescence, the atmosphere seemed darker when I ventured there, like a reflection of my emotions and what was going on in my life. Every single time I visited, one thing remained the same: I was always alone.

Myla and I always took the bus home from school together, but one beautiful, autumnal day, I decided to walk. Myla had gone over on her ankle in PE in the last period and couldn't walk with me, so I waved her goodbye at the bus stop and set off walking.

Autumn is my favourite season. The temperature is cooler and the air feels fresher. I adore the colours of the changing leaves, the cosy feeling of being wrapped up beneath layers of coats and scarves, and the excitement of the festive season to come. For me, it always felt like a time of change: trees baring their branches, the new year visible on the horizon and the beginning of a new school year.

The route home was rather pretty: a rocky path winding its way through nature. It was always quiet so I didn't see many other people along the way, except for an old couple and the occasional dog-walker. I loved how secluded and peaceful it was; one could almost imagine they were far away from civilisation. It was a wonderful opportunity for reflection and spending some quality time with myself.

That autumn was warmer than I was used to, but I had still been overprepared and worn my winter coat, scarf and gloves. I was sweating beneath all those layers, so I took off my gloves and scarf, shoving them carelessly inside my bag and unzipped my coat. I instantly felt a fresh breeze on my stomach and back, cooling down the droplets of sweat on my skin.

I chose the longer, more scenic route, taking me forty-five minutes from school to home, thirty if I was walking at a brisk pace. The beaten, winding path snaked between hills and fields, partway through woodland and part-way alongside the canal. I was kicking wet leaves and revelling in the snap of twigs beneath my feet, when I finally reached the halfway point. I had been taking my time, enjoying the views—already forty-five minutes had passed since I'd left the school—but I was in no rush to get home.

Forking off from my path, a narrower track led off to the left. I decided to take a little detour and have a wander down there as I'd not been that way before. I had no intention of following it all the way as I wasn't sure where it would bring me out, plus it was foggy and had started to drizzle. I kept meaning to turn back, but when I saw Moraine Manor peeking out through the trees ahead, curiosity got the better of me.

The path led out in the Manor grounds—a hidden, wild garden. Sequestered amongst the overgrowth were relics of a time when the Manor had been in use: a mossy, dried-up water fountain, crumbling statues of angelic figures and dirty stone benches. There were also some discarded, old crisp packets and drink cans for a touch of authenticity. I abhor littering, so I found myself gathering the rubbish and stuffing it in my bag angrily, with the intention of binning it all when I got home.

After my litter-picking, I took the time to take in my surroundings. I glimpsed the back of the house through the trees and stepped closer, hoping for a better view. At first the scene was still and concrete, but then, something changed. It suddenly felt dreamlike, like I'd fallen asleep and was seeing my minds projection of the garden rather than the real thing. The garden awoke; I could hear birds and critters where before it had been lifeless and quiet. Everything was now in motion, no longer dead and abandoned.

Now, I don't want to say that the air was sparkling, like it would be described in a children's story, but it had taken on a strange quality. White orbs danced before my eyes, creating a magical, yet eerie, illusion. All sound was muffled like just after a heavy snowfall.

I walked deeper into the wilderness, becoming very aware of the changes occurring around me. A large, iridescent insect darted past me, the likes of which I had never seen before and that's when I knew where I was. Here and there, I saw shadows and movement in the undergrowth; pixies and faeries.

I pressed on, following my route to a clearing. At the centre, stood an enormous oak tree. Its branches were so long, they sheltered the entire clearing. I walked beneath its boughs in awe; I had never seen a tree so huge and ancient. I arrived at its trunk and skimmed my fingers over the rough bark. I sat down beneath it, nestling myself between its roots and took a deep, relieved breath. I wanted to stay there forever. Before I knew it, I had nodded off.

Despite my tranquillity, I strayed through dark dreams. Dreams of half-forgotten memories and dreams my imagination had devised. Dreams so dark I was crying out in my semi-conscious state: of demons, haunting spirits and terrifying forms. In the distance, I saw a dim light approaching. It was tangible. Into the light I fell, drifting, suspended in time, before it engulfed me.

When I came to, it was dark. I used the torch on my phone to guide my way out of the garden. All feelings of magic and otherworldly fear had evaporated at the thought of being murdered by my aunts for being so late home. I had no missed calls, but then I realised I had no signal. They were not going to be happy.

I stumbled blindly back to the main path and, to my surprise, found Myla and my aunts looking lost and calling my name. When they spotted me, they looked positively furious and I braced myself. 'Where the hell have you been?' one of them—or all of them—asked, shining a bright light in my face.

'I am so sorry! I took a detour and may have fallen asleep,' I answered sheepishly.

'Fallen asleep?' Lyanna screeched breathlessly. 'Are you out of your damn mind?'

'Lyanna's right, anything could have happened to you out here on your own in the dark. Do you know how dangerous that was?' Serafina scorned.

'I'm sorry, I didn't mean—'

'Fuck me, Sara, I was terrified,' Myla added.

'Language,' Lyanna reminded her.

'Sorry.'

'I'm so sorry, Myla, your ankle must be killing you.'

'Don't worry about it.'

'Come on, let's get you guys home,' Serafina sighed.

My aunts walked ahead, angrily whispering to each other. Myla hung back to walk with me.

'Where were you really?' she asked me conspiratorially, a look of scepticism and mischief in her eyes.

'I'm not quite sure,' I replied truthfully.

Myla continued to watch me, her eyes analysing my expression. 'What were you searching for?'

I didn't reply.

Chapter Nine

At sixteen, I got my first boyfriend—he was also my first kiss. Quite a few lads had tried, especially at the 'pop and crisps' nights at the local night club but, like my virginity, I'd wanted to save my first kiss for someone I cared about, not some spotty, random adolescent who was trying it on just so he could go back and tell his friends how far he'd gotten with me.

It was year eleven, the final year of high school, when I should have been focussing on exam prep, that my boobs finally began to sprout and my mouth-to-teeth size ratio balanced out. I was tall and slim and my face was relatively in proportion, I suppose. I had long, dark hair and had started putting more effort into my appearance: wearing make-up and experimenting with my style.

Joel Underwood, two years above, began to show an interest in me. He left notes on my desk asking me out on dates and sent me cute pictures of animals on MSN. At first, I didn't think much of it—and I suppose part of me didn't believe he was serious—but then he finally asked me out face-to-face. Blindsided, on the spur of the moment, I said yes, even though I wasn't entirely sure if I was attracted to him. I'd never put much thought into the opposite sex and had had no plans for a boyfriend, so my reaction took me by surprise.

As soon as I said yes, he grabbed my face and kissed me—my first kiss, tongues and everything. I was happy about this for two reasons. One, I thought it was romantic and I felt like I was in a film. Two, it meant I'd had no time to worry about how bad I was going to be. In hindsight, him kissing me like that should have given me a clear indication of the kind of person he was: taking anything he wanted regardless of what I wanted. I just thought, because he was older and more experienced, he was a passionate romantic.

After the kiss, I was speechless. Somehow, while shaking with nerves, I managed to give him my phone number before he stalked away, leaving me breathless.

Naturally, the first thing I did was rush to find Myla in the canteen. She was sat in the corner in our usual spot, munching on her Nutella sandwich and doodling in her battered sketchpad. I blew in like a hurricane with a look of disbelief and elation on my face and interrupted her peace. She almost choked on her sandwich in surprise.

I explained excitedly all that had happened, not pausing for a single breath. We screeched excitedly and discussed the details of the kiss, like it was the most exciting news story we'd ever heard. Our voices were so high-pitched and ridiculously girly that pupils on other tables shot us irritated glances, but we ignored them.

*****

Joel called me that night and we arranged to meet up. We went on quite a few drives in his car over the following weeks. We talked endlessly about everything: our families, our studies, our hobbies, and we seemed to have a lot in common.

Sometimes, I took Myla along, especially at the beginning, for moral support. They genuinely seemed to get along. I loved hanging out with my best friend and my new boyfriend; I felt like such an adult.

On the occasions when Myla didn't join us, and sometimes when she did, we made out—A LOT. I'd never experienced that feeling before; that burning, squirming heat in my lower abdomen, my fingers and neck sweating, my entire body tingling. I finally understood why people gave in to their urges. I didn't feel like I was ready for sex, but I knew it was in my near future.

My aunts didn't mind us going for drives, especially when I took Myla with us. We'd had open conversations about sex and safety, and in truth, they trusted me. I think part of them were actually relieved that I'd shown some interest in dating as I'd been quite a late bloomer.

I can honestly say, even now as an adult knowing what went on in my teenage years, that my aunts being open and trusting with me was a great thing. I never felt the need to rebel or do anything I might have regretted. They not only trusted me, but I trusted myself and my instincts. I knew my limits and right from wrong, but I also knew that if anything bad *did* happen, I could talk to them about it and not be ashamed or embarrassed.

So many girls I knew were repressed by their parents, and when they were away from home, they lived the lives of porn stars, going home feeling dirty and ashamed, yet unable to confide in anyone about it. Sex is a natural thing and at that age, kids are bound to be curious about it. If they want to do it, they're going to do it—isn't it best that they're given the right information and support so that they can make intelligent decisions instead of fumbling about blindly in the dark? I am so grateful to my aunts for being open with me and allowing me to make my own educated decisions, and mistakes.

*****

I remember the first time I was ever concerned by Joel's behaviour. It was a few months into our relationship; Myla and I were hanging out at her house, as was usual for a Saturday. I was painting my nails when Joel called. 'Hey, Sara, what are you up to today?' he asked when I answered the phone.

'I'm just at Myla's, why?'

He gave a derogatory grunt. 'Can I come pick you up?'

'Myla, is it okay if Joel comes to pick us up?' I asked her.

'Yeah, s—' she began.

'No!' Joel barked in my ear. 'Just you and me, Sara, not Myla.'

'Oh, okay.' I turned to Myla. 'Sorry, he just meant me,' I told Myla regretfully, before turning back to my conversation with Joel. 'Why don't you want Myla to come?'

'I just… Look, can we talk please?'

'We're talking now.'

'No, face to face. I'm coming over.' He hung up.

I put the phone down on the windowsill, confused. 'What was that about?' I wondered aloud.

'Was he funny with you?'

'Yeah, he seemed really moody. I don't like that he wants to "talk" with me.'

'Look,' Myla sighed, turning to face me with a troubled expression, 'maybe he just wants to see you alone? You're a couple, I get it. You don't always want me there.'

'I do! It's the best hanging out with you both.'

'Yeah, that's great for you, but not for me and him.'

'What do you mean?' I asked cluelessly.

'Well, he obviously wants to be alone with you, and I, well, don't always want to be the third wheel.' She averted my gaze, afraid that she'd offended me. I admit I did feel a little hurt. How could I have been so naïve to not see this coming? Was I that immature?

'I get that,' I replied at length.

A horn honked outside. I went out to Joel's car, expecting to have a short talk before going back inside the house, but instead, as soon as I'd closed the car door, Joel set off driving. 'Where are we going?' I asked, unnerved and hastily fastening my seatbelt.

'I don't know, anywhere. I just want to get away from her.'

Surprised at his nasty tone of voice, I snapped, 'What do you mean by *her*? And will you slow down?'

Joel pulled into a layby, the tyres screeching in protest, and shuffled agitatedly in his seat. 'You're always together!'

'So?'

'So, I'm your boyfriend, Sara, don't I ever get you to myself?'

'We see each other alone all the time!'

'Well, not often enough.'

'What do you dislike so much about Myla?'

'It's not her, it's us!'

'What do you mean?'

'It's just not normal, is it?'

'What isn't?'

'I've never had to wait this long before.'

'What are you talking about?'

He mulled something over in his head for a moment before continuing, 'When are we going to have sex? I'm going crazy.'

I was taken back by the abruptness of his question. 'So, that's what all this comes down to, is it?'

'No, Sara, you know I really like you.'

'Yeah, exactly. You *like* me and I *like* you. We've only been going out a few months. I'm not ready for that. I hardly know you, really.'

'Well, we can do other stuff.'

'We do other stuff.'

'Feeling your boobs while we make out is *not* other stuff.'

'Oh well, I am sorry!' I fumed, my cheeks turning scarlet.

'Don't be like that.'

'Like what?'

'Overdramatic, childish. It's not a big deal.'

'It might not be to you, but it is to me. Take me back please, now.'

'Take you back?'

'Yes, to Myla's.'

'You're going back?'

'What did you think would happen? That I'd give in and have sex with you for the first time, right here in this layby? That might be what the other girls you've been with might do, but not me. I'm not going to waste my Saturday afternoon arguing with you about it.'

'But—'

'Take me back. Now. Or I'll get out and walk.'

Joel dropped me back off at Myla's parents' place without either of us saying another word to one another. Myla watched me through the window as I made my way up the path to the front door. Back in her front room, she asked me where I'd gone. 'He just drove off! I didn't even want to go anywhere with him!'

'What did he want to talk to you about? Me?'

'The bottom line is, he's frustrated because we haven't had sex yet.'

'Jerk.'

And that's all we had to say on the matter.

Joel did apologise later for the way he'd handled the situation, but I still had my doubts about him. Whenever we were alone, he'd try to push it that bit further each time; each time I'd push him away, he'd get angry and punch things like an overgrown toddler.

Up until this point, the only men present in my life were my male teachers and Jack Radcliffe, Serafina's on-off abusive partner. I'd seen him shout at her, demean her, try to control her and I knew that he'd hit her on a couple of occasions. Now, I had a boyfriend that was exhibiting similar behaviour and I hadn't realised until then how much Jack's actions had impacted me. When Joel lashed out or raised his voice, I would flinch and even cry sometimes. That made him even angrier, louder and more aggressive.

I will stress that neither Joel nor Jack ever laid a hand on me, but even still, it hadn't set me up with a great view of men. I thought they were stupid, dramatic, nasty and quite pathetic.

I thought dating was going to be fun and exciting, a new adventure, but instead, it turned out to be stressful and unenjoyable. I don't know why I didn't call it quits, why I continued to see him and get into the same predicaments. I suppose I kept hoping that he'd get over it, or that my body would just give in and let him have what he wanted to shut him up, but it didn't, thankfully. I wasn't ready and that was that. He was going to have to like it or lump it.

During my relationship with Joel, I visited the Other Place often. I saw enchanting waterfalls, pixies hiding in the grass, exotic and unusual creatures, but I also saw a shadow. Sometimes, the atmosphere was magical and pleasant; other times, it was oppressive. On those occasions, I would leave as quickly as I'd gone.

Although I was aware that I was there, I had no idea if the place itself, or the things in it, were aware of me. After that morning all those years ago when the faerie had shown herself to me, I hadn't interacted with any other being. I was just an observer, like I was watching from behind a glass screen.

I didn't tell anyone about the Other Place. When I was away from it, I pushed it out my mind. Part of me wondered if it was real, or if I was just going mad, but then another part of me believed in it and loved my little secret. I felt special; I was the only one, I thought, who had access to this other world, so surely that meant I was important or different in some way? I loved going there and the more I went, the less I wanted to return.

Chapter Ten

The first party I ever attended began as an exhilarating yet nerve-wracking experience but by the end, it was truly quite horrible. The house was crammed with Joel's adult friends and I somehow felt like I shouldn't have been there, like I was trespassing on something forbidden. Of course, Myla went with me; one, because I needed her, and two, because she would have never forgiven me if I hadn't invited her.

The party was thrown at Joel's house while his parents were abroad on holiday. Myla and I went straight there after school, with the permission of my aunts, of course. Myla didn't need her parents' permission; she'd just told them she was going to be home late and they hadn't questioned her further, whether out of trust or disinterest, I'm not sure.

Joel brought us alcopops, most of which we drank while we were getting ready upstairs in the bathroom. *Metallica* was blasting out of the sound system, filling the whole house with the sound of deep, chugging riffs. We could feel the bass vibrating beneath our feet.

Myla wore a dungaree dress and her Converse All Stars, whereas I'd opted for a slinky red dress in the hope of impressing Joel. I wanted to look grown up so that his friends would accept me. 'You look amazing!' Myla exclaimed excitedly.

'Are you sure?' I asked, fiddling with the hem of my dress self-consciously.

'Yeah! I've never seen you look like that!'

'Thanks.' I smiled. 'Do you feel underdressed?' I asked and regretted it instantly. I hadn't meant it to sound so derisive.

Myla didn't look offended. I don't know if she was even capable of taking offense, but she did look annoyed. 'You know me, Sara, I'd never wear anything like that.'

Now, I was annoyed. Was she suggesting I looked slutty? 'No, I didn't mean you *have* to wear a skimpy dress, it's just that you always wear that.'

'Exactly, so why would I change my style for some stupid party?'

The atmosphere had gone from jubilant to icy in the space of a few minutes. 'Well, if you think it's stupid, you can just go home, you know.'

'I don't want to leave,' she admitted, looking hurt.

'Well, I don't want you to either! I was just thinking of you.'

Neither of us knew if we were still mad at the other or if we'd just accidentally made up. We both said sorry, then took a last look in the mirror and headed downstairs to the party.

We drank a lot of alcopops, not daring to try anything harder, which didn't really get us tipsy, but instead made us hyperactive and giggly. In between dancing to *Limp Bizkit*, laughing and chatting with Joel's friends, Joel cornered me every chance he got. He told me he couldn't resist me in my red dress.

Later on, Myla and I went up to the bathroom for our third wee that hour and inadvertently walked in on two partygoers snorting cocaine off the toilet seat. Rather than looking angry or surprised, they casually offered us some like it was a slice of pizza. The looks on our faces must have been quite comical because they both broke out into hysterical laughter. We declined their offer and speedily made an exit.

That party was the first time I'd encountered drugs. I found it surprising how casual people's attitudes were towards them, especially after having it drilled into us at school that drugs were the devil's food. I'd never had any interest in trying them, and innocently, I believed I would probably never come in to contact with them. Anyway, it's a good job I never tried them because I have an incredibly addictive personality.

I never tried drugs as I stepped into adulthood either. It wasn't because I'd seen first-hand what they can do to people, or even for health or moral reasons, or even because they can ruin lives and potentially kill you. I have been paranoid and insecure for most of my life. I have been high and I've been low, curled up inside my own mind at times, overthinking everything. I felt like my mind was too big for my brain. I could be extremely sad or extremely happy and suffered from bouts of depression in my early adulthood. I always kept my emotions bubbling close to the surface. I would lock myself away from the world, then let it all out in an eruption of emotion.

I have many different sides to my personality: happy, positive and bubbly versus sad, dark and even slightly twisted. I have a vivid and wicked imagination and have always been a creature of the night, finding it hard to sleep and suffering from nightmares; therefore, night-time was the time when I would be at my most creative. I am a person of extremes, not in my lifestyle but in my personality and emotions. If I were to take drugs, I feared they would either amplify these qualities—which would be much too intense—or worse, dull them.

I am a freak, but sometimes, it makes life more interesting. There were things that I wanted to change about myself, but it sure as hell beat going through life totally neutral. And you know what? Despite all the horrible things that have happened to me in my life and the impact that they've had on me, despite never having tried drugs or fucking with my body or mind, I can honestly say that I've never felt like I've missed out on anything.

I get high on life, on love, on words, on human interaction, friendships and relationships. These things alone have been enough to pull me through some difficult, lonely and dark times.

*****

It was 11 pm. Myla turned to me and said, 'I think I'm going to get going, I don't like the atmosphere in here so much anymore.'

'No, stay!' I pleaded. 'It's only eleven, stay a little longer, for me?'

'Are you enjoying this?' she asked, gesturing around to the people surrounding us, in various stages of undress, stumbling around and quite a few blatantly high as kites.

'Well, yeah. It's kind of thrilling actually,' I admitted.

Myla looked at me incredulously. 'I'll stay a little longer, but only for you.' She smiled half-heartedly.

'Thank you!' I hugged her tightly. At that moment, Joel appeared, looking glassy-eyed.

'Ooh, some girl-on-girl action,' he exclaimed.

'Urgh, Joel,' I grunted, disgusted. Myla and I pushed away from each other, both with looks of revulsion on our faces. 'That's a gross thing to say. Why do you have to make everything smutty?'

'Oh, come on, I was only joking. Lighten up a little! Come on, let's dance.' He dragged me away to the living room, leaving Myla stood alone awkwardly.

As the song grew louder and heavier, Joel and I ground up against each other, kissing and moving to the beat. Some of his friends cheered us on and tried to lift up my dress while I was distracted. Caught up in the moment, I let them.

When the song ended, I returned to Myla's side, sweaty and flustered. 'What did you let them do that for?' she demanded.

'It was just a bit of fun,' I answered coolly, though inside I felt dirty and embarrassed.

'No, it wasn't. You should have told them to stop.'

What I wanted to say was, 'Yeah, you're right. Let's get out of here,' but instead I said, 'Don't be so boring.'

Myla seethed visibly, her eyes lasering holes in me. 'I'd prefer to be boring than a whore. Who even are you?'

I didn't get time to reply. She turned on her heel and stormed out. I didn't follow her. I felt lonely and ashamed and I felt that I deserved to get left behind. Myla was right—that wasn't me. I'd done it all to impress a stupid boy and his stupid friends, who, quite frankly, I didn't give a shit about, but I did give a shit about Myla and what she thought about me.

I called Lyanna and asked her to pick me up, which she did happily. I didn't say goodbye to Joel; when Lyanna's car appeared outside, I got straight in. I spent the entire journey avoiding questions about the night and why Myla wasn't with me, a stone of regret and guilt lodged firmly in my gut.

Myla and I made up, of course. I went around to her parents' place the following day and apologised sincerely for the way I'd behaved. As always, she had a deep insight prepared to knock me off my feet. 'Why are you trying to be something you're not?' she'd asked me. 'You're a dreamer, Sara. You have this blue-sky, starry-eyed view of what you think life should be, of what you think you should be, but one day, you're going to wake up and realise that none of it is all it's cracked up to be.'

I promised her that I'd never act that way again. That's all I could think to say in response.

Myla forgave me and took me at my word. I vowed not to let boys interfere with our friendship ever again.

Chapter Eleven

I lost my virginity at the age of sixteen. It was not a good experience; I didn't want to do it. I spoke to friends about this later in life and some believe that it constitutes as rape, though I'm not sure. Although I didn't want to do it, I let him. Whether he knew if I wanted to or not remains a mystery and therefore, I can't categorically call it rape. It's a grey area, a blurred line. I said no, but then I stopped saying no. Did I give off 'no' vibes? In fact, did I say anything? My memory's sketchy of the whole thing, to be honest.

I don't hate him, but I really hated myself for a long time. I barely remember the experience, not because I was drunk or anything like that, but because it was so, well, horrible. I can't call it rape because I can't actually remember what happened. It was traumatic. I was numb during and upset afterwards, so I think my brain has taken an eraser to the memory. It's now nothing more than a half-blurry pencil drawing inside my head and a knot in my stomach when I think about it. I had no idea I felt this strongly but writing about it now, after all these years, makes me feel sick. No one should ever feel that way when they think about their first time.

The other reason I refuse to call it rape is because he wasn't a 'bad' person. I believe that if I had shouted and screamed and sent him away, he would have gone. So, why, if I really didn't want to do it, did I not scream and shout and send him away? I have never, ever, regretted anything in my life, except that. That is one thing I would change about my past. It's also something I still struggle to understand. Why did I let it happen?

I woke up at 10 am in Joel's bed, the morning after another one of his house parties. I hadn't drunk the night before so I wasn't hungover, just tired.

The sunlight shone around the sides of his blind and I lay a while, quietly watching the dust motes swirling in the beams, waiting for Joel to wake up beside me.

Joel had been almost paralytic when we'd finally gone to bed at about 3 am. This was the second time I'd slept in his bed and neither time had he tried to have sex with me, which I thought was progress. The previous time, I had enjoyed lying in his arms and talking the morning after. I felt comfortable and content finally, like I was part of a real, grown-up couple.

That morning began just as cosy; he woke up and immediately turned over to embrace me. We lay there, breathing in each other's scent, feeling skin on skin, not speaking, just being. Then, out of the blue, he told me he loved me for the first time. I said it back. Whether I truly did love him and whether he loved me, I'm not sure. I was swept up in the moment; for the first time, a boy, sorry, a man, had told me he loved me. It felt right to say it back. And who knows, maybe I did? Teenage hormones make you feel things so much deeper, so it's hard to tell.

He kissed me passionately and held me close, and for a moment I did truly feel like I could be in love. But it didn't stop there and that's when my memory gets hazy.

Did I tell him no? Did I push him away? Did I make a fuss? Struggle? I'm sure I did, at least a little, because I know, for definite, that I didn't want to do it, but I still let him. I don't know how long it lasted, what it felt like, nothing. I just remember being laid on my back, trying to think of anything but what we were doing, or should I say, what he was doing to me. I didn't like it—in fact, I hated it—but I was then forced to lay in his arms afterwards and pretend that everything was normal when inside, I was screaming at myself to get out of that bed and out of that house.

I lay in his arms, silent tears streaming down my face, and he didn't say a word to me. He didn't ask me how I was, how I felt, nothing. I wanted to go home, where I would feel safe and normal again. I wanted to be a child again, to be back at the lake, paddling with my aunties, with no knowledge of this adult world, no knowledge of what it feels like to be invaded by someone.

Myla was staying in the room next to us. Somehow, just the knowledge that she was close by gave me much-needed comfort. I made my excuses to Joel, who didn't protest as he was already half-asleep, got dressed and crept into the next room to wake up Myla.

I shook her, rather forcefully, and whispered aggressively, 'Myla! Wake up!'

'Woah! What? What time is it?' she asked blearily.

'10:30. Please, we have to go.'

She must have sensed something in my demeanour or caught on to the urgency in my voice, because she practically bolted out of bed, threw on her coat and shoes and followed me out of the house. 'What's wrong?' she asked me as we walked hurriedly down the garden path and out on to the street. 'You look like you've seen a ghost.'

I gulped, tasting bile in my mouth. 'We did it. Had sex, I mean.' Myla stopped walking. 'Don't stop! Come on, keep going,' I urged, continuing at a brisk pace.

'What's wrong? What happened?' she asked, hurrying after me.

We turned a corner and crossed the road, making our way onto the path that led over the field to my house. It washed over me then, a sudden relief that Joel's house was no longer in view, like it had been watching me. I couldn't speak.

Myla stopped me and forced me to look at her. 'You're scaring me! What's going on?'

'It was horrible, like really horrible,' I managed.

'Did it hurt?'

'No, no. Nothing like that. I just, I…'

Myla waited patiently, scanning my face for a clue of what I was going to say next. 'I didn't want to,' I admitted, before bursting into tears.

Myla held me for a few moments, probably unsure of what to say. When I looked at her face, I could see sympathy, but also anger simmering beneath the surface. 'Did he force you?'

'No, yes. I don't know. I'm so confused.'

'Sara, please try to explain it to me, I don't understand.'

'I don't either.' I took a deep breath and looked around. The bleak sky cast a gloomy light down on the scene. The morning was cold, I suddenly realised, and I wanted to get as far from Joel's house as possible. 'Can we not talk about it here?'

'Sure,' she agreed, rubbing my arms. 'Let's go to yours.'

We walked home in silence, neither of us sure what to say. We reached the passage that led to the end of my street and I stopped dead. The faerie I had met seven years before was standing at the gate. Once again, she was cloaked. 'What is it?' Myla asked, breaking my trance.

'Can you see her?' I questioned, pointing to where the faerie was stood.

'Who?' She looked in the direction I was pointing, confused.

'Her, there.'

'I can't see anyone. Are you okay? You're drip-white.'

I fought back bile once again and blinked. The faerie took down her hood and smiled warmly at me. More than anything in the world, right then, I wanted to go to her and follow her back to that golden field. This time, I knew I would have followed her into that forest. The only thing that stopped me was Myla's presence. 'Sara? You're scaring me. Are you okay?'

I snapped out of my trance and looked into Myla's worried eyes. When I turned back to the gate, the faerie was gone. I'd missed my chance. I felt like I was drowning in a well of sadness. 'Let's go, I want to get home,' I said, setting off down the path and through the gate.

The smell of sausages greeted us as we entered the house. Lyanna was cooking in the kitchen and the air was dusky with smoke. 'Hey, you two! I've made sausages. I thought you might be needing some sustenance,' Lyanna announced as we closed the front door behind us.

'Thanks, maybe later,' I mumbled, before heading upstairs.

'Thanks, Lyanna,' Myla said as my aunt entered the hallway. They exchanged meaningful glances at my hasty exit up to my room.

Myla followed me into my bedroom and sat herself down on my bed while I took off my clothes. She waited for me while I showered, thoroughly. After the shower, I felt slightly better but still sickly. I put on my favourite pyjamas, the ones decorated with sleeping, smiling clouds. Even they couldn't make me feel better that day.

Back in my room, I recounted the whole incident to Myla. She was as confused as I was but offered me some consolation. 'I think you froze, that's all I can guess.'

'Maybe,' I shrugged, feeling deeply disappointed in myself. This was not how it was supposed to be. We should have been discussing every detail and getting all excited and girly. Instead, all I wanted to do was curl up in a ball and forget the whole thing.

'Is it because you were caught up in the moment, then changed your mind halfway through but didn't have the guts to stop it?'

'No, I definitely didn't want to do it at any point. I told him no, I think, but then I let him carry on. I don't know what came over me. It's like I was trapped inside my body and I couldn't do anything.'

'Then, you froze.'

'Yes and no. I don't know.'

'Were you worried he was going to break up with you?'

'No, it's not that. Look, I don't know. I don't want to talk about it anymore. I'm so disappointed in myself and I can't bear to think about it.'

Myla shuffled over and put her arm around me. 'Sara,' she said sweetly, moving my hair out of my eyes, 'whatever happened, you did nothing wrong. Don't torment yourself like this.'

I cried for a while and Myla let me. I was so grateful to have her in my life at that moment. I don't know what I'd have done if she hadn't been there to comfort me.

At length, she asked, 'What are you going to do? About Joel, I mean.'

'I don't know. I can't see him, not yet. It hurts, you know, that he will see this whole thing from a different point of view. He has no idea what he's done to me.'

'That's debatable.'

'No, Myla, I genuinely don't think he'll know. I didn't put up enough of a fight. I should have stopped him.' I began to cry again.

'Hey, hey,' she said, rocking me soothingly. 'Don't worry about that now. We'll cross that bridge when we come to it. What can we do, right now, to help you? Do you want sausages? Can you face Lyanna?'

I thought about it for a moment, unsure. My stomach was painful with hunger, but did I want to see Lyanna? How could I look her in the eye?

Myla filled the silence for me. 'Will you tell her?'

'Yes,' I replied without hesitation. I noticed Myla relax a little, relieved. 'But not yet,' I added.

'Right, so we'll go get breakfast, or dinner, or whatever time it is, and then we'll take it from there, okay?'

Thank the gods for Myla.

*****

Alongside me walked a handsome, rugged man. In my dream I knew him, and even trusted him, but I had never seen him before in my life. We were passing through an unfamiliar, peculiar place. In every direction was a seemingly endless expanse of bare, gnarled trees. The air was icy cold and my head had begun to ache with it. I could no longer feel my fingers or toes but, feeling on edge, I trudged on without complaint.

Eventually, we reached a pretty glade. In its centre stood a small cottage. The man stopped suddenly and raised his finger to his lips, signalling for me to stay quiet. The look of concern on his face terrified me; there was obviously something there to be afraid of.

We ducked down behind a felled tree and watched from our hiding place. I wanted to ask him what was wrong, but I dared not breathe let alone speak. The sound of breaking twigs underfoot caught my attention.

Two young women carrying logs emerged from the cottage. Both had porcelain skin but looked entirely different. The first had ebony black hair and dark, sultry eyes. She wore a long, layered frock and a velvet cape of sapphire blue. The other lady had flaming red hair, piercing hazel eyes and was attired in amber silk. Their lips were full and scarlet, like beads of blood decorating pearly snow.

While they were going about their business obliviously, I noticed, as did the man beside me, thick, blue ice, hard as glass, creeping up the trunk of the tree. I pulled my hand away quickly, wincing as though burned. On the ground about us, ice crystals and stalagmites formed, defying the laws of physics, and above our heads, impossibly fast, icicles dripped down, dangerously sharp and close to our heads. I instinctively shielded myself.

My breath froze in great swirls of mist the instant it left my mouth. I closed my mouth, terrified of giving away our position, and attempted to hold my breath.

At that moment, a strange, female creature entered the glade from the opposite side to where we were hidden. Her silver hair fell all the way down to her hips, and her lips and eyes were a deathly, sinister violet. She was naked, covered only in a layer of glittering frost. She appeared as fragile as a crystal vase, though her demeanour revealed a malevolent danger.

She began to laugh menacingly, causing the two young women to drop their wood in fright, having only just noticed her presence. The sky darkened and all the ice surrounding us groaned eerily, before cracking and splintering. The sorceress continued to laugh insanely.

A great *smash!* echoed all around, like the sound of a thousand glasses crashing against a stone floor. The ground rumbled and I felt shards of ice hitting me from all angles. The man's body weighed down on me as he shielded me from the worst of it.

I heard the terrified screams of the two women and then all was still and silent. The earth held its breath.

The man continued to hold me, not moving or speaking for some time, until eventually, he let me go and got to his feet stiffly. After he checked the coast was clear, he gestured for me to join him in the clearing. I stood reluctantly, fear still gripping me.

The two women were dead. Their bodies lay impaled on great shards of ice, the tips sticking obscenely out through their otherwise pristine, alabaster skin. Bright blood splattered the bright snow.

I will never forget their eyes; those deep, dark, lifeless eyes, open and staring in horror, forever remembering their last shocking, tragic moments on this earth.

I woke up abruptly, panting and sweating profusely. It was one of the most vivid dreams I'd ever had, and I knew precisely what it meant—all innocence and purity was lost to me now. My childhood was gone, over. My virginity had been stolen and there was no way of ever reclaiming it. I was tainted, changed, a dark moth shedding its beautiful cocoon.

I laid my head back down on the pillow and cried myself back to sleep.

*****

Joel didn't call me for two weeks. Part of me was glad; I couldn't bear to face him, but another part of me was sad. Did I mean so little to him? As the days passed by, my sadness gave way to anger. Did he know he'd done something wrong? Was he avoiding me out of shame? Myla was furious that he'd used me and dumped me, as she saw it, and was desperate to give him a piece of her mind.

On the second Sunday after it had happened, in the evening, he finally called me. 'Hey,' he greeted me when I answered the phone.

'Hey,' I replied croakily.

There was a pause. 'How are you doing?' he asked.

'Fine, you?'

'Okay, I guess.' Another pause. 'I miss you.'

'Why?'

'What do you mean?'

'Well, why do you miss me? You can see me any time. I'm right here.'

'I, er, didn't think it was a good idea.'

'Oh, didn't you? Thank you for making that decision for me.'

All of a sudden, his arrogance made me want to explode with fury. I had been so worried, so terrified of this moment, terrified of him, angry with myself, that I hadn't stopped to think of what he had actually done. Even if it had been enjoyable, consensual sex, he had told me he loved me, fucked me then ignored me for two whole weeks.

'Don't be like that.'

'Don't you dare!' I shouted, standing up in anger. 'Don't you dare tell me how I should be, what I should do. You're a worthless, nasty piece of shit! Well, you finally got what you wanted, didn't you? And the fact that you didn't call, text, email, nothing for a fortnight just proves that that was ALL you wanted.'

'I'm calling you now, aren't I?'

'Ooh, well done you. You're a brave man.'

Joel sighed on the other end of the line. 'Look, it's obvious that nothing I say will reason with you.'

'You haven't even tried! You scumbag. You always make me feel like a stupid little girl, like I don't know anything, but I'm not an idiot. I know what you are now, so thank you for showing me your true colours.'

There was silence, and for a moment I thought he'd hung up, then, 'I meant it, you know. I do love you.'

'Whatever,' I retorted and hung up.

My hands were shaking but I didn't feel like crying; I felt like trashing my bedroom and screaming and stamping my feet.

A knock at my door startled me back to sense before I did anything I would regret. 'Sara?' It was Lyanna. Obviously, she'd heard my half of the phone conversation. 'Are you okay?'

'No!' I shouted in a nastier tone than I'd intended.

'Do you want to talk?' she asked, sounding worried.

I slumped down on to my bed and sighed. There was no point trying to put it off any longer. 'Yeah, I'll be down in a minute.'

'Okay, whenever you're ready,' she told me kindly and I heard her footsteps retreat down the stairs.

I took a moment to compose myself before heading downstairs to face the music. Serafina, who had come over for Sunday dinner, and Lyanna were sat in the kitchen, blatantly apprehensive about what I was going to tell them. Of course, they already knew, or had an idea—I'd been acting strange since it had happened—but they needed to hear it from my mouth.

I told them everything, not in any great detail, but enough. They didn't say a word until I was finished, then they both came over to hug me. 'I'm sorry you went through that,' Serafina said.

Lyanna nodded in agreement. 'You could have come to us at any time.'

'I know. I never intended to not tell you at all, I just didn't want to relive it. It was so raw, and I was so confused and angry at myself.'

'You should *not* be angry at yourself,' Serafina told me forcefully. 'The mind does strange things to protect itself. You experienced a trauma and your body reacted accordingly. No matter what anyone tells you, having sex is a huge deal. You never know how you're going to feel until it happens.'

I flinched when she said the word 'sex'. It sounded like a dirty word to me now, associated with feeling sick and vulnerable and scared.

Lyanna, noticing my visible flinch, gave me another hug. Serafina was the logical, problem-solving aunt and Lyanna the affectionate, caring aunt. I needed them both equally. 'Why is everything falling apart?' I asked them hopelessly. 'None of this was supposed to happen to me.'

They exchanged a look that said they'd never wanted anything bad to ever happen to me. They wanted to shield me from the world and all its atrocities forever. I think, like me, they wanted to go back to that day at the lake, when I was innocent and untainted by the world. 'A perfect world is not real. Shit happens to everyone at some point, I'm just sorry it happened to you so soon. I was hoping that it would be at least another few years until you got your heart broken,' Serafina said.

'If not ever,' Lyanna added.

'Of course,' Serafina agreed. 'Heartbreak is all part and parcel of growing up though, unfortunately. But the other stuff…that should never have happened. Ever. He should never have put you in that position.'

'I put myself in that position. I was naïve. He was too old for me. I thought I was mature enough, that I could handle it. I thought I was grown up, but now I've never wanted to go back to being a kid more in my life.'

Lyanna hugged me yet again and stroked my hair. 'You did nothing wrong,' she said, mirroring Myla's words. 'Don't let this break you. You'll always be our little gummy bear.'

I didn't know whether to smile or cry. 'Let it go now, Sara,' Serafina advised. 'You've told us and you've spoken to Joel,' she said his name like it tasted bitter, 'so now, you can let it go. You're strong and you're brave—you'll be okay.'

Then she said something that stuck with me for the rest of my life. 'Any rubbish that life throws at you, you have to take it on the chin and learn from it. It all shapes you, the good and the bad. Don't let it wear you down, let it mould you into a better person.'

Serafina left after our hearty Sunday dinner and Lyanna bade me goodnight not long after as she had an early start the next morning. I stayed up to get my bag ready for school. I could hear her shuffling around upstairs, getting ready for bed, and the sound comforted me.

I went outside into the back garden for some peace and fresh air. I was now resolved to take on board what my aunts had said, focus on my schoolwork— GCSE exams were coming up—and forget all about boys for a while.

I was a thoughtful teenager and I liked being alone with my own mind. I was deeply emotional and felt things, I was sure, more than others my age seemed to. I guess that came with being a writer, a creative type.

I sat on a stone bench just outside the patio doors and took in a deep lungful of cool air. The sky was furious. There was a flash in the distance, then the thunder began, like ominous drums rolling. Next came the terrific flashes of lightning, splintering across the sky, illuminating the hills in the distance, the valley, the tops of the trees, all for split seconds at a time.

I sat and observed the spectacle in the pouring rain for what seemed like hours, thinking of nothing but the scene unfolding before my eyes. It was a release, a moment in time when I didn't need to think, when my troubles escaped me, and I was utterly alone with the force of nature.

The rain ceased and the clouds parted. I could see the stars, piercingly bright, so clear; like diamonds washed up on the dark shore after the depths of the ocean have spat them out.

I went upstairs, locking up behind me, and dried myself off, then sat on my bed and looked out of the window into the night. I lit some candles and incense to soothe my aching mind and heart, then opened the window to feel closer to nature.

A gust of wind blew in, causing the soft candlelight to flicker. As it did, the deep shadows around the bed and door began to move, as though there were great, dark demons shifting around the room. I fancied I saw something scurry across the carpet and dart behind my bookcase, but it hadn't felt threatening, so I paid it no mind. I stayed up late into the night writing and thinking and clearing my head. It was my own therapy, my way of extinguishing the demons.

I wrote about the universe: it's endless, beautiful state. I questioned the idea of God, religion and faith, its rights and wrongs and general absurdity. I questioned the meaning of life. Was there one? Was it ever possible to find an answer?

I thought about happiness and sadness, love and hate, and the fine line between things that at first seem so opposing. I thought on depression and the human mind—the seeds planted earlier that evening by Serafina—it's depths and abilities, both known and unknown, shrouded in mystery.

I tried to comprehend freedom and whether anyone can ever truly achieve it. I even considered the subject of death. Always, as the night drew deeper, my mind would wander to darker territory. I wrote about the emotion death draws out of us, and the impossibility of reason while enduring grief. Despite never experiencing bereavement myself, I had read many books and watched many films that dealt with these themes and I felt a certain amount of sympathy for it. For some reason, I found it fascinating.

Ultimately, as I always did, I went back to the subject of inevitability; the concept that my life was laid out before me and there was no way to change my fate or future because it was already written in my genes, my childhood, the part of me that I had no control over.

I dwelled on the Other Place, why I could see it, why it came to me at such important moments in my life. As I didn't know my parents, I couldn't help but wonder if it was all because of them.

Chapter Twelve

I did focus on my schoolwork for a while and Myla and I were back to normal: no more parties, no more dragging her along on dates, no more constantly analysing different aspects of mine and Joel's relationship, just us being us. I showed her my writing from the night of the storm and it inspired her enough to create some illustrations to go alongside it.

One weekend, a month or two later, there was a knock at the front door and I answered. It was Joel, looking tired, strained and sheepish. I didn't know what to say, so I stood there dumbly with my mouth wide open. 'Can we talk?' he asked, his voice hoarse.

'What about?' I replied, shocked.

'I just have some things I want to say.'

I looked around guiltily. I don't know why, I knew Lyanna was at work and I wasn't expecting Myla for another few hours, but still, I felt guilty for even entertaining the notion of talking to the creep. Even so, I was curious as to what he'd possibly have to say to me, so I reluctantly let him in.

We sat at the dining room table and I let him speak first. In my house, on my time, I felt in control of the situation somehow. 'I can't sleep,' he started. 'I just feel so guilty. I'm so sorry for what I did to you. I was a total arsehole. I'm shocked you let me in actually.' He studied my face as though to find the answer written there.

'I was curious,' I shrugged, trying to lessen the intensity of the atmosphere.

'Well, I just couldn't bear to leave it as it was. My guilty conscience wouldn't let me sleep, and I thought the only way to ease the guilt and get my life back was to come over and apologise.'

I have to admit, I was pleasantly surprised. I don't know what I'd expected, but it hadn't been this. 'What do you want me to say?' I asked genuinely.

'Nothing,' he answered and I believed him. He looked awful, like he hadn't slept since we'd last talked. I racked my brain for some underlying, duplicitous reason for his visit, but I couldn't think of any other reason than the one he'd given me.

'So, this is just to ease your conscience?'

'No, also because you deserve my apology. I treated you appallingly. I've missed your company so much. I never realised how great you are until you were gone.'

'How come you've left it so long then?'

'I figured you'd never want to see me again and I couldn't face seeing you. Sometimes, I'd drive past the school just to catch a glimpse of you. I drove myself crazy until I just couldn't take it anymore and I knew I had to come see you.' His voice caught in his throat. I thought he was going to start crying but he composed himself. 'Can you forgive me?'

I honestly felt bad for him. Fighting every instinct in my body, I said yes. After all the reflection, going backwards and forwards in my mind, I'd finally started to put it all behind me, so to forgive him felt right, like the final nail in the coffin of the whole shitty situation.

'Really?' He looked astounded.

'Yeah. I've done a lot of thinking these past months and it won't do you, or me, any good to hold a grudge. What happened, happened. There's no going back, it's over.'

He seemed both relieved and disappointed. 'So, you forgive me, but you'd never take me back?'

'I thought that you didn't want anything from me? That this was just an apology?'

'It was, but hearing those words, *it's over*. I don't want it to be over.'

I didn't know what to say, yet again. After everything that had happened, how could I take him back? What kind of person would that make me? But, I did. Not straight away, but I did take him back. I shouldn't have.

We talked for a while longer before I asked him to leave. Myla or Lyanna were going to arrive at any moment and I couldn't face their reactions if they found Joel sitting there. He left as soon as I asked him. Then, secretly, over the next few weeks, he went out of his way to prove his love for me. I knew I was playing a dangerous game, unsure if I could really trust him, but I couldn't help feeling that if it was all just a front to get me back into bed then it was awfully long-winded. The thing I hated most about it all was lying to Myla.

Eventually, I had to tell the truth. After love letters, flowers, declarations of love and multiple promises, I took him back and I couldn't hide it any longer. As you can imagine, the conversation didn't go very well. They were livid, beyond furious. They couldn't believe what I was doing, but then, they hadn't heard all the amazing things he'd said to me.

I admit that I did have my concerns and at times I thought, *What the hell am I doing!* but every time I raised these doubts with Joel, he said all the right things to put my mind at rest. I couldn't help but fall hook, line and sinker for every word he uttered. I felt like a goddess, truly wanted and adored.

It drove a wedge between myself and Myla, which I hated, but I was blinded by 'love' and the craving I had for his attention. I was a teenage fool, swept away on flimsy promises and whispers of romance.

*****

It all came to a nasty, heart-breaking conclusion not a month or two after we got back together. I started frequenting parties with him again, but this time I was without my best friend. Things weren't quite as romantic and beautiful as I'd imagined. I ended up in some nasty scenarios, feeling uneasy and homesick. I felt a million miles away from my comfort zone.

It started with manipulation, breaking me down, making me feel small and worthless. He played mind games with me, preying on my trusting, innocent nature. He would flirt with other girls in front of me and on some occasions, he even groped them brazenly. It was like he was trying to see how far he could push me, to provoke me. Whenever I pulled him up on his behaviour, which wasn't as often as it should have been, he told me it was just a bit of fun and it didn't mean anything. For some reason, I let it go.

One thing I couldn't let go, however, was him sleeping with somebody else. I saw the way he looked at Elena, a friend of his from college. She had huge breasts and enormous hazel eyes. She didn't disguise the fact that she wanted him: laughing loudly at his lame jokes, stroking his arms whenever she spoke to him, even putting me down and belittling me in front of everyone. I felt like a tiny, insignificant person whenever she was around. How could I ever compete with someone like her? Sometimes though, I did wonder if I even wanted to compete with someone like her. I didn't want to be lascivious and so openly shameless. I couldn't imagine anything worse than displaying myself like she did.

Ever since I'd lost my virginity, I got an odd feeling in my stomach whenever I was alone with any men, and not just with boyfriends and people I was intimate with, or even with strangers, but men I know and trust, like teachers, friends or friend's relatives. I felt dirty, vulnerable and panicked around them, like I wanted to cover up every inch of my body. I could almost feel their hands and eyes crawling all over me like bugs. I irrationally felt like they wanted to undress me. I shrank into myself, playing with my baggy clothes nervously. I still get that feeling to this day, every now and then. Joel had broken something deep inside of me, and I wondered if it could ever be fixed. It couldn't, not really, but I learned how to live with it.

Of course, because of the issues I was working through, I didn't want to have sex again or do anything intimate at all, so we were back to square one: him hounding me every chance he got and getting angry when I rejected him. And so, one night at one of his parties, I escaped upstairs to his room for some peace and quiet. Why I didn't just go home, I have no idea. Part of me is glad that I didn't however as when I opened the door, I found Elena straddling Joel, rocking back and forth, moaning ridiculously like a wannabe porn star, her dress pulled down below those huge breasts of hers. I stood there for about half a minute (though it felt like hours) just watching them, feeling sick and completely gobsmacked.

They didn't notice I was there until I made an involuntary half-cough, half-sob. Elena noticed me first and sniggered, still riding my boyfriend like a mule. He then noticed me and I saw a fleeting recognition in his eyes, a look of guilt or shock passed over his features, but then, his face contorted into a nasty grin. That wasn't the same man who had come to me weeks before, begging my forgiveness and promising me the world. He was high and he was a monster, sneering back at me through the haze of drugs. I couldn't watch anymore. I walked away and never looked back. I never heard from him again.

Why he crawled back to me and reeled me in—what his motivation was—I'll never know. Was it some sick, twisted game? Maybe a bet with his friends to see if he could pull it off? Or had he been genuine and then quickly gone back to his old ways? I guess some questions are never supposed to be answered.

I didn't want to go home that night, or to Myla's. I couldn't face the humiliation of having to explain what had happened: that I'd let him stamp all over my fragile heart once again. They'd warned me, seen right through him, especially my aunts. They'd encountered men like him before. So, I wandered all night. It was the early hours when I'd left Joel's and by the time I found where I was going, it was breaking dawn.

Before me was a vast, empty space occupied solely by long grass and an enormous, ancient oak tree; the same tree within the grounds of Moraine Manor that I'd greeted before on my walk home from school. It towered over me, blinding me to everything else. Calmly, I approached it with a smile on my face, the way one would greet an old friend. At its base, I touched the rough bark remembering the feel beneath my fingertips. I settled down on the grass beneath it, between its mighty roots; my natural throne. It felt like home. This was my safe place, my quiet place.

I thought at length about everything that had happened. How could I have been so stupid? How could I have let that happen? I'd never been particularly interested in having a boyfriend, so why had I allowed such a monster inside my heart, and let him crush it so completely, and on more than one occasion? Worse than that, he'd crushed my spirit. The one thing that was so unique to me—my lust for life, my intelligence, my optimism—now all shredded and torn like old rags. How could I have let it come to this? I asked myself this question over and over, but I couldn't pinpoint exactly where it had all gone wrong.

I thought about Serafina's words the night I'd confessed to losing my virginity, but at that moment they didn't offer me any warmth or comfort. It had gone too far, too much had happened. Things would never be the same. I was at the pivotal moment between adulthood and childhood—I couldn't ever go back, but I couldn't bring myself to step forward. The future was an abyss, a deep well of uncertainty and darkness. My stomach lurched as I was about to step over the edge. The sun was rising, the clouds scudding across the sky in the dawns light, like a time-lapse film, casting shadows across the land. Everything seemed to be moving too fast for my tired mind; the trees swaying in the wind, the leaves shaking, the birds darting from branch to branch just blurs in the sky. And yet, inside my head, everything was in slow motion. My thoughts were sluggish, my head and eyes heavy.

I sat there for hours, numb, aware of nothing. Then, across the glade, I saw a figure moving. It wasn't the graceful form of the faerie, this was something sinister. It was a shadow, formlessly drifting from side to side as though searching for something. Then, it stopped. Though no eyes were visible, I could sense its stare upon me. Slowly, it advanced. I felt fear like nothing I'd felt before. As the figure moved closer, the space around me darkened visibly and a sense of foreboding weighed down on me.

Panicking, I tried to move. I wanted more than anything to run and never look back, but my body had turned to stone. The shadow was before me, its ghostly arms outstretched. I felt it brush against my skin, its touch soft yet prickly. I couldn't do anything but stare, petrified, as its long, claw-like fingers extended. All the hairs on my body stood on end. I closed my eyes, clenching them tight, tears of fear trickling down my cheeks.

The prickling strokes on my face became sharp stings and I realised, with utter horror, that the abomination was running its claws down my face. When I thought I couldn't handle the terror any longer, the sun peeked over the tops of the trees and the demon vanished.

Whether out of shock or exhaustion, I passed out. When I came around, I had no clue where I was or what time it was. Overhead, the crisp, bright early morning light had been buried beneath dense, black cloud, and the refreshing breeze had transformed into a thick, stuffy atmosphere promising rain. The cold had spread to my bones, like fingers of ice reaching out beneath my skin. I was reminded of the shadowy figure and was jolted out of my daze. It was time to leave and make my journey home to my aunts to come clean.

Chapter Thirteen

You would have thought that after all I'd been through, I'd want to go back to my quiet life of studying, reading and writing, pick up what remained of my relationship with Myla and focus on my education. But no; instead, I took the opposite path. I wanted something to distract me from my guilt, pain and sense of worthlessness, so I continued to party and headed down a road of self-destruction. I thought I would have had enough of those juvenile gatherings of imbeciles, but somehow, I became hooked on them, drawn to the empty-headed hedonism of losing myself in a room full of strangers.

I think Myla had been asked by my aunts to accompany me and keep an eye on me, because I know she never wanted to be a part of that scene. I wasn't acting myself, but I suspect that my aunts didn't want to ground me or fight with me in fear of pushing me further away. So, they used the only tool at their disposal: my level-headed, forgiving, loyal best friend. Myla didn't try to tame me or make me see reason, she let me play it out, get it out of my system. Maybe, that was what I needed: escapism.

Where before I had turned to Tolkien or JK Rowling for my fix of escapism, I now turned to parties and alcohol. It sounds strange, but I felt like I wasn't worthy of my normal interests, like I'd muddied myself, so I didn't deserve to relax and enjoy my real passions. I was trying to fill an unfillable hole inside myself.

*****

At the end of spring, things came to a head. Myla and I made friends with two guys in the year above us at school: Benji and James. They enjoyed heavy metal and cult 80's movies like us and invited us to every party they knew of. I made it clear from day one to both of them that I wasn't interested in a relationship or sex.

It was spring bank holiday weekend. The night was going well; I'd had a few drinks and was feeling a bit looser, less shy. I was sat chatting with Myla when Benji came over and asked Myla to join him outside. They'd taken a shine to each other lately, so I nodded for them to go ahead. I never felt awkward sat alone at these things, I knew pretty much everyone there. I watched them all having a good time and enjoyed not having to talk for a few brief moments.

'Hey, what are you doing sat there all by yourself?' James asked, standing over me at the end of the sofa.

'Myla's outside with Benji,' I told him.

James raised his eyebrows. 'Right,' he said with a glint in his eye.

'She's not like that,' I grunted, reading his mind.

'Everyone's like that when they meet the right person.'

Joel flashed up in my memory. 'If you say so.'

'Come on, let's get you another drink,' he suggested, eyeing up my empty glass.

'I've had enough for tonight, I think. I'm pretty tired, I might head home.'

'Nah! I'm going to make you one of my famous cocktails!' He took me by the hand, smiling cheekily like he knew something I didn't. I felt like I knew James pretty well and was comfortable enough in his presence to not be perturbed by this. I was tired, but I knew I could be a while waiting for Myla, so I let him lead me down the stairs into the basement kitchen.

I looked around in awe. I'd never ventured into that part of Benji's house before. The marble worktops, sparkling clean chrome finishes and showy spotlights all looked super luxurious. 'Benji's parents must have a bit of money. This is like a whole extra house. Some people live in flats smaller than this!' I exclaimed.

'A bit, yeah. That's right,' he said, turning to me, 'you've never been down here before, have you?'

I shook my head. 'Benji doesn't let anyone down here in case they damage anything. Nobody in the upstairs bedrooms or basement, that's the rule, but I'm sure he'd make an exception for you.'

I smiled. 'So, where's this cocktail you're making me?'

'Right!' He turned and began rifling through the cupboards. 'What do we have in here?' He pulled out bottles of rum, whiskey, vodka, gin, sour apple alcopops and some cookie mix.

'You can't be serious? That'll be disgusting!' I laughed.

'Just a sip, it'll be funny! Benji and I used to do stuff like this all the time whenever his parents weren't home.'

I reluctantly agreed and watched as he mixed all the ingredients together in a plastic jug. I took one sip and nearly vomited. The intoxicating taste and smell were nearly as bad as the texture; the powdery cookie mix had turned into pockets of thick sludge. We decided not to finish the mixture off and laughed and joked as we cleaned up the mess we'd made. I felt some warmth towards him, stirrings of feelings that could lead to something more between us. It felt like we had a secret friendship that existed only between us, there in that basement where nobody else was allowed. He was the first guy I felt I could trust since everything that had happened with Joel. 'Let me give you the grand tour then,' he said, gesturing to the doors leading off into other rooms.

He showed me a neat and tidy guest bedroom, a study crammed full of books and art posters, a chic, small bathroom and then finally, 'his' room. 'This is where I stay whenever I sleep over. Pretty cool, huh?'

'Yeah, sweet,' I agreed.

He didn't switch on the light, which I thought was odd as he had done so in every other room, but then, we were just standing in the doorway and the light from the kitchen was enough to illuminate most of the bedroom. It wasn't anything special anyway: a single bed with a few shirts thrown on it, a wardrobe with its doors hanging half-open and a standing lamp in the corner looking stark and lonely. 'Go in,' he said, prodding me in the back.

'Why?' I asked, giggling nervously. He was going to play a trick on me, I knew it. 'I don't trust you,' I laughed, turning to face him.

'Course you do,' he laughed back half-heartedly. 'We've had some fun down here tonight, haven't we? It's been nice to get some time alone with you.' He stepped closer, forcing me step backwards into the bedroom.

'Yeah, it's been nice,' I agreed, starting to feel uncomfortable.

He closed the door behind him. I could just make out his face in the moonlight seeping in through the undressed window. He now looked serious, all jokes forgotten. 'What are you doing?' I asked nervously, giggling lightly, trying to recreate the casual atmosphere we'd had in the kitchen.

'I want you,' he told me, and I instantly got flashbacks to my time with Joel.

'No, you don't,' I responded, trying to brush off his comment. My mind refused to believe that I'd found myself in this position yet again.

'I do. I've been watching you.'

Any other girl might have taken his advance as a compliment. He was an attractive guy, a really attractive guy, in fact, but the way my mind was wired at that time meant I had zero interest. All the thoughts I'd had in the kitchen, the feelings that might have begun to bloom, had now withered and died.

'Don't do this,' I pleaded.

'I want to be more than friends.' His voice was hoarse and whispery, filled with lust. He kissed me hard on the lips and for a brief moment, shocked, I kissed him back. His hands ran through my hair, down my spine, then he forced his way down the back of my jeans, until he grabbed a great handful of my backside. I felt that familiar lurch in my stomach, bile rising in my throat, and I let out a cry.

'Stop it,' I said breathlessly, pushing him away. His hands released me and he moved away. I backed myself into the corner. I should have made for the door, but I was frightened, like a deer in the headlights.

He advanced on me and gripped my waist, trying to kiss me. His breath reeked of beer. I turned my head away, disgusted, causing him to miss my mouth. He seized the opportunity and kissed my neck instead. I struggled to break free of his grasp, squirming and protesting, but his mouth made its way to the top of my breasts and his hands found them too. He squeezed, hard, causing me to yelp in pain. 'Get off me!' I yelled and smacked him as hard as I could around the side of his head.

'Ow!' He backed off then, seemingly coming to his senses. I saw the look on his face, illuminated by the moonlight. He looked shocked, but not at my actions, at his own. 'I'm sorry,' he growled and stormed out of the room, slamming the door behind him.

I felt the wall at my back and realised I was falling. I slumped down onto the floor, hugging my knees. I felt sick and dizzy, so I let myself fall to one side, the hard, laminate floor cool against my face. I lay there and let the tears come. I heard rain pattering against the window, so I focussed on that. *Pitter patter, pitter patter.* Soothing rain. Safe, cold rain. The tears formed a pool between the floor and my cheek, but I paid it no mind. I felt the sadness in my heart drain away with every tear.

After a short while, the rain ceased and the room became cocooned in silence. Suddenly, the light flicked on and Myla appeared in the doorway, Benji close behind her. 'Sara, what are you doing in here?' she asked, surprised. 'We've been looking everywhere for you. What's wrong? What happened?' She crouched down and brushed my hair out of my face.

I struggled up into a sitting position. Benji, now crouched down beside Myla, looked genuinely worried. 'He assaulted me,' I told them. 'He tried to…' I couldn't say the word.

'What? Who?' Benji raged. 'Tell me it wasn't James.'

I nodded. 'No! I can't believe it!' he shouted. 'I'm going to kick his arse!' He paced up and down the room, running his hands through his hair anxiously.

'Oh, Sara,' Myla sighed sympathetically. I knew she was thinking, *How are we here again?* She smoothed my knotted hair and rubbed my shoulders while Benji continued to pace up and down.

'I knew there was something up when I saw him leave. He would never leave without telling me where he was going, and he almost always stays over, but I never thought it could be anything like this. I just can't believe it. I never thought he could do something like that.' He seemed to remember we were both in the room with him. 'Are you okay?' he asked, turning to me.

I nodded. My tears had dried up and I just wanted to leave. 'Take me home, Myla.'

Benji called us a taxi and paid for it. He hugged me before we climbed in and apologised that this had happened to me under his roof. I told him it wasn't his fault and he promised me he'd never speak to James again. At least I knew there were some decent men in the world.

'Well, you can say it now: I told you so,' I said to Myla once we were belted in and on our way home.

'What?' Myla questioned, looking horrified. 'Why would I say that?' She clutched my hand desperately.

'You warned me. I have a rose-tinted view, you called it. I was swanning around, head in the clouds, like a brainless idiot, and I got burned, just like you said I would.'

'You're not stupid—don't say that! It's just the way you are, Sara. You're learning and growing, making mistakes. You're human! I would never say I told you so!'

'How come you're not in this mess then? How do you have it all so bloody sorted?'

'I don't, Sara, trust me. I have my own stuff going on, just maybe not as,' she struggled to think of a word, 'deep as yours.'

'My problems aren't deep. They're pitiful. *I'm* pitiful. I hate myself.'

'Don't hate yourself. You're beautiful, inside and out. You're just going through a rough patch, that's all.'

'I can't help it. What's wrong with me?' I sighed heavily and slumped back against the backrest. I was completely miserable. 'I can't help thinking, is this all there is?'

My words hung between us like a heavy, black cloud. Myla broke the silence. 'Don't beat yourself up, please. You're scaring me. There's just something missing, a hole you keep trying to fill. Maybe you'll fill it one day, maybe you won't, but you need to keep fighting these bleak thoughts you're having.'

'But I don't know how.'

Chapter Fourteen

Back at home, things didn't get any better. My aunts had stayed up watching movies and at the sound of the door, came out of the living room to greet us. At the sight of me, they looked something like disgusted. 'What happened to you?' Serafina asked harshly.

'Leave it,' I grumbled.

'Excuse me?'

'Just leave it,' I said, a little more forcefully.

'Look at you,' she tutted.

I caught sight of myself in the hallway mirror. Mascara was running down my face, bra straps hanging off my shoulders and, somewhere along the way, I'd ripped my top. Well, James had ripped my top.

'Sara, what's going on?' Lyanna asked in a calmer tone.

'What do you mean?' I snapped.

'You look like you're doing the walk of shame,' Serafina observed, looking me up and down distastefully.

'Yeah? Well, maybe I am!' I shouted. 'Shows what you think of me!'

'Who even are you?' Serafina snapped back.

'Serafina!' Lyanna hissed, shooting her a look of disdain.

'Well, just look at her! Coming in at early hours of the morning, looking like a prostitute!'

'Hold on a minute! Don't you want to hear her side of the story?'

'No, I don't want to hear it. I've heard enough!'

'You don't even live here!' Lyanna scolded her.

'She's my niece too!'

I took their argument as the perfect opportunity to escape upstairs. I couldn't face another conversation about somebody taking advantage of me, nor could I handle a fight if I didn't tell them. Myla followed me up to my bedroom, awkwardly quiet. 'It's all my fault,' I said, slumping down on my bed.

'It is NOT your fault,' Myla protested.

'Well, nothing like this ever happens to you. How do I keep getting myself into these positions?'

'You don't; you haven't done anything wrong. Apart from maybe being too trusting. Look, you're a beautiful girl, and that obviously brings out the worst in some men.'

Beautiful? I'd never thought of myself as beautiful, never in my life. I was surprised to think that somebody thought of me that way, even if it was my biased best friend. 'I am not beautiful!' I argued. 'And if I am, I don't want to be. I never want to speak to another guy in my life.'

'They're not all like that,' Myla assured me.

'Aren't they? Who isn't? Benji?'

'Well, yeah, Benji. He was disgusted at what James did.'

'Well, good for you! I'm glad you've found someone decent,' I said, rather bitterly.

'That's not what I meant. I was just trying to comfort you.'

'It didn't work!' I shouted. 'Now, I just feel foolish for always getting close to the wankers. I must be a really bad judge of character.'

'Calm down, Sara, please.'

I exhaled long and hard. 'I'm sorry. I just don't think I want to deal with this all over again. It took me long enough to get over all that stuff with Joel and now I'm back to square one.'

'I know, and I wish I could take some of that pain away, but you'll be alright. You were alright before; you can be alright again.'

'I wasn't alright before. I'm not alright now. I feel like I'll never be okay ever again.'

Myla wanted to tell me I would be, I knew, but she held back. I didn't need to hear that right then. So, instead, she put an episode of the *Big Bang Theory* on my tiny television and let me be for a while.

*****

The next morning, I was woken up by a knock on the bedroom door. Myla had slept over to keep me company. I felt her stir in the bed next to me, but she made no sign of waking up. 'What?' I whispered.

'Sara? Can I talk to you downstairs please?' Lyanna asked quietly.

I dragged myself out of bed, threw my dressing gown on and followed Lyanna downstairs into the living room. I sat myself down in the shabby armchair facing her on the sofa. 'We need to talk,' she said ominously.

'I guess we do,' I agreed, bracing myself for what was to come.

'Can you let me speak? And don't talk until I'm finished?'

I nodded apprehensively. 'I love you, Sara,' she began. 'I really do, more than I've ever loved anything in my life.'

I shifted in my seat, uncomfortable. So, it was going to be a guilt trip. 'And that's why it upsets me so much to see you throwing your life away,' she continued.

I opened my mouth, intending to defend myself, but she held her hand up to stop me. No problem, I'd just drop the bombshell of last night *after* she'd finished making me feel the size of an ant. 'I haven't seen you studying in weeks, you barely read or write, or any of the things you used to love to do. I don't ever see you anymore.' She paused and sighed. 'And it hurts me, do you know that?'

I didn't know if I was supposed to answer or if this was some kind of test, so I kept my mouth shut. Her eyes looked genuinely affected. I had to look away. 'It hurts me. Where's my little girl gone?' Her voice caught in her throat. 'I don't know who you are anymore. I don't recognise you.' She stood up and walked cheerlessly to the window. 'I'm really lonely, Sara. Of course, I don't expect you to be here all the time; you're sixteen years old, you have a social life, but I wouldn't mind so much if I knew you were out and about having fun with Myla like you used to. You used to go to the cinema or for long walks. You'd come back all rosy-cheeked and breathless and happy! I'd make you both tea and we'd sit and talk. Talk! Remember that? I feel like I haven't spoken to you in so long. You're practically my daughter and I have no idea what's going on in your life.

'What hurts me most is knowing you'd prefer to be out there doing god-knows what, instead of being here with me. It's like you're trying to torture me. I get up and go to work and you're asleep, I come home and you're out. Serafina loves the solitude and silence—she's always been happiest in her own company—but that's just not me. I don't do good on my own; I get sad.'

She was still facing away from me, looking out through the window. It was the saddest sight I'd ever seen.

When we're growing up, we believe our parents are invincible. We believe that they can handle anything, that they don't need the same things as us: companionship, conversation. We assume they'll always be there whenever we need them, no matter how nasty we are, how distant we become; whenever we need them, they'll be there, all forgiven, ready to comfort us as though nothing has ever changed. To hear my aunt tell me she was lonely and describe her sad, lonely days, filled me with guilt and sadness. 'I guess, I just don't want you to end up like me,' she added.

I broke my pact of silence. 'Why wouldn't I want to end up like you?' I asked genuinely.

'I was a singer in a band before I worked in the café. I travelled all over the country, drinking, partying, playing gigs, going out with a string of guys. I didn't have any responsibilities or cares. I was totally free to do whatever I wanted, but I had a huge, gaping hole inside me that I was desperate to fill. No amount of alcohol or sex or singing would fill it, and I went down a dangerous path. I wasn't happy, not at all. It was all so meaningless and empty. You saved my life, I think.'

I was startled at her revelation. 'How?' I questioned.

'If it wasn't for you, and I suppose your mother leaving, I have no idea what would have happened to me. You gave me a focus and I couldn't live selfishly anymore. I gave up singing, got a job and focussed all my attention on you. I didn't have the time or capacity to be self-destructive anymore. It was actually nice to have someone else to think about except myself.'

I'd never heard any of that before. I'd had no idea what Lyanna's life was like before I'd come into it. Teenagers assume that their parents' lives started the moment they were born and never stop to think that they lived a whole other life before them. 'You see, that's why Sef is so hard on you. She's not soft like me. She's seen it all before, seen me make the same mistakes you're making now. The same mistakes your mother made.'

The silence was deafening. We'd never really discussed my mum before, not in any great detail anyway. I'd asked Lyanna things like what my mum's interests were, what she looked like—trivial things—but part of me had never wanted to know anything more than these flimsy details. 'What do you mean?' I probed.

'She was a wild card, your mum,' she said, a ghost of a smile on her lips. 'She was my wingman. We did everything together until she met your dad.'

Sometimes, I forgot that my mum was Lyanna's sister, that she'd known her inside out at some point in her life. 'How did you feel?' I asked, surprised as the words tumbled out of my mouth.

'What?' Lyanna turned to face me, finally.

'When she left—how did you feel?'

'Well, your mum and I grew apart long before you came along. She grew up, or seemed to, and moved on with her life, while I was still pretending that I was forever young. It still crushed me, of course, but by the time she left, I'd already formed a bond with you and I was as much angry at her for leaving you as I was upset at her for leaving me. That's when I knew that I'd changed; when I cared more for your feelings than my own.'

'So, you have no idea what happened to her then?' I wasn't sure if I really wanted to know. I'd gone nearly seventeen years without asking that question and I still wasn't sure if I was ready for the answer.

Lyanna sat back down on the sofa. 'No, I really don't. Sometimes,' she hesitated, 'I wonder if she's even still alive.'

I gulped. Despite never knowing the woman, the thought my mum could be dead cut deep. 'I'm sorry. I shouldn't have said that.'

'I asked.'

'I just can't marry the two people together—the sister I knew and the sister that left.'

'What happened to make her leave?' I couldn't believe we'd never discussed all this before, but it had just never occurred to me. My mother was like a fictional character, a one-dimensional being from the pages of a book. I wondered if I'd never asked these questions so that I could lock her away in my mind, so that I wouldn't have to face the truth.

'After she became pregnant with you and your dad died,' we both cringed when she said the words, 'she just wasn't the same. They'd had all these plans, your mum and dad—travelling, starting a family, making a home and life together—and then they were over, just like that.'

In that moment, I felt something I'd never felt before; sympathy for my mother who'd abandoned me. 'She brought you home from the hospital and Sef and I were there to greet you. And, there was nothing.'

A tear crept down Lyanna's cheek. I sat myself down next to her for comfort, as much my own as Lyanna's.

She wiped her face and turned to me. 'There was nothing in her eyes. They were blank, like all the life had been sucked out of her. She had post-natal depression bad, really bad. And on top of that, she was still grieving the loss of her husband. Oh God, I should have told you all this sooner. It's all my fault.' She held her head in her hands as though ashamed.

'What's your fault?'

'I feel like, a part of you is broken because somewhere deep inside you're bitter. Bitter and sad. You were abandoned as a child, and I suppose it would be natural for you to feel angry and hurt, and maybe even blame yourself.'

'I don't feel that way,' I assured her, though inside me something clicked, like a missing piece of a puzzle falling into place.

'I don't think your mother thought that it would hurt you. What you have to understand about depression, is the worthlessness one feels. She thought you'd be better off without her. I don't think it helped that you looked so much like your dad.'

I swallowed, my mouth dry. I looked like my dad? I suddenly felt their loss bearing down on me and it was more than I could bear.

'I looked after you a lot in the beginning, even while Evelien was still around. We were so close, you and me. She left me a note one day saying that we weren't to worry about her, that she would be alright and for us not to look for her. Of course, we did, for months and months without any luck. We didn't think she'd try to kill herself, though we weren't sure, what with the last part of her note.'

'What did it say?' I asked and regretted it straightaway.

'It said, well, it was very odd phrasing, you see. It said something like *don't worry, I've gone to the quiet place*. I wasn't sure at first. It sounded ominous, but the more I thought about it, I truly believed that she meant the quiet place in her mind.'

I felt sick. If there was one thing I'd written of more than anything else, it was the quiet place. It was the running theme of all my work and my most overused phrase. I couldn't help but feel that it wasn't a coincidence. 'You see, that's why I can't let you go down that road. I promised your mother that I'd look after you and I won't let you end up like either of us.'

All the drama of the night before felt insignificant now, trivial. I'd wanted, so bad, to let her rant at me and make me feel bad, then I could tell her about what had happened with James and guilt trip her in return. Looking into the deep well of pain and sadness in her eyes, I couldn't bring myself to tell her, so I never did.

'Don't worry,' I said at length, 'I'm not going to any more parties; I don't want to do that anymore. I want things to go back to how they used to be, more than anything.'

Lyanna didn't say anything, only stared at me in a way that told me she could see something inside me that nobody else could. 'Did something happen last night?'

'Well, yeah,' I began, then paused. 'I saw my reflection in the mirror and I didn't recognise myself. I never want that to happen again, I want to be me again.'

Lyanna looked sceptical. 'You're not just saying that, are you?'

'No.'

'Promise?'

'I promise,' I confirmed and I meant it whole-heartedly. When I'd woken up that morning, I'd felt utterly hopeless, lost and full of self-pity, but after that conversation, everything had changed. I felt a weight of new emotion, but I also felt refreshed as all the truths washed over me, like I knew myself better.

Lyanna began to cry, silent tears coursing down her face. Then, I began to cry too, and so, we held each other and let it all out. It was therapeutic. I felt closer to her in those moments than I had ever before. She was my mother.

Lyanna left later in the morning to run errands in the city, so I took the opportunity to catch Myla up on all that we'd spoken of. By the end of my story, Myla was crying as well. 'There's something else I need to tell you,' I confided. And so, I told her all about the other place; the visions I'd had, the faerie I'd seen, the feelings I got, and how I somehow felt that it was all connected to my mother and her quiet place.

'I knew you were hiding something from me,' Myla admitted.

'How?'

'Sometimes, you can act just, um, different, I suppose. You don't seem like you're really present. Your body's there but your mind isn't. Little things, like that time in the alley behind your house when you asked me if I could see her. I'd never seen that look on your face before. That was it, wasn't it? The faerie?'

I nodded. 'God, you must think I'm crazy.'

'Well, not crazy.'

'Admit it! I don't blame you. Faeries and hidden worlds. I totally get why you'd think I was mad.'

'I could hear the conviction in your voice though. I know, whether it's real or not, you believe it's real and, I have to admit, the mention of the quiet place in your mum's note is kind of creepy.'

'What do you mean?'

'I've seen it written, in black and white, by your own hand. It's all over your work, like an obsession. Are you sure Lyanna's never told you about that before? Or Serafina?'

'I told you, we've never really talked about my parents before.'

'I know, I know. I just find it so hard to believe.'

'Me too. The whole thing is unbelievable.' I heaved a great sigh. 'Myla?'

'Yeah?'

'Is there something wrong with me? Am I broken?'

'No, I don't think so. The mind is an intricate, complex thing.'

We sat there, in silence for a while, both feeling quite baffled and sombre. This was not how we'd expected the day to go. I think in an effort to lighten the mood, Myla said, 'But it would be cool if, you know, it was real, all that magical stuff. If it was a place you could actually go visit.' She looked genuinely excited.

'Yeah,' I laughed. 'I guess it would be.'

Chapter Fifteen

I officially finished high school in a positive place. I stopped going to parties and hanging out with that crowd, just like I'd promised Lyanna. In fact, I stopped hanging out with anybody except Myla and it was just like old times. I finally felt like myself again. We went back to writing and drawing, going on mini outdoor adventures and visiting our old haunts. I even took her to see 'my' tree. Nothing out of the ordinary happened though, and we both went away feeling rather disappointed.

Everything felt like it used to with Myla and my aunts, but also different. I felt older in my mind, like I'd been woken out of a dreamy sleep to find that reality was starker and grittier than I'd ever imagined, like my eyes had been opened to the truth of the world. I could now see all the colours, and all the shadows. Life was no longer simple, and I knew there was no way of going back to how it used to be. Childhood was utterly lost to me, but it's lost to everyone eventually. I realised it had actually been creeping up on me for a long time.

I focussed on my schoolwork and started enjoying classes once again. Bullying was now a thing of the past—I think everyone had grown up that year—so school was a much more enjoyable experience. English language, art and history were my favourite subjects. I re-realised my passion for learning and threw myself head-first into my work and revision. Our GCSEs were fast-approaching, and it had dawned on me how much I had missed and brushed off. I'm glad I sorted my priorities out just in time to turn it all around.

My most hated class was math; I really struggled with that subject, even though I was in the top set. My math teacher could tell I was struggling and paid particular attention to me because of that. At the time, I believed he was picking on me and trying to make me miserable, but now I know he saw potential in me and genuinely wanted to help me. So, when he forced me to take extracurricular classes and told me off in front of the whole class for not trying hard enough, he wasn't trying to embarrass me or piss me off like I thought; he was trying to help me reach my potential. I am forever grateful for the help he gave me, even if I never got to tell him that. I can't even remember his name.

My favourite memories of that summer were our trips to the beach. The four of us—Myla, Lyanna, Sef and I—were so much closer and would, whenever we got a chance, take off to the seaside. We chose a different beach each time; pointing to a random spot on the map and driving there. We saw it all: timeless, eerie ghost towns with shingly, misty beaches; bright, sunny piers with two-penny slot machines; fish and chip shops; stripy, pastel-coloured bunting blowing in the sea breeze.

The day we went to collect our GCSE results, my stomach was in my mouth. I was absolutely certain I had failed at everything and was mentally preparing myself for having to break the news to my aunts that I'd ruined my life, but when I saw my results written in black and white on that little slip of paper, I nearly broke down crying in relief. I got an A in English and, surprisingly, an A in science; Bs in history, art, graphics and IT, and the result I was most proud of—a B in math! All my hard work had paid off and I left the auditorium beaming with pride. Myla did amazingly well too and we celebrated that night—while all our friends went out drinking—with pizza and a *Jurassic Park* film marathon at home.

As I'd been wasting most of my school year partying and dealing with drama in my personal life, I'd not had the chance, or inclination, to figure out what I wanted to do after high school. So, I did what all sixteen-year-olds do when faced with that last-minute choice—I enrolled in sixth form. I was older, more mature, but I wasn't ready to leave school and step out into the big, wide world just yet.

I was jealous of those in my year who already knew, categorically, where they wanted to go and what they wanted to do, and even knew how they were going to get there. Some of our friends had already started putting together their portfolios for universities. I had no clue whatsoever about any of it, so I did what I did best: I winged it. I chose English language, history and art for my A-levels, excited to get to focus on my three favourite subjects for the next two years. I was hoping dearly that at some point, I'd have a light-bulb moment and just realise what I wanted to do for the rest of my life. Of course, that never happened.

I'd always dreamed of being an author—I felt like it was my true calling—but now, faced with the prospect of actually having to work to get there and with the little faith that I had in my own talents, I thought it was just that; a dream, like winning the lottery.

Before we knew it, the summer had gone with the wind and we were starting sixth form. Things were still going well at home; I was spending more quality time with Lyanna as Myla was living out her summer fling with Benji. I wasn't bothered by this. I didn't give a crap about dating. I just enjoyed gaining back lost time with my family.

Myla's summer fling fizzled out with the coming of the rainy season and I was excited to get back to school, especially as we were taking art and English together. Myla had chosen science instead of history.

The freedom of sixth form was refreshing. The teachers treated us like young adults and even let us call them by their forenames. There were no uniforms and we got free periods. These were for studying and working on assignments, but I have to admit, Myla and I used some of the spare time to go shopping.

I worked hard that first year and got good grades. I didn't lose focus and I was looking forward to entering my second and final year with a thirst for more knowledge and a good head on my shoulders, but it wasn't meant to be. The second year brought with it fresh troubles and issues and, it turned out, I hadn't grown up at all.

Chapter Sixteen

It was the end of July, the beginning of summer break, and the UK was suffering through an intense heatwave. Outside my bedroom window, the sun shone down mercilessly on the parched fields and cracked earth. My entire body was sweating, even my eyelids. I'd only just taken a shower, but I could already feel the sweat droplets rolling down my back and the grimy, unwashed feeling developing under my armpits, despite only wearing a vest and shorts.

Lyanna was working and I briefly thought how sorry I felt for her inside that stuffy café, serving overheated, grumpy customers. I trudged downstairs into the kitchen and poured myself a glass of cold pineapple juice straight from the fridge. 'Hey there, stranger.'

Startled, I let go of the carton, managing to catch it before the juice spilled everywhere. Serafina had entered the kitchen from the front room. 'I didn't know you were here,' I squeaked.

'Sorry,' she replied, eyeing up the mess I'd made. 'I got here this morning, but I didn't want to disturb you.'

'What are you doing here?' I asked, tearing off a sheet of kitchen roll and mopping up the small spillage. I took a seat at the island and took a deep, long drink.

'I haven't seen you for a while because I've been so busy at the library. I thought I'd swing by and check in on you.'

'Well, thanks.' I sensed there was more to her visit than she was suggesting but figured it'd come out when she was ready.

'How are you doing?'

'Not bad. How are you? Any plans for the summer?'

'No, actually. Not yet anyway.'

Serafina looked apprehensive, like there was something on the tip of her tongue trying to show itself.

'What have you really come here for?' I questioned, wiping the sweat from my forehead.

She looked mildly offended. 'What do you mean?'

'Look, just spit it out. I know there's something you want to say.' Serafina never just dropped by to check in on me.

She sighed, obviously giving into her internal struggle. 'I was thinking that maybe you should think about getting a job.'

'Oh, so that's what this is about.'

'I just think that it would help Lyanna out.'

'What, like you do?' I countered scathingly.

'Excuse me?'

'Well, you've never been worried about helping Lyanna before, so why are you so bothered now?' I didn't quite understand where all my animosity was coming from, but apparently it had been brewing inside of me for a while. I suddenly felt very defensive.

Serafina and I had been butting heads a lot lately. She seemed to be picking on every little thing I did, wore or said, and one day, I'd exploded and told her to fuck off. That was the real reason I hadn't seen her in a while. It had been playing on my mind, and I hated both of our stubborn arses for not sucking it up and making things right. 'I don't know who you think you're talking to but—'

'What's that?' I interrupted, for the first time noticing a yellowing bruise on the inside of her arm.

'What?' she asked, looking down at herself.

'That!' I hissed, grabbing her by the arm.

'Get off me!' she yelped, her face turning grey.

'Don't tell me you're back with Jack.'

'It's none of your business who I'm with.'

'If they do that to you, it is.'

'No, it's not!' she snapped.

'I don't know who the hell you think you are, talking to me like that. You're just a stupid little girl. You need to grow up.'

'Sorry, but I don't take orders from grown women who allow their boyfriends to do things like that to them.'

'What the hell did you just say to me?'

'You heard me,' I replied, getting off the stool and turning my back to her. I could feel her eyes like daggers in my back. I felt a deep shame for stooping so low, but I held my nerve and started running water in the washing-up bowl as though nothing had happened.

There was quiet for some time; all I could hear was the sound of soapy water sloshing around in the bowl while I washed my plates and glasses from the night before. I finally finished and Serafina still hadn't said a word, so I found myself standing there stiffly, too terrified to turn around. The silence stretched on awkwardly, so I bit the bullet and turned away from the sink.

Serafina was sat down, looking ghostly and sad. 'Look, I'm sorry. I—'

'Didn't mean it?' Serafina finished my sentence.

'You're just like your mother.'

'What do you mean?' I demanded. I didn't know if she had meant that as an insult or a compliment.

'She was a bitch too.'

Her words were like a slap across my face. I stepped back as though I'd really been struck. I didn't know what to say, I had no witty retorts for that. 'She always knew how to dig the knife in too. How to say the cruellest words to really hurt me.' Serafina began to shake violently. I'd never seen her like that before, so enraged and out of control.

It came to light later that Serafina had been going through a tough time and that old bruise on her arm was just the tip of the iceberg. That day, she had come over fresh from a fight with Jack. She was heading for a nervous breakdown and struggling to cope. I was so hurt and shocked by her words however that I only saw a vindictive, nasty woman sat before me. 'Don't talk about my mum that way!' I yelled.

'Why? I have a right, more so than you, to say whatever I like about her. She was my sister. I grew up with her, and she made my life miserable.'

'You made your own life miserable, Serafina.'

'There you go again, sounding just like her. *You're boring, Serafina, a loser, you have no life.* Blah, blah, blah. Making me feel like I was worthless.'

'She didn't! She wouldn't.' I suddenly felt like a child again, being told something I didn't want to hear. I wanted to cover my ears and sing 'lalala!' at the top of my lungs so that I could block out her mad ravings.

'Oh yes she did, your lovely mother. The one who abandoned you and dumped you on us.'

So, here we were. This is what it all came down to. All my childhood fears and worries—that she resented me—were being proved true. Something inside of me snapped and I felt an urge to run away or curl up in a corner and cry. 'Yeah, she was no angel,' Serafina continued. 'It was the best thing she ever did, leaving, ridding us of her stupid petty dramas and her nastiness. Good riddance,' she seethed.

'Stop it!' I screamed, breaking. 'Stop it, stop it, stop it, stop it!'

Lyanna arrived home in the midst of it all, stepping through the door obliviously. I was vaguely aware of her running footsteps at the sound of our yelling. 'What on earth is going on?' she shouted, trying to be heard over our raging argument.

'She's gone mental, that's what,' I told her through tears, my voice livid and shaking.

Serafina continued to rage on and on about my mum and I could no longer stand it. I lunged at her. I just wanted to shut her up. For the first time, I felt protective of my mum, who was no longer there to defend herself.

Lyanna stopped me, pushing me back forcefully. 'Sara! What's gotten into you?' I thought she was going to start yelling at me too, or even hit me, but instead, she turned to Serafina, who was now hyperventilating. Lyanna stooped down to make eye contact with her. It dawned on me that she was having a panic attack.

'Serafina, sshh,' Lyanna soothed. 'Breathe with me.' She took a deep breath and exhaled through her nose.

All I wanted to do was get the hell out of there. It was like a bad dream. This was not how I'd pictured my day turning out. Instead of doing the decent thing and helping Lyanna calm Serafina down, I ran for the front door.

Outside, the heat was stifling, but I knew I needed to get as far away as I possibly could. My body protesting furiously, I ran down the street and out of sight of the house as fast as my legs would allow. I stopped, short of breath and sweltering in the heat. I knew I didn't have long before they'd come looking for me—only until Serafina had recovered from her meltdown—so I made a hasty decision and dashed into the wooded area behind our street.

I ran and ran until my chest tightened and my limbs gave way. I sat down on the hard, dusty ground to catch my breath. Where was I going? How long did I think I'd be able to run for? What had even happened back there? Where had all that pent-up anger come from, on both sides? It had gone from exchanging pleasantries to full-blown war in a matter of minutes. All because of what? I didn't have a job? She was mad at my mum? Had Jack really upset her so badly to have caused all that fury to erupt out of her? I was so consumed by my own anger and pain, that I didn't want to rationalise her mania. I wanted to be angry at her and to feel every hurt she'd inflicted.

I contemplated seeking refuge at Myla's place, but I realised that would be the first place they'd look for me and I didn't want to be found. Some sick, twisted part of me wanted them to worry, wanted them to care where I was. Then, it dawned on me that I'd left my phone in my room. My first, and only, thought was, *Great, now they'll worry even more.*

After a few miles, I stopped running and slowed down my pace to a brisk walk. I kept to the wooded areas as I was sure that by then they would be driving around looking for me. I passed the hill that overlooked the valley and stopped briefly to spy Moraine Manor through the trees. As always, the sight of it gave me the chills.

I carried on for a few more hours, until my feet were throbbing so severely that I couldn't walk any further. The sky had turned a purply-pink as dusk approached. One thing was for certain, I was no longer in Moraine.

I was flanked by trees, but I could still see the motorway in the distance; the white and red twinkling lights of the traffic travelling north and south to their various destinations. It briefly crossed my mind to try and hitchhike, but I decided that was a foolish idea at that time of the evening for a solitary seventeen-year-old girl. The prospect of staying in the woods didn't excite me all that much either, however.

I realised then that I had no food or water, and my stomach growled at my stupidity. I slumped down against a tree trunk and let the dark creep in around me. What was I doing there? Had I really intended to run away? Wouldn't I prefer to be back in my nice, cosy house with all my belongings? Back where I was safe, loved and comfortable. But it was too late for that now; I had to see it through.

I sat for a while as the night closed in, mulling things over in my head. My heart rate had slowed, and my fury no longer felt so compelling, but I was still upset. It looked like that stony, hard floor was going to be my bed for the night.

It was pitch black and the temperature had dropped. I folded my arms across my chest in a feeble attempt to warm myself up. Something glittered at the other end of the clearing in which I was sat, before blinking out again rapidly. At first, I thought I'd just imagined it, but then, further around the clearing, closer to where I was sat, something glinted again. It was a pair of eyes. I looked around desperately, trying to find an escape route, but the velvety blackness revealed nothing. More eyes appeared all around me. My heart seemed to stop beating. I wanted to run, but I couldn't. My body was exhausted and refused to move.

Then, voices could be heard, not far off; some in converse, some chattering wildly, some shouting, some whispering, some shrieking in pain, some angry and some giggling mischievously. I felt as though my ears were going to explode with the pressure.

I began to cry quietly, still unable to move, petrified, confused and exhausted.

I cried because I didn't understand what was happening.

I cried because my mind was playing tricks on me.

I cried because I was drained, emotionally and physically.

I cried because I was alone, completely alone.

I cried because I wanted someone to hold me: my mum, Lyanna, Myla, a man, anyone.

I cried because I was sure that this wasn't my imagination. It was all too realistic and horrifying.

Mostly, I cried because there was nothing else to do but cry.

I wept for a long time, surrounded by bodiless voices and socket-less eyes. Then, the voices ceased and silence fell over the woods. The darkness wrapped its wings around me, thick, cold and heavy. It pulled me down into a fitful sleep in which I dreamt of demons, shadows and wicked eyes.

*****

I awoke the following morning to the sounds of birds tweeting in the branches above and creatures rustling in the undergrowth. Daylight streamed in through the leafy roof, and the fear I had felt the night before had evaporated with the coming of the sun.

I stretched my aching limbs and felt all the troubles of the previous day scurry away into the woods. I needed to go home. What had I been thinking to put my aunts through that? I was wrong in the head. An attention-seeking lowlife.

I had no idea where I was or how I was going to get back. I couldn't face that long walk again, and I longed for my bed and some stodgy food to fill my empty stomach. So, I did what I'd decided against the night before and hitchhiked. Looking as hopeless and dishevelled as I did, it wasn't long before a kind, old man took pity on me and let me into his car.

He attempted to get me to open up about how I'd ended up in such a sorry situation, but he soon realised this was a futile exercise and gave it up to talk about the unusually hot weather. He seemed satisfied enough to know that I was going home.

He dropped me off in Moraine city centre and I got the bus home from there, feeling thoroughly ashamed and full of remorse.

Chapter Seventeen

I knocked on Myla's front door timidly. When she opened it, she looked like she wanted to hug me and hit me at the same time. 'Where have you been!' she demanded, dragging me inside as though she was terrified that I would run away again.

Her parents' home was a modern, sprawling, open-plan house. Even after all my years of visiting, I still couldn't get used to its size or sparkling cleanliness. As usual, her parents weren't there. Myla led me into the front room, which was immaculate except for Myla's sketchpads and pencils laid out on nearly every surface. Scrunched up pieces of paper littered the floor and her drawings were spread out across the gleaming glass coffee table. 'You've been busy,' I observed, sitting down on the plush, impeccably white rug.

Myla took a seat beside me. 'Yeah, well, I had to find something to do to keep me occupied while I was awake all night worrying about you,' she said scornfully.

'I'm so sorry. I wanted to let you know what was going on, but I accidentally left my phone at home.' I looked down at my hands and picked at my nails.

'I'll have to call Lyanna now. You can't stay here.'

'I wasn't intending on hiding out, I just can't face going home yet. Can you just give me a little longer?'

Myla appraised me sceptically, then nodded. 'You might want to take a shower.'

I looked down at my muddy clothes and blotchy, scuzzy skin and nodded in agreement.

When I came back downstairs after a much-needed wash, I found Myla waiting for me in the now tidy front room, looking less than impressed. 'So, what happened?' she asked as I took a seat on the cream leather sofa.

'We argued.'

'I got that. What about?'

'Family stuff,' I shrugged.

Myla sat forward. 'Come on, Sara. You can tell me. What drove you to run off like that? To not come to me?'

'I couldn't come here because this would be the first place they'd look for me. I needed to get away.'

'But what did you fight about that was so bad that you felt you had to get away?'

I paused, unsure where to start. 'To be honest, I don't really know. It all made sense last night. It all seemed to come from nowhere. We were both really horrible to each other.' I became teary and tried to swallow my emotion. 'We both said things we shouldn't have. I don't know, it was a mixture of things. I don't really want to go into it.'

Myla sat back. 'Okay, you don't have to tell me. I get it. You and Serafina have never quite seen eye to eye.' We sat in silence for a little while, then she said, 'I'm glad you came to me first,' and smiled at me warmly.

I smiled in return. 'Were they really mad?'

'No, not mad. Just worried. Like, crazy with worry.'

'I'm in deep shit, aren't I?'

'Probably. And speaking of which, you're going to have to go back, or at least let me call them to let them know you're safe.'

'I know, I know. Call them once I'm gone, please. Give them a heads up that I'm on my way home.'

We hugged, for longer than usual, then I trudged home, not so fast.

When I arrived home, unsettlingly, there was no drama, no shouting, no exclamation as I walked through the door, just an awkward quiet. I wasn't sure which I would have preferred. 'Hi,' I greeted my aunts as I stood in the kitchen, fumbling awkwardly with my clothes. They were both sat at the table, looking spent. Lyanna got up sombrely and came over to hug me, instantly relieving the tension I felt. They both looked awful, I thought, as I stepped back and studied them. Especially Sef. Her wild hair was a matted mess and deep, dark circles ringed her eyes, which were all puffy and red, like she'd been crying, heavily.

I didn't know what to say next and it seemed that neither did they. The silence dragged on and still I couldn't muster the right words. Serafina couldn't even bring herself to look at me. The warm feeling from Lyanna's hug had faded fast. Then, I realised, it was so simple. 'I'm sorry,' I said, my voice seeming to echo around the room.

Serafina finally looked up at me. 'I shouldn't have run away like that,' I continued. 'And Serafina, I shouldn't have said all those things to you. I was way out of line. It's all kind of a blur; everything was okay and then it wasn't, and I don't know why.'

Serafina got up and hugged me as well. I was surprised at her sudden display of affection. I had thought I would have been lucky if I ever got a hug from her again after what I'd said to her.

She stepped away. 'I'm sorry, too. I was awful. We both were.' She sat back down, heavily, like the weight of the world was on her shoulders.

Lyanna finally spoke. 'Sara, you do realise what we thought, don't you?'

'No,' I replied, unsure what she meant.

'Well, it was very much like history repeating itself, or so we thought.'

It took me a moment to understand what she was referring to, but then it dawned on me, the realisation crashing over me like a tidal wave. 'You mean, because my mum left?'

Lyanna nodded. 'You seriously thought I might not come back?'

'Part of me, yes. We both did, or at least, we worried that you wouldn't.'

I hadn't at any point connected what I'd done with what my mum had done seventeen years before, but now, it seemed so obvious. I was acutely aware of how much pain and panic I must have caused. I also briefly entertained the notion that I was indeed like my mother: impulsive, emotional and selfish. 'Oh God, I hadn't thought of that at all! I really am sorry for putting you through that.'

Lyanna shook her head. 'We're just so glad you're home,' she assured me.

'Where did you go?'

'I actually have no idea,' I confessed.

'A wood somewhere.'

'You slept in a wood? Alone?' Lyanna asked, mortified.

'Yeah, it was pretty horrible.' An image of gleaming eyes in the pitch black surfaced in my mind but I pushed it back down.

We talked for a while and I recounted most of my journey to them, omitting the part with the eyes and voices. Serafina still didn't say much and seemed to be thinking of something else entirely, but eventually, things seemed to return to normal between us all and I was glad for it.

I climbed into my own bed that night and revelled in the comfort of my clean sheets and being surrounded by own belongings. I swiftly drifted off into a contented, easy sleep.

Chapter Eighteen

The hot, dry summer dragged on lazily. Myla and I had taken to swimming at the public baths in the city centre a few times a week, just to cool down.

One Wednesday afternoon, the blazing sun beating down on our tanned shoulders and wet heads, we were walking home from a particularly active session. 'How's things at home?' Myla asked conversationally while we walked.

'Not bad, I suppose. Sef's still acting a little odd though. She's around a lot,' I answered.

'Is that what's odd?'

'Yes and no. She's around a lot, but then she sits around reading all the time, barely speaking to either of us. It's like, she doesn't want to be there, but she doesn't want to be at home even more so.'

'That's weird, even for Serafina.'

I dabbed at my forehead, wiping away the droplets of sweat. There wasn't a cloud in the sky and despite moaning for years how England never got a real summer, everyone in the land was hoping for a cool spell, or even some summer rain. No matter what the weather, Brits always find something to complain about.

'Can you think of any reason why she wouldn't want to be at home?' Myla continued.

'Well,' I said, reluctantly, 'the last time she behaved this way, Jack was around.'

'Jack's her ex, right? The violent one?'

'Yep.'

'I don't know the whole story of that.'

'No, he came and went, came and went. Always the same. There's not much to say, really, except that he was a grade A nobhead.'

'You think she could be seeing another grade A nobhead?'

'I bloody hope not!' The thought of another lowlife interfering with my family made me feel both angry and tired. 'She wouldn't make the same mistake twice, would she?'

'People do tend to do that.'

'Urgh.' I remembered my own mistakes with Joel and James the previous year.

'You have to be there for her, no matter how infuriating it is. It's not about you.'

'Yeah, well, we'll cross that bridge if and when we get to it. We don't even know if that's what it is. Though, now I come to think of it, I did see a bruise on her arm a few weeks ago.'

Myla looked concerned. 'Well, I hope it isn't that, but maybe, prepare yourself in case it is.'

But the reality was so much worse. Serafina had, in fact, not met a new grade A nobhead but had gone back to the same one.

I said goodbye to Myla at the end of her street. When I walked through my front door, I knew instantly that something wasn't right. I could hear a strange whimpering sound, and for a second, I thought there was a dog in the house. Then, I saw Lyanna standing over Serafina, who was curled up on the kitchen floor crying. I couldn't see her fully at first as her head and shoulders were obscured by Lyanna's body, but then, as I stepped further into the room, I saw something I don't think I'll ever forget.

Serafina's face was unrecognisable; her eyes were swollen and purple, her mouth was cut and raw and dark bruises covered her neck and shoulders. There was blood, so much blood; it stained her clothes, matted her hair and streaked down her face in rivulets. 'What the hell happened?' I erupted, fighting the urge to break down sobbing. Although I had previously called Serafina weak in a moment of anger, I had actually always thought of her as a pillar of strength; someone who could never be moved or broken down, like a stern, unyielding cliff wall. To see her in that state was heart-breaking and deeply shocking.

Serafina flinched at the sound of my raised voice.

Lyanna hushed me. 'Help me with her.'

Struck dumb, I helped Lyanna take her up the stairs to the bathroom, where we ran her a bath, undressed her and helped her in. Serafina screeched as the warm water stung her sore skin.

Lyanna closed the bathroom door quietly, leaving Serafina alone. She must have seen right inside my mind as she shook her head as though to say, 'not here', and gestured back down the stairs.

I followed her into the dining room, where we took seats facing each other at opposite sides of the table. 'Well? Are you going to fill me in?' I asked, barely concealing my horror.

'It was Jack,' she confirmed.

'What!' I raged, standing up and pounding my fists on the table. 'I didn't even know she was seeing him again.'

'We didn't tell you, we knew how you'd react.'

'Damn right! How could you let her?'

'She's a grown woman, she makes her own decisions. I did want to tell you, but she made me promise not to. She didn't want to undo all the progress the two of you have made. I think she really thought that it'd be different this time.'

'Did you?'

'No, of course not. I did warn her, you know.'

'How did she get here, in that state?'

'She walked as far as she could, then she called me and I picked her up.'

I felt a twinge in my heart at the thought of her walking all that way and nobody offering to help her. 'And you didn't think to take her to the hospital?'

'She wouldn't let me.'

'You should have forced her.'

'It's her decision.'

'Have you at least called the police?'

'No, she won't let me do that either.'

'Who cares? Call them! Call them now!'

'No, Sara, it's her choice! She explicitly told me not to call them.'

'So fucking what? He needs locking up!'

'I know, I know, but she's my sister.'

'That's even more of a reason to call them! Look at what he did to her!'

'Sara, please keep your voice down. Calm down.'

'How are you so calm?'

'I am NOT calm. This is just how I'm dealing with it.'

'Well, if I'm the only one thinking clearly, I'll take it into my own hands.' I stalked back into the kitchen.

'Sara, no, leave it! I need you here to help me. Please!'

My rational mind, which may have told me to stay at home and support them both, was stifled by the overwhelming need to see Jack, to hurt him. 'Don't worry about me, I'll be fine. You take care of Sef.'

'You're just a kid! I am NOT going to let you do something so stupid.' Lyanna followed me into the kitchen and took hold of my arm firmly, pleading with me. I shook her off.

'No, it's not right. I can't just sit here and do nothing. I can't let him get away with it.'

'He won't get away with it, this is just not the right time.'

'It IS the time—they need to see her like this! They need to see what he's done.'

'Please, Sara. Look, if you stay, I'll call the police,' she bargained.

I thought about it for a moment. My main goal was to get the police involved, but I still felt that it wouldn't satisfy my need to make Jack pay. 'Okay,' I agreed at length.

'Go check on her while I call them. I don't want her to overhear.'

'I think she'll realise, you know, once they're here and asking her questions,' I replied sarcastically.

'I know, I just don't want her to know until then. I have no idea how she'll react.'

I headed upstairs and knocked softly on the bathroom door, so as not to startle her. 'Sef? It's only me.'

There was a low moan from behind the door, which I took to mean "come in".

When I walked in, my rage roared inside of me. I wanted to yell or burst into tears; she looked so vulnerable lying there in the murky, copper-tinted water, completely naked and covered in cuts and bruises. That image will never fade from my memory. 'How are you feeling?' I asked, closing the door behind me as though that would somehow give her back her dignity.

She mouthed words in reply, yet nothing came out but a groan. I realised then that he'd tried to strangle her, again. The bruises and swelling around her neck showed all the signs and the fact that she couldn't speak confirmed my fears. 'Okay. Don't try to talk. Do you want to get out?'

She nodded weakly and tried to lift herself up. 'No, stop, I'll get Lyanna,' I told her, urging her to lay back down. She was shivering, the bath water had cooled down considerably. I opened the door and called down to Lyanna, who appeared almost instantly at the sound of my voice.

'She wants to get out now.'

As she passed me on the stairs, I raised my eyebrows questioningly. She nodded in response, confirming silently that she had called the police. 'Do you need any help?' I asked.

'No thanks, I don't think she'll want us both in there.'

I nodded and headed back downstairs slowly, so as not to raise any suspicion. I heard a squeak and a thump as Serafina climbed out of the bath in the room above. I grabbed the car keys from their hook by the magazine rack and, as quietly as I could, I snuck out of the front door, closing it carefully behind me.

Lyanna had taught me how to drive, though I'd had no official lessons nor had I taken my test. I'd never had any interest in learning to drive, but Lyanna had insisted on showing me the basics as she believed it was a useful skill to have. I was now proving her right, though I don't think that was what she'd had in mind when she'd told me that.

I was extra careful not to draw any attention to myself; this was not a good time to turn Grand Theft Auto. I used the indicator, drove to the exact speed limit and eventually found myself outside Serafina's place, unscathed. All the curtains were drawn despite it being the middle of the day and I briefly wondered if he was even going to still be there—what idiot would remain at the scene of a crime? —but then I remembered the kind of man I was dealing with, and decided he would definitely still be there. Hell, he was probably sat by the door, waiting for Serafina to walk back in and forgive him.

I took a deep breath and walked, not too fast, up to the front of the house. I entered the small front garden through the gate and fished for the spare key under the plant pot, where it always resided waiting for me.

On entering the house, I didn't call out. For a moment, I felt like toying with him, making him believe I was his battered girlfriend, home at last. A moment later, I heard him call out 'Serafina?' from upstairs. I slipped past the foot of the stairs swiftly and quietly, trying not to be seen or heard, and took a seat at the dining table in the centre of the kitchen.

I took a minute to take in my surroundings. The house was a complete tip. Serafina had never been an overly tidy person. She was a fan of organised chaos—books and papers strewn about haphazardly, sweet wrappers and used coffee mugs left out, things like that—but it had always made the house look lived-in, homely. The house I was sat in now looked like a crack-den, or what I imagined a crack-den to look like.

Jack had completely taken over her beautiful home. The place stank of stale beer, cigarettes and bins that hadn't been emptied in weeks. Beer cans, magazines, dirty clothes and used takeaway containers littered the floors and surfaces, and there was a thick layer of dust carpeting everything. With the kitchen blinds lowered, the room was gloomy and miserable, not the lovely, inviting home I was used to. This utter lack of respect just added to my list of reasons to hate the guy.

I heard shuffling footsteps coming down the stairs and my stomach clenched. 'Sef?' he called out again. 'Listen sweetheart, I didn't mean t—' He entered the kitchen and saw me sat there. 'Oh, it's you,' he said, looking annoyed and disappointed.

I could not believe how calm he was being, as though they'd merely had a small quarrel that could be easily fixed with some nice words. He had nearly killed her and yet, he was stood there in his boxer shorts, like it was just a normal, lazy day. He looked at me like I was an irritating fly buzzing around his head that needed to be swatted. I figured that he probably saw most women that way.

I didn't say anything. I was trying to think of the right words and stop myself from lunging across the room at him. 'Where's Serafina?' he asked, visibly perturbed by my silence.

'At ours.'

'And what? Has she sent you sent you to break up with me?'

'I don't need to do that. I think you know this time isn't like all the others. You know it's over.'

He didn't respond.

'Or do you?' I asked. 'Are you so delusional, so arrogant, that you think she'll come back to you?'

'She will come back,' he said with swaggering conviction.

'You'll never see her again. I'll make sure of it.'

'You've been watching too many films, kid.'

'Don't call me that,' I barked.

'What, kid? That's what you are, isn't it? You don't know anything about adult relationships. Just run along home now.'

His patronising tone was infuriating. I wanted to smash his face in. I wanted him to end up looking like Serafina did at that very moment. 'I may not know about adult relationships,' I retorted, 'but I know that what you did isn't right and can't be forgiven. Not even by Serafina, no matter what she's forgiven you for in the past.'

'She always comes back,' he shrugged and I knew for certain that he was utterly deranged. He really had no idea what he'd done or how much pain he'd inflicted, emotionally and physically. My patience was wearing thin and I was done with talking. Men like him only respond to violence.

I stood up. He didn't seem to notice. It had not yet crossed his feeble mind that a young girl could feel so much anger and hatred towards him. He was astonished when I marched over to him and struck him across the face. I didn't cause him any damage, nor did he seem to feel the blow, but the amazement etched across his face assured me that he at least hadn't been expecting it.

He grabbed hold of my arms and I suddenly realised just how strong he was for such a scrawny, bony guy. For the first time, I realised what danger I'd put myself in.

Luckily for me, at that moment, the sound of police sirens drifted towards us and Jack released his vice-like grip. 'They're not here for me, are they?' he asked, looking concerned.

'Probably,' I shrugged, trying to keep my cool. He looked like a cornered animal, his eyes darting side to side, trying to think of a way out, his brow sweating. His logical mind took over his flight instinct and he bolted out of the room and up the stairs, apparently to put some clothes on.

I stood stock-still, unsure what to do next. I supposed the best I could do was try to hinder him, so I stationed myself at the bottom of the stairs and braced my arms against either wall, in a weak yet well-meaning attempt to stop him from getting away.

The sirens were outside the house and I heard car doors *slam!* Just a little longer…

Jack, now fully clothed, came barrelling down the stairs two at a time with a crazed look in his eyes. 'Get out of the way, Sara!' he screamed at me and barged me as hard as he could with his elbow. I shrieked in pain as his elbow collided with my ribs and I impacted the wall, hitting my head.

The police stormed through the door, jumped over my crumpled form on the floor and managed, just in time, to grab hold of Jack by the back of his shirt before he could escape through the back door.

A female officer, entering behind the first two officers, bent down and asked me if I was alright. I nodded gently, clutching my throbbing head.

I was taken to the hospital where I was checked over by a doctor. Just a bang on the head and a bruised rib, nothing fractured, luckily. Lyanna joined me at the hospital once she'd retrieved her car from the police. She didn't press charges against me for the theft. I thanked her, then kept quiet. We both gave our statements in separate rooms before she drove us home.

Lyanna looked tired, exhausted even, and stressed out. It had been an immeasurably long day, but the sun was finally setting. All of a sudden, she pulled the car over at the side of the road and began to weep. I was so surprised, I just sat there like a useless lump, unsure what to do. Then, I came to my senses, unclipped my seatbelt and put my arm around her. We sat there like that for a while. I didn't cry, though I don't know why. I wanted to, but I also wanted to stay strong for her.

At last, she pulled herself together, wiped the tears away and sat up straight. 'What were you thinking?' she asked, exasperated.

'I wasn't. I was just acting.'

'You don't say! He could have killed you!'

'He wouldn't kill me,' I replied with more conviction than I felt. 'He's just a pathetic loser who likes to exert his power over women. He doesn't have the balls to kill someone.'

'You don't know what people are capable of when they're backed into a corner.'

'All I know is, I couldn't just sit there and do nothing! That's all I was thinking,' I sighed. 'I am sorry for stealing your car though.'

Lyanna's mouth turned up slightly at the corners, like she wanted to smile but didn't think it was appropriate. 'Have they locked him up?' I asked.

'Yes,' she confirmed with a hint of relief in her voice.

'Then it was all worth it.' I leaned back and snapped my seatbelt back into place.

We drove the rest of the way home in silence.

When we arrived home, Serafina was sat with an officer. The paramedics had been and gone. Apparently, they had wanted to take her into hospital to be treated properly, but she had refused profusely. So, they had checked her over at the house, given her some string painkillers, stitched up some of her cuts and left her with a kindly, old officer. The officer was chewing her ear off about fishing, or something, most likely in an effort to take her mind off things and lighten the mood, as is the older generation's way.

On our entrance, he stopped talking and looked in our direction. I saw a look of genuine relief pass over Serafina's face. Whether it was relief because I was safe, or relief because we'd saved her from the old guy's wittering, I wasn't sure. 'Ah, look, your family's back now,' he pointed out needlessly, and Serafina managed a weak smile at his words. 'I'll be off then. Unless there's anything else you need from me?' She shook her head sadly.

After the officer left, we sat quietly while Lyanna heated up some soup for Serafina and toasted some bagels for me. I scoffed the whole lot down too fast, as I hadn't eaten since breakfast, giving myself a stomach ache. Once I had finished, Lyanna and I sat and watched Serafina attempt, painfully slowly, to eat her soup. She must have really hated us for sitting there watching her like that, our faces full of pity.

I expected her, for some reason, to open up and talk about what had happened, but instead, once she had finished eating, she excused herself and made her way up to the spare room to bed.

That night, lying awake listening to Serafina crying in the next room, it finally dawned on me what I'd done. A seventeen-year-old girl, stealing her aunt's car, going alone to see a violent criminal, hitting him, trying to stop him from leaving…things could have gone a whole lot worse for me.

I didn't understand what had come over me, but I was once again reminded of my impulsive, dramatic mother. Something had taken over, like an angry fog, a feeling I'd had no control over. And, while I lay in bed, thinking, I feared I'd gone mad. I'd had no idea I'd had that kind of rage and courage inside of me. Who was I? What was I doing? Why had I reacted that way? But I was glad that I had. Now, he was locked away where he belonged and it was all because of my recklessness.

*****

Serafina didn't talk about what had happened for weeks afterwards. Her voice took a while to recover and she shrunk inside herself, still barely communicating, unable to look us in the eyes like she was ashamed.

One day, while we were in the middle of eating our evening meal and I was daydreaming as I stared out at the dusky garden, she blurted out, 'I bet you're really ashamed of me, aren't you?'

Lyanna and I exchanged glances, dumbfounded. We hastened to assure her that no, of course not. 'Why would you think that?' we asked.

Serafina turned to me. 'Your words, Sara, have haunted me these past few weeks. You said I'm weak and you were right—I am weak.'

'No! I never meant what I said! I've never, *never* thought you were weak, not for one moment,' I reassured her.

'But I was.'

Lyanna placed her hand over Serafina's and said softly, 'No, you weren't. He manipulated you, played mind games with you. None of it was your fault.'

Despite hating what Serafina was thinking and saying, I was glad that she was finally opening up. It's not good, ever, to bottle up powerful emotions. 'Please don't think about what I said to you in anger. I said it to hurt you during a stupid argument. Not one word of it was true.'

'Don't let me go there ever again,' she pleaded with us.

'Sef, I did try to warn you before, but it's not easy once you've set your mind on something. You've got the Black stubbornness,' Lyanna said with a hint of joviality in her voice.

Serafina smiled a little, but her eyes remained serious and thoughtful. 'I suppose I should thank you, Sara.'

'What for?' I questioned, genuinely.

'For getting the police involved. I don't agree with your methods,' and at this she stared at me pointedly, 'but you were right. He does deserve to be punished. This is bigger than me; I don't want him to hurt anybody else.'

I nodded but said nothing more. 'Don't do anything like that again though. I mean it. Putting yourself in danger like that; it was reckless. I never would have forgiven myself if anything had happened to you.'

Lyanna nodded vigorously in agreement. 'I'm afraid I can't promise anything.'

'You bloody well can. Promise me, right now!'

'No, I can't.'

'Why not?'

'I don't know,' I answered thoughtfully, looking back out into the garden, which was now bathed in the shadows cast by the moon and the solar-powered fairy lights that twinkled and glowed prettily. 'I feel like something has woken up inside of me, something I have no control over. Another side of me, a darker side.' In my head, the words felt full of truth and authenticity but out loud, they made me sound like an imperious little cow.

When I was a teen, I often thought that I couldn't wait for my twenties, to be an actual adult. I'd long thought I was grown-up for my age and wanted nothing more than to be taken seriously. No matter what you say as a young person, no matter how wise or thought-provoking your words, you'll always sound precocious or high-handed. Say those same words as an adult and people will listen to you.

My aunts exchanged looks that I couldn't read.

I laughed nervously. 'That's what I feel anyway.'

'You really do live in a fantasy world, don't you?' Serafina observed and fixed Lyanna with another look that suggested she meant more by that statement than she'd meant it to sound. 'Teenagers,' she tutted.

Chapter Nineteen

The day finally came when I decided to tell my aunts what was really going on inside my head—about the Other Place. For the past year or so, it had seemed to be lying dormant. Nothing much out of the ordinary had occurred, and I'd started to think I had grown out of it. It all seemed so removed from reality that it even crossed my mind that I'd imagined it all, but after what happened with Serafina and Jack things had started to unravel.

I kept having recurring, vivid dreams; dreams that felt so real that when I awoke, I had no idea where I was or what century I was in. I was seeing things wherever I went, things that other people couldn't. Some of these things were horrifying and unnerving, some were alluring and beautiful.

Those around me—my friends and my aunts—had started to pick up on my strange behaviour. I was spending most of my time alone, dwelling on my thoughts and visions, writing about them, and when I was around others, I didn't feel wholly myself, like I wasn't really there. I was distracted, short-tempered and found it difficult to concentrate on what was going on around me. Instead, I would stare off into the distance and I'd often find myself coming to and realising that everyone was staring at me as though there was something wrong with me. Myla told me I had been talking to myself on one occasion, which made me extremely uncomfortable. I was beginning to feel like I couldn't control it (not that I ever could), like my body was no longer my own.

It was Myla who persuaded me to talk to someone about it. I didn't want to talk to a shrink; they specialised in psychology and therefore, there was already the preconception that it was all in my head. I still wasn't convinced that it wasn't psychological, but I definitely didn't want it deciding for me before I'd even opened my mouth. Besides, being under eighteen years of age, Lyanna would have had to give her permission for me to see a psych, so I would have had to tell her anyway.

It was the end of September; the leaves had started turning russet and gold and despite the temperature still being quite mild, I could feel autumn approaching.

I arrived home from school and found my aunts in the dining room, drinking tea and looking out at the garden. They were deep in conversation when I entered and sat down heavily beside them at the table. They cut off their discussion and smiled at me. I sighed heavily in greeting. The workload in the second year of sixth form was double that of the first year and I was feeling the strain. 'How was school?' Lyanna asked cheerily.

'Not bad, thanks,' I shrugged, not wanting to go into further detail.

'That bad, huh?' Serafina teased.

'I've got to go do some coursework soon, but for now, I'd just like to relax and forget all about World War Two, Rembrandt and Shakespeare.'

'Point taken,' Serafina nodded.

We sat for a while, watching the leaves flutter down from the trees, talking about nothing in particular, then I suddenly blurted out, 'Can I talk to you both about something?' I didn't really want to have this conversation, ever, but I knew I should and now was as good a time as any.

Lyanna and Serafina immediately stiffened, probably expecting me to say I was dropping out of school or that I was pregnant. 'Of course, anything,' Lyanna replied warmly.

'Well, I don't really know where to begin.'

'Anywhere you want,' Lyanna prompted. Serafina remained silent and watchful.

'Well, there's something that's been happening to me—all my life, actually.'

Now they looked truly concerned, like I was going to tell them I'd been abused or something. 'It's nothing horrible,' I added hastily, 'it's just something going on in here.' I pointed at my head, then paused. 'Although I'm not really sure if it is inside my head.'

'Sara, spit it out. You're talking in riddles.'

Lyanna looked mortified at Serafina's abruptness. 'Yeah, right. Well, ever since I was a kid, I've been visited by *things*.'

'What sort of things?' Serafina asked sceptically. 'Like, in your dreams?'

'Sometimes, yeah. But then it happens when I'm awake too. I've seen things inside this house, in our garden, in the street, at school. Basically, wherever I go.

And, sometimes,' I sighed, working up the courage to say it aloud, 'I go somewhere else.'

They were both rendered speechless, their brows furrowed in concern. This was not at all what they'd expected me to say. 'Where do you go, honey?' Lyanna asked me, in a slightly patronising tone.

'I can't describe it. It's somewhere else; in this world and not, at the same time.'

Serafina and Lyanna looked at each other nervously. 'What do you call this place?' Serafina questioned.

I was confused at how specific her question was. 'What do you mean?'

'What I said; what do you call it? You say you've been going there all your life so you must have a name for it.'

'The Other Place.'

They looked at each other like they'd just been told some really disturbing news. 'What is it?' I asked nervously.

'Well, it's just that…' Lyanna didn't seem to know how to finish her sentence.

'What?' I asked again, panicked at their reactions. Were they going to send me away to be sectioned?

'That's what your mum called it,' Serafina divulged.

My whole body tensed. I was cold to the bone, but my palms and back were sweating. 'What do you mean?'

'Look, we haven't told you everything that went on with your mum. We didn't think it was necessary but now, it obviously is.'

'So, tell me now. I want to know.'

'It's very strange. I don't want you to get upset.'

'I won't.'

'Let me tell her, Serafina,' Lyanna interrupted. 'You're not very, umm, tactile.'

Serafina nodded, apparently unoffended by this observation. 'After your dad died, your mum changed, as you know. Of course, we thought it was just grief, the fear of bringing a child into the world alone, and all the other stresses she was dealing with, but things got progressively worse. It wasn't just how distracted or ill-tempered or emotional she could be; she started raving about things, talking to herself.'

I gulped. This was already starting to sound incredibly familiar. 'She always came back to the *other place*. We thought it was metaphorical, maybe a figurative place in her head, or a nice area that she liked to visit, but then things turned a lot darker. I'd wake up to her screaming in the middle of the night and she would insist that something had been there in the room with her. It was terrifying. We were both so worried about her.'

Serafina interjected, 'One day, she came home after disappearing for hours—we have no idea where—and she was covered in scratches.'

Lyanna shot Serafina an angry look. 'What had happened to her?' I asked, my voice shaky.

Lyanna looked terribly sad. 'We don't know. She tried to tell us, but her words were all fragmented. We only caught the gist of it.'

'And?' I questioned forcefully.

'She said she started somewhere and it had been pretty and it was right, or something like that. Something about meeting someone, or a few people. Seeing things clearly. But then it had gotten dark there; she kept saying the word dark over and over again, like she was stuck on it. Something had changed—the people went away, and she was left with a monster.' Lyanna sighed.

'And then she started screaming hysterically, and we couldn't get any more out of her about it,' Serafina finished, leaning back in her chair and folding her arms across her chest.

I took a moment to digest this information and tried to get my head around what they'd told me. Every fibre of my being was telling me that my mum had been out of her mind, had completely lost the plot, but how could I possibly believe that when the same things had happened to me? That would mean I'd gone mad too. I didn't know what to say or think, so I just sat there staring at the glass fruit bowl in the centre of the table and the lonely apple that resided there.

Lyanna and Serafina gave me time to mull everything over and didn't add anything more. Eventually, I said, 'What do I do with that?'

Neither of them had an answer for me. They mumbled and fidgeted uncomfortably. 'I mean, what does it mean?' I stood up and paced back and forth in front of the patio doors. 'How can we both have thought and felt and seen the same things, when I don't even remember her?'

'Well, she is your mother,' Serafina observed.

'What, so I inherited this? But what even is it? A condition? Am I schizophrenic? Bipolar? Psychopathic? What's even wrong with me?'

114

'We don't even know that anything *is* wrong with you,' Lyanna said, attempting to reassure me. 'You don't seem as bad with it as she was. It might be—'

'Bullshit!' I blurted. 'This isn't a coincidence. This isn't something that can be brushed aside.' My voice was high-pitched and panic-stricken, so I took a deep breath and steadied myself. 'And, *this* is really what I wanted to tell you, I don't think it's in my mind.' The silence was excruciating, so I carried on determinedly, 'All the way through this, I've questioned myself, questioned my sanity. I've been terrified of what's been happening to me but instead of confirming what I feared, all this about my mum has proven to me that it is real! I mean, think about it—even if it was a mental illness, some kind of hereditary thing, we wouldn't both have had the exact same dreams and visions, go to the same place and we definitely wouldn't call it by the same name.'

The look of concern on my aunts' faces halted my train of thought. I'd been talking as though to myself, momentarily forgetting they were even there with me. 'Would we?' I asked earnestly.

'Sara,' Serafina responded, 'there's something you have to understand about Evelien. This other place, it was an idea that had taken hold of her mind, slowly worming its way inside, until it completely took over and eventually, it broke her. Don't you see? This was why she left. It was an effect of all the stress she'd been under, her mind had created it to protect her from the pain she felt.'

'I don't believe that,' I answered.

'Why not?'

'Because your mind wouldn't create something to protect you that actually hurt you. How do you explain the negative things that happened? The nightmares? The cuts?'

'That was just her grief creeping through, finding a way to show itself through the imaginary world she'd created. I hate to say it, but the cuts were probably a product of self-harm. I've read about this stuff, I—'

'Oh, so now you're an expert, Sef?'

'That's not what I'm saying—'

'Look, I understand why this would be so hard for you to believe. That's what your precious books have told you, that's how you've explained it to yourselves all this time, so it would be difficult for me to change your minds now, but I know what I've seen, what I've felt, and it's not made up.'

Serafina exhaled, exasperated, but Lyanna looked straight at me and sincerely told me, 'I believe you.'

'You do?' I asked, incredulously.

'I do. Just like I believed your mum.'

'You didn't sound like you believed her,' I pointed out, dubious.

'You liar!' Serafina exploded. 'You never once said you believed her!'

'Sef, you were always different to us: logical, realistic, rational. There were things that Evelien told me that she would never say in front of you.'

'Like what?' Serafina looked hurt.

'Like the fact that she walked and talked with these other people, that time was different there. She told me that she'd left for days one time, and when she returned, barely an hour had passed. And, just like Sara, she confided in me that she truly thought it was real. She wasn't in one of her hysterical states when she told me this, before you say anything; she was coherent and alert. She looked me straight in the eyes and told me that it was real. From then on, I took her seriously.'

'Why didn't you tell me?' Serafina whispered, clearly astonished and dismayed at the turn the conversation had taken.

'Because you never would have believed her. You may have even laughed at her. Then after she left, it didn't seem so important anymore.'

'Of course, it was important! I can't believe you kept that from me.' Serafina stood as though ready to leave.

'Why are you so upset? You know you never could have believed her.'

'Oh, so because it's not something I could get on board with, because I'm logical, as you put it, I don't have feelings? It still hurts that you both thought so little of me that you whispered behind my back and hid things from me.'

'It wasn't like that.'

'Don't. I don't want to hear anymore.' Tears spilled down Serafina's face. I'd never seen her emotionally hurt before. Even after Jack had beaten her to a pulp, I'd never seen her cry, except from physical pain. My heart went out to her and I didn't at all blame her for wanting to leave and get away from the situation.

'It's just like Sef to make it all about her,' Lyanna said bitterly, as the front door slammed shut.

'Don't, Lyanna. It doesn't matter. She just needs some time to digest everything. I know that feeling, I don't judge her for it.'

'I know, but you need us.'

'Right now, I only need you. Like you said, you believe me, but she never could. Maybe it's for the best that we're left alone to talk for now.'

Lyanna nodded faintly. 'I suppose so. You know, it all started when your dad went away, before he died.'

'What, the visions?'

'I think so. When I thought back on it afterwards, the signs had been there for a long time, longer than I'd realised.'

'Why do you think we can see it?'

'I honestly don't know, honey, I'm sorry. I mean, she always was unique, imaginative, creative; her head was in the clouds. She was different to everyone else our age, well, from anyone I'd ever met, really. Maybe that spirituality, that innate ability she had for seeing everything for what it really was, made her susceptible to it? And you, well, you're so much like her, and you're her blood, so it would make sense that you'd be susceptible to it too.'

'Do you really believe us?' The word 'us' rolled off my tongue. I found joy in talking about my mum and I as though we were a team, both on the same side. 'Do you really believe there's a place in this world, a magical place that only we can see?'

Lyanna considered her reply carefully. 'I believe there is a lot in this universe that we don't know about, that we don't understand, that can't be rationalised or explained. I also believe, if it is real, you two probably aren't the only people in the world that have experienced it. There'll be others out there.'

I considered this. 'I think that makes a lot of sense.'

'Oh, Sara. I'm so sorry you've been dealing with this all alone.' Lyanna was suddenly overcome with emotion. She embraced me tightly.

'I haven't,' I confessed. 'Myla knows.'

She let me go and eyed me curiously. 'Does she?'

'Yes; I told her last year. She was the one who convinced me to tell you guys.'

'And, what does she think?'

'I don't think she really thinks anything, to be honest. Myla has the gift of being able to just let things be. She doesn't worry about ifs or whys; she just accepts things as they are.'

'Well, that really is a gift. She's special, that one.'

'She really is.'

At that moment, the front door clicked open and shut. Myla strolled into the kitchen. 'How's it going?' she asked casually.

I laughed. 'Okay,' I told her, but those two syllables fell short of the events of the past hour.

Lyanna left me to catch Myla up on all that had been discussed and when she returned twenty minutes later, she was watery-eyed and melancholy. 'I have something you might like to see.' She handed me a wooden box, plain and nothing special to behold, but when I opened it up, my heart skipped a beat. Inside were letters exchanged between my mum and dad. 'These are the letters they wrote to one another while he was away, before and after she got pregnant with you.'

'So, he came back on leave?'

'Yeah, he came back for a couple of months before being redeployed. It was a gift that she found out she was pregnant while he was still home, but it made leaving again that much harder.'

'I can imagine.'

Myla posed the question I wanted to ask but dare wouldn't. 'How far along was she when he died?'

Lyanna pondered this for a moment. 'About six, seven months.'

My chest tightened. I didn't say anything more for a while.

Myla, Lyanna and I sat and read each letter together, entangled within the story of their romance. Their words were poignant and beautiful, yet straight to the point, as though they knew they only had a limited amount of time left together.

On reading the final letter, from my dad to my mum, we all got choked up. The letter didn't say anything much different to the others, but knowing it was the last one he ever wrote, and the last one she'd ever read from him, made it so much more heart-breaking. 'The day after she received that letter, she got the news that he'd been killed. She never even got the chance to write her reply. It's tragic.' Lyanna wiped he tears away.

We talked a while longer about my parent's relationship. I asked questions and for the first time in my life, I felt joy at the thought of them and their love, like they were finally three-dimensional human beings, who walked and talked and felt, deeply, rather than formless shadows hovering over my thoughts.

I thought about those letters constantly for a few weeks after reading them, and I re-read them whenever I got the chance between essays and studying. I realised, on reading them again, that my mum had been trying to tell him about what was happening to her. She had attempted to press him to ask her by hiding hints and clues within her writing. She'd secretly wanted to tell him everything but had obviously not wanted to add more weight to his shoulders than he already had. And though she didn't tell him explicitly, I could read the words that were left unsaid, something she couldn't talk about but wanted to say more than anything. It hung between the words, in the empty spaces between the lines, like a dark cloud threatening rain on an otherwise fine day.

It had haunted my mum, the Other Place, and all she'd wanted was to tell the one person she loved more than anything in the world, to share her fears and her burden with him, but she had never gotten the chance.

Chapter Twenty

My final year of sixth form passed me by in a blur. My concentration levels dropped and I lost all interest in the subjects. I didn't care about the Corn Laws or the use of light in a painting; I wanted to learn about the blood and lust of our extravagant, gritty history and draw the things from my dreams. I somehow scraped by and came out with a C in English and art and a D in history. My aunts were disappointed in me, but they soon came around when I was accepted into art college.

The 'choice' to go to college hadn't actually been a choice, just like all my other 'choices' so far in life. Once again, while everyone was achieving the grades they'd strived for and were taking their pick of the best universities in the country, I was like a car stuck in mud, wheels spinning uncontrollably yet getting nowhere, with no clue of where I wanted to go or what I wanted to do. Art college seemed to me the only place I really stood a chance of getting in. Plus, Myla had enrolled there as well.

I wonder now if things would have been different had I not been so consumed by the Other Place. Would I have enjoyed my subjects instead of being constantly distracted? Would I have received better grades and been able to choose better options for higher education? Would I have been more focussed in my studies and been able to make long-term decisions about my future instead of living purely in the present? The Other Place was starting to take over my life. Hey, I suppose there's no point in wondering about it now; what happened, happened, as it always did.

Art gave me something to channel my energy into; it brought me back down to earth and allowed me to be distracted from the distraction itself. It was definitely the best thing for me at that time; I had started to wonder if I was ever going to return to a normal life in which faeries and other worlds didn't exist.

Myla and I made new friends and formed a tight-knit group with Aron, Lori, Jon and Daphne. Aron was a lackadaisical, moony sort of boy with a half-shaved head and a penchant for skateboarding. I believe he had joined the course for the same reasons as me; he didn't know what else to do and probably thought it'd be a laugh. Jon was his polar opposite; an intense, dark-haired, dark-eyed lad who took himself and his work incredibly seriously. Somehow though, they meshed together well and were fast friends.

Lori and Daphne were very similar young women; arty and cool with a don't-give-a-fuck attitude. Myla and I gelled with them instantly. They were creative without the pretension. Like us, they just really enjoyed what they did and didn't have the same snobbery about their work that some others in the class had.

The college was situated in the heart of Grosvenor Park—a huge woodland area on the outskirts of Moraine. Every evening, at the end of the school day, we'd all stroll home through the Park together, deep in conversation about TV programmes, films, music, our plans for the future, style, society—all those subjects that young adults have such passionate opinions on. I finally felt like an independent grown-up, in charge of my own workload and time, hanging out with similar-minded friends, creating whatever I wanted and coming and going from home as I pleased. It was exactly as I'd pictured college life. I'd finally found somewhere I felt I belonged.

My work still had the theme of the written word running through it. Above all, writing was always my passion above imagery. I could never stifle my love for words and script. I made collages; layers of charcoal and ink illustrations and photographs inscribed with elegant, handwritten verses of poetry. The results were plastered all over my bedroom walls and every surface was cluttered with sketchbooks, big and small, bursting with my imaginations creations. My work gave me a channel through which the fantasia in my mind could meet the real world, and in some ways, it helped me work through my warring thoughts and make sense of it all.

Myla and I collaborated extensively. She had become increasingly fascinated with photography and together, we'd develop the moody, other-worldly pictures that she had such a unique talent for capturing, and draw and write all over them, creating visual stories for each one.

The seeds of inspiration were firmly planted inside my mind, flourishing and growing into great branches of inventiveness. I was ensnared; my every waking minute was spent creating and experimenting.

There was something else in class which also took up a lot of my attention, or should I say *someone*. Zak Slater—a tall, handsome man of nineteen years, with a flair for oil painting. He had a sweet, kind, boyish face and he was somewhat awkward, in an endearing way. He listened to film scores and admired the work of Vermeer.

The first time I ever spoke to Zak, he squeaked shyly and seemed to be having a hard time believing that a woman was talking to him. I found this surprising considering his lean, muscular build and good looks, but it also made me like him more. There was no hint of conceitedness or ego, only a nervous, self-effacing man looking out through those grey eyes.

We got to know each other slowly, at a pace that suited me. All my past encounters with 'love' had been swift and brutal, nothing like what a young girl should experience. What I had with Zak was natural and easy, a friendship that was blossoming subtly into something more under the watchful gaze of our friends. They, especially Myla, encouraged me to open up and take things further, but I was content with that pace of progression. I didn't want to rush into anything for fear of ruining the relationship we'd so carefully nurtured. He seemed to feel the same way, or so I thought.

Now eighteen years old and being surrounded by young adults, parties became a frequent occurrence for Myla and me. These, however, were nothing like the parties we'd been to before. Everybody drank and things got silly, but there was no sinister, uncomfortable atmosphere. This was probably because I knew everyone there and more importantly, I trusted them. Nobody was trying to show off or impress anyone else; they were just casual, fun gatherings; what a party was supposed to be.

At the Christmas party held at Daphne's house, Zak officially asked me to be his girlfriend. I said yes because it felt right at that moment. I was seized by the festive spirit and we had been flirting back and forth for long enough. However, after the spirit of Christmas withered away and we headed into the bleak beginning-of-the-year months, I started to regret my decision.

There was nothing wrong with Zak, not at all. In fact, he was as close to perfect as you could get—kind, respectful, artistic, sensitive, and he was also protective and made me feel safe—yet something inside me screamed when we were alone together. The wisdom of many years' experience and contemplation has allowed me to see that this reaction stemmed from my previous encounters with the opposite sex. I still couldn't let myself totally relax around them and I sensed danger in every movement, every word spoken, every touch, intentional or otherwise.

I'd had my heart broken and as a result, I broke Zak's heart and became the kind of person I had so despised. I started to avoid him and never let myself be alone with him. I gave him mixed messages about my feelings; whenever I was drunk, I would fawn over him, and when we were apart, I sent him gushing text messages saying how much I cared about him. Then, when I was sober, I'd be flippant with him and sometimes even outright ignored him. It was obviously affecting him; he pulled me up on my behaviour on a few occasions. Every time, he told me how much I was hurting him and how confused he was, and I would apologise profusely, genuinely feeling sorry for the way I'd treated him, and then I'd vow to him, and myself, that I'd somehow find a way through it and be the girlfriend we both wanted me to be.

Only, the mind doesn't work that way, unfortunately. It won't let you just brush those kinds of feelings aside. It would not let me forget, and no matter how hard I tried, I couldn't bring myself to feel the way I wanted to. Despite trusting him and caring for him deeply, I couldn't rid myself of the fear and vulnerability I felt whenever we were alone. I tried to act like everything was alright, but inside I was screaming at myself to get out of there, to get to a quiet, safe place where the screaming would stop.

It all came to an abrupt, nasty end at my nineteenth birthday party that April. I'd been dodging Zak for a few weeks. Part of me had hoped that he'd get the message without me having to break it to him directly. I was a coward.

I was stood outside in my garden smoking a cigarette (as most of the students did in my class—it had started on our class trip to Paris in January), talking to Myla and Lori, when Myla interrupted me suddenly. 'He's here,' she whispered harshly.

'Who?' I asked, looking around expectantly.

Zak poked his head out of the patio doors. 'I should have known you'd be out here,' he said rather bitterly. He'd never taken up the habit of smoking and didn't approve of it either.

Myla and Lori scurried off inside the house awkwardly, not even bothering to make up any excuses. 'Happy birthday to me,' I said sarcastically, then took a deep drag on my cigarette in defiance. 'Where's my hug?'

He just stared at me, uncomprehending. 'What?' I asked sulkily, though I knew why he was there, and it wasn't to wish me a happy birthday.

'I need to talk to you.'

'You always need to talk to me.'

There were other people dotted around the garden in groups, keeping their distance so as not to disturb our conversation. I turned away from Zak and joined in on a debate over Star Wars versus Star Trek.

Zak tapped me on the shoulder, a look of deep hurt written across his sweet face. 'Please can we talk?'

I groaned and broke away from the group, as though he was a parent calling me in off the streets for bedtime. 'Fine.'

'What's going on, Sara?' he asked me, clearly upset.

'What do you mean?' I feigned ignorance.

I looked over at my party guests distractedly. When I looked back at him, the smile was immediately wiped from my face. 'What?'

'I'm trying to talk to you.'

I was being deliberately evasive, and it was so plainly obvious. 'Well then, talk!' I laughed derisively and stroked his arm in a playful attempt to lighten the mood. I didn't want to be acting that way. Every fibre of my being was telling me not to be that bitch, to stop hurting him, to stop blocking him out and just allow myself to be happy with him, but I couldn't. 'This isn't a joke to me, but I'm glad to know how you really feel.' He shook my hand away from his arm.

'How I feel? What are you talking about? You're being so sensitive.' I regretted the words they moment they left my lips and my stomach clenched with guilt. His sensitivity was one of the traits I loved so much about him, and there I was, using them as a weapon against him in my twisted game.

'Don't belittle me. Don't make me feel like less of a man because I care about you and I want to know what's going on inside your head.'

'Look, you're just making it into too much of a big deal.' Though I knew he wasn't. If the tables were turned, I'd be acting in exactly the same way. In fact, I'd probably be acting psychopathic. 'We're just having fun.'

'Is this all this is to you? A bit of fun?'

'I just meant tonight, the party—'

'There's always a party, there's always a reason not to be alone with me, not to have this conversation. You've been avoiding me. You're dragging my feelings and dignity through the dirt.'

'I'm not, I just—'

'Just what?'

'It's just, maybe, maybe we're in different places?'

'Obviously.'

There was an awkward pause. I wanted to throw my arms around him, tell him how much I loved spending time with him, how much I respected him, how much I really didn't want to hurt him, how much I valued him and his feelings. But I didn't. I laughed. Right in his face. 'This is stupid,' I told him heartlessly.

'Oh really, my feelings are stupid?'

'Well, yeah.'

'That really hurts, you know.'

I could see it all written on his face. I was deeply cutting him. He looked crushed and tired. I wondered how many sleepless nights I'd caused him, how many times he'd obsessively checked his phone, hoping for a message from me, hoping that I'd wake up and be the person he'd originally fallen for, but I couldn't help myself. There was a mental block between my brain and my mouth. My thoughts would not form into speech. 'I love you, Sara.'

My stomach flipped. It should have been the happiest moment and maybe in a different life, I would have said it back. This wasn't some stupid teenage romance; I knew he would do anything for me (he'd put up with me for that long for a reason), he would have followed me to the ends of the earth if I'd asked him to, and that's why I had to end it. I couldn't let him in, I couldn't let him do that for me, I couldn't let that twisted, cruel situation continue. I dug the knife in deeper. 'Love?' I scoffed. 'It's not love. You're acting crazy! You're smothering me—it's too much. You're too needy.' Urgh. That word: needy. The most derogatory word you can use to describe someone showing their love for you.

His face changed then; his expression hardened. He no longer appeared upset—he was angry. 'You're lying to yourself. I can see straight through your act.'

He was right, of course he was, but that was exactly why I couldn't let him close. I wasn't ready to let someone in; the walls my mind had built around me were an impenetrable fortress, my only form of protection. He already knew me too well.

I watched him walk away and after college finished in July, I never saw him again. I often wonder where he ended up, what he ended up doing with his life and who he ended up with. I hope beyond hope that he found happiness and I didn't screw him up too much. I hope he didn't build his own walls because of me. Maybe I'm being too vainglorious? He was a strong, determined young man and I'm sure he was alright, eventually.

Myla came straight out into the garden after he left to find me crying on the floor by the plant pots. She hugged me and asked, 'What happened? Did he upset you?'

'No, it's worse—I hurt him.' I wanted to run after him and tell him the truth, but I couldn't.

'Oh, Sara.'

'Don't,' I sniffed, pushing her away, 'I deserve to feel this guilt. I was awful to him, like really awful. It hurts because I care about him so much.'

'I know, I know. It's okay.'

'It's not okay. It's all their fault. I wouldn't be like this if it wasn't for them and what they did to me,' I spat. 'If they hadn't fucked me up so badly, Zak and I could be happy together.'

She knew who 'they' were, I didn't need to say their names. 'I know.'

'You know how much I care for him, don't you?' I pleaded. 'You know I didn't want to hurt him?'

'Of course I do. I know you better than you know yourself, and I think he did too.'

I nodded and sniffed sadly. 'I hope so.' The idea comforted me and his parting words to me echoed inside my mind. 'I don't want to feel this way anymore.'

'You won't. You're obviously just not ready for an intimate relationship yet and that's okay.'

I could always count on Myla to offer me wisdom and comfort, even after I'd acted like a complete bitch. What are friends for?

Chapter Twenty-One

The college year was coming to an end and it had crept up on me like a rising tide. I was just beginning to acclimatise to my carefree lifestyle when, all of a sudden, it was time for our final projects and all around me, the other students were stressing about university applications. I wasn't.

Lyanna had attempted, many times throughout the year, to discuss my future plans and goals with me, or lack thereof. She told me repeatedly that I needed to be focussing on what came next. Within the first month of the course, I was told I was already supposed to be considering my options for when the course was finished the following year, but I wasn't the sort of person to plan that far ahead; I lived in the moment and recklessly only thought about anything of any importance at the absolute last moment.

Myla knew from the minute she set foot in that class that she wanted to be a photographer and was now applying for photography courses at universities across the country. She had it all planned out. I envied her drive and determination, but it just wasn't in my nature. My aunts, Serafina more so than Lyanna, scolded me, telling me I was lazy and 'living in a dream world'—that I needed to take responsibility of my life. I shrugged it off and ignored them, still clinging onto the hope that one day, it would all just work out as it had so far.

*****

The final project was based on family. We were each to create a study, in our own style and preferred medium, that represented family and what it meant to us. The work was to be showcased in the park grounds and we were told to utilise the environment. My idea was basic, at best, and my love of nature influenced my entire project. I found an ethereal willow tree and hung my work in its branches, the idea being that I was creating a literal family tree. It was whimsical and somewhat primitive.

I created three intricate drawings of Lyanna, Serafina and Myla (because family doesn't necessarily mean what we were born into) and hung them in the tree. I surrounded them with prints and sketches of inspiring quotes on family and relationships written by my favourite authors and poets. Suspended above it all, in the highest branches, I strung cut-out silhouettes of my parents. In the centre of the images, I painted large, white question marks, stark and ominous.

I hadn't thought outside the box, but then, I never did. I liked art to be a recreation of what was inside my head. Myla, on the other hand, had given her work much thought. Her idea was also simple, yet more effective in its execution. She suspended photographs of her home and her parents in various stages of development along a row of silver birches. Her vision was to portray the journey she had been on to learn about her family and to truly get to know them and understand them. The first set of prints were hazy, under-developed and as you walked along the line, the images gradually came into focus. The final prints were crisp and stark, revealing clearly all her parents' flaws, yet these were somehow more beautiful than the grainy, dreamy photographs. Through her eyes, you could see the beauty in her imperfect family; she loved them because of their flaws as much as for the strengths. Needless to say, her parents came to the exhibition and were veritably proud of what Myla had accomplished.

Myla was awarded a Distinction for her efforts while I received a Merit. I'll be honest though; I was undoubtedly pleased with my grade and over the moon that I'd gotten more than a standard Pass.

Myla gained entry to her top-choice university and though I felt uneasy both at the thought of not knowing what to do with myself and at losing her to another city, I was genuinely pleased for her. She deserved it—she had her head screwed on, unlike me.

Myla didn't attend her top-choice university in Edinburgh; instead, she accepted an offer in York, only a few miles west of Moraine. I never asked her why she did this, though now I have an inkling. I was so elated that I would still get to see her at weekends that I never even entertained the notion that she had actually turned down one of the best photography courses in the UK for me.

She lived in student accommodation during the school week, firstly to get a feel for the full university experience, and secondly—so she could roll straight out of bed fifteen minutes before her classes started. She could sleep, that girl.

I, on the other hand, instead of starting a whole new adventure of my own, was facing the reality of having to find a full-time job. I had still not decided what I'd wanted to do next and, after missing the enrolment window and with no safety net to fall back on, was going to have to make the giant leap into adulthood. Serafina couldn't help but point out that I'd just wasted the last three years of my life living selfishly, just to resign myself to finding a menial job and completely invalidating all the work I'd spent the last three years completing. I could have found myself a menial job straight out of high school and made Lyanna's life easier. Lyanna told me not to listen to Sef, but deep down, we both knew that there was truth in her words.

What *were* the past three years in aid of? What was I possibly going to do with all the knowledge I'd gained in sixth form and college? I realised I'd been on a narcissistic ego-trip, hiding from any kind of responsibility and disguising it as a journey to a better future. I wondered how I'd ended up where I was. I'd been plodding along, assuming that, eventually, I'd find my path and it would all work out, but it hadn't. I'd reached a dead-end and now there was nowhere left for me to run. I was getting left behind.

Myla and I drifted apart, of course we did. She led a separate life to me, filled with new friends, new places and goals. At first, our routine had been successful. Myla would come home on the weekends and we would enjoy our usual activities as though nothing had changed. She aided me with my CV and job applications, and I got an insight into her new, exciting life. I lived vicariously through her.

After a few months, however, she would return home less and less, claiming she had a stack of work to do, but then I'd see photos of her partying with people I'd never met on social media. That's when I began to resent her. I was jealous, but at the same time, I thought everything was her fault. She had betrayed me, left me behind, abandoned me. On the weekends that she did return home, I made her miserable. I made digs at her new life and her new friends and I'd act paranoid and jealous like she was my lover. The final straw came when I told her she was just like my mother. I told her she didn't care about me and was leaving me to go onto bigger and better things. She countered that I needed to grow up, stormed out and that was that. I pushed away the only decent thing in my life. We didn't speak for months afterwards, the longest we'd gone without keeping in touch since we'd met all those years before.

*****

I found myself a job in a bookstore. One day, I was out and about, handing out copies of my CV (whilst doing a spot of window shopping) when I stumbled upon Armchair Books. I'd browsed in the shop on many occasions, but I'd always thought of it as a place for pleasure and leisure. Now, I was viewing it as a place of possibility and a chance to earn my own money. I imagined spending every day of my working life surrounded by books and getting paid for the privilege. In the store window was a hand-written, shabby advertisement confirming they were hiring and needed somebody flexible. That was me!

I went in, handed over my CV to a friendly member of staff and filled in the application form there and then as I had nowhere else to be. They were impressed with my CV despite my lack of work experience and became visibly excited when I divulged that I was available for an immediate start as I was unemployed. I attended an interview there less than a week later and, on the very same day, I was offered the job over the phone. I agreed, enthusiastically, to start the following Monday, excited that I'd finally found a new path. It wasn't the path I'd always pictured for myself, but it was better than the desolate wasteland I'd found myself wandering aimlessly in. Lyanna was over the moon for me and even Serafina showed some enthusiasm once I told her I would be working with books.

On my first day at my first job, I was wracked with nerves. A job was nothing at all like school; rules had to be followed religiously, there was no slacking off, and I knew it was going to be a shock to my system. Once I got there, fifteen minutes early, my mind was immediately put at ease.

I stepped through the door, the bell tinkling as I did so, and approached the counter. My palms were clammy and I had a giant knot in my stomach. It was like my first day at high school all over again, but this time, Myla wasn't by my side. 'Hi,' I greeted the assistant shyly, attempting to look as friendly as possible.

'Hi,' the man behind the counter replied, looking up from the hefty logbook he was currently flicking through. 'Can I help you?'

'Yes, I'm Sara. I'm starting work here today.'

His face lit up in recognition. 'Oh, great! It's good to meet you, Sara. I'm Isaac, your new manager.'

'Nice to meet you.'

'Sara's here!' he shouted to an absent person. 'Of course, you've met Anna the supervisor.'

I nodded at the tall, curvy redhead, who stepped out through the doorway leading into the back of the store. Anna had interviewed me. 'Morning, Sara. It's good to see you again,' she welcomed me.

We exchanged greetings and pleasantries—them asking me how I'd found using the public transport and where I'd travelled from—then Isaac began training me. By the end of the first week, we were like one small, happy unit, and I settled in well.

The shop was pokey and packed full of stock; every available surface was piled high with books, both new and second-hand, not unlike my bedroom back at home. In the special section, there were some tomes that were over a hundred years old. Even after the end of my shifts, I found myself hanging around, fawning over the dusty, worn volumes, searching for hidden treasures and marvelling at the old English text and quaint illustrations.

The place was never busy with customers. There were only two of us working a shift at any one time, except on delivery days or the occasional Saturday due to the town's tourism. It was closed on Sundays, although I probably would have offered myself up for those shifts as well, had they let me. I loved the energy of the place; the staff were intelligent and like-minded, and we all loved our jobs. Isaac and Anna were good bosses—lenient, fair and approachable—which made the job itself that much more enjoyable.

Things started to pick up at home too. I went home content and tired each day, relieved not to have any homework. My spare time was now my own and I could finally pay Lyanna money for board. I was independent and happy.

*****

The months ticked by and the novelty wore off, like it did with everything in my life. I plodded on, still enjoying my job, but the feeling that something was missing nagged at me. Once you settle into a routine and things are no longer shiny and new, but instead familiar, you begin to notice the silence in the gaps. For me, the missing piece was friendship, companionship.

I'd made new friends at the bookstore, but they were just colleagues. I didn't talk about my personal life with them and they definitely didn't know my 'secret'. I missed being around someone I could share anything with, someone I could laugh with until my stomach hurt, someone I could be completely myself with. In short, I missed Myla.

The visions returned with a vengeance, occurring frequently and growing ever more vivid. I was constantly paranoid that someone, or something, was following me. I saw movements out of the corner of my eye and sensed somebody watching me whenever I was between work and home. I started to dread leaving the house because of it.

One night, I was walking home from the bus stop and reached the alley that ran behind my house. I was lost in my own thoughts, daydreaming, when I was sure I heard footsteps approaching me from behind. I whirled around instinctively but there was nobody there. On edge, I pulled my coat collar up to my chin and headed back in the right direction, intent on getting home as fast as I possibly could, but there was a shape in the shadows ahead.

I stopped dead in my tracks, unsure what to do. I could retrace my steps back the other way and walk all the way around to the other side of the estate, but this would lead me through the park, which at night was just as creepy. However, the prospect of walking right up to that shadow among the shadows gave me chills right down to my toes. I could see the lights on in my house through the trees and knowing it was so close, picturing my cosy, warm bedroom, spurred me on. I just had to put my head down, walk right past it and I'd be almost there.

I forced my feet onwards, one in front of the other, and pulled my collar as high as it would possibly go. I couldn't bring myself to look up, as though if I couldn't see it then it wasn't there. My heart was beating out of my chest, but still I forced myself forward. As I passed it by, I glimpsed briefly a horrifying figure, not human but unlike any creature I'd ever seen before. It was reaching out to me.

I ran. I didn't scream as I had no breath in me; I just ran as fast as I could until I was safe inside my house, in my bedroom with the door firmly closed behind me. I was sure that I was truly insane, yet that couldn't possibly have been a figment of my imagination, could it? What is the mind capable of? Could it really create visions and feelings as visceral as those I'd felt and seen or was it really happening? I didn't know which prospect frightened me more.

I dropped to my knees, tears coursing rivers down my face. I was inconsolable and there was nobody there to comfort me. My best friend was miles away and likely not even thinking of me right then.

I sat and thought deeply about myself and my history and the position I'd found myself in. The foundation of my life was rocky and unstable, a lot of it unknown to me, which meant I could never really grow as a person. Instead, I'd been formed from a million unanswerable questions. My whole life, there had been a large question mark hovering over me. I now saw the meaning in my final project, with the silhouettes of my parents lingering above me, just out of reach.

I wrote in my journal:

I feel empty. Nothingness. I'm standing on the edge knowing I should be doing something but there is nothing to do and yet, everything to do. I feel this complete lack of purpose. I am unnecessary, alone, with nothing to work towards. I have a feeling that I can't quite put my finger on, laying just beneath the surface.

I feel lost, unsure, empty, heavy. My body is heavy, my eyes are heavy. It feels like such an effort to get up. All the gravity in the universe is centred on me, pulling me in, crushing me. No, it's emotionally heavy. It's like that feeling you get when you know something big is about to happen. I'm on edge, waiting nervously, erratic, paranoid, jumpy—I'm waiting but I know nothing is going to happen. I'm searching and waiting but nothing will ever come.

All my fantasies and dreams have been smashed by the cold, hard realisation that this is it. This is it. I'm in the wrong place, the wrong time, and I'm here alone.

Nothing but words on a page. Feelings are hard to put into words and they always seem to fall short.

That night, brought on by the horror in the alleyway, I strayed through dark dreams of half-forgotten memories and creations from the murky depths of my imagination. Nightmares so dark that I cried out in my semi-conscious state; of demons, haunting shapes and terrifying, leering faces. In the distance, I could see a dim light slowly approaching. I could feel its faint warmth and into the light I fell, drifting slowly, suspended in time, before it engulfed me. 'Sara? Sara?' Lyanna shook me awake.

I sat up, sweating profusely, tears streaming down my face, my throat sore from screaming in my sleep. 'What is it?' she asked me frantically, stroking my hair, trying desperately to calm me.

I couldn't talk. I was drowning in my own sobs.

A few miles away, Myla was looking up at her shaded ceiling, unable to sleep. She was remembering the ghosts of our past: her and I strolling through the forest, playing games and tricks on each other. She could hear our laughter echoing through the halls of her mind. There had always been so much laughter.

She remembered our innocence, when we were afraid of nothing, full of youth and vigour, the days before reality bore down on us and snatched us away to different places. Then she thought of me as she knew me now: confused and tainted by time and bad experiences, yet still childlike as though those years had never passed. It made her sad and she drifted off to sleep as her tears fell.

*****

It was time I faced facts—although the bookstore job was a temporary relief and relatively enjoyable, it just wasn't fulfilling. When Myla and I dreamed of our futures, it had never ever crossed my mind that I would ever be doing anything other than what I love: travelling the world, seeing new places, going on adventures and writing about them. I had been determined that I would be a rich, best-selling author, and at no point had that felt out of my reach. Now, it felt as far away as the Andromeda galaxy and I had no idea how I could ever get there. I hadn't written or even thought of any stories lately. All my drive for storytelling had deserted me and the blank page filled me with dread. I was beginning to resign myself to working in a bookshop all my life and never following my dreams, despite being only twenty years old.

I always thought I had a firm grasp of who I was and who I wanted to be, but now I wasn't sure at all. Who was I? What had I become? What was going to happen to me? Life wasn't going to hand me anything, I realised, but I'd lost all the will to try to change my fate. So, where did that leave me? Once again, that nagging, restless voice inside my head asked, *Is this all there is?*

Chapter Twenty-Two

Myla had a boyfriend, Leo. I found out about him when I saw she was in a relationship on Facebook. Finding out that way made me feel desperately cut-off. I'd always known everything that was going on in Myla's life, so for her to be in her first 'real' relationship and for me to know nothing about the guy—what they did together, how he treated her, how she felt about him—crushed me. I considered many times reaching out to her and making things right between us, but I was still so angry. The silence from her end told me that she was still angry too. We both needed more time.

Weeks turned into months and nothing changed. Get up, go to work, come home, eat, read, sleep, repeat. Still no contact from Myla. I spent a lot of my time in the company of my aunts but other than them and my work colleagues, I had no friends. Already, I'd lost touch with all my school and college friends. I assumed I was just a forgettable person. It was a lonely, desperate time and my thoughts were always bleak, like there was a dark storm constantly raging inside my head. My nightmares continued to be graphic and horrifying, and I was so tired all the time from broken sleep. Lyanna ceased coming into my room to see if I was alright every time I woke up screaming, as it now happened so frequently. She tried to get me to open up, to seek help, but I wasn't interested. Part of me wanted to feel it all; I felt I didn't deserve to feel better.

*****

Five months after Myla had stormed out of my life, I was finally spurned into getting back in touch with her by none other than those terrible dreams of mine.

It was 2 am and I'd dropped off to sleep not ten minutes earlier. In my sleep, I was lying in my bed, looking up at my ceiling just as I had been when I'd drifted off. My brain believed I was still awake. I felt something heavy and wet drip on to my face and slowly trickle down my cheek. I wiped my face and found my hand smeared with sticky, congealed blood. I looked back up, confused and appalled. The ceiling had mutated from wood and plaster into flesh, the surface opening up before my eyes into a monstrous wound right above my head. Blood oozed and dripped from the wound as it stretched wider and wider. I could hear the sound of skin and muscle ripping apart. How could this be happening?

I awoke with a start, my eyes darting around wildly. The ceiling was once again smooth and white, and I breathed a sigh of relief as I realised that I'd dreamt the whole thing. What could that have meant? Part of me knew that if I'd carried on sleeping, that wound would have opened up wide and sucked me right in.

The feeling of relief I'd felt on first waking soon deserted me as I heard a noise at the foot of my bed. My whole body was rigid with fear and I seriously contemplated shouting for Lyanna like a frightened young child. Fear pulsed through my veins. I was petrified, unable to move, but I had no idea why such a small sound had perturbed me so fiercely. I couldn't see anything out of place from where I lay and no more sounds could be heard, but as I laid there, cold sweat exuding from every pore, it felt to me as though the demons of Hell itself were present.

As always after these visions and dreams, I was left with the sense that the divide between worlds, between me and the Other Place, was gradually collapsing. I was sure that soon, I wouldn't be able to distinguish between what was real and what wasn't.

I drifted back into an uneasy sleep. Always I hoped it would be dreamless and always I was disappointed. My slumber now took me back to the woods where Myla and I had always walked when we were younger. Myla was far ahead of me and I was following cautiously, watching her.

Something appeared from between the trees. I stopped, rooted to the spot with shock and fear. Looking down on her, at least three times her size, was a huge, dark, shaggy beast. It was a monstrosity, hellish; the sight of it made me wretch in disgust. I could wait no longer to see what it was going to do, so I moved fast, terrified I would be too late. I leapt out from my hiding place. The beast turned its coal eyes on me and I saw nothing but red. The beast retreated into the darkness of the woods, allowing me closer to Myla.

She was sprawled out on the sodden earth. It had been raining so the grass was deliciously vibrant. Her damp, golden hair curled around her face and clung to her bare arms and neck. Eyelashes, long, dark and soft as feathers, fluttered on her cheeks, her eyes closed as though she was sleeping peacefully. Her cheeks were a delicate, pale pink, matching the blossom petals resting on and around her. They drifted down gently from the branches overhead.

I stood over her, a hunched figure in black watching the rainwater mingle with the cherry-red blood that streamed out of the vicious wound in her head. She was the prettiest sight I'd ever seen. Black shapes were now massing all around us and I became aware that I was floating up, rising above the scene. Through the trees I could see the monster returning, ready to take the rest of Myla. It was angry, seething with hate—I could feel the fire burning within it, yearning for her life.

Below me, Myla slept on in her bed of petals. Was she asleep? No, she was dying. The blood was still draining from her in a steady stream. I couldn't move, I couldn't save her. As the life left my one and only true friend, all I could do was watch and wait for the monster to break her apart until there was nothing left.

That was the darkest dream I'd ever had. It had been so visceral, so realistic. The next day, the image of Myla laying in a pool of her own blood remained ingrained on my retinas. The thought of that loss was too much to bear.

I texted Myla a simple message: 'Hey, how are you?' and awaited her reply.

*****

Myla had never felt a loneliness so stark. Even at Uni, surrounded by friendly, familiar people, she felt completely alone. Her dorm had lost its comfort and joy. Her everyday activities—her work, her classes, her downtime—were all scarred with sadness. She had been forced into a heavy, melancholy reflection that had come with what she saw as the loss of her best friend. She had nobody to share her life with, nobody to pick her up. She felt outcast, vacant, and couldn't believe how long it had been since we'd spoken, that I'd just walked right out of her life.

Sometimes, the pain gave way to anger. *Why did I push her away? Let her leave? I was selfish and immature*, she thought. The anger was only fleeting; always, the sorrow clawed its way back, extinguishing the flames, and she would remember that she loved me. How had we let it go so far? She had been sure I would run after her when she'd left, or at the very least, call her later that night to apologise, but I never had.

137

Often, Myla would find herself turning to me to tell me something or picking up her phone to call me, only to remember there was only an empty space where I had once been. We were both entirely separated from the one person who had always been there, and now neither of us had any idea where the other was, what they were doing or if they'd ever return to our lives. That was the hardest thing. Of course, we both had control over the situation to an extent, but neither of us wanted to be the person who gave in, in fear of rejection.

Myla had been hopeful and positive in the beginning, certain I'd crawl back to her seeing as it was all, in fact, my fault, then everything could just go back to the way it was before. But, as time crept by, it dawned on her that I wasn't going to swallow my pride, that we'd both let it go too far and it was now going to be difficult to return our friendship to its original state.

Myla was sat in her dorm one evening, collecting her thoughts. She looked out through the small, high window across the quad, as she did at some point every single day, wondering where I was and what I was doing at that moment. She opened the window, letting in the cool, fresh air. It was a humid evening for March and the air buzzed with static from an impending storm. A sweet, soft breeze brushed against her face through the gap.

Looking out on the world that evening—students and professors rushing by, carrying books and chattering in groups—she spoke inwardly to herself, pleading me to stop being such a bloody baby and suck it up. *Why won't she just reach out to me?*

As always, she finished her daily ritual by wishing me well. She hoped I was happy and had no regrets.

Her phone vibrated and a text from me shone out from the small screen. Her reply? 'Okay, how are you?'

Things had not been great for Myla. Despite what the photos on Facebook would have me believe, she was not content and had not forgotten all about me.

The romance with Leo had been a whirlwind; they'd met, started dating, made it official and within a couple of months, he'd become possessive and paranoid, always wanting to be with her. Whenever they were apart, he would call and text her constantly, asking where she was, who she was with, and when she'd be back. She had wanted to focus on her work, but he caused her so much stress that she couldn't concentrate and her grades had taken a hit because of it. She made the right decision to end it and she was honest with him. She admitted that he had become too much for her—it had gotten too intense, too fast—but she told him that she still cared for him and wished him well.

Everything started to get back on track after that; her grades improved and she was creating her best work, but then, it had all taken a sinister turn. She saw Leo wherever she went. He was attending the same university so at first, she hadn't thought much of it, but he was also appearing in unexpected places. It seemed wherever she went, he was there. She called him to ask him if her was following her, but he'd reacted sharply, calling her a vain bitch, as though she was self-obsessed for thinking such a thing. She'd taken him at his word and put it all down to coincidence.

She remained uneasy, however. Stalking was a terrifying ordeal and it did seem to be something he was capable of. He had technically been stalking her when they were together so why would anything change now that they were apart? She didn't see him quite as often after that call, but it did cross her mind that he may have just been taking more care not to be seen. Whenever she did see him, he was standing oddly, rigid, not appearing to have any purpose.

One night, he followed her at a distance all the way back to her dorm, even though his room was at the other side of campus, and she knew then, categorically, that she was being stalked. He stood outside in the quad for hours that evening, just staring up at her window. Myla phoned one of her male friends, Joe, who lived in the next block over, and Leo finally left when Joe asked him to, rather forcefully.

This happened on a number of occasions. He would stand in the quad on a night, like he was waiting for her. Unfortunately, Joe wasn't always around to tell him to leave so she then considered telling the university about his behaviour. However, knowing what she did about Leo's personality and family history, she couldn't bring herself to ruin his education over this. He hadn't physically hurt her in any way; he had issues but was he actually doing anything wrong? Of course, the answer was yes, he was, but it's difficult to see things as they really are when you're on the inside. Maybe if I'd been around to offer her advice, things might have been different.

At Easter, she took the opportunity to go home to Moraine for the week and hoped that when she returned, he'd be over his obsession.

*****

139

It was a stormy spring afternoon and Myla was sat in the living room window at her parents' house, enjoying some peace and quiet. A flash could be seen on the horizon, so far away that it looked to her like it was at the very edge of the world. Following the lightning, a distant grumble. The cherry blossoms were coming to the end of their bloom and petals fluttered down in flurries of pink, carried on the fresh breeze.

The sky was darkening quickly, the shadows stretching longer and longer. Out of the shadows, a figure emerged. The shape was barely visible in the gloom—the last light of day was fading rapidly with the coming of the storm—but Myla didn't need to see any features to work out who it was.

She ducked down beneath the window ledge and scrambled on her hands and knees to the front door, locking it as fast as she could. She sat with her back against the door, breathing heavily and scared to move.

After a few moments of quiet, she regained her composure. She expected to have heard some sign of his presence by now so, curious, she crept along the floor, back beneath the window to look outside.

Peering over the sill, she couldn't see a sign of anyone. The dark rainclouds had consumed the sky and the sun, which had almost dropped below the horizon, tinged the sky with an angry red glow. Myla didn't dare relax however—she needed to stay alert. Her parents were out for the evening at a convention and the neighbours weren't within shouting distance.

Knock! Myla stiffened. Knock! She dropped back down to the floor. Knock! Three drawn-out raps upon the door. Myla waited, her breath held. She judged the distance between her current position by the window to her phone resting on the coffee table.

Knock! Knock! Knock! Louder, faster, more urgent. Trying desperately not to be heard, she crawled across to the table, grabbed her phone and ducked behind the sofa.

The wind was now starting to blow and drizzle splattered the window, but the thunder and lightning had run their course. The sky was a little brighter now, or maybe her eyes had adjusted to the gloom? Perhaps the storm would blow over soon.

Myla was trying to occupy her thoughts with anything but the maniac stood outside her door. Why hadn't he called out? Why hadn't he looked through the window? Was he playing a game?

The wind blew stronger, howling and whistling over the roof and down the chimney. A voice carried on the wind; he was calling her name, but the wind was distorting the sound, morphing it into a distant-sounding wail.

Stay hidden, stay quiet, she thought. Luckily, all the lights in the house were off. She regretted not closing the curtains, yet she still hoped he would think that she wasn't home. Who knew how long he was going to stay out there?

A thought occurred to her. To find her house, he must have followed her all the way from York, but she'd been back hours. Why had it taken him so long to show himself? The only logical explanation was to check that she was alone. She'd been sat in the window for a good half an hour before he'd made his presence known to her. A chill ran down her spine to think that he'd been watching her that whole time, waiting for the right moment, like a predator stalking its prey. To do what? What would he actually do if she went to the door? She dreaded to think.

Myla sat there a long, dreadful while in the creeping darkness, waiting for a sign that he'd left. He hadn't knocked again. She needed to brave it. She couldn't sit there until morning and she wouldn't be able to sleep if she didn't check it out.

Since the brief text conversation we'd had the previous month, things had remained awkwardly quiet between Myla and I, but now she needed help and I was the first person she thought of. She sent me a brief text—she was too scared of calling me in case he heard her—saying: 'Need help. Please come to mine quick.'

She peered around the side of the sofa. Through the rain-spattered glass, she could see the sky had cleared but it was now almost fully dark. A faint glow of pinks and oranges highlighted the smoky darkness in the west. The wind was now nothing more than a sighing breeze.

Still trying to keep quiet, Myla cautiously tiptoed over to the window and looked out on the garden. She could see nothing but the wet, petal-covered lawn and the trees swaying slightly beneath the dusk sky. She visibly sighed with relief, yet she still needed to be absolutely certain he'd gone, or she wouldn't be able to relax.

Her phone still clutched firmly in her fist, she opened the front door and stepped outside timidly. Something moved in her peripheral vision, but she noticed too late to get back inside the safety of the house.

I ran all the way to Myla's place, as fast as my legs would allow. We hadn't spoken properly for so long, so I knew something was terribly wrong for her to text me so urgently. In all the time I'd known her, she'd never asked me for help. I was the one who was always in trouble and she my knight in shining armour. I couldn't help fearing the worst.

I rushed through the gate at the bottom of the front garden and found her lying there on the grass. My nightmare, the one in which she'd died, came back to me in a powerful rush. I choked out, 'Myla?'

I ran over to her still form, but I didn't dare touch her. To touch her, to feel her chill skin, would make it real. My nightmare had come true. I'd crossed some kind of boundary between reality and dream. It was all the same: the wet grass after the storm, the blossom petals strewn around her body, her clothes, her hair, her peaceful face, it was all as it had been in the dream. Except for one difference—there was no blood. Hope returned to me and I crouched down beside her.

I stroked her damp face. It was warm, not deadly cold as I'd envisaged. Her eyes flickered and she sighed. 'Oh, thank the Gods!' I cried. I lifted her head carefully and placed it on my lap. 'Can you hear me?'

Her eyes opened and she looked up at me, bewildered. 'Sara?'

'Yeah, I'm here,' I soothed her. The roles were reversed and I was glad to be the one to be there for her for a change. 'What happened?' I asked.

Recognition sparked in her icy blue eyes. 'Where is he?' she questioned, suddenly panic-stricken. She pushed herself up on to her elbows, looking around wildly.

'Who?'

'Leo.'

'Your boyfriend?'

She nodded. She must have noticed my face contort in anger because she hastily added, 'It's not what you think. It's not like Jack, but it's not good either.' Seemingly satisfied that he was no longer in the vicinity, she slumped back down onto the grass.

'Come on, let's get you inside and dry.'

I helped her up and back inside the house. I took her upstairs to the bathroom, and grabbed her a large, fluffy bath towel from the airing cupboard so that she could dry herself off.

Once she was dry and changed into some clean clothes, she told me everything. I sat and listened, shocked, angry, guilt-ridden and saddened. 'Why didn't you reach out to me?' I asked.

'Why didn't *you* reach out to *me*?' she retorted.

'I didn't think you'd want me to,' I answered her honestly.

'Did you really think I wouldn't have helped you? That these past few months wouldn't have been totally forgotten had I known what you were going through?'

'I never took it seriously, not really. Not until today. Today, I fully grasped the danger I've put myself in, and then I reached out to you.'

I nodded. There was no point in arguing now—it all seemed so trivial and pointless. 'Do you know where he is?'

'I doubt he'll have gone home, so he could be anywhere.'

'We need to call the police.'

I called them for her, and they arrived a short time later. Myla recounted the whole story to the officers, from the beginning to the end. When she had stepped outside after messaging me, he had grabbed her, but she'd fought back. It was all a blur as it had happened so fast, but he obviously hadn't counted on her fighting back and, in panic, had struck her around the head. That was all she remembered until she awoke to find me by her side.

They did eventually arrest him and he admitted to everything. At the trial, he'd received a three-year sentence for stalking and assault and he showed great remorse for his actions. Myla was lucky that, even after he was released, she never saw him again. I read somewhere that while he was in prison, he'd received therapy for his issues from his childhood and once he got out, he went on to work with a charity for people facing the same issues he'd faced.

I never forgave him for what he did to Myla—he'd left her after a blow to the head, with no idea if she was alive or dying—but part of me was glad that he'd turned his life around. It gave me a bit more faith in mankind.

Chapter Twenty-Three

Myla and I moved in together that summer. I'd saved up most of my wages as I'd not had anything to spend money on for so long and Myla was receiving her student loan. Her parents helped us with the bond for the flat, so we were on good footing.

We never spoke, in any detail anyway, about our months of silence. After the events with Leo, it no longer seemed important. It was all over now and that was all that mattered. Our friendship resumed its normality, and if anything, it was stronger than before. Moving in together was a natural transition; Myla no longer felt comfortable living on campus, so she hadn't signed herself up for another term and I finally wanted to fly the nest. Both Lyanna and Sef helped us on moving day and Lyanna cried, even though our flat was only a few streets away from her house.

The flat was basic yet cosy; perfect for two young women in their first home. It was open-plan with a modern kitchen overlooking a fairly spacious lounge. We bought a faux-suede corner sofa on finance and covered the walls in movie posters and photographs of us and our families. There were two bedrooms; one large and one medium-sized. I took the large one, which we agreed was fair as I'd put most of my savings into the bond and the décor.

I painted my room pale grey and lined the walls with bookshelves. It became my own private library and study. Myla's room was decorated more to a teenager's taste: bright purple walls covered with band posters, piles of mismatched rugs littered the floor and sentimental items haphazardly arranged on her shelves, plus her enormous collection of teddy bears stuffed in every corner.

We'd each retreat to our rooms to study and create every evening (I'd finally gotten back to my writing again) and then we sat and watched films all night until the early hours. We felt like kids again, enjoying an eternal sleepover, only now, there were no adults around to tell us to stop eating junk food or when to go to bed. It was the best time of my life. I enjoyed my job at the bookstore again now that I had something to look forward to when I returned home each evening.

Our weekends—when I wasn't at work—were spent outdoors, working on Myla's photography projects (I became her unofficial model) and bouncing ideas off each other for my stories. On Sundays, we wrapped our duvets around ourselves and created a bedding-fort on the sofa. We'd stay there all day in our pyjamas, enjoying movie marathons or binge-watching the most recent TV series. That autumn and the beginning of winter were wet, even by British standards, so we listened to the rain hammering against the windows, drew the curtains and shut the world out. It was just me, Myla and our eternal youth.

*****

The underlying theme of the following summer was, *if not now, when?* Myla had passed her driving test at the beginning of the year, and her parents had bought her a second-hand old banger of a car. I have to hand it to Betsy (the car). I thought she'd never make it to the end of the street, but she took us on journeys to the seaside, walking trips in Northumberland (Myla's old stomping ground from a previous life) and to as many rock festivals as we could afford.

I felt truly content for the first time since college. I even began opening myself up to partners, well, more so than before, anyway. In truth, I went in the opposite direction and became promiscuous. Some people sleep around when they're sad, I did it because I was happy.

My one true summer romance that year was Ryan Hurst. We met in May at a cover band festival and we had dirty, nasty, exciting sex in his tent on the first night. We could hear the voices of our friends chatting and laughing just feet away, with only a thin piece of fabric separating them and our naked bodies. I remember I wanted to enjoy and prolong every moment, feel every part of his body and for him to feel every part of mine. I revelled in the excitement of the unknown; someone new, who I'd never met before, and would probably never see again. I felt like I'd finally broke down that barrier and I was enjoying what I found on the other side.

We did see each other again. It turned out he had tickets to pretty much every festival we did, and so, we hooked up at every single one. Every time I saw him, with his long hair, tattoos, high cheekbones, a beast awoke inside of me. We'd screw and laugh and screw some more, and then, at the end of the weekend, we'd

145

say goodbye and that would be that until next time. Although, I have to admit, I often thought about our trysts when I was lying in bed alone back at home.

Myla didn't mind my distraction. As mine and Ryan's relationship (if you can call it that) was so casual, we had as much fun in the company of our friends as we did alone in each other's. Plus, Myla was enjoying some no-strings fun of her own.

Once September came and the festival season ended, Ryan and I said goodbye to each other with the knowledge that we'd probably never see each other again and while that gave me a twinge of longing for the summer to begin all over again, I knew that we'd remember each other, the feel of each other's skin, the scent of the other's hair, the taste of each other and the sound of our laughter on those long, mild, starry summer nights for the rest of our lives.

Memories are sometimes enough and we both knew that to take our love—of a kind—out of those fields and those circumstances, would be to taint and ruin something that had been so wholly perfect. It existed purely within that universe and could never be brought into the real world.

*****

Since I'd moved out, Lyanna too seemed to be gaining her own independence. She had started singing again and formed a band who performed gigs in local pubs at the weekends. Myla and I often stopped by to see her in action. I loved watching her up there; seeing her as an individual and a woman with her own life and passion, rather than just my aunt who'd have tea ready for me when I got home from school or tidy my bedroom without me asking. I was seeing the real her, a siren belting out rock ballads with her husky, powerful vocals, while the whole room listened in awe. She was a human being, now able to live for herself and not for her niece.

One of the things I'd been worried about when I'd left was how Lyanna was going to cope without me. For so many years, I had been her whole world. It turned out, me moving out was the best thing that could have happened to either of us.

Sef and I, on the other hand, were still wading through our layers of issues. Serafina was still somewhat reclusive and we had to prise her away from her books to spend any time with her. Part of me accepted that that was just who she was, but another part of me thought her to be selfish, hiding herself away from me, depriving me of our relationship.

Once again, it all ended in a heated row, calling each other nasty names, dragging up the past, trying to see who could inflict the most painful blow. Eventually, we made up, as we always did, and we arranged to go see Lyanna's band at the Labyrinth that Friday night. Myla and I swung by the library to pick Sef up as she was working late, as usual. 'I'm glad you decided to come out,' I said to Serafina from the back seat of the car.

'Me too, kid.' She still called me "kid" when the mood took her and I didn't mind, but I did often wonder if she was being affectionate or condescending.

'Yeah, I haven't seen you for ages, Sef,' Myla chimed in. 'How are you doing?'

'Good, thanks; you?'

'Yeah, we're great.'

'You haven't visited the flat as much as we'd like,' I added.

'I know, I know. I'm sorry. I get caught up—you know how I am. And time, it just passes by so fast.'

I agreed with that. 'I know. Let's just enjoy tonight. Because who knows when I'll see you again!' We both laughed.

The Labyrinth was packed to the rafters, as all pubs were when *Evie and the Wildhearts* played. Lyanna had named the band after my mother and her passionate, loving nature. They mostly played covers, but lately, they'd been showcasing some of Lyanna's own songs, which had both meaty riffs and profound lyrics. I was so proud of her.

We each got a drink from the bar and waited for the band to come on stage. I glanced at Serafina, who seemed distracted and withdrawn, and noticed for the first time how thin she looked. I was about to ask her if she was eating properly, when the first notes of AC/DC's *Thunderstruck* sounded out around the room. I decided I'd ask her about it later, but I knew her answer would be that she didn't have time to eat when she had so much work to do, as it always was. Next, the band moved on to a rendition of Johnny Cash's *Riders in the Sky*. The three of us sang along, cheered the band on and caught up. It felt really good for us all to be together, in that time and place. Music can bring anyone together.

Halfway through the set, I noticed a guy standing across the room at the other end of the bar. I'd seen him in the Labyrinth before, so assumed he must have lived somewhere nearby, but I'd never truly *noticed* him. He had shoulder-length dark hair, with dark eyes to match, and I realised that he was watching me intently, like I was the only person in the room. I felt myself blush, embarrassed and suddenly conscious of every part of my body and what it was doing at that moment, but I also relished the feeling of being wanted. My lower abdomen clenched and a hot finger stroked my spine. When *Sara's Song* began, Lyanna's latest composition, I decided to take the plunge and introduce myself. 'Excuse me a minute,' I said to Sef and Myla. 'I won't be long.'

Myla gave me that cheeky, knowing look and Serafina merely nodded, still singing along to her sister's song.

I approached the stranger with feigned confidence and the first thing I said to him was, 'This song's about me, you know.'

He looked at me with a glint in his eye and replied, deadpan, 'Really? That's your line?'

I laughed. 'I meant it as a joke, sort of.'

'Well, is it about you or not?'

'It is, actually. Sara Black, nice to meet you.' I smiled.

'Richard,' he offered in return.

'That's my aunt up there,' I told him, shouting to be heard above the music and the rowdy crowd.

'Cool! She's great.'

'She really is.'

'I come here whenever they play.'

'Me too. Well, obviously.'

'I know you do.'

'You do?' I didn't know whether to be creeped out or flattered. His casual tone put me at ease, however.

'Yeah, I've seen you here a few times.'

'And do you always watch me so intensely?'

'I try not to, but it's hard.'

'Oh, really?'

'Yeah, I mean, you're mesmerising.'

I laughed, sure he was joking, but when I looked into his eyes, I saw no hint of the playfulness that had been there a moment before. Right then, I knew how that night was going to end. Nobody had ever called me mesmerising before and I'd never seen anybody want me so bad, except maybe Ryan. 'Wow, thank you,'

I said after a pause. It might have just been a line, but it had the desired effect. 'Do you live around here?'

'Right around the corner.'

My lower abdomen clenched again and I felt a flutter in my stomach. This was hot. 'After the set, why don't you show me where?'

He looked half-excited, half-surprised. 'Are you always so forward?'

'Truthfully, no. But then, nobody looks at me the way you do.'

This seemed to please him. 'Well then, you're on. How many songs are left?'

I chuckled at his brazen impatience. 'Not many, I don't think. *Sara's Song* is usually one of the last. Excuse me, I just need to tell my friend what I'm doing.'

'And, what are you doing?'

'Going back to a stranger's house.'

'Will she be okay with that?'

'That's not for you to worry about.' I smiled and disappeared back into the crowd.

As the last song of the set rang out, I explained to Myla and Serafina what my plans were. Myla laughed and told me to be safe but to have fun. Serafina, on the other hand, wasn't quite so understanding. 'Are you mad?' she asked me seriously.

'What do you mean?'

'Well, if it's not bad enough that you're leaving early, but you're leaving early to go back to a stranger's house for a shag.'

'Keep your voice down! It's just a bit of fun. I didn't think you'd be so offended.'

Lyanna finished singing and accepted praise from the audience. Everyone except us were clapping and whistling. She stepped down from the stage gracefully and made her way through the crowd to us. 'I'm not offended, I just can't believe you.'

'Look, I'm sorry, okay? I didn't think of it that way. You're right, I'll stay here with you guys.'

'Nah, forget it, Sara. You go ahead, sleep your way through half the city. I was planning on going home now anyway.'

'Hey! What's going on?' Lyanna interjected.

Neither of us acknowledged her. 'How dare you? It's one guy! Are you calling me a slut?'

'Maybe I am.'

149

'Well, I'd prefer to be a slut than a recluse who spends all her time shut off from the world with no life or friends.' Serafina gawped at me, dumbfounded. I turned to Lyanna. 'That was amazing, as always.' I congratulated her and kissed her on the cheek. 'Now, I've got a hot date, so I'll see you on Sunday for our shopping trip.' I waved goodbye to Lyanna and Myla as I made my way back through the crowd.

Richard was stood in the same spot, nursing his whiskey. His face brightened when he saw me returning. I grabbed his hand and led him out of the pub. I needed to let off some steam. We only made it to the end of the road before his hands were all over my body, my hands reaching up the back of his shirt, our lips locking, searching for each other in the darkness.

His house was small but fairly clean for a guy living alone. In the hallway, we took each other's clothes off and kissed passionately. He pulled away from me and appraised my body. 'Wow, you're beautiful,' he told me. I grabbed hold of him and his hands found me. 'Do you want to go upstairs?' he asked me between kisses.

'I don't think I'll make it,' I replied. I wasn't lying; my legs had turned to jelly.

He led me into his front room and pushed me firmly down on to the sofa. As he went down on me, his hands gripped my breasts, my waist, my thighs, as though he wanted to feel it all at once.

I pulled him up, so we were eye to eye and kissed him long and hard. We continued for what felt like hours; neither of us could get enough of the other. Once finished, we both lay exhausted and carpet-burned on the floor, breathing heavily. All the anger I'd felt at Serafina's words had been burnt out.

The next day, I stayed at his all day. In the afternoon, we invited Myla around to join us. Although we'd intended it to be a one-night stand, we actually got on well and there was no morning-after awkwardness. It was an unusually hot, late September day, and we sat in the garden all day chatting about films and history and science.

In a flash, it was dusk. The stars started to peek out and last embers of the sun guttered out. After a while, Myla headed inside the house, leaving Richard and I laid out on the grass gazing up at the nights sky. The stars twinkled magically and all was peaceful and quiet. The glow of the moon created ethereal shadows. Then, everything was turned upside down.

Chapter Twenty-Four

Myla came out into the garden and called my name. I looked over to where she was stood in the doorway. The moonlight cast deep shadows around her eyes and under her cheekbones, emaciating her. Her ghostly form swayed and I thought she might faint. 'What is it?' I asked, immediately sensing something was terribly wrong.

'We have to go,' she told me flatly.

'Why?' I sat up, panicking. 'What's wrong?'

'Something's happened…to…' She couldn't get the words out.

'To who?' I urged.

'Sef.'

I jumped up. 'What? What's happened?'

'I don't know. We need to go.'

I sprinted across the lawn, shouting back to Richard, 'Sorry! We have to go!'

'Of course, yeah. I'll see you…' I vaguely heard him reply. I never saw him again.

Myla drove erratically. Usually, she was calm and confident behind the wheel, but for the first time I felt unsafe. It scared me—not fear of getting into an accident, but at what could have caused her to react that way. 'Lyanna called me,' she explained. 'She sounded distraught.'

'Oh no, oh no.' Every horrible possibility raced through my mind. My thoughts strayed to the worst scenarios, but every time I envisioned what it could be, I gagged and my mind blocked the thoughts. Not that. It couldn't be that. 'What did she tell you?' I asked, hoping that she would give me some words of comfort and rid me of my dark thoughts.

'She wouldn't tell me. She just said that it was Serafina and I had to take you to the house. But, Sara,' she paused, trying to compose herself, I assumed for my sake, 'it doesn't sound good. I'm sorry.'

I wanted to cry, but I didn't know what I wanted to cry for. I both wanted to get to the house and get as far away from it as possible. Did I really want to know? If I ran away now, I'd never know, I'd never have to feel any pain, but I had to know. I had to be there for Lyanna, no matter what had happened. 'Myla, you've taken the wrong turn,' I pointed out as we drove past the end of Lyanna's street.

'I haven't. We're going to Serafina's.'

No, not there, I thought. I wanted to go to Lyanna's house. I could take in any news better if I was in a place where I would feel safe and comfortable.

As we turned onto the street, we could see blue flashing lights illuminating the pavements and homes on either side of the road. There was an ambulance and police car parked outside Serafina's house, so Myla had to park further down the road.

As I got out of the car, my legs gave way and I fell, banging my knee hard on the stone pavement. I didn't feel it. Myla helped me to my feet and supported me as we walked to the house.

The house looked the same as always—charming and quaint—but to me it was a looming terror, a huge bodiless mouth threatening to swallow me whole. What lay in wait within those walls? What was I going to find? As we approached, the door opened and two paramedics exited, guiding a gurney with a long thin mass lying atop it, covered completely by what looked like a black tarp. A body. The face was covered. A dead body. I felt Myla shiver head to toe next to me but still she held onto me firmly. My brain couldn't grasp what was happening or what it meant. Who was in that bag?

I heard a wail of agony from within the house, but it sounded so very far away. The world was spinning. Once the gurney had been wheeled inside the ambulance, I stepped slowly, dazed and disorientated, over the threshold. The wailing grew louder and I found Lyanna sat at the kitchen table, her face a mask of pain and grief. A police officer sat beside her, resting a hand comfortingly on her arm. Lyanna looked up at me and I saw it in her eyes. I knew everything from that look and I crumpled onto the floor under the weight of it all.

The police and paramedics left, time ticked by unbearably slowly and still nobody spoke. What could any of us say? I had a million questions I wanted to ask and yet I didn't want to know the answers. To know would make it real.

Serafina's life and belongings surrounded us on all sides. I wanted to be close to it, but I couldn't bring myself to look directly at any of it. I stared down at my hands instead.

Myla eventually broke the silence. 'I think I should drive you both to Lyanna's.'

I contemplated this. I wanted to get away from that house, but I also couldn't bear to leave it.

Lyanna made the decision for us. 'Yeah, you're right,' she croaked.

Myla drove us to Lyanna's place where Lyanna instinctively began preparing hot drinks and toast for us all. She placed a steaming mug of hot chocolate before me and overly buttery burnt toast. I merely stared at it, feeling sick.

None of us felt capable of speech. It was such a shock, such a loss. How could we ever get past this? How would any of us talk ever again?

That night, we all slept in Lyanna's bedroom: Lyanna and I in her bed, Myla in a sleeping bag on the floor. The next day dawned, bleak and overcast. We spent the day pottering around the house, barely speaking, still deeply in shock. I phoned work and made them aware of what had happened. When I spoke the words "my auntie died", they sounded like they weren't coming out of my mouth, like it wasn't my aunt that had died. Somehow, the words fell short of what I had lost. I was given a few days compassionate leave, but I didn't feel any better. I was utterly numb.

As the days passed, that numbness gave way to a raw, sickening guilt. I cried constantly; the slightest thing would set me off. Every time I thought of her, instead of remembering all the wonderful things we'd done together and the good times, I could only seem to recall the last conversation we'd had, the last words we'd spoken to each other. How could I ever forgive myself? How could I live with that guilt? I never told her how much I loved her, flaws and all.

We started talking again, trying to get back to some kind of normality, when we received another blow. Serafina had had cancer. Her body was riddled with it, invading her like a plague, and she'd known about it. We were told that she'd been given the diagnosis months before and was told, basically, that they couldn't help her. It was too late—it had spread too far. She had refused any medicine, not wanting to spend the last months of her life feeling terrible. Only the week before, she'd been hospitalised after collapsing at the library and yet, she'd not once told any of us. She'd chosen to face the end of her life alone.

She'd hidden herself away, no doubt to hide her symptoms, and only seen us when she'd felt well enough. Sef had always been rake-thin but I realised now why I'd noticed a difference in her on the Friday night. She'd also always kept to herself so even her behaviour hadn't caused us much concern. It all made sense; she'd wanted me to stay that Friday, that's why she'd been so angry at me for wanting to leave. She knew we may never see each other again, but I'd left anyway, and in such a horrible way. I'd not even bid her goodbye because I was so wrapped up in myself and my own wants and needs. Grief wholly consumed me, Lyanna too. We were angry, at Sef for keeping this from us and robbing us of our final goodbyes, and at ourselves for not noticing the changes in her, for not being there for her when she most needed it.

For so many years, I struggled with that guilt, for letting my own selfishness deprive me of my last night with my aunt. I stopped meeting guys, stopped enjoying myself, or doing anything at all that would give me pleasure. It was my penance, my punishment for what I'd done. The pain never left me. Time did not heal the deep wound, but eventually, a long way in the future, I forgave myself. It was a long, difficult road to that place though, and life got a lot worse before it got any better.

*****

We didn't put the house up for sale for months and months after we lost Sef; neither of us could bring ourselves to face it. I remember the last time I went in, to help Lyanna sort through some of Serafina's belongings. Did I want to forget or not? Part of me secretly wanted to hold on to the pain, as some kind of self-persecution, when in truth, I was just wallowing in self-pity. That was my greatest insult to her memory: using her loss of life and my own grief as a means to hurt myself. I was indulging in the pain and misery of all that had been lost.

Sef left me her whole book collection, which was hefty, and a decent bulk of her savings. I wasn't pleased about this in any way—I didn't feel that I deserved any of it. The books sat in dusty boxes in my loft and the money sat in a savings account, both untouched for many years. I couldn't bear to feel any joy out of her passing.

Myla was my rock throughout it all; she held me when I cried, she comforted me when I tortured myself, she put up with my mood swings, and listened to me rant and moan, working through my emotions in any way I could. She became my therapist and almost always succeeded in distracting me. We were both there for Lyanna too. She had now lost both of her sisters and the tragedy of it all was more than any of us could comprehend. I never let on to Lyanna the guilt I felt. She was the only family I had left and I was determined to be the best niece I could be, though I admit, I perhaps didn't make her life as easy as I could have. Despite my good intentions, I was too self-absorbed to see how much I was hurting her.

Chapter Twenty-Five

Six months later, I diagnosed myself with depression. I'd felt low before, but I knew this was something different. Some days, I physically couldn't drag myself out of bed, like there was a great weight bearing down on me whenever I tried. I called in sick at work at least once a week, and on the days that I did manage to force myself to show up, I was always late. But I refused to let myself be vulnerable and tell them the truth, though I'm sure they had a grasp of what was going on inside my head. I was like an entirely different person. The light in my eyes and my soul had been extinguished.

I was always exhausted, physically and mentally, despite sleeping most of the time. Whenever I wasn't at work, I was in bed. Sometimes, on good days, I'd make it to the sofa, but still, I'd sleep and sleep and sleep like I could never get enough. Truth be told, I didn't fight it. I didn't want to be conscious. I didn't want to feel anything. When I was asleep, I wasn't suffering.

Myla spoke to Lyanna as she was worried for me. She'd never seen me in that state before. Lyanna visited me one afternoon to try and get through to me.

I was in bed, my greasy hair plastered to my head as I hadn't been able to bring myself to wash it in so long, trying to drift off, when Lyanna entered my room and took a seat at the edge of my bed.

'It's 3 pm, Sara,' she sighed, exhausted. 'Why are you in bed?'

'What else is there to do?' I mumbled.

'Myla's worried about you, you know?'

'I know.' What did she want from me? I didn't want to feel that way.

'The poor girl may as well just be living here alone for all the company you are.'

'She understands.'

'She shouldn't. She's too soft, that girl. She's not helping you, she's enabling you.'

I wanted to feel angry and normally, I would. I'd tell her to stop going on at me and get the hell out of my room, but I couldn't muster any emotions whatsoever. I couldn't even be bothered to open my mouth and form any kind of response. 'I lost my sister, Sara, and you don't see me spending all my time moping around in bed.'

'I know,' I said flatly. I agreed. Yet another reason to hate myself. Just let it all pile on, I didn't care.

'Is that all you have to say?'

'Yeah.'

'Sara, get a grip!' she shouted. She pulled open the curtains, letting in the grey afternoon light. Right then, it felt like knives piercing my retinas. 'It's not all about you. I'm still grieving too!'

'I know,' I responded, squinting. I turned over, facing away from the window, unable to stand the harsh daylight.

'Please, give me something. I can't bear this hollow shell you've become.' I started to cry then. Lyanna cried too. 'I can't lose you too.'

I felt a twinge of sympathy for her. I knew she was right and I wanted to make myself better, both for her sake and Myla's as much as my own, but the trouble with depression is you can't force yourself out of it or think about anybody else; you can barely even think about yourself. However, at the sound of Lyanna—my strong, responsible aunt—whimpering helplessly like a lost child at my side, I couldn't help but reach out.

'You won't lose me,' I promised her. 'I just don't know what's happening to me. It's like I can't feel anything and yet I'm feeling everything all at once. I just want to be me again.'

I turned back over and Lyanna stroked my hair, like she had when I was a child. We stayed there for a while quietly, thinking our own thoughts. Nothing more needed to be said. We were both still hurting terribly and each dealing with it in our own way and that was okay.

I quit my job. I was hardly ever there and when I was, I was only there in body, not in spirit. I had enough savings to help Myla cover bills for a while, while I figured out what the hell I was going to do. I saw a doctor, but they just wanted to drug me. I disagreed with western medicine for the most part, so I declined as politely as I could. I figured, not having the added stress of trying to force myself to go to work every day and act like everything was normal when it wasn't, would relieve some of the pressure in my head, but I was wrong;

instead, I stayed in bed longer and stopped bothering looking after myself altogether. It was probably the worst idea I'd ever had as I now had no purpose at all. I was jobless and completely lost.

*****

I was asleep on the sofa one afternoon. Myla was at Uni, so the flat was cocooned in a lonely, grim silence. I was dreaming of something eerie, half asleep, half awake, in that strange, paralysing limbo between the two consciousnesses. I was vaguely aware that something was in the flat with me, but alternately, somewhere in my logical mind, I knew Myla wasn't due home for another few hours.

Scratch! Scratch! Scratch!

I stirred slightly, fighting the paralysis.

Scratch! Scratch! Scratch!

My eyelids were glued shut. I strained to open them, but I felt heavy all over, like I'd been drugged.

Scratch, scratch, scratch. Scratchscratchscratchscratchscratchscratch!

Fingernails down a wooden door. No, it was too deep-sounding, too loud: claws, not fingernails. I waited, unable to move, for what would come next.

The door was suddenly flung wide open and banged loudly as it hit the wall and bounced back. The scratching became background noise to a peculiar skittering sound all around the room. The sound brought an image to my mind of a clawed beast climbing and jumping from wall to wall.

All of a sudden, the noise ceased. I could hear quiet shuffling on the wall above my head, barely audible. Then, I felt hot breath on my face and a foul stench clogged my nostrils.

I stared, immobilised, up at where the smell was emanating from, but nothing was visible. The room seemed to be rapidly darkening, as though time had hit fast-forward. The darkness spread from one corner of the room to the other and the fire in the hearth, which I had lit a few hours earlier, was steadily dwindling until eventually it extinguished, hissing into extinction.

The panting above my head mutated into a low, heavy grunting and the vile odour became intolerable. I retched. The whole room creaked, a long, deep, eerie *creak*, like its very foundations were groaning. I continued to lay there, paralysed.

There was a loud *thump!* Then *scratchscratchscratch* along the walls and the door closed with an almighty *slam!*

The darkness lifted and the fire roared back into life as though nothing had happened, but I remained staring at the ceiling, frozen in fear.

For the first time in a while, I felt an overwhelming desire to leave the flat. Not desire—need. Every corner, every shadow, every shape held the possibility of terror. I needed to get out, straight away.

I threw on some clothes and ran out of the door as fast as my weak, stiff legs would carry me. I needed to get to the quiet place and away from the endless noise inside my head. I went to the only place I could think of—Moraine Manor.

Something always called me there, like a siren drawing me in. Once I reached the grounds, the derelict ruins of times passed, I slowed down and felt the place awaken around me. Its essence flowed through me, soothing me, helping me forget. It was like entering a new world, leaving the old behind.

I slumped down on the grass and screamed at the top of my lungs. I let it all wash over me: grief, anger, hurt, pain, confusion, all of it poured out of me like a waterfall. It flowed over me, under me, through me, until there was nothing left. I was wrong to go there at that time. After the visit from the unknown entity at my home, the last place I should have gone was there. I didn't know that at the time, of course, but I'd been drawn there by the Other Place; it was a trap.

I suddenly felt more alert than I had done in months, like I'd been woken from a long, deep slumber. I'd been dying and now I was alive. I could hear all the sounds of nature, see all the colours, everything was more distinct than ever before. My elation was only temporary for then the atmosphere changed, imperceptibly at first, but it dawned on me that I wasn't safe. That same creeping fear clawed its way back into my heart and I saw it. It had been there all along but only now was it able to show itself to me.

It hadn't been able to touch me in my home, not even show itself to me, because my home was not in the Other Place, but here, I was trespassing on its land.

I stared in complete horror at the most hideous, abhorrent creature I had ever set eyes on, worse than anything that could be drawn on paper or designed to life on film. It could only be described as a daemon, something that only your mind could imagine in the dark depths of the night, when all joy and hope had escaped you. The daemon was hoofed and horned, its grey, leathery skin wrinkled, its stomach bulbous and its hairy face grotesquely disfigured. Its grin was contorted and wicked, but its eyes were dead and blackened. I stared into those eyes for too long, like something was holding me there. I thought I would be driven mad by them.

I managed to break through the invisible bindings and forced myself to move. The creature's eyes followed me as I made for a gap in the tangled brush, but it did not move or make to follow me. It appeared before me once again further along my path, but I wouldn't stop. I ran and still it appeared on all sides, taunting me, grinning that grin. It could catch me any time it wanted to, but it was choosing instead to play with me, like a predator with its prey.

When I finally thought it was going in for the kill and my time was up, a hand reached out of the earth and I instinctively went for it, allowing it to drag me below. Darkness enveloped me, my legs gave way and I dropped to the cold floor, curling up. I hugged my knees, rocking back and forth, listening intently for the sound of hooves above, sure that at any moment the daemon would burst through and claim me. Then, I heard it shuffling through the bracken directly above my head, but it didn't come for me.

I heard it speak a harsh, evil tongue that was not of this world, then it left and no more could be heard. A faint light glowed ahead of me and a strange creature stepped into it. It was small, maybe five feet high, and dainty, with pointed ears and large, glittering eyes. It spoke to me in a language I'd never heard before but understood. 'It was trying to find you. I couldn't let it.'

'Thank you,' I whispered in its tongue.

'Why couldn't you let it?'

'Because you are good. Only bad can be taken by the daemons. He was not following the rules. He wanted your flesh, blood and bone.'

I shivered. 'Is it safe for me to leave?' As much as I didn't want to go back above ground, I also didn't want to sit in this dark, damp hole any longer.

'I think so, yes.'

'Well, thank you, once again.' I almost said I was in their debt, but something inside warned me not to.

The light blinked out, plunging me into darkness once more, and for a moment I thought I was in yet more danger. Daylight streamed in from above and the creature reached down to help me out of the hole. It was surprisingly strong for such a slight little thing.

I brushed myself off and turned to say thank you once more, but the creature had already disappeared.

I headed home, awed and shaken. I thought, as I dismally lumbered along, that had the daemon caught me, nobody would have ever found my body, and Myla and Lyanna would have never known what had happened to me.

When I arrived back at the flat, Myla was already home. She looked both relieved and apprehensive when I walked through the door, covered in dirt. She looked me up and down and asked me where I'd been. 'You wouldn't believe me if I told you.'

'Try me.'

I took a shower first and despite the events earlier, I found that I didn't feel on edge in the flat. In fact, I felt the opposite: safe and comfortable again. It couldn't get at me here.

I told Myla all that'd happened. I didn't want sympathy and Myla sensed that, so she put her logical head on for me. 'You don't think it was all brought on by what you're going through?'

'What, you mean I imagined it?'

'No, I don't mean that, but maybe that you're more susceptible to it when you're in a bad place?'

I thought on that. It did actually make sense. 'Oh, Myla. I'm so tired of feeling this way. So tired of feeling at all.'

'I know, but you have to feel, feel it all, to get through to the other side.' She sat down beside me and rested a hand on my knee. 'It's what makes us human; emotion. Stop trying to fight it. It's natural to feel lost and scared and sad sometimes, but you have to keep fighting.'

'I don't know how to fight.'

'You do—you've done it before, you can do it again. You have to be patient, take small steps every day.'

'Tell me how.'

'What makes you happy? Even for a moment? All I need is to get outdoors, or be with you on peaceful nights, just simple pleasures. It's the small things that matter, remember that. You're searching for something big; you always have been. I don't know exactly what for, but I can sense it. You're waiting for some kind of epiphany and I don't think Sef's death is the root cause.'

I looked at her, both pained at the reminder of my loss and curious as to what she meant. 'I think,' she hesitated, 'that you're in a rut. I think you've always had this darkness, this restlessness inside of you. It took Serafina's passing to bring it out of you in such an all-consuming way, but it's always been there lurking beneath the surface. I think you're unhappy, tired of your life. I also think her death has reminded you of your own mortality, which would explain why you have such a deep need to have a purpose, to want to do something. I think you needed an excuse to escape your menial job because it wasn't enough for you.'

'So, you think I'm using her…death…as an excuse?'

'No, you know I don't mean that, but it's just one of many factors. My point is, if you don't enjoy the small things in life, how will you know what to do with yourself when something huge does come along? And, more to the point, what will you do if it never comes? Be like this for the rest of your life? Live and die depressed and alone? Eternally trapped in the waiting room of your own life? You can only enjoy what you do have, and you have a lot; people who love you, a nice home, your own possessions and treasures, your health. Stop waiting for your life to start because this is it. You're in it now and time is something you can never get back.'

What do you say to that? I felt stripped bare, vulnerable, like she could read me as easy as words on a page. 'You're right, of course you are, but I can't seem to climb out of this hole. I thought time would help—'

'Time? Time doesn't change anything,' Myla interrupted. 'People and events change you. You've got to stop letting the world break you and start taking control.'

'But I'm weak. I hate this world. Everything that's happened has tainted me. I'm negative and I used to be so optimistic and happy. Not to mention all the other crap going on right now in the world—murder, rape, war—and on social media—casual racism, sexism, inequality, the rich, the poor, celebrity and the social media culture of trash. I'm so sick of it all, so worn down. There are so many people in the world who just don't give a shit about anything but themselves, and it hurts me. Everyone is killing themselves and each other.'

I felt exhausted at my sudden outburst. Some of it, I'd had no idea I'd been carrying. 'Sara,' Myla replied, 'the brightest of humankind are the most afflicted.

162

Those who 'don't give a shit' don't have these worries and that's exactly why they don't give a shit. They either can't comprehend a life outside their own, or they don't want to. It's the hard-working, caring people who want to make something of themselves and act in a way that influences for the better, that carry the weight of the world. Don't carry that weight for them. Focus on your own life,' she grasped my arm urgently, 'and the people you love, and help them by helping yourself. You're still you, I promise. You're still in there somewhere, we just need to scrape off all the dirt you've collected and start again.'

Chapter Twenty-Six

After my conversation with Myla, I felt ready for a change. The veil of depression didn't completely lift, but it loosened its hold on me. I could still feel the melancholy fog clouding my mind and judgement, but I knew I had to take some action, take a different path to the one I'd ended up on. There was something that I'd always needed to do, and now that I was jobless, lifeless and lost, it felt like the right time to do it. I needed to find out what the Other Place was, what it really was. I needed to go there—if it was possible—and discover why it had chosen me and what it all meant. I could no longer linger on in the world without purpose or direction. The only way to quiet my mind was to dig deep into its chasm, in the hope of finding answers—answers to my past and my current misery.

I couldn't tell Lyanna and Myla. How could I tell them that I was leaving them, but that I didn't really know where I was going or when I'd be back? They were going to tell me I was mad. They were going to be heartbroken. I planned it all carefully; what I would pack to take with me, the money I would leave for Myla to take care of the bills (courtesy of Serafina) and how I'd pull it all off without raising any suspicion.

I thought carefully about my reasons for going. Was I going in search of my mother? No, it wasn't anything as human as that. I'd be lying if I said I hadn't considered the possibility that she may be there, but it wasn't my sole purpose. My reasoning was if I didn't go then, I never would. Was I scared? Yes—terrified, in fact. Part of me wished I could tell them so at least they'd know where to look for me if I didn't return, but it just wasn't feasible. This was something I had to do alone.

The night before I intended to leave, Lyanna stayed at ours, drinking, eating good food, laughing, watching terrible movies, listening to 80's music and trying to forget about all that had come before and all that was still to come. We reminisced about all the good times we'd shared with Sef and we toasted her.

Her presence was sorely missed. They didn't know it, but it was my farewell party.

In my room, my bag was packed, ready to go. After they took themselves off to bed, I snuck into the kitchen to pack some food (snack bars, crisps, tinned goods, that sort of thing), then I spent a good forty-five minutes writing a goodbye note to them both. I don't remember precisely what it said, but I told them that I loved them both, I would look after myself to the best of my ability and I promised I intended to return as soon as I could. I made it clear I didn't want them to come looking for me. I was viscerally aware that I was treading a well-worn path and I worried briefly how it might affect Lyanna to receive a note so similar to the one my mother had left her, but there was no other way.

I went to bed and slept for a few hours before my alarm woke me up at 5 am. I showered for a full half an hour, enjoying the sensation as the hot water washed over me and the scent of my jasmine body wash filled my nostrils. Who knew when I'd be getting a decent shower again?

I crept back into my bedroom, threw on my favourite *Black Sabbath* t-shirt, cargo pants and a fleecy hoodie, took one last look at my room filled with all my favourite things and headed down the hall as quietly as I could. In the kitchen, I checked I'd packed everything I needed in my large rucksack. I smiled at the sight of one of Myla's teddies, Snufflebump, staring back at me. I'd thieved it from her bedroom the previous evening, knowing it might bring me comfort sometime in the near future. Everything was there—it was time to leave.

I closed the front door behind me as quietly as I could. I stood there dumbly for a few moments, knowing I could go back inside, unpack my things, get back into bed and nobody would be any the wiser. No. I was going. As I walked away from the apartment, I felt so terribly sad. I was leaving the two most important people in my life behind and I had no idea when I'd be seeing them again, but when I reached the bottom floor and exited the front of the building, I was filled with anticipation. I was Bilbo Baggins setting out on my very own adventure.

*****

The great oak tree loomed up ahead, solid and unchanging as it ever was. It was now 8 am and I knew, back at the flat, Myla and Lyanna would likely be waking up about to find out that I'd gone. I pushed the thought from my mind—

165

I could only focus on what was ahead. It would be too difficult to continue if I kept looking behind.

I sat down on the ground beneath my tree and waited. I didn't know what I was waiting for, but I felt it in my bones; that was where I was supposed to be. The sun climbed lazily in the sky and nothing happened. Doubt started to plague my thoughts. What if it wasn't the right time? What if I never found the Other Place? What if I never found my answers? What if I had to return home, feeling foolish, and explain to them that nothing had happened? What if I had to go back to the way things were before, find another menial job and continue on that path that led to nowhere? No. I could not let that happen. I would have preferred to sit and wither away beneath that tree than let that happen.

Sure enough, just before midday, a figure crossed the clearing towards me. I was so racked with doubt that for a brief second, I thought it could be Lyanna coming to take me home, but it wasn't. It was the faerie who'd led me out of my garden so many years before. Once again, she was cloaked, her face concealed within the shade of her hood. I knew somewhere beneath that soft, green fabric, her wings were secreted away.

As before, when I was a child, she spoke to me in her language inside my own head and, as before, I understood every word she spoke. She told me to follow her, so follow her I did. All lingering thoughts of home were forgotten as I was led deeper and deeper into the grounds of the Manor. The house appeared on our right side, emerging ominously through the trees, but we passed it by and continued through the wild gardens.

Soon after, we approached a derelict yet pretty cottage. It was suffocated by dense foliage and woodland, except its front which faced us from across a small field. Nestled there, it appeared to be a fairy-tale cottage, but not taken from a children's story—it was straight from the pages of a twisted tale by the Brothers Grimm. I could feel a darkness dwelling in the midst of that beauty. 'Are we going in there?' I asked the faerie nervously.

She nodded her head gracefully in response. 'Death walks these lands. This place belongs to him and we are just passing through. I think he will allow it,' she told me in her ethereal, soft voice.

I shivered and pulled my fleece tight around my neck. I looked about, expecting "death" to appear at any moment. 'Don't worry, Wanderer; he will not harm you while I'm by your side.' That comforted me, though only a little.

The 'Wanderer' was her name for me. She didn't ask my real name—I'm sure she had no need for it. I wondered what her name was but didn't dare ask. I was still in awe of what she was and only spoke to her when she addressed me directly. I found out her name many years later and I'm glad I didn't ask at the time. 'Before we enter, I must tell you the history of Snowmist.'

'Is that its name?'

'Yes. It's a story from long ago, but it's important that I tell you.'

'Why?'

'Before you enter any place where there is a deep or tragic history, you must learn it in order to respect the place. Places hold memories; to go in unarmed with that knowledge is to invite misfortune.'

This is the story she told me, word for word. I remember it as clearly as the day I heard it.

It was a summer, long ago. The air was damp and teemed with buzzing insects and the sound of splashing pondlife. Snowmist was a grey land, overcast and misty all year round, but on this day, the atmosphere was vibrant and full of energy. The air, the water, the earth—it all shimmered and hummed with life.

A man and his wife lived in this cottage all those ages ago: Koen and Elie. They were a happy, simple couple, content with their small plot of land and they never wanted for anything.

Elie was gazing out of her kitchen window, across the pond that lay within the garden at the back of the house. Others may have viewed the place as miserable, cold and wet, but Elie loved its serenity.

Elie was gravely ill. She had hidden it from her husband as long as she could, but she could hide it no longer. Her skin was deathly pale and clammy and over the past weeks, her body had shrunk into that of an emaciated corpse.

This is not the story of Elie and her illness; this is the story of Koen and his grief. They had been married for many years, quietly living their uncomplicated, comfortable life. They rarely saw other people in their neck of the woods and did not feel the need to venture out of these parts, which made Elie's passing harder to bear for Koen.

At the moment of her death, she was lying in his arms in that very house. The last word she heard on this earth was her own name, spoken in a loving whisper by the man she had loved her whole life. Koen gripped Elie fiercely and for a few brief minutes, she embraced him in kind. Eventually, her arms became limp and she was gone. He laid her peacefully down upon their marital bed, wrapped the covers tightly around them both and wept until dawn broke the following day.

Koen continued to weep for a whole week without barely a pause for breath. He had left her body in their bed, unable to let her go, and there he had slept beside her each night. Elie's body had begun to reek and finally, he knew he had to bid her goodbye. So, a week to the day after her death, he dug her grave.

Despite the season, the ground at Snowmist was frozen solid, for it was a harsh and unforgiving place. A dense fog hung over the land, obscuring his vision. He dug for the whole day and into the night, stopping intermittently to wipe away his tears. By dawn the following day, the hole was finally deep and wide enough for his wife's fragile body to lay undisturbed.

Koen dressed his beloved Elie in her sheer white wedding dress for she was delicate and sweet like a lily. He placed her body carefully inside her cherished mahogany ottoman and covered her with petals from her favourite garden flowers. He placed some of her prized possessions inside with her, then closed the lid and with great, painstaking effort, he lowered the ottoman into her grave. Once inside, he sprinkled yet more petals and some earth onto the closed lid of her coffin. The heavy beating of his heart uttered farewell as he filled the hole back in.

For the rest of that day, Koen sat by her grave, beneath the great willow tree that hung over the pond; the pond where they had first laid eyes on each other as children, where they had lived and loved for many years.

Koen watched the floating lily pads and sprouts of pond grass swaying in the gentle breeze. The green, cloudy water rippled serenely and he wondered if it was cold within.

The air felt freezing as a swirling mist rolled in. It felt below zero, but the water was not at all frozen. It rippled silently, ignorant to its surroundings, oblivious to his grief and suffering. He wanted to climb in and let it wash away his pain and heartache.

When darkness finally fell, he could no longer sit outside for fear of freezing to death, so he retreated inside the cottage, lit a fire in the hearth and curled up in front of it. Sleep did not take him.

Koen sat every day beside her grave for many months from dawn until dusk. It helped him to feel close to her, but still his heart would not heal. He longed for her touch, her kindness and warmth. He wished to hear her laugh, her breath on his skin, her calling his name. His life now held no joy or purpose.

After such a long time being immersed in his own grief, Koen could no longer handle the pain and he longed to leave this life of sorrow behind. He got down on his knees and kissed her grave. He took a last look at their humble home, the house where all their treasured memories were locked away, the place where they had been supposed to grow old together. He stood at the edge of the pond and slowly stepped back, letting himself fall back into the murky water.

Below the surface, Koen saw strange sights—faces, flowers, visions. It was warm and still within, not icy cold and suffocating like he'd anticipated. The pond seemed to have no bed and he continued floating down and down and down. He closed his eyes, inhaled deeply and waited to die, to be reunited with Elie, but death never came and neither did she.

Looking at the cottage, after hearing that harrowing story, the atmosphere now felt oppressive and haunting. Why had she told me that story? Was there some underlying moral that I hadn't fathomed? 'What happened to him?' I asked curiously.

'You will see,' she answered cryptically.

The faerie walked the path to the cottage and I followed reluctantly. What was I doing there? Why was I choosing to do this when I had a lovely flat and family back home?

I looked at the solitary gate that stood between us and the awful yet beautiful history of Snowmist. Beyond the gate lay the cottage gardens, now overgrown and wild. Not even the pathway remained visible. My guide pushed the gate open and it creaked creepily on its rusty hinges. I wondered who the last person was to enter or leave through that gate, and how long ago that had been.

I followed the faerie through the garden, pushing branches aside and flattening the lengthy grass with my steps. On our right loomed the abandoned cottage, mostly concealed within the greenery. Some morbid part of me wanted to venture inside and see what remained of Koen and Elie's life.

The place was formidable. Elie had died there and Koen had suffered terribly, alone, before disappearing. It haunted me; I could feel the heartache and grief emanating from within it.

We came to a clearing in the wilderness, a place where no life could touch. The pond lay ahead of us, hushed, lying in wait. There was no sight nor sound of any wildlife like there had been back on the path. It was almost as if we had entered another dimension, completely cut off from the rest of the world. Everything was muted, entirely still, like we'd stepped inside a photograph.

There was no breeze to stir the rushes or weeds. The place had remained exactly the same as it had been the day he'd disappeared, frozen in time.

The water was like glass: reflective and smooth, untouched since that bleak period. The mist hung there heavily, like it did everywhere in Snowmist, but there in the clearing, it was ghostly and calm rather than damp and heavy.

The faerie stepped into the water. I watched, horror-struck. Did she expect me to follow? You would think that nothing could persuade me to enter that pond, but I heard her majestic voice inside my head, beckoning me, and all sense deserted me. I followed her in.

The water rose inch by inch until it was up to our necks. We lifted our feet off the ground, inhaled deeply and ducked beneath the surface. I felt my body being pulled down and the warm water embraced me like an old friend. Did I think I was going to die? No. No worries or fears crossed my mind. The faerie had altered my thoughts, pacified me. If I had had any of my wits left, I would not have followed her in a million years.

Below, the water was perfectly clear. I could see the faerie as clearly as I had above in the broad daylight. No silt obscured my vision, yet I could not see the bottom, or the top. There was nothing but impenetrable darkness rising up to meet me from below.

The pond was an abyss and I was peering down into the great void. It was pulling me down to my death. My senses came back to me and I started to panic. I opened my mouth to scream but all that left me were tiny air bubbles, escaping quickly up to the surface high above. I grabbed the faerie by the arm, unashamedly terrified, but she barely acknowledged my touch. She gave me a look that told me to remain calm and trust her. Her eyes, reflecting the glimmer of daylight from above, distracted and entranced me until I felt calm once more. There was no more air in my lungs, but they did not constrict or burn and I didn't struggle for breath. I exhaled, letting what little oxygen remained escape, and I felt a great relief wash over me. It felt natural.

Darkness swallowed us and pulled us down into the great, dark nothingness.

Black changed to a deep, purplish blue and the water twinkled like the night sky. We were floating in the heavens. The world opened up around us and I was aware that we were no longer in Snowmist pond. There was no end in any direction, just an endless expanse of tranquil water.

The faerie swam ahead of me in what I assumed was the direction of the surface, but I couldn't be certain. Like in space, there was no up or down here.

Soon, I saw a pale light far away, dispersing the imperious darkness. I wondered what would greet us there.

A dark form flashed across my vision. It happened so fast that I wasn't sure if it had been a deception of the light or my eyes adjusting to the gloom. The faerie gave no sign that she had seen anything amiss.

My eyes were weary and my limbs weak. Another dark shape darted across my field of sight and this time, it had been obvious. I kicked my legs faster, panic running through my veins. Who knew what lurked in these unknown waters? We were both swimming faster now; the faerie too had noticed the strange shadows. More and more were swarming around us. The closer we swam to the light, the clearer the forms became. They were circling us, hunting us—we were surrounded.

I caught a glimpse of a tail, a definite fish-like tail, shimmering and scaly, but I could make no more of the creatures as they closed in and pulled away, playing their wicked games.

My chest was aching and I was beginning to feel human again. Every second became a fight to stay conscious, to defeat the urge to breathe in and inhale the deadly water. My only chance was to make it to the surface, even if only to take another breath. With my very last reserve of strength and intransigent will to live, I made my final push.

Suddenly, the air exploded and my lungs burned with the sudden intake of oxygen after being so starved. The sound of waves crashing on a shore somewhere nearby thundered in my ears. I looked around but the faerie had disappeared. I looked in every direction but all I could see was the endless water and sky—shades of black and grey and purple, and the twinkling reflection of the stars on the water.

I trod water until my breathing returned to normal and I regained some of my strength. Then, I laughed hysterically, momentarily forgetting my peril. I was brimming with emotion. I'd made it! I was alive. It was an ecstatic, disbelieving laugh of relief, but my mirth was cut short as I felt something tug on my leg and I was pulled back down below.

The sea engulfed me once more; I'd had barely any time to take a breath. I struggled against my captor, but whatever it was, it was strong and swift. I was descending at an alarming rate and now all I could see was the deepest black. The light had deserted me. I looked around wildly, searching for the faerie, but I could see nothing.

By some miracle, the space around me lightened, the water glittered green and eerie forms came into view. Surrounding me was a shoal of merpeople. The few mermen—pasty, bare-chested and bony with shimmering, white tails—each held a torch: long silver poles topped with ghostly orbs of light.

My captor released its hold on me, but I wasn't free. The group slowly closed in on me. One of the mermaids—an orange-haired beauty with a glimmering bronze tail—swam ahead of the others with her golden arms wrapped around a figure. It seemed to be a young boy. His head hung limply from his neck and his skin was ashen. His hair floated in a wispy cloud around his face, preventing me from seeing if he was conscious or even alive.

Strange, ringing voices called to me from all directions, disorientating me. I couldn't understand their language, but from their tone, I knew they were angry. The mermaid let go of the boy and I wanted to reach out to him, to shake him awake, comfort him, save him, but the lack of oxygen and the weakness of my limbs prevented me from doing anything but watch him float dreamily before me.

The voices ceased and a deathly silence fell. The pressure of the water and the sudden silence of the merpeople intensified. I thought I might faint. Once again, I stopped breathing, but once again, I remained awake and most importantly, alive. I didn't have time to wonder at this as, without warning, the mermaids rushed at the boy. I gasped in terror as one by one, piece by piece, they ripped him apart. His inky, crimson blood swirled in the water, creeping its way towards me. His entrails and shattered bones were flung far and wide, as the monsters clawed and swiped at him, pulled at him and broke him, until all that remained was mushed meat. There was so much blood, I could taste it.

The mermaids, as the mermen watched on vacantly still holding their unearthly torches, seemed to rejoice in the bloodbath. They swam around and around in it, savouring it, all the while laughing and shrieking wildly.

I was in a trance, unable to believe what I'd witnessed. I looked on, dumbstruck and dazed, as their colours flashed before my eyes. Some were all white with pale bejewelled headdresses, like slivers of ice. Some were dark and filthy, with black tendrils of hair like seaweed and shadowed eyes. Others had dazzling scales of all the colours of the rainbow. All were magnificent to behold, enchanting and beautiful yet savage and terrifying. They were the ultimate predator; seductive, clever, crazed and strong.

I snapped out of my reverie—I needed to escape and fast. They were now turning their attention to me and I had no doubt they intended the same fate for me. I fought down the urge to vomit as pieces of the boy floated by. I looked around desperately for some way to escape but they had blocked me off on all sides. They were closing in fast, their elongated canines bared, clawed fingers reaching out, thirsty for blood. I coiled my body up tightly and focussed my mind inwardly, calling out for help. My life flashed before my eyes—Myla, Serafina and Lyanna all appeared to me.

I felt no regret, no repentance for anything I'd ever done, only sorrow, a melancholy nostalgia and a deep longing to see them again. If I had been on land, the grief would have brought me to my knees.

I used these thoughts and emotions to give me strength. I let them build up inside of me until they became a force of energy to use as protection and comfort in my final moments.

At the very last second, a shockwave hit the water. It was so great and powerful that the merpeople were flung away from me in all directions. They were scattered effortlessly like dandelion seeds on a breeze. I remained stationary, dumfounded.

I came to my senses and began my ascent back to the surface. As before, my lungs seemed to come back to life and I began to choke and gasp for air as water filled up my lungs and sent a burning pain through my chest. Within seconds, I lost consciousness. First, my body lost its mobility, then my eyes closed and finally, I felt myself drifting back down into the abyss below.

Chapter Twenty-Seven

I awoke on land, the feel of wet sand between my fingers, the sound of the waves crashing nearby and a cool breeze whispering over my skin. I could feel the frothy, cold water lapping at me on one side before retreating. I was dazed and weak. Someone was calling my name, but I couldn't tell if they were nearby or far away. I suddenly felt aware of my skull—it felt heavy and ached fiercely. A soft voice coaxed me back to consciousness.

Stiffly, I pushed myself up and rested my weight on my elbows. I looked around, straining to see through the fog in my head.

Strewn across the shoreline were a dozen or so mermaids laying lifeless. They appeared peaceful and angelic in death, stunning to behold with their shimmering scales and iridescent skin. Nonetheless, I shivered at the memory of what these deceiving creatures had done to that poor boy. 'Sara?' I turned my head at the sound of my name, remembering I was not alone. The faerie was crouched down low beside me.

'Where did you go?' I asked with great effort. My lungs were tight and my throat raw.

'Nowhere.'

'But you were gone.'

'No, I was still here—in the sea, in the air, in the earth. I was calling on my sisters for help. We saved you.'

I jolted, suddenly remembering the shockwave that had stopped the advancing mermaids. 'That was you?'

'Yes.'

I looked at her, my mouth wide open, in awe of her power. 'I am, I suppose you would say, part of nature.'

I nodded, though I didn't really understand. A pain shot through my stomach as I remembered the boy. 'Why didn't you save him?' My voice cracked on the last word.

I could see the deep sadness in her eyes. 'A great force of energy is required to create a shockwave that impactful. I couldn't do it without my sisters. We weren't quick enough.'

I felt guilty. 'You saved mine,' I offered in an attempt to assuage her sadness.

'Yes,' she agreed, giving no more emotion away, 'and death is a part of nature. That is the way of it.'

My head swam; I was too weak for this conversation. I merely nodded and asked no more about it. Somewhere close by, I heard a woman crying. 'Who's that?'

The faerie stood and I could see beyond her the form of a woman weeping on her knees. The faerie walked over to the stranger and placed a hand on her shoulder. The woman sniffed loudly and wiped away her tears. The faerie pointed to me and the pair exchanged quiet words before the woman got to her feet, brushed the sand from her ragged clothes and walked in my direction.

Time appeared to slow as I watched the pair walked over, taking what seemed to be a long while for such a short distance. I was exhausted. 'Sara?' the lady asked.

'Yes?' I croaked.

'Hello,' she greeted me, extending her hand.

I took it, using her to pull myself onto my feet. 'Sorry, who are you?' I asked suspiciously. She was human. There was nothing supernatural or out of the ordinary about her. In fact, she was not at all the kind of person I had expected to meet in another realm. Then it hit me; I was in the Other Place. I'd made it, just. I swayed on my feet, uncomprehending. I just couldn't believe it. Part of me was sure I was dreaming, as though at any moment I would wake up, back in my own bed at home. It wasn't inconceivable as all the dreams I'd ever had of the Other Place had felt as real as that.

I realised the woman was looking at me, concerned and expectant. 'The Wanderer, I think, has finally realised where she is,' the faerie said to the stranger.

The stranger smiled affectionately. 'I remember when you called me that.'

'Wait,' I interjected. 'You called me Sara earlier, but I never told you my name,' I said to the faerie.

'I have always known your name, since the day you were born,' she confirmed.

'How?'

'That is not my story,' she replied, looking pointedly at the stranger. 'Sara, this is Evelien.'

*****

I stared, gobsmacked, at my mother. At first, my mind could not connect the dots and I remember briefly thinking what a coincidence that this woman had the same name as my mother. I appraised the woman before me—she was tall, like me, with waist-length flaming hair. Her lips were scarlet and her eyes dark, shining with emotion. Her strong nose and caramel skin were like mine. Could this really be my mother?

The stranger nodded as though reading my mind. 'Sara,' she breathed.

'Mum?'

She nodded again, stepping forwards as though to embrace me, but I instinctively backed away. If she was hurt by this, she didn't show it. I felt affection for her instantaneously and a longing to know her, but I was in such a deep state of shock that I couldn't process all the thoughts and feelings whizzing around my body and brain, so I stood there like a statue with my mouth agape. 'I know this must be difficult for you, for so many reasons. I'm still getting my head around this myself.'

'Did she bring you here?' I asked, gesturing to where the faerie had been stood mere moments before, before realising she was no longer there.

Evelien didn't acknowledge her disappearance, as though she was used to such behaviour. She shook her head in response to my question. 'I was looking for the village boy. He had been missing for many moons and I was sent to search for him. She told me what had happened.'

I thought of the boy who had been killed. 'You knew him?'

'Yes, his family are my neighbours. Now I'll have to deliver the awful news to his parents.'

'I'm sorry,' I said, looking at my feet.

'This wasn't how I imagined our reunion,' Evelien admitted.

'But you have imagined it?' I asked, looking up hopefully, unable to disguise my feelings.

Evelien's face softened and a light sprang into her eyes. 'Of course I have. I think of you every day.'

'Then why didn't you come back?'

'It's not easy to explain. Not here, in this moment, but in time, I will answer all your questions.'

'So, I'm coming with you?'

'Where else would you go?'

I looked ahead at the seemingly endless expanse of white sand and nodded in understanding. I didn't know how I felt: lost maybe, scared, even hopeful? But there was no going back. I could only go forward.

We set off, trekking across the beach in the blazing sun, neither of us speaking. The weight of everything that we wanted to say hung heavy on our minds and hearts, but neither of us knew where to start. How do you begin a conversation like that?

We seemed to walk for an eternity, the landscape never changing, just the bleached, white-hot sand and the glaring daylight. After what felt like days, we finally reached the end of the beach. Tall mountains loomed up ahead and Evelien led us through a mountain pass at the lowest point. It was green there and treacherously rocky, in stark contrast to the flat, wide whiteness we'd come through.

I lost all concept of time. Sometimes, the sun seemed to have set twice in one day, and on others, it seemed to hang in the sky for weeks, never wavering from its spot high above. We saw many landscapes, some cold, empty and lifeless, some vibrant and colourful, tropical even. Still, neither of us spoke. The longer the silence dragged on, the harder it was to break. Despite finally being reunited with my mother, it was the loneliest I'd ever felt.

One day, shortly after sunrise, I was sat looking out over a deep valley. Evelien informed me that within that valley lay her village. She was packing away her things, preparing for the final leg of the journey, while I sat pondering my life. I was thinking of home and watching the sun rays beating down on the tops of the trees and lush green fields.

Evelien came to stand beside me, taking in the breath-taking view. I spoke then, for the first time since we'd left the shore, of something other than the weather or where we were going to make camp. Something about the open space and sky above, made me want to *be* open. 'I prepared myself for death back there in the sea,' I began. 'I saw death right in front of me and I faced it. I was ready for it. It was Lyanna who came to me. Not you, Lyanna. She was my weapon, my hope, the only reason for my sadness and my happiness. I was sad to lose her, happy to have had her in my life. I wanted, more than anything, to see her again, but I also resigned myself to knowing that if I was going to die then at least we'd had all that time together, you know? I was grateful. And now, here I am, a million miles away with my mother, and all I want to do is get back to her and never let her go.'

Evelien continued to look out over the valley, her face an unreadable mask. She patted me on the shoulder and told me it was time to go.

The Other Place, so far, had not been what I'd expected. All my dreams and visions had led me to believe the place would be magical, full of strange creatures and wondrous landscapes and while the scenery was beautiful, it was no different to any of the places I'd visited on my travels back home. Nothing out of the ordinary had occurred. The only difference between the Other Place and home was the lack of life for miles around. On our long journey thus far, we'd not encountered a single soul and apart from the sound of birds twittering high above in the trees, we'd encountered no wildlife either. I actually found it quite disturbing, despite appreciating the peace and quiet.

As we walked steadily down the hill into the valley, Evelien began to sing beside me. It was a beautiful, serene sound—her voice was rhythmic and gentle. The tune vaguely reminded me of an old Celtic folk song I'd heard as a child. It relaxed and soothed me and before long, I had forgotten my irritation at things not going quite as I'd planned. I felt I was walking through the air, being carried on the music of my mother's voice.

For those moments, I felt like nothing had happened in my life. The song had me under its spell. I was weightless, free from the memories of pain, grief and fear. Long after Evelien had finished her lullaby, the sensation stayed with me.

We stopped by a stream at the roots of the mountain. Stretching out from beneath my feet lay rolling hills, lush fields and great trees of all shapes and sizes. Eerie, white orbs sparkled and floated through the air, like the translucent, bright spots you can see when you stare up into the clear, blue sky on a sunny day, and for the first time, I truly felt like I was no longer on the same plane.

I took the opportunity to take a wash in the stream, stripping off entirely, as Evelien had assured me it was okay to do, and immersing myself in the cool water. I felt overcome with a sense of freedom and warmth. The water washed away my troubles, refuelled my system, rejuvenated me. It brought me back to life.

I felt as though I'd been trapped in a long, dark tunnel, trudging endlessly towards a bleak end. Every day had been an effort just to get up, put on a smile, but this new air, this new place was breathing life back into my soul.

I was very aware that I was under a spell, either cast by a living being or the place itself. I didn't dwell on this however, I just let it be. I was filled with a thirst for love; not just the love of another person but for the love of life itself. I had lost the will to live—not to keep breathing, survive, but to really live. To feel life in all its glory and to feel free, like anything could happen.

Something about that place helped me to see the light at the end of that long, dark tunnel, and it came from the great, shining sun beating down on my naked body as I lay in the middle of that unknown world, surrounded only by nature.

I climbed out, somewhat reluctantly, and as I let myself dry off in the warmth of the day, Evelien asked me, 'Did you feel it?'

'Feel what?' I asked dreamily, still in a state of deep relaxation.

'That's not an ordinary stream.' She smiled knowingly.

'What's extraordinary about it?'

'It flows down from the great mountains up in the north. They call it the giver of life.'

'Why? Is it a religious thing?'

'No, we don't have religion here. Not as you know it, anyway. This is a spiritual place, a place where people come to heal the sick and wounded, to meditate and be reborn. The stream can bring you back from the very brink of death.'

I wondered at this. So, that was why I'd felt restored from taking a dip in the waters. 'Is it real?' I asked. 'Or is it the power of suggestion? In the mind, so to speak.'

'Is it not real if it exists in the mind? Surely if it's real in your mind then it's real to you?'

'Hmm…' I murmured thoughtfully.

'Anyway, how could it be the power of suggestion if I only told you about it after you'd experienced its magic?'

'I suppose so.' My mind was still trying to adjust to the new environment, coming to terms with where I was. I was still not entirely open to the fact that I had indeed travelled to a different realm. I couldn't yet hand myself over completely to such a notion until I'd witnessed something truly unimaginable.

We continued through the valley, the pretty views passing us by on all sides. At the bottom of the mountain by the stream, the colours had been rich, the atmosphere ethereal, the air alive with the sound of life, but now we had arrived in a desolate landscape: a wasteland of blackened trees and dead fields, all drained of colour. I wondered why I hadn't seen this from my viewpoint at the top of the mountain. I was feeling increasingly on edge and I sensed that Evelien was feeling the same, so we quickened our pace.

We walked for miles and miles without the scene changing, but eventually we stepped into what could only be described as a winter wonderland. Snow fluttered down from the clouds high above, glittering in the sun rays. We'd entered a wintry forest where the trees were densely packed, closing in on all sides. Drips and splashes could be heard all around as the snow melted overhead and dropped from the great heights down to the forest floor.

Finally, we reached a break in the seemingly boundless expanse of woodland. Just ahead was a small house built solely from logs, twigs and branches. I stopped, taking in the sight. Beyond the house lay many more houses, similarly built. It was a whole village of them. 'Welcome to my home,' Evelien announced.

'It's…' I paused, '…lovely.' It astounded me that my mother lived in such a simple place. I was curious to know how the houses stayed standing, but I was also in awe of the earthy charm of the village.

'This is my house,' she told me, pointing to the first house I'd seen. 'Now, I suggest you go in and make yourself comfortable while I go take news to the people.'

'What news?'

'I'll tell them of my new guest, but I must also tell the parents of the young boy that…' Evelien clearly couldn't bring herself to finish her sentence.

I nodded sadly in understanding, having forgotten until that moment about the young lad who had been killed. I was glad Evelien had not asked me to bear witness to that conversation.

I settled myself inside my mother's house and drifted off to sleep, curled up in a hand-carved, uncomfortable chair. I awoke sometime later, confused and stiff, to the sound of Evelien entering through the door. 'How did it go?' I asked her sluggishly, as she sat down across from me.

Evelien looked drained. 'As you can imagine, horrible. They're inconsolable. They never imagined he would make it as far as the shore.'

'How *did* he make it that far? Surely he didn't take the same route as us?'

She shook her head. 'There is something you must understand about this place, Sara—it's never the same. It changes. It can be helpful at times, when you are in dire need, and other times, it can betray you. The same journey has taken me less than half the time it took us. Though that's not entirely accurate as time isn't linear here. It's not like back in our world; it can't be measured. Even after all these years, I still can't quite grasp it. I'm programmed to think the way you do. I don't think I'll ever understand it, really.'

'I see,' I replied, though I didn't. I suddenly felt overcome with exhaustion. I needed to sleep for at least a week. So, that's what I did. Well, for what felt like a week.

Evelien put me up in her bed, tucking an enormous feather duvet around me and singing me to sleep. As the sleep took me, I remember thinking for the first time that I had an actual, living, breathing mother. I felt like a beloved child and soon drifted off into the deepest slumber of my life.

When I awoke, I was vaguely aware that it was light outside and I could hear Evelien shuffling around in the next room.

The house was comprised of two rooms: the bedroom I was currently inhabiting, furnished with a bed and dilapidated cupboard, and the main room with is fireplace, seating area and cooking space. I had yet to find out where the bathroom was.

While I had been asleep, Evelien appeared to have washed and dried my clothes as they were now laid over the end of the bedframe. I put them on gratefully, before venturing out into the other room to find a steaming bowl of stew and a tired-looking Evelien waiting for me. 'How do you feel?' she asked.

'Good. Thanks for letting me use your bed. Where have you been sleeping?'

'Out here,' she replied, gesturing to a large, thick fur rug laid out in front of the fireplace.

'How long have I been out for?'

'Days, by your reckoning.'

'Days?'

'Yes, but the sun hasn't set yet. It's been bright for a while now. I think it will go down soon.'

I couldn't even begin to understand what she was telling me and I had no desire to know more. The science behind the Other Place was not something that

I would ever understand, so I resolved to just accept it as it was. 'Sara, I know you've only just woken up, but I think it's time we spoke.'

I agreed, unsure if I wanted to or not, but I knew I couldn't put it off any longer.

As I ate my stew, Evelien told me of all that had led up to her disappearance: the grief of losing her husband so young, the post-natal depression after my birth and the visions that had consumed her and led her here. 'Please understand that I didn't want to leave you, but I couldn't bring you here with me and I couldn't stay there any longer. You must know the pull this place has. Once it shows itself to you, it's not something you can just ignore or forget about. You have to know, you have to follow it.'

'I do know, but I also know that I wouldn't have deserted my child for it.'

'You say that, but—'

'Don't tell me I don't know because I've not been in that situation. I do know; I know myself. It was hard enough to leave Lyanna and she's a grown woman who can look after herself.'

'Lyanna is one of the reasons I left. I saw how she was with you. I knew you'd be better off with her than me.'

'You're right about that,' I agreed coldly.

'I deserve that. I deserve all your bitterness. I'm not making excuses, believe me, I'm just telling you my side of the story.'

'And I've listened. Part of me understands, in some weird way, but what I don't understand is why you never came back.'

'It's not so easy to leave once you're here.'

'Not even for a little while, just to see me?'

'No. I couldn't. How could I? I had no idea what it would be like if I went back. Lyanna might have hated me, refused to let me see you.'

'So, you were a coward?'

'Yes, I suppose I was. Look, you'll understand soon enough. You won't go back either.'

'I bloody well will!'

'Maybe, I don't know you. You might be stronger than me, but this place, it takes hold of you.'

'Well, I'll be returning home, no matter what. You can bet your life on it.'

'You set out here with that intention, I suppose. I left with the intention of never returning.'

'But why? That's what I don't understand. Once you felt better, you could have come home.'

'I got better, yes, but if I ever went back there, even now, my mind wouldn't survive it. The loss of your father was too great. I still grieve him even now and I always will. Here is the only place I can distance myself from that.'

'You can't grieve him forever.'

'I can.'

'How do you know you'll feel that way if you go back?'

'Because that's all that world holds for me now. Loss, pain and memories of a loving man that I'll never see again.'

'Not even to see your sister? Not even to see your daughter?'

'Don't you understand? You can't live between the worlds, Sara. You can only exist in one or the other, and I exist here.'

Why?'

'Because to wander between the worlds will rip your soul in two. The mind can't comprehend the existence of both places at the same time.'

'I'm doing that right now.'

'Yes, and before long, you'll understand what I mean. You'll have to make a choice: this world or the old one.'

Her words sat heavy on my heart. She was out of her mind. The Other Place had changed her. She was no longer my mother, if she ever had been. She was of another world now and there was no going back.

'Did you know I was coming?' I asked after a brief silence.

'Part of me felt you, but I thought that was our bond. I didn't know you were aware of this place though.'

'Do you know why we can see the Other Place? Is it genetic?'

'I assume so, but I'm not going to pretend to know its secrets. I've never sought out answers here. I came here to let all the questions go.'

'So, you don't even understand the world you live in?'

'No, but do you understand the world *you* live in?'

'To an extent. I know how the days, months and seasons work, for instance,' I answered snidely.

'And does that give you a deeper understanding of your place in the universe?'

'Well, no, but—'

'Then it's not useful, it doesn't matter. So many things I used to worry about, I don't have to now. They all seem so trivial and irrelevant. All I want to do is live my life quietly and peacefully here, away from that world and all its toxicity.'

I understood where she was coming from, but I still couldn't help feeling that she'd completely missed the point. How could she have walked away from her family so easily? 'Sara, earlier, you said "sister".'

'What do you mean?'

'You said sister, not *sisters*.'

I gulped. I hadn't thought once to tell her of Serafina's death. Despite knowing they were sisters, my mind still hadn't fitted the pieces together. Perhaps part of me still couldn't quite believe this woman was my mother. It seemed Evelien was right about the schism between the two worlds and the inability to let them exist side by side in my mind.

'Serafina died,' I told her, cringing at my own bluntness.

Evelien looked perturbed, but not upset. 'I'm sorry to hear that.'

'Are you though?'

'Of course I am. She was my sister, but we never really got along and I haven't seen her for so long, the words don't really mean that much to me.'

I stared at her, horrified. 'Do you have any humanity left?'

'Yes. I feel sorry for your loss, but I can't feel any sense of loss myself as I already lost her when I left.'

'Do you not even wish that you could have seen her one last time?'

'No,' she replied firmly. 'I told you, when I left, I never intended to return. I made peace with that a long time ago.'

*****

I stayed with Evelien for as long as I could, knowing full well that once I moved on, I would likely never see her again and unlike her, I still held some sentiment. Despite the sour taste she'd left in my mouth, for so many reasons, I still could not so willingly leave her without at least getting to know her and her way of life first.

I learnt how they got rid of waste, how they grew and prepared their food, their customs, how they protected themselves from the elements and much more. I volunteered my assistance with chores around the village and got to know the other inhabitants. They were all like my mother: friendly, yet completely lacking that human depth. They were two-dimensional to me.

I wasn't going to learn anything more there, that much was clear, and I wasn't content to not achieve what I had set out to do—find a reason for all this, the reason I was there.

So, at last, it was time to say goodbye. Evelien hugged me and told me she was going to miss me. I genuinely believed she meant it, in her own unique way. I told her that I was glad to have had the time we'd shared together, and I genuinely meant it.

What do you say when you meet your mother for the first time as an adult? And then, what do you say when you say goodbye for the first time? What do you think or feel when you realise that she's not human? When she shows barely any emotion at saying goodbye to her only child, possibly forever? I was surprised to find that I felt emotionless too. At first, I'd felt angry but then I realised that none of it mattered.

I already had a family. I already had a mother: a woman who had raised me and taught me manners and morals, who loved me unconditionally and who would always be there for me.

So, as I turned away from my mother for good and continued on my journey, neither of us shed a tear.

Chapter Twenty-Eight

I was now alone in the wild. I realised that when I had felt alone back home, the knowledge that my family was within arm's reach, there waiting for me whenever I needed them, had provided me with comfort. It enabled me to feel what I felt without fear, to know that I had a foundation on which to steady myself no matter how dark my thoughts became. Out there, I had no protection, no solace, no escape. I was stripped bare. When I awoke from a nightmare, there were no home comforts or sounds of someone nearby to chase the fear away, only a dense darkness, offering no warmth or remedy.

Past the open fields and grasslands of my mother's community, I entered great woodlands. I saw awe-inspiring landscapes, passed through dark, enchanting forests, washed myself in sparkling pools beneath waterfalls, crossed raging rivers and climbed over felled trees.

The going was tough at times. The terrain was uneven and insidious, yet despite that, I relished the freedom and nothing but fantastic views as far as the eye could see. I saw places and spectacles I never knew existed.

What is freedom? Is it really achievable? I felt free, especially at the beginning, but I also felt weighed down with responsibility. I was in complete control of my time and, most importantly, my own survival. I had no schedules or plans and my options were limited. I was restricted by my emotions, my fears and the ultimate knowledge that everything was entirely out of my hands.

Luckily, I'd learned a few skills at the community, such as what berries, mushrooms and plants I could eat, what to watch out for, how to start a fire, how to keep warm and dry, but the fact was that the nature that surrounded me—the weather, the terrain, the wildlife—all determined my fate and weighed my success.

Freedom sometimes felt within my grasp, like it belonged to me, such as at times when I looked out across the land and saw the noble sun setting or a great stretch of water glittering in the fading light. Then, at other times, it slipped away from me and I felt a suffocating pressure to keep myself alive and an overwhelming fear of the unknown. I had no idea where I was going, what I was going to encounter or what I was even searching for.

The sun was merciless. It was my only friend, a mercurial companion. She was deceitful; she could love me and leave me, with no remorse. She made me feel safe, then would take away her warmth in the next breath. I felt a better person in her presence, but when she hid from me, I was isolated and mournful. And when it rained, those times were the hardest to bear. The world was black. The rain would hammer down on me in torrential violence, washing away my sanity, deafening me and blinding me. The thunder would growl ominously, the lightning would streak across the sky, and I would long for my sun.

I had so much time to think and to dwell. When the sun peeked out after a particularly miserable night, my creativity would be ignited. I thought long and hard about myself and my life back home. I looked up at that burning orb and knew that that same sun was beating down on everyone in the world no matter who or where they were—those on holiday in tropical climates, the workers on their commutes in the big cities and in the countryside, those who were lonely or sad, those who were content, the young, the old. Everyone. The same sun. It connected me to life, the rest of the humankind, the planet and, beyond that, the universe. It comforted me and helped me feel closer to home.

At first, the solitary living had given me a great deal of satisfaction. It was just me, my path, the sun, the moon, discovering and exploring in the peace and quiet. Eventually, however, the novelty wore off and I missed company and conversation. I felt anomalous and forgotten by the world. I wondered if I really existed anymore, like one would wonder at if a tree makes a sound when it falls and there is nobody to hear it. I feared, more than anything, getting lost out there and no-one ever finding me. I could die and be erased from all memory, my soul condemned to roam the wilderness for all eternity.

My emotions were extreme. My spirit absorbed the new experiences like nourishment, and I felt a joy in living so powerful, finding meaning in natural beauty. Then, my isolation would overshadow my exhilaration, and drag me down back into the great pit of despair. The nights were the longest; so dark and so cold.

Despite the hard times, I still felt better off than I had been before, stuck at home, imprisoned in my misery. I grew as a person, learning and beginning my great journey. All I truly yearned for was company. Snufflebump comforted me—I became curiously attached to that fuzzy little bear. Knowing he was there inside my backpack kept me going, like I was carrying a piece of Myla everywhere I went.

My thinking time, which was pretty much every waking minute, was nothing like any quiet time I'd had at home. Back at home, I felt like my thoughts were trapped inside a cage, unable to bloom. In the endless, open wild, my thoughts floated around me and drifted out to the horizon and into the great beyond.

I wished I had taken my journal and a pen with me. I wanted to document my days, my musings, my journey. Instead, I marked boulders and rocks using small stones, leaving chalky letters like a breadcrumb trail. Often, after leaving my inscriptions behind, I wondered if anyone would find them and speculate over the identity of their author. I wondered if I would ever return to those spots and remember the emotions that had inspired me to write them. What person would I be then? What would have happened in my life between this point in time and that?

I soon came to the mountains. They had been looming threateningly on the horizon, but I finally reached their roots. The ground beneath my feet was uneven and unsympathetic. I thought I was close to death on many occasions. The constant ups and downs, going around, going through, climbing, and falling wearied me to the point of exhaustion, but those views when I reached the high points were worth all the effort. I felt like a God, looking down on my creation.

*****

One morning, bright-eyed and feeling refreshed after a decent night's sleep, I set off into a new day, thinking it would be the same as all the others. The hazy sun hung low in the sky, peeking above the distant horizon, tinting the sky and clouds hues of vivid pinks and oranges, like the timid flames of a growing fire.

The day turned out clear, warm and radiant. The brilliant blue sky was almost completely unmarred except for a few wispy, cotton clouds. The vibrant green of the trees and hills in the daylight were trimmed with gold. In the distance lay more grey mountains, partially obscured by mist. I wondered when I would finally see an end to it all or if I would continue wandering forever.

Then, out of the blue, I glimpsed what appeared to be a man-made structure in the valley below, the first since I'd left the community. I made my way down to it carefully. It was a great archway, ornately carved with runes and symbols. I examined the structure, running my hands over its bumpy yet smooth surface. I felt peaceful, docile even, and I wondered if there was more magic at work like there had been at the stream with my mother so long ago.

I heard a soothing voice and a woman stepped out from behind the arch. A woven band of spikes was seated upon her brow, her golden hair cascading down from beneath it. Looking closer, I realised she was wearing a crown of beastly teeth. Translucent, purpling bruises circled her eyes, highlighting her violet irises. There was a wild glint in those eyes. I took a step back, startled.

The stranger spoke to me in a strange, melodic language and I felt myself being drawn closer to her. She appeared pleased to see me and I didn't fathom why until she involuntarily licked her lips. Her violet eyes turned jet-black and she reached out to me with long, bony, claw-like fingers. I wanted to run but I was rooted to the spot.

I heard a male voice, deep and gruff. He was speaking in yet another language I couldn't understand. The woman looked around, alarmed, before running away without a second glance in my direction. I regained my ability to move and physically relaxed. I knew it had been a close call.

A striking man appeared through the archway. He wore a dark grey worn and shabby leather jacket, stitched haphazardly together, black trousers made of some thick, rough material and chunky boots. About his person he carried various weapons: a sword, which he was currently re-sheathing, a longbow strapped across his back and an array of different-sized daggers and knives. His azure eyes were shining, full of knowledge and humour. His multi-toned hair, which reflected the golden sunlight, hung dishevelled and matted around his shoulders. Stubble flecked his weather-battered skin, all the way up to his high cheekbones. I hadn't realised how handsome he was beneath all that dirt, but now I could see him. 'Thanks,' I breathed, unsure what to say.

'You should thank me,' he grinned devilishly. 'Do you have any idea who that was?'

I shook my head in reply. 'She was a sorceress, and not a good one. She roams these lands feeding on the flesh of anything that lives and dares cross her path. She enjoys the blood of humans above all,' he told me pointedly.

I shuddered. I guessed I really did need to be grateful he was there. 'How do you know I'm human?' I asked. My voice sounded strange to me after so long in silence.

'You glow.'

'What?'

'Humans glow. Not like a light, it's something else that you can't really see, only sense.'

'Why?'

'Because you crossed the line between the worlds. It leaves a mark on you.'

'Really? Nobody's mentioned it before.'

'Who have you seen out here?' he asked me, one of his eyebrows raised in genuine curiosity.

'I came from a community back there,' I answered, gesturing in the direction I'd come.

'Ah, them. Well, they wouldn't tell you.'

'Why not?'

'Well, they don't say anything that's not worth saying. They don't have time for frivolous chatter, they only do what's necessary.'

'Yeah, I suppose that sums them up well.'

'What were you doing with them, anyway?'

I really didn't want to go into any great detail of my relationship with my mother and what had led me to her, so I just told him, 'I was passing through.'

'To where?'

'What?'

'To where? You were just passing through on your way to where?'

'Well, actually, I don't know.'

'Why?'

'You ask a lot of questions, don't you?'

'Well, you're very mysterious and invite a lot of questions,' he quipped.

I laughed. The sound rang in my ears. 'I ask because it's my job to know. My folk govern these lands and we know everything that happens within it.'

'Well, I've passed through unchecked so far,' I countered.

'Have you? So, you think it's coincidence that I happened upon you at the same time as the witch?'

'You've been following me?' I questioned, perturbed.

'No, I've been observing you, from afar. In the interests of protecting our land, of course.'

I was sceptical at the least but didn't push it any further. 'So, what are you?'

'What do you mean?'

'You said your folk govern these lands—what are you? Do you have a name at least?'

'My name is Thane.'

It was a good name. 'That's not quite what I meant.' I sighed, exasperated. How did you describe something that you've never needed to describe before? 'Your group—you must have a collective name.'

He raised an eyebrow attractively, distracting me. 'No name.'

'I've noticed that nothing here has a name. I've been travelling for a long time now and I don't even know the name of the place itself.'

'This,' he gestured about him, 'is just the earth.'

'How can it not have a name?'

'Because we have no need for names, they hold no meaning.'

'I disagree. Names can hold a lot of meaning, actually.'

'Really? And you know so much about names because…?'

'I read,' I retorted, brushing off his condescending tone.

He laughed a hearty laugh that instantly calmed my frustrations. 'I meant no offence. You will have to get used to my bluntness.'

'Will I?'

'Well, I have to get going and I assume you'll be joining me?'

'And why would you assume that?'

'A number of reasons. You were heading in this direction anyway, you've probably become unnerved by the sorceress and may want to stay close in case any more unsavoury characters choose to prey on you, you have no idea where you're going but I do, or you may even just want some company on your long, lonely journey.'

I smiled. He had me there. Why wouldn't I follow him? He had, however, missed one other possible reason from the list.

We returned to the path I had been following and he continued to ask me probing questions about my reasons for being there, where I'd come from and the like. I delivered vague answers, unwilling to reveal my life story to a complete stranger.

Before long, I became thoroughly grateful for his company as the landscape changed drastically. The daylight dimmed, despite the sun being no closer to setting, and the air was smoggy. The atmosphere was oppressive and malevolent. I felt paranoid and twitchy, convinced that we were being watched. 'We have entered the sorceress' lair,' Thane whispered to me, apparently also sensing a presence.

'The same one?'

He nodded gravely. 'We must keep our wits about us.'

Chapter Twenty-Nine

We stumbled upon a storybook cottage nestled deep in the heart of the woods. The cottage would have been pretty and well-tended once upon a time; I imagined smoke puffing dreamily out of the stone chimney, candlelight flickering through the leaded windows and the smell of freshly baked pastries and pies wafting out the open door. Now, however, it was derelict and stern, the walls grimy and crumbling, no light shining out from within and worse, the entire place reeked of death. All around us, the vegetation had withered and died.

Thane stopped and outstretched his arm to prevent me from taking a step further. He raised a finger to his lips to signal quiet. 'Something terrible has happened here,' he announced.

I opened my mouth to ask what but he shook his head.

Suddenly, a brisk breeze picked up. The leaves whispered and the blackened grass shivered. A creeping sense of doom passed through me and I realised, with sudden terror, that we were not alone. The sky darkened above and the walls of the forest closed in on us. I watched on, viewing the cottage through fearful eyes, as the windows and door appeared to morph into a tormented, furious face.

There was laughter, but not humorous laughter; the sound was entirely devoid of mirth, cruel and harsh. I couldn't pinpoint the source as it seemed to be coming from all around us, echoing between the trees and the house. The pitch rose, higher and higher, until it sounded like laughter no more but a crazed, grief-stricken wailing.

The scene was familiar to me and I was overcome with a sense of déjà vu, and then it dawned on me why. I remembered a dream from long ago, like a clear spotlight shining through the mist of time.

Eventually, the forest was quiet once more and the shadow passed. I let my breath out in a long, relieved sigh and realised I had been holding it instinctively. Thane crept closer to the cottage and I followed closely behind. He stopped abruptly, causing me to bump right into his back. 'What is it?' I asked, peering over his shoulder. He remained motionless and unresponsive.

I saw them then, the two bodies. Two corpses: brown, decayed skeletons with nothing but scraps of hair and cloth still hanging limply from them, serving as a reminder of what, or who, they once were.

I knew who they were, I had seen them many years before in my mind's eye. I didn't mention this to Thane, it didn't seem appropriate. The fact remained they were dead.

I stumbled around the side of the cottage and vomited violently. When I returned, Thane was still standing guard over the corpses, seemingly deep in thought. 'Did you know them?' I asked him.

Thane shook his head grimly. 'No.'

'We can't just leave them here, not like this,' I thought aloud, suddenly overcome with emotion.

'No,' he agreed, 'but we must be quick. She'll be back before long.'

I shivered, staring around nervously.

Thane disappeared inside the house and returned carrying a shovel to dig their grave. He dug a hole large enough to rest them both in comfortably, while I went in search of blankets to wrap them up in.

I helped him carry the bodies to the deep hole and, as gently as we could, laid them to rest together. We had no time to say any words. Thane filled the hole back in and we set off from that evil place in haste.

*****

The land grew no more cheerful as we trudged on into the evening. The temperature remained below freezing and the world about us dark and gloomy. 'I don't like this place. Where are we?' I asked, pulling my fleece tightly around myself.

'I know where we are—on the borders of the Fells—but I feel something here that I haven't before.'

'Like what?' I was unnerved.

'A shadow. Some kind of dark presence.'

'Is it her?'

'No, this is something else.'

I stumbled, my legs and eyes tired and heavy. Thane caught me. 'Come on, I know you're weary, but we can't stay here.'

Further along our road, Thane stopped in his tracks, looking alarmed. 'There's something here.'

'What is it?' I hissed, trying to get as close to him as possible, terrified.

Ahead, through a gap in the trees, I could see something moving, something huge. I closed my eyes, not wanting to find out what it was. 'Stay here, I'll take a closer look.'

'No, I won't stay here on my own!' I insisted and followed anxiously behind.

As we came to the edge of the treeline, the sight that greeted us stopped us dead in our tracks. A great, nebulous, dark fog hovered in mid-air, only visible against the purple, dusky sky. It was not a fog like anything I'd seen before; its mass was stationary, floating in one spot high above the ground. I pictured a black hole, or what I thought one might look like: a dense, dark, swirling mass. This was no black hole, however. Although parts of the shadow were an impenetrable black, other parts were lighter and, here and there, smoky tendrils crept out as though reaching out to pull us in. It was the creepiest, most unnerving sight I'd ever seen.

The churning mass was blocking our entire path. I dreaded to think what might happen should we venture any closer. 'What should we do?' I asked Thane. The thought of retreating into the woods filled my heart with dread, yet we couldn't go forwards. 'We'll have to go around. Follow me.'

As quickly and as quietly as we could, as though in fear of waking a sleeping monster, we crept along the treeline. The shadow had been deceiving; we continued along the path for at least a mile before there was any sign of leaving it behind. We walked on a little further, not wanting to risk getting too close.

When we deemed that we were far enough past the shadow's perimeter, we ran across the open plain. We didn't stop until the thing was a small spot far behind.

Breathless, we slumped down on the cold, hard ground. 'What the hell was that?' I turned to Thane once my breathing had returned to normal.

'I've never seen anything like it before,' Thane replied.

'Never?' I asked disbelievingly.

'Never. It was the queerest thing. I find it hard to believe that its appearance on the same day I meet you is a coincidence.'

I blanched, confused at his accusatory tone, but I was in no mood to question him further.

Thane kindled a fire and the warm glow of the flames chased away our dark thoughts for a short while. We talked way into the night, trying to speak only of cheerful things to lift our spirits, but something about that shadow haunted both of us. It felt like all the joy and light had been sucked out of the world into that great void.

I told Thane of my childhood. I confided in him of my mother's part in my story and the great darkness within me that I was trying to quell. Thane, too, shared with me stories of his life and family. He and his kin were protectors of the land. I gathered they were a kind of tribe, supremely strong, with keen senses, a deep love of all living things and unnaturally long lives. Thane could not tell me his age as there was no measure of time in their world, but from what he told me, I guessed he was hundreds of years old.

I felt comfortable around him, easily sharing stories with him about my own life and listening eagerly to all that he had to say. The greatest stories are told around a campfire.

We found that there were many differences between our cultures. Their idea of beauty appeared to be concerned mostly with inner beauty. They held stock in knowledge, thoughtfulness, friendship, compassion, bravery and humour. They were a passionate people, acting on impulses and unafraid of emotion. There appeared to be no social etiquette: no what's wrong to say and no what's right, only what *was* said. They talked openly of their feelings and because of that, there were rarely any disagreements. They did not believe in possession, nothing belonged to them—the world was the world and they were merely passing through. Their beliefs resonated with me and I felt a deeper affinity to their race than my own.

Love was a hot topic between us. When I explained my meagre experiences with it, he became stony-faced. 'That is not how love should be. Love should be uplifting and inspiring. I'm sorry for you,' he told me.

'But surely, if you're from a place where you freely share each other, you won't understand why my experience was so hurtful?'

'We share freely, but we don't hide it. We are open about it and we would never use love as a weapon or to gain advantage. It is tragic.'

I agreed wholeheartedly. Despite all my terrible experiences with the opposite sex, I was a true romantic at heart. To hear him speak the very words that I had written in my journals, warmed me. Although I'd never experienced true love, I still longed for and had faith in it.

I have always relished reading about love, writing about it, hearing about it, watching it unfold but I was yet to experience it—and I mean the real, passionate, end-of-the-world love. It is the best thing in all humanity. 'Don't get me wrong,' Thane continued, 'love can destroy you, hurt you, force you into making the worst decisions imaginable—it can even drive you to kill—but it also inspires, comforts and provides the most joyous, rapturous moments of your entire life. It is the most amazing thing, when it burns you *and* when it lifts you up. It's more intoxicating than any drug and more beautiful than any vista. Love makes the whole universe more beautiful.'

My heart ached; how I longed to feel that with someone. I felt lonelier then than I ever had done out in the wild on my own. 'I wish I could go back in time,' I mumbled, thinking of all the things I would have done or not done.

'There is only one way to look back in time, and that is to gaze up at the stars.' Sensing my melancholy, he added, 'Besides, I see a bright future ahead of you.'

'You do?' I asked, my voice brimming with hope, despite knowing he was just trying to console me.

'Of course; you're a special person.'

I smiled, silently thanking him for attempting to comfort me.

That night, as we stared up at the nights sky, we fell asleep on the flat of our backs thinking of our pasts and our futures.

*****

We walked on for many more sunsets and sunrises. The landscape became hospitable and attractive, the weather warmer and calmer, and soon, the great shadow we had encountered felt like a distant memory.

Thane and I got on well. We shared a similar, dry sense of humour and we talked endlessly about all things. We bathed in each other's energy and something more developed between us. Despite the enormous age gap, he still had the spirit and looks of someone not much older than me. If anything, his wisdom, experience and rugged looks made him more charming.

We made love for the first time one morning beside a tranquil river. The sun had not yet appeared over the horizon and our bodies were illuminated by the ghostly light that comes just before the break of day. As we entwined, eager and lustful, the sun rose silently and unnoticed. We were blind to our surroundings, blind to everything but our act.

Afterwards, we laid side by side, breathing heavily, our chests and stomachs rising and falling rapidly. A chill breeze gently skimmed over my bare skin, cooling the sweat that had pooled between my breasts and the cleft of my stomach. The sun, still low in the sky, barely offered any warmth. I didn't notice the cold however as I was daydreaming of the moments that had led up to us having sex.

We had woken in the dark, ready to set off on the next leg of our journey and while we had been fumbling around trying to collect our belongings, we had brushed up against one another. There had been an instant electricity between us and before I knew it, his hands were in my hair, his lips brushing against my face and my shoulders, whatever bare skin he could find. It had felt completely natural. I had felt lust before on many occasions, but this ran deeper. Thane was gentle with me, passionate yet careful, like I was fragile and precious to him. I felt a connection to him deeper than I'd had with any man before and I was surprised to find this intensified my pleasure.

We didn't speak afterwards; there was nothing to say. It was what it was, and I didn't want to ruin the state of elation we were both in with clumsy words. We dressed and packed up, then set off along the riverside into the new day.

A mile or so downriver, we came to a bridge. It wasn't a rickety old bridge like I would have expected but a sturdy wooden bridge, complete with hand-carved handrails and a beautiful view of the river. Thane informed me that he and his brothers had built the bridge a long time ago and I marvelled at their craftmanship which had stood the test of time.

We passed over the river without incident, stopping only to appreciate the view: the water swirling beneath our feet and low-hanging willow trees on either side, trailing their leaves in the sparkling, clear water.

At the other side of the river, we came to a steep, grassy hill. At the top, after an arduous climb, I stopped to take in my surroundings while Thane scouted the easiest route to take down the other side. I sat myself down on a flat-surfaced boulder and looked out over the great, green valley below. The sun was now setting and her red haze ignited the world. I turned to see where Thane was and found him watching me, his face bathed in a sensuous, rubescent glow. He didn't look away when I caught him watching me. 'My shirt suits you,' he observed. I had taken to wearing one of his long, white shirts as a dress to cool me down. It created a soft breeze on my legs when I walked.

'It's comfy. Thanks for letting me borrow it.' I smiled, turning back to the stunning view.

The next day, we entered yet another forest, but this was like no forest I had ever seen before. The air was thick and close beneath the golden trees and all around us, as we walked side by side, leaves were falling and twirling about us. Outside the forest, it was summer. Fresh, colourful, rich lands spread out beneath a high, hot sun, but here within the enchanted walls of the forest, it was forever autumn.

I watched the strange leaves fall from the branches and new ones sprout in their place, ready to fall after them. The leaves on the forest floor were only a few layers deep as they crumbled and decayed swiftly, absorbed back into the earth, nourishing the roots. On and on it went in an endless cycle. 'This is the forest of the Phoenix,' Thane told me, breaking through the musical quiet. I felt truly in another world. 'It is a place of rebirth, a place to be humbled, a reminder of our place in the universe. We are but one of these leaves.' He stopped, watching a pure golden leaf flutter down to join its kin on the ground.

I didn't wholly understand what he meant and part of me wondered if he was talking to himself. I stayed quiet and observed the magic unfolding all around me. 'We can never truly exist,' he mused.

'What do you mean?' I asked earnestly. I loved the way he sometimes spoke in riddles.

'We're just a speck on the face of the universe,' he answered. 'The cosmos, nature, time, everything, it all goes on forever. It's eternal, constant. Our time on this planet, living, breathing, is just a tiny, tiny, *tiny* fraction of that. If you were to see forever in the space of a day, we would not be seen, not any of us. You, me, your people, my people, we would not even be perceived as a dot or a blur. We would be non-existent.' He paused, looking up at something that I hadn't noticed. 'But *they* would be here from the beginning to the end and beyond.'

I looked to where he was staring and saw there a beautiful female, her hair crowned with golden flowers, her body cloaked in a shawl of leaves. I heard her voice in my mind and all around us, like the forest itself was speaking. Her voice was loud yet barely a whisper, deep and high, welcoming and uninviting, kind and cruel. She seemed to have many voices, each one saying something different to the last. 'Come on,' Thane urged. 'We've outstayed our welcome.'

We exited the forest and I asked Thane who the woman was. 'They are what you people would refer to as Gods. They created this land and they protect it.'

'But I thought your people protected it?'

'We do, to an extent. We keep order and peace, maintain and observe but they are the real keepers.'

'You say they—are there more of them?'

'Yes, many more. They are in the sky, in the air, in the earth, in the seas and rivers, in the forests. They are called Elementals.'

I suddenly remembered the faerie who had led me to the Other Place and how she had said that she was a part of nature. How she and her sisters had created the shockwave that had killed some of the merpeople. Something told me to keep that memory to myself, however. 'That's beautiful. It reminds me of the Norse Gods. Are there any evil ones?' I questioned.

'There's no evil in them. Evil is a mortal curse and they don't have dealings with us. As I said, they were here at the beginning and they'll be here at the end, if there is such a thing. We are nothing to them. They don't feel mortal emotions. They are solitary, each the keeper of their own realm.'

Once again, my mind drifted back to the Elemental who had appeared to me so often in my life, and I wondered, if what Thane said was true, why she'd appeared to me at all.

Somehow, despite the magnificence of his story, I felt sad. I was miniscule and pointless. If all this was truly real, it was too big for me to comprehend. What was the point in my life? I thought back to my life at home and what little I'd achieved. Compared to these beings, my life was unspeakably short, and I'd not done anything with it yet. I was suddenly overwhelmed with fear at the prospect that I was wasting my precious life. 'What's wrong?' Thane asked, concerned. 'You've gone pale.'

'All this,' I said, gesturing around me. 'I feel so small and insignificant.'

Thane sat down beside me and put his arm around my shoulders. 'Sara, you can't think like that. You can't search for reason and meaning in chaos or worry if you'll ever make a mark on this world, because truthfully, not many of us will. If we all thought that way, it would be the end of us.'

His words didn't have the desired effect and instead made me feel even more dismal and unimportant. 'What I mean to say is, life is what you make of it. The meaning is different for everyone—there is no answer. To live, to love, to reproduce, to learn, to progress, to share; these hold true meaning. Don't search for answers as you'll likely never find them. I still haven't found any great meaning in mine yet and I doubt I ever will, but life is in the journey, the discovering. The answer, I believe, will not be found until the end.'

I found more comfort in these words than the previous, but still I felt downcast. I had come on a journey of discovery and instead had opened a Pandora's Box of questions and riddles I never knew I wanted answers to. Even after all the time I'd had to contemplate and after all our discussions, I still had absolutely no idea where I was, what I was doing there or where I was going. But then, is that not life summed up?

Chapter Thirty

We came to a quaint, closed-in woodland, more akin to those back at home than the ethereal, sweeping forests we had ventured through so far. I was put instantly at ease but of course, nothing in that place would be as simple as it first seemed. This was not an ordinary wood but the home of the Fae.

Set into the trunks of the trees were tiny doors and windows. They were so small that it took me a while to even notice they were there. Every door was a different bright colour; some adorned with numbers, others with miniscule letterboxes and doorknockers. I noticed tiny washing lines strung up in the neat gardens and some even had benches positioned outside the doors.

Through the windows I could see rooms full of everyday objects, only a fraction of the normal size. Lights beamed out through some of those windows but there was no sign of any inhabitants who, judging by the size of their homes, were only a few inches tall. 'Are these faerie homes?' I asked Thane, my voice disbelieving and full of joy.

'Yes, the Fae folk. Don't be fooled by their size—they're not always as sweet as they appear.'

'But still, I dreamed of a place like this as a kid! Where are they all?'

'My guess is they're having a gathering.'

'Like a party?'

'I suppose you could call it that.'

'I hope we see them. I would hate to miss my one chance of meeting some faeries.'

I was not disappointed. Before long, we happened across the Fae gathering. It was held in a clearing; the boughs of the trees high above arched over and intertwined so that it appeared we had entered a grand, golden hall. Thane and I stayed within the cover of trees on the outskirts, trying not to draw attention to ourselves.

The hall was alight with a thousand fireflies and the trees were decorated with pretty banners and ribbons. The scene was straight from a children's storybook. Tables and benches were set up all around the clearing and at the far end, a group of musicians played merry songs on strange instruments. I had never seen anything like it before.

The feast was truly a feast: fresh meats of all kinds were laid out amongst nuts, berries and pastries. My stomach growled at the sight of all the delicious food and I longed to join the celebrations.

The Fae, it seemed, came in all shapes and sizes. There were some who were tiny, as I'd expected, with fluttering, delicate wings and others taller than Thane with luminescent skin and ghostly, flowing garments. 'You want to join in, don't you?' Thane asked me.

'More than anything,' I replied, my eyes twinkling with excitement and longing.

'Come on then.' He took my hand and led me into the clearing. The Fae didn't stop to look at us or ask who we were. They appeared to know Thane and it seemed it was enough for them that I was accompanying him. Our first stop was the food tables. The feast was delicious, but I was soon full after eating so little for so long. We drank syrupy sweet mead and ate the scrumptious food until we were stuffed full and merry. The enchanting, spritely music drifted on the air, lighting fires in the minds of all who heard it for miles around.

The band began to play a twinkling, catchy tune and I instantly felt a tingling sensation in my fingers and toes. The faeries all took their places in a circle at the centre of the clearing and clapped gently in time to the beat.

I felt like my body was no longer my own; I was enchanted by the music. Thane took my hand and walked me into the centre of the circle. He turned to face me and began a slow, rhythmic dance. I followed suit, picking up the moves easily. As the tempo quickened, the faeries continued to clap and stamp their feet in time, some even shouted and jumped for joy. All around us, a sea of gleeful faces watched us as we stepped and swayed along to the melody. When the song was about to reach its summit, it stopped abruptly. The sound of a violin, or the Fae form of a violin, echoed around the hall, the haunting notes stretching out into the night.

Thane grasped me by the waist and pulled me to him. Our noses were almost touching. I looked into his eyes and was mesmerised. He twirled me and spun me; we glided around the circle as gracefully as lilies swaying in the summer breeze.

The rest of the crowd joined in at once as the song resumed its upbeat tempo, the beat getting faster and faster. We danced and danced until I was sure I would collapse. The song reached its almighty climax with applause and cheers from the crowd. Thane and I remained entwined in the middle of it all, unable to tear our eyes away from each other. It took us a few moments but eventually, we broke our gazes and re-joined the party.

Never have I ever felt part of something so magical, so extraordinary, in all my life. I felt a joy so powerful and all-consuming that for one glorious night all the bad in the world was completely forgotten. I later learned that the Fae name for that hall was Utopia.

The party went on late into the night. Dawn was approaching when I finally felt tired and Thane led me away from the clearing. Nearby, hung between the trees, were many pale, sheer drapes, rippling gently in the breeze. Thane pulled aside one such veil and revealed within a bed of flowers. He guided me inside as fireflies buzzed around us, bathing our surroundings in a warm glow.

He kissed my mouth, my cheeks, my shoulders, and then laid me down tenderly on the bed of flowers.

*****

The sun's morning rays piercing through the boughs overhead awoke me. I breathed in the sweet, fresh air and listened to the sound of fluttering wings and chattering faeries all around us.

Thane was laid awake beside me, looking troubled. Something was happening to him that he didn't understand. He felt close to me in a way that was much akin to his relationship with his brothers, yet with all the passion he usually felt for his female lovers. He had never felt so close to a woman before, not in all his years. The women hunters were like his brothers, sharing respect and camaraderie, and the women he had loved he'd never shared the bond of friendship with as well as lust. To find someone he felt both things for was such a new and confusing feeling.

That morning when we had made love, it had felt entirely different to our previous sexual encounters. It hadn't been animalistic, purely about the pleasure; it had been emotional. We had each relished every intake of breath, every movement the other had made, and we'd watched each other, memorising every part of each other's bodies.

We both laid awake a while, not speaking, just enjoying the sounds of the woods and the tranquillity. I was truly comfortable for the first time in…what? Days? Weeks? Months? We made the most of not having to rush off to the next place.

The sun climbed high in the sky and we knew it was time to move on. Reluctantly, we exited our sanctuary, only to find our clothes missing. A stooped, wrinkly, tiny man led us to a beautiful pool where he suggested we wash. We obliged happily, dropping the sheets we had wrapped around ourselves unashamedly and dipping ourselves into the cool, refreshing waters.

When we exited sometime later, our clothes were waiting for us, freshly washed and dried. We thanked the faeries as we passed them by on our way through the woods and continued on our journey.

The trees fell away and we left the thickness of the woods behind. A vast field of bluebells sprawled out before us. In the centre of the field, amongst the vibrant flowers, sat a faerie. She was human-size, maybe a little more petite. Her hair was pulled into a severe bun and she wore a dress of black threaded with gold. Her eyes were sad and her demeanour downcast. 'She looks miserable. Should we see what's wrong?' I whispered.

Thane shook his head. 'I think she wishes to be left alone.'

'But what can she be so sad about?' I enquired, gesturing to the beautiful, lush field.

'She lives in an enchanted kingdom. I don't think I'd ever be sad if I lived here.'

'There is pain, corruption, secrets and grief in all societies, no matter where in the world you are,' Thane replied. 'Come on, we need to get going.'

We passed the grief-stricken faerie and my heart was filled with a deep sadness.

*****

It was a warm and fragrant night. Thane sat by the fireside, sharpening his sword, keeping watch while I dozed beside him. We were camped by the side of a river, overlooking golden fields that appeared to stretch all the way to the ends of the Earth.

Thane wasn't comfortable with the idea of us sleeping in the dark, out in the open and unprotected. He believed we were vulnerable, though I didn't sense any danger there. There was no arguing with him though, so he kept watch and let me sleep.

That night was the first full darkness we'd had in three days, by my reckoning, so I was taking full advantage of it. It had been three terribly long days of walking in the blistering heat with no shade or refuge, no sunset and barely any rest. We were both exhausted and nauseous.

My sleep was unbroken and deep. I was out for the count for a good few hours without even slightly stirring. Thane was watching my chest rise and fall as I breathed, enjoying the peaceful look on my face. He stood and sheathed his sword then scouted in a tight circle around our camp. Each viewpoint was the same as the last: the solid black line of the Earth resting beneath a deep indigo sky. Nothing else; no clouds, no shadows, no movement, not even any sounds. But still, he kept watch.

Something was whispering to me, flutters of familiar words drifting through the dark. Harsh hisses and soft murmurs. In my mind's eye, I could see where my mortal body lay sleeping. In the dream, I was alone and Thane was no longer watching over me.

The dim light and deep shadows were moving, chasing each other, but one shadow remained static; a substantial form of darkness deeper than the black of night. It was talking to me. I didn't understand the alien words but, in my dream, I knew their meaning.

The rushing of the nearby river seemed closer now, louder. The once gentle sound which had eased me into sleep was now a raucous din, thundering in my ears. My chest was tight, my lungs burning. I was reminded instantly of my terrifying experience in the sea with the mermaids and it set my heart racing. I could see my still body laying deeply asleep below me, but I could feel myself drowning.

Thane could see something moving in the darkness, but he couldn't tell for sure how close it was. The endless uniformity of the landscape muddied his depth perception. Then, he heard a scuffling sound and felt a vibration in the ground beneath his feet, but still the darkness continued to confuse his senses. He thought that it must only be a wild animal, yet he stayed stock-still, his eyes wide and ears alert, listening intently.

The shadowy form, which a mortal eye wouldn't have spotted in the blackness, was still ahead, unmoving. Again came the scuffling sound in the dry dirt. Something wasn't right. He felt eyes watching him.

All of a sudden, the form was before him. It had moved whip-fast without detection and before he could react, Thane was knocked unconscious.

Inside Thane's mind, he could see me in a long, white gown, still sleeping soundly. I was in the arms of a cloaked, dark figure. Its face wasn't visible but he could see the outline of its spindly antlers protruding from beneath its hood. Long, bony fingers stroked my hair and my face, soothing me, and still, I slept soundly.

Stone-cold dread filled Thane until his veins felt full of lead. He fought the overwhelming urge to sleep. After what felt like a long time, rather than the mere seconds it had been, he brought himself around. As quickly as his stiff legs would allow, he got to his feet and searched around for me.

I was no longer laying peacefully where he'd left me. A devastating need to find me overtook him and he focussed all his senses, his strong body coiled and ready to take action.

Water—splashing, gurgling. Thane spun around. I was in the river. He ran to me, but I was now deathly still. He jumped into the icy water without hesitation, his arms instinctively reaching out for me. He wrapped his arms tightly around me and dragged me from those bitter depths.

First, he checked my airways were clear, then he pressed on my chest rhythmically. The seconds dragged on and Thane's heart was in his mouth. Eventually, I spluttered back to life, a surge of murky water erupting from my lungs. Thane held me sat upright, keeping his arm firmly around my shoulders until all the filth had come out. 'Sara! Are you okay?' he gasped.

I coughed violently in reply. My throat and chest felt like they had been scrubbed with sandpaper. 'I thought I'd lost you,' he murmured, holding me tight.

It took a while for me to get over that experience. I didn't sleep well for a long time, constantly fearing daemons would come for me in my sleep.

Something changed inside me after that. I didn't want to die; not there, not a million miles away from my family and my home, not when I'd achieved so little. I felt an overwhelming desire to leave that place and never look back, but I still hadn't found any answers and had no idea how to get home.

Thane sensed the change in me. As the sun began to set on yet another long, exhausting day, he couldn't help but feel that it was a metaphor. He'd thought that his heroism and act of love in saving me would strengthen my love for him, but it wasn't enough to douse the terror and sadness I now felt. He felt the sun was now setting on our day in the sun.

*****

Finally, after a long journey of ups and downs, we reached Thane's home. The village was made up of log cabins and large canvas tents, and the whole place was bursting with life. His people were weathered and dirty, but their eyes were full of mirth and wit, much like Thane's.

Thane greeted each and every person with open arms and inside jokes that I couldn't understand. He introduced me to as many of his people as he could, though I don't remember their names now. Except one: Elezra.

Elezra was a true warrior—she was exceptionally tall and lithe, Amazonian even. She stood in the fashion of one who was a natural-born fighter: legs spread apart and anchored to the ground with heavy boots, heels dug in, anticipating the next move, and her hands on her hips, fists clenched.

Her face was pretty—not in a youthful, innocent way but strong and striking. Her hardened expression and intelligent eyes did away with any appearance of loveliness. Her hair was dirty and matted, dreadlocks and plaits hidden within its thick, dark mass. She was as wild and untameable as the wind and the sea.

At first, I thought she hated me, but we soon became fast friends. As much as I'd enjoyed my time alone with Thane, it was refreshing to be around other people, and such interesting people at that. They all welcomed me into their fold and I found such pleasure in seeing first-hand their way of life and hearing their tales of great battles, far-off lands and magic.

Sometimes, I let my mind wander and imagined remaining there. It was a beautiful, simple, earthy place and the people were both wise and humble, easy to get along with, but I knew I couldn't. I remembered my near-death experience all too clearly and I longed for my home and my family.

Although I still had no answers for my purpose in the Other Place, I felt I'd at least found my own reason for being there. I may not have learned much about the place itself, but I was gaining knowledge about myself every day.

Thane and I remained close, though I refused to let our relationship develop as I knew it would make it harder to leave when the time came. I resolved to enjoy the time we had left together and to not think too much about the future. We talked and we laughed, and we made love endlessly, until the time came that I had to finally face the road ahead—the way back.

Chapter Thirty-One

'Is the only way back through the sea?' I asked Thane one stormy night while we were huddled around the fire inside his hut.

He shook his head. 'No, it can't take you back.'

'So, how do I get home?'

Thane sighed deeply. 'I've asked you before so I think I know the answer, but is there any way you could ever call this home?'

As much as I'd grown to love Thane's village and the people who dwelled there, I was not my mother. I would never forgive myself if I didn't return home. I longed to see Myla and Lyanna and feel the warmth and comfort of their presence. 'If I had no family, I could easily stay here. You know how I feel about this place, but I—'

Thane raised his hand. 'Please, don't finish. I understand.' Thane gazed into the fire, his mind far away, possibly imagining another life where I was his and he was mine. 'Will you ever return?'

'I can't see into the future.'

'But do you intend to?'

'Of course, but so much could happen! Who knows what I would return to?'

'If you told me you were coming back, I'd wait for you. I wouldn't take another.'

'I know you would and that's why I can't tell you that. I couldn't tie myself to this place, to promise you that I'll return when I don't know if I will, knowing that you would be waiting for me. It's too cruel.'

'You have such a beautiful, honest heart.'

'Thanks.' I smiled. 'Do you know if you can cross over?'

'I admit it's something I've wondered about. The truth is, I don't know. None of my people have managed it and I wouldn't like to be the first to try.'

'I get that.'

We both sat quietly watching the flickering flames for a while. 'So,' I said, at length, 'how do I get home?'

'There's only one way back: the Pool of Infinity.'

'How long will it take me to get there?'

'Sara, you know we don't measure time.'

'I know, I know, but surely you have a measure of distance?'

'The land shifts and changes as you well know. If the land wants us to get there quickly, it will let us. Part of me hopes that it hinders us.'

'Us?'

'I'm coming with you, of course.'

'But surely you have things to do here? You've been away for so long already.'

'Nothing is as important as cherishing every moment with you.'

His gaze was penetrating me, seeing beneath my exterior and into my soul. I kissed him then and we grasped each other as though we never wanted to let go.

Times like that, lying together before the fire, sharing each other's energy and love, weakened my resolve. How could I leave when I'd found something so perfect? This was not what I'd come searching for, but it was better than anything I could have imagined. Even though I was leaving without any answers to the questions I'd so badly desired, I knew I'd found something I truly needed: knowledge of myself, of the world and a reason to live.

*****

The next morning, just before sunrise, Thane and I set out on the last leg of our journey. Our hearts were heavy and our thoughts were black. Neither of us spoke for a good long while, each of us wallowing in our own pits of misery.

The downward slope of our road eased our legs for a short time but before long, we began to climb steadily uphill. The autumnal, golden scenery of Thane's village turned austere and gloomy. The sun disappeared behind the ashen clouds and the vibrant colours dissolved into endless shades of grey. The trees were leafless and twisted, the grass worn and dying, and the atmosphere cold, stiff and uninviting. The land reflected our moods. 'There's something I didn't tell you about our road,' Thane confessed.

'What's that?'

211

'I didn't want to tell you because I didn't want you to worry. There's no other way to get to the Pool. We must pass through the Veil.'

'And that is?'

'It's what your people may think of as a purgatory.'

I swallowed nervously. 'But you must remember that whatever you see, whatever we encounter, they can't hurt you. They are wandering souls, caught in the cracks between our worlds.'

'H-how did they get there?'

'Well, that's the other reason I didn't tell you.'

'What?' I asked, frustrated. 'Tell me. Stop trying to shield me.'

'They were wanderers like you, trapped between the planes, unable to live in either.'

'Why though? How did they get there?'

'They couldn't choose. They didn't completely want to be in either place, so they're doomed to wander for all eternity between the planes of existence.' He turned to me, stopping me in my stride. His expression was intent and solemn. 'Sara, when you enter the Pool, you must be whole-heartedly resolved to go back. There can't be any trace of doubt in your mind.'

A revelation struck me; this could go some way to explain why my mother had never returned to us. She had been drawn into her new life, had forged new relationships and, as much as she'd wanted to see her daughter and her sisters again, it had been too much of a risk. Deep down, she knew she was not resolved in her decision to enter the Pool and the risk of getting caught in the Veil was too great. 'Sara? Sara?' Thane shook me by the shoulders, jolting me out of my reverie. 'Promise me.'

'I promise,' I replied, though in my heart I was uncertain. It was all so much to take in. 'Do we absolutely have to go through the Veil? Is there no other way?'

'I already told you—no. It's the only way.'

'Why is it like that? Why is the land laid out that way?'

'The land uses it as a tool to keep people here.'

'You say that like the land can think and feel and act.'

'It can. It's a warning, showing you what you could become. Most won't attempt to cross over once they've seen those trapped in the Veil.'

'But why would the land want to keep us here?'

'Because it's greedy. It feeds off life, off our energy.'

'Well,' I exhaled, steeling myself. 'What are we waiting for then?'

After miles of nothing but bleak desolation, fear set in, though I tried to hide it from Thane. Here and there, souls strayed, and I knew we'd reached the Veil. 'Are they dead or alive?' I whispered.

'Both. They're conscious beings, but they can't be described as living. They don't eat or sleep or feel like living things.'

'And they stay this way forever?'

Thane nodded. 'It's just awful,' I stammered, tears filling my eyes.

The pale, ghostly figures didn't acknowledge us, which I was extremely grateful for, yet I felt terribly wrong being there amongst them, like I was trespassing on something secret. I found myself thinking, over and over, that we shouldn't have been there, but I couldn't help fearing that I might be joining them on the other side very soon.

We trudged further into the haunted land and more and more souls appeared around us. I was shocked at how many there were, having once been so sure I was the only person on the planet who could visit the Other Place. How wrong I'd been. Before long, we were walking among a whole host of them. I remember thinking how eerily beautiful they were. Well, as beautiful as death can be.

Through the hoards, I could see a long, narrow, stone bridge leading to enormous, ornate gates. All along the bridge, ominous stone daemons watched and waited, their lifeless eyes searing into us. Part of me expected to see a scorching inferno through those gates, but there was only a faint azure glow. Everything was creepily calm, quiet and dark. A spooky glimmer hung about the place like a phantom vapour; bluish and pale. 'Where do those gates lead?' I asked, trembling.

'That's where they leave. They are herded there from the Pool, the gates open and they're left to roam the land.'

I had never been truly scared until that moment. Even when I had been nearly drowned by the daemon in the river, I hadn't been fully conscious, so I had been unaware of the mortal danger I'd been in. Now, I was all too aware and alert.

Before I had reached that place, fear had been a weightless, superficial emotion, felt during horror movies or after a particularly bad dream. It had always been fleeting and would pass at the flick of a light switch. Now, I knew what real fear was. It gripped my bones, my organs, my every nerve. This was true fear, not the kind I felt when there was a moth in my bedroom; this was life or death. I could become one of them, very soon.

Thane gripped my hand and led me through the mass of bodies and at the feel of his firm grip, something amazing happened. Through the dread and despair, my mind broke free and I was filled with the will to keep going. This was life or death and I chose life.

We made it through the Veil and at the other end, we took some time to rest and reflect. 'I understand why some would choose not to attempt to cross over after seeing those poor people,' I observed.

'Nobody has attempted it in your lifetime,' Thane responded.

'How can you possibly know that?'

'I don't *know* it, but I do know that it has almost passed from my memory the last I heard of someone crossing over.'

'That fills me with hope,' I answered sarcastically.

We made camp and remained there to sleep. The ground was frosty and the air felt cold and damp. We didn't sleep easily.

When we awoke, we set off in haste, walking for miles and miles until the sun began to set. The scenery remained unchanging. Our path didn't turn, go uphill or downhill; it remained flat and straight. The dark, brooding trees continued to wall us in on either side and the chill mist and drizzle were unceasing. The place was miserable yet sombrely pretty.

Yet again, we set up camp, both of us stalling for time before we reached the place where I would depart, possibly forever. We set up a tent and attempted to start a fire, though the conditions made this a long and arduous task. We managed to start a small fire, but it soon dampened and fizzled out.

We sat in the entrance to our tent, looking out into the darkness, listening to the sounds of nature all around us. The drizzle was only light, but the drops filtered down from leaf to leaf, getting heavier and heavier, building momentum, until they dropped loudly on to the roof of the tent and the hard ground. The atmosphere was hushed, time was paused, waiting for the rain to cease and joy to be returned to the world once more.

At next light, we reached the end of the trees and entered vast, open fields. The rain finally stopped but a mist still hung heavy in the air, shielding us from unwelcome gazes.

After a long while walking through stark fields, the weather changing from dismal to miserable and back again, the endless fields gave way to hills and moorlands. Jagged rocks jutted out from the earth and, instead of pale green peeping through the mist, the colours were earthy deep greens and browns. I was reminded of my beloved Yorkshire.

We found ourselves upon a rocky precipice, overlooking a boggy marshland. Ahead, as far as the eye could see, were wet, heavy hills and a blackening sky. The atmosphere was oppressive and creepily quiet as the dark clouds above sunk lower, ready to offload their mass.

We emerged out of the marshes onto a network of stony paths. The path we took was sheltered by trees, so the ground was less wet and muddy. My mood lifted as my hair and clothes finally started to dry out.

Our last night together was much more cheerful than any other night since we'd left the home comforts of the village. We sang songs and told stories around the fire, laughed heartily and made love one final, glorious time. 'I think we will arrive at the Pool before the next sundown,' Thane admitted as I lay in his arms.

I sighed heavily, a great weight settling on my shoulders. 'I don't want to leave you, but I have to,' I said as tears spilled down my cheeks.

'Please, don't cry. We're not at the end yet,' he told me, wiping my tears away.

'I know, but I just can't bear it. I hate goodbyes.'

'I think we'll meet again.'

'Do you really?'

'I do. Our fates are entwined.'

'I hope so.'

'You know though, don't you, that I'll wait for you?'

'Please, don't put that on me as well. I couldn't bear to break your heart.'

'But it's already broken.'

'So's mine.'

'If we don't see each other again, and I mean *if*,' he stressed, 'you know I'll always love you and I'll think of you every day.'

'And I you.'

We fell asleep in each other's arms, though we didn't sleep soundly. We were fighting sleep; every time one of us dropped off, we would jolt awake suddenly, hold each other tighter and fight the weariness once more, until eventually, the sun rose on our last day together.

As predicted, we arrived at our destination not long before the following sunset. We reached the top of a steep hill and below us lay the Pool of Infinity. From where we were stood, it appeared to be an ordinary waterfall pouring down into a peaceful lake, attractive but not unique in any way. We climbed down the mountainside until we reached the water's edge.

The sun had now set. We stood looking out over the Pool; its glass-like surface reflecting the galaxies, the stars, the nebulas, which were so magnificently lighting up the sky above. 'I understand now why it's named the Pool of Infinity.'

Thane remained silent. 'Is this it now? Is it time?' I asked. 'Must I go now?'

He turned to me and kissed me.

'That's your choice. And remember, make it wholly; there must be no doubt in your mind.'

I think he hoped I would tell him that I wanted to go back with him and forget all about my other life but of course, I couldn't do that. 'I suppose it's now or never.'

I was gripped with nerves and fear. I didn't want to leave him. Every part of me was screaming to stay with him. How often did people find a love like this? I grabbed him and embraced him fiercely, weeping uncontrollably. 'Why do I have to make such an impossible choice?'

'Ssh, ssh,' he soothed, stroking my hair. 'I'm sorry but you must make it, whether you want to or not.'

I looked up into his glistening eyes. 'I know, but I feel as though I'm being torn in two.'

'You're not. You are whole and I will always be a part of you. Sara, it's time.'

He helped me tighten my bag straps and smoothed down my hair affectionately. 'How do I do it?' I asked, feeling like a child leaving their parent for the first time.

'Swim out as far as you can until your feet no longer touch the ground, then fully immerse yourself. Don't think of me, think only of your destination, your home. You mustn't think of me, Sara. Do you understand?'

I nodded, entirely distraught and unable to bring myself to leave his side. 'You have to be strong. Focus on your family. Don't think of me until you reach the other side.'

I nodded again, still unable to speak.

He kissed me one last time then let go of my hand, signalling it was time for me to leave. 'I love you, Sara,' he breathed.

'I love you too.'

Unbearably, I tore my eyes away from his, knowing that I couldn't look back again. I waded out into the Pool until the water rose up to my chin. Then, I let go. I couldn't look back, but I could still feel his presence, those deep eyes watching me, comforting me.

I let myself float there on my back and then I saw it—the universe. I was transported through space and time; all the galaxies and colours and flecks of light swirled around me. I was a giant swimming in the ocean of space, running my hands through nebulous mists, sending planets and stars spiralling away in all directions. I was weightless, floating through the great endless beyond.

I closed my eyes, cleared my mind and focussed all my thoughts on home: the faces of Myla and Lyanna, smiling with excitement at my return, welcoming me with open arms. I could hear their voices, smell their scents, feel the warmth of their skin on mine.

There was a sudden lurch, like I'd been dropped from a great height, and then, I heard the sound of birds and the feel of the ground beneath me. I opened my eyes.

Chapter Thirty-Two

It took me a while to get back on my feet; I was shaky and dizzy, feeling like I'd plummeted from the top of a skyscraper. I looked around, getting my bearings, and sighed with relief as I realised that I was back in the grounds of Moraine Manor.

I yelled at the top of my lungs with glee, my voice echoing all around. I heard the flutter of bird's wings as they took flight in fright. After a few seconds, their twittering resumed.

The day was overcast yet bright. Somehow, I'd expected things to look different, but of course, the grounds had remained the same for many decades. I was apprehensive at the thought of what I was going to find once I returned home. I had two options: go to Lyanna's or Myla's first? I chose Lyanna's—I owed her that much.

I caught the bus home. It felt strange being back amongst 'ordinary people' and hearing the sounds of traffic and other mundane, every-day noises. There was so much concrete everywhere. I was changed and I would never look at the world in the same way again. I thought about Thane and my heart ached. I wondered what he was doing at that moment and how he was feeling.

Surprisingly, I actually felt glad to be back. I missed Thane greatly, but I was also eager to see Lyanna and Myla, to tell them all about my journey and find out how they were.

As I approached Lyanna's front door, I hesitated. I don't know why, but I felt nervous. I steeled myself and knocked on the door. I had never knocked on that door in my entire life, but I now felt like a stranger. I hoped that she wasn't at work; I had no idea what day or month it was.

Lyanna opened the door, much to my relief, and at the sight of me, nearly collapsed in shock. 'Sara?' She threw her arms around me desperately, before ushering me inside.

Out of habit, I made my way through to the kitchen and took a seat at the island. 'Wow, you really stink, do you know that?'

I laughed. 'I suppose I will. Sorry.'

'Oh my God, I don't care. I just can't believe you're back,' she exclaimed, tears rolling down her face.

'I'm so sorry. Were you really worried?'

'Of course I was—I was so mad at you for doing that to me! Furious, even, but you're back and it's been barely any time at all. I'm so glad you're back, I don't even care how mad I was.'

I looked at her, puzzled. 'What do you mean?'

'I've been going out of my mind with worry. I don't think I could have taken it another week.'

'No, I mean, what do you mean, *barely any time at all*?'

Now, she looked puzzled. Then her expression changed to joy and she embraced me. 'I'm just so glad you're home safe, back with me where you belong.'

'Me too.' I smiled, inhaling her familiar scent. 'But Lyanna,' I pulled away, 'how long have I been gone?'

'Don't tell me you've lost track of the days already?' she joked, busying herself filling the kettle with water.

'No, I'm being serious,' I said. I felt off, like the world was tilting.

'You've been gone a week.'

My jaw quite literally dropped and I choked on my words, unable to speak. 'What's wrong?' she asked, looking concerned.

'A week?' I managed.

'Yes, why?'

'Lyanna, I've been gone months, maybe even a year.'

'What are you talking about?'

'I'm being serious. I've been gone a long time.'

Lyanna still looked sceptical and worried. 'Look, if you don't believe me,' I pulled the elastic out of my hair, proving that my hair had grown considerably since I'd last seen her.

Lyanna stared at me in disbelief. 'I've been gone a long, long time. I travelled for miles and miles, stayed with two different communities, I…' I stopped talking. A realisation struck me full force.

'What is it?'

'Oh my God,' I breathed, as the whole world shifted beneath my feet.

'Sara, you've gone grey. What is it?'

I did the math in my head. If time passed so much faster there than it did here, then I may never see Thane again. If each week here was roughly a year there then, despite Thane's long lifespan, it could mean if I went back in a year, he could be gone.

I was overwhelmed with emotion. It hit me—everything I'd seen, done, experienced—it all dawned on me in one great tidal wave. I started to cry.

Lyanna came over and put her arms around me. I rested my head against her chest and let the tears fall. 'Come on, tell me about it.'

'I will, but first, I want to get a shower and eat and sleep in a bed.' I was utterly exhausted and suddenly felt it, all the way to my bones. I stood up and staggered across the kitchen, wondering how I was going to make it up the stairs. 'Lyanna, will you let Myla know for me?' I slurred.

'Of course.'

I washed away the filth of what felt like a thousand days, put on a pair of Lyanna's pyjamas and climbed into my old, huge, soft bed. I slept for hours, deeply and undisturbed. When I awoke, it was evening according to the clock on my bedside table.

I padded downstairs, feeling like a new person, though still groggy. My heart leapt at the sight of Myla, sitting in the front room watching the television with Lyanna. I had missed them both so much. 'Myla!' I exclaimed as I entered the room.

'Sara!' She stood up and went to embrace me, then stopped herself short. 'You arsehole! How could you do that to us! How could you do that to *me*?' She punched me, not softly, in the shoulder.

I was gobsmacked and hurt, though part of me had been expecting it. Then she grabbed me and hugged me forcefully and I knew she hadn't meant it. 'I'm glad you're back,' she whispered into my ear.

Lyanna ordered us some food—my favourite, pizza—and after we ate, me savouring every single mouthful, I told them everything.

I told them how I got to the Other Place, how I'd met my mother on the other side and spent time with her in her village and then, how I'd gone on ahead, alone. I told them about Thane, how we'd fallen in love, all the things we saw and experienced together and how we'd lived together a while in his community.

I explained the Veil, as best I could, and the Pool of Infinity and how I'd returned home. By the time I'd finished my tale, it was pitch black outside.

They couldn't believe all that I'd done and yet, to them, it had been such a short space of time. They'd barely had time to miss me whereas I had begun to forget the details of their faces.

Although they'd listened intently, engrossed in my story, and asked me questions, especially about my mum and Thane, I could tell that part of them was struggling to place that world in their reality. How could they go to work and university, pay bills and watch the news *and* believe everything I had told them? Of course, they didn't think I was lying, but without seeing it for themselves, I had to accept that part of them would never truly believe it was real. Hell, part of me couldn't believe it was real. Being back in the real world, where nothing had changed, I felt like my time in the Other Place had been nothing more than an extremely vivid dream.

Once again—and not for the last time—my mother's words played over in my mind: *You can't live in both worlds, they can't exist simultaneously in your mind.* When I had been there, the thought of returning home had filled me with dread, like it wasn't mine anymore, like I didn't belong there. Back home, with all my home comforts, the thought of returning to the Other Place made me feel scared and tired. I couldn't believe what I'd done, what I'd accomplished on my own. The person I was at home was a different person to who I'd been there. How could I ever reconcile the two?

One thing that remained unchanged were my feelings for Thane. I wished I could see him again. I wished he could have come back with me and been by my side, telling my aunt and my best friend our story together. But I knew now, that could never happen. I couldn't merge the two worlds, as much as I couldn't merge the two people inside of me. They existed on two separate planes and to try and force them together, would be paradoxical. I was an anomaly, able to walk between the two worlds. The wanderer, that was my true name.

Could I accept that? Could I be two people? Could I be the wanderer without knowing why? Could I accept that I may never know why?

Life went back to 'normal'. After reflection, soul-searching and some much less romantic job-searching, after all I'd been through, the journey I'd embarked upon, I ended up back at the beginning—back at Armchair Books. I explained to Isaac that I'd received help with my depression and was now doing a lot better.

He didn't need much persuading as we'd gotten on so well before, so he rehired me there and then.

Sometimes, back in that place, back to my old way of life, it really did feel like I'd never actually been to the Other Place. Thane, and the love I still harboured for him, was the only thing that convinced me it had all really happened. Nobody could dream up something that realistic, could they? I missed him terribly and spoke of him all the time to Myla and Lyanna, trying to keep him close and convince myself that he was still a part of my life. I wished there was a postal service between our worlds; I would have written to him every day. That was a humorous, yet pleasing, daydream.

The years passed by and my love for him never dwindled. I didn't even entertain the notion of dating again; my heart was wholly his and I held onto hope that I would one day return to him. That was, until I met Bastian.

*****

It was the winter of my 25th year and I was wrapped up in layers of jumpers and scarves, working in the cold bookshop. Outside, the rain was hammering down hard, bouncing off the pavement, obscuring the view. I was in the back of the shop when I heard the heavy creak of the door opening and closing, and the little bell tinkled to make me aware someone had entered the shop. I peered through the gaps in the shelves and saw the figure of a man shaking the droplets of water from his umbrella before placing it in the stand by the door. 'I won't be a minute!' I called.

'That's okay,' he replied. 'I'm just browsing.'

'Okay, well, I'm right here if you need me for anything,' I assured him and continued ordering the stock.

It was mid-week, so there were only two of us working. Isaac had gone out for his lunch and I was holding the fort alone.

The customer worked his way around to the back of the store, stopping in the science fiction and fantasy section, right beside the horror section where I was currently working. I didn't look up; I sensed that he was the sort of customer who liked to browse in peace.

I sensed the man getting closer to me until I saw out of the corner of my eye that he was right beside me. I suddenly felt very uncomfortable, aware that he was watching me and that I was completely alone, backed into a corner. 'Sorry,' he apologised. 'I didn't mean to make you feel uncomfortable, but do I know you from somewhere?'

I turned, looking at him properly for the first time, and gasped loudly, my eyes wide with shock. It was Thane. 'I...I...' I stammered, unsure what to say.

'You recognise me, don't you?' he said, telling me, rather than asking me.

I nodded, uncomprehending. 'I can't work out where I know you from, though.'

The man before me was both Thane and not Thane. He looked exactly like him, down to his cornflower blue eyes, strong, slightly wonky nose, salt and pepper facial hair, the deep laughter lines around his mouth and eyes, his build and even his demeanour. The only difference was his shorter hair and modern clothing. The fact that he didn't know who I was confirmed to me that he wasn't Thane, yet somehow, he recognised me. I knew for certain that we had never met—our only connection was how much he looked like the man I loved. The divide between worlds was slipping, I could feel it, deep inside of me, like a great schism ripping everything apart. Suddenly, a piercing, throbbing ache shot through my head and I pressed my hands to my temples, wincing in agony. 'Are you okay?' he asked, concerned.

'Yes, sorry. Just a headache.' Unsure of what to say and entirely unsettled, I asked, 'Is there anything I can do for you?'

The man frowned in confusion. 'You do recognise me, don't you?'

I shook my head vehemently and turned back to the shelf I was working on. 'Have I offended you?'

I shook my head again, biting my lip nervously. 'Well, I'm sorry to have bothered you,' he mumbled, scratching his head in bewilderment, then strode out of the store, leaving his umbrella behind.

My knees buckled and I slumped down to the floor, inhaling a deep lungful of oxygen. What had just happened? Why did he look so much like Thane? How had *he* recognised *me*? I had too many questions; my head was spinning and my mind felt like it was going to split into two.

I worked the rest of my shift on autopilot, barely speaking a word to Isaac when he returned from his break. When I arrived home, I told Myla everything, but she could make no more sense of it than I could.

A few days later, I was working in the stockroom when Isaac came through and told me there was a customer asking after me. Wracking my brain to think who it could be, I walked out on to the shop floor and stopped as soon as I saw who it was. It was him. 'Hi,' he greeted me, looking nervous. He held up his umbrella. 'I came back for this,' he lied.

'Hi,' I replied, a wave of emotion rippling through me at the sight of his handsome, familiar face.

'Anyway,' he said, 'I was just wondering if you'd maybe like to come for a coffee?'

I heard Isaac snigger childishly behind me, before disappearing into the stockroom to give us some privacy. 'I don't think that's a good idea,' I replied flatly.

'Can I ask why not?'

'It's just not, okay?'

He nodded. 'Okay, but this isn't the last you've seen of me,' he promised and walked out of the shop, umbrella in hand.

'What was that all about?' Isaac asked, emerging from the stockroom.

'Don't ask,' I muttered.

'Do you know him?'

'No.'

'He seemed taken with you. Why don't you want to go out for coffee? He's a good-looking guy.'

'He came in the other day. I just don't like the look of him.'

'Why? Is he bothering you?' Isaac suddenly sounded concerned.

'No, no. Nothing like that. Look, not that it's any of my boss' business,' I grinned, 'but I'm just not in the frame of mind for dating.'

'And, not that it's any of my business, like you say,' he smiled, 'but it wouldn't hurt to go for coffee.'

He was right, except that *just going for coffee* could be the most complicated, terrifying thing I'd ever do.

When I left work at 5 pm, the man was waiting for me outside. I attempted to ignore him, put my hood up to shield myself from the biting wind and walked on by, but he wasn't giving up easily. 'Sara?'

The sound of my name spoken in Thane's voice sent a shiver down my spine. I swung around. 'How do you know my name?' I demanded.

'It's on your badge.'

'Oh, right.' I turned back around and continued walking.

'Why won't you talk to me?' he asked, following me.

'You ought to be careful—I could accuse you of stalking me.'

The sound of his footsteps ceased. 'Fine, I'll leave you alone.'

I stopped walking, feeling guilty. 'I'm sorry.'

'What's going on here?' he asked.

I stood there, my back to him, willing myself to turn around and look him in the eyes, but I couldn't. 'You wouldn't believe me if I told you,' I replied.

'Please, can we talk?'

I nodded, turning around to face him, but still unable to look up from the pavement. We walked in silence to the nearest café. I ordered myself a hot chocolate and sandwich, then we sat down awkwardly on the high stools facing out of the glass storefront onto the wintry scene. We sat quietly for a while, looking out at passers-by as they rushed from place to place trying to escape the cold.

At last, he said, 'I'm Bastian.'

I nodded. 'Look, I'm just going to come out with it. Since I came into the shop the other day, I haven't been able to get you out of my mind. I feel like I know you, and I know you recognise me by the way you looked at me. How do we know each other?'

'We don't,' I told him bluntly, taking a sip of my hot chocolate and still refusing to look at him.

'Will you look at me?' he asked, irritated.

I sighed and turned to face him. My eyes met his and I was transported through time and space, back into the arms of the man I loved. 'You do know me.'

I shook my head. 'I don't, I honestly don't. You just look like someone I know, that's all.'

'It's more than that.'

'It is. When I say, you look like him, I mean, you are his doppelganger.'

'And he is?'

'We were in love.'

'Right, so that's it?'

'That's it.'

'Then, how do I recognise *you*?'

'That I don't have an answer for. That's why it's so disturbing. I should know you, but you shouldn't know me.'

'This is weird.'

'I know.'

'Are you still together?'

'No,' I sighed. 'I haven't seen him in a long time.'

'Where is he?'

'In another place.' How else could I explain?

'If you don't mind me asking, how did you guys break up?'

'Long-distance relationship.'

He nodded, believing he understood when he really, really didn't.

I felt at ease with him. The encounter hadn't been as terrifying as I'd built it up in my head to be and I'd found it surprisingly easy to explain the situation away. 'So, Bastian, what do you do?' I asked, diverting the course of the conversation.

He raised his eyebrow at the change in topic and my tone of voice. He looked so much like Thane in that moment that I almost choked.

'I'm a photographer,' he answered.

I pulled myself together. 'Really? My best friend's a photographer.'

'Freelance?'

'Yeah.'

'Tough going, isn't it?'

'It can be, but she does alright for herself. What do you photograph?'

'I do music photography mostly: gig photos, album covers, magazine shoots, that sort of thing. I do landscapes as a hobby. I like to travel.'

'Wow, that sounds like fun.'

We chatted for hours until we were asked to leave by the staff who were ready to close up. Somehow, after actively avoiding him, I now didn't want to leave his company. 'Can I see you again?' he asked as we stepped outside into the biting cold night.

'Yeah,' I replied.

'When's your next shift at the shop?'

'Tomorrow. I get off at the same time.'

'I'll meet you outside the shop at five then.'

'Okay,' I agreed, then we parted ways.

On the way home, I thought about how fucked up the situation was. Did I like him for who he was? Or was I trying to feel closer to Thane? He wasn't him, I had to keep reminding myself. The lines were blurred and I had absolutely no idea how I was feeling or what was real. I was excited to see him again, but was I excited to see Bastian or Thane?

I thought about it all night and the following day at work, but as the end of my shift and the time to see him again approached, I felt no closer to figuring out my feelings. I supposed the only way to find out was to spend more time with him. At ten minutes to five, I saw him waiting outside and my heart skipped a beat. Love is a dangerous game.

Chapter Thirty-Three

'I thought we could go for a drink. There's a bar not far from here I usually go to,' Bastian suggested as we walked side by side down the tree-lined street. The lamplight glistened on the cobblestones and the wind blew bitterly, biting at my nose and cheeks.

'Drinking on a Wednesday?' I joked, my eyebrows raised mockingly.

'Hey, I'm not suggesting we get trashed.' He smiled. 'Just a little something to warm us up and settle the nerves.'

'You're nervous?'

'Aren't you?'

'Yeah, but I wasn't stupid enough to say it out loud.'

'You just did!'

I blushed. 'So, where's this bar?'

'Just around the corner.'

I let him lead the way. I found myself in a poky drinking establishment called Stewie's; I have to admit, it was pretty cool inside. Movie and gig posters covered the peeling walls and fake skeletons hung from the ceiling. Metallica's *Creeping Death* blared out as we took a seat in a booth, drinks in hand.

I sipped at my strawberry cider and looked around, appreciating the interesting décor. 'I can't believe I've never been here before—it's right up my street,' I mused.

'You approve?'

I nodded. 'What kind of music are you into?' he asked.

'Eighties stuff: rock, metal, a bit of pop. Sometimes, I feel like I was born in the wrong era.'

'I've always said that about myself, but I prefer the seventies.'

'Yeah, I love the seventies too. I don't like any modern music, really. I honestly couldn't tell you who's in the charts right now.'

'Me neither,' he concurred. 'Chart music all sounds the same to me; there's no substance to it. Although, I have to disagree about *all modern music*. There are tonnes of underground bands trying to rise up and some of them wouldn't have been out of place in the seventies and eighties.'

'Well, I just don't have time to keep up with it all, I guess. You're on the inside of the industry so it's easier for you to follow.'

'I suppose. I do get to go to a lot of great gigs.'

'It's been such a long time since I went to a gig,' I thought aloud, feeling nostalgic. 'I used to go to local gigs with my aunt. She was in a band herself but after her sister died, she lost her passion for it. It's a shame.'

'I'm sorry to hear that. What kind of band was she in?'

'Oh, it was just a cover band, but she did write some of her own stuff. She was great.'

'What did she play?'

'She played guitar every now and then, but she's a singer.'

'She sounds like a cool lady.'

'Very. She raised me; she's pretty much my mum.'

'Really? Where are your parents, if you don't mind me asking?'

I told him the first thing that popped into my head. 'Dead,' I responded, deadpan. I supposed I wasn't exactly lying.

'I'm really sorry to hear that. It sounds like you've had a pretty rough time.'

'Thanks, but my aunt raised me well. I never missed out on anything.'

'Well, good.'

'What about you?'

'My parents are Scottish. They're still up there, living in Edinburgh.'

'What made you move down here?'

'Uni. And then, I made friends and didn't want to leave. It's a great place.'

'You don't have a Scottish accent,' I observed.

'No, they moved to York before I was born and we lived in Leeds for a while as well. We didn't move up to Edinburgh until I was in high school, then I moved back to York to go to university. I prefer Moraine though. It's quieter—less tourism—but it's still easy enough to get to all the main cities for my work.'

'You've moved around a lot then! How was that?'

'I loved it. I mean, sometimes, especially when I was younger, I'd get annoyed—leaving friends behind and whatnot—but I'm pretty adaptable. I'm drawn to adventure and change.'

'I think I'd like to get around more. I've lived here my whole life and because my aunt raised me alone, we could never really afford to go on any holidays. Not abroad anyway.'

'I get that. We haven't been on many overseas trips either. Where do you want to go?'

'As cliché as it sounds, I've always wanted to go on an American road trip. I just love that they have *everything* over there.'

'Right? Some people look down on America. They think it's all capitalism, bimbos, sugar and plastic, but it's one of the most diverse, beautiful places on the planet.'

'I know! Thank you! I mean, you've got volcanoes, forests, mountains, deserts, lakes, plains, farms, enormous cities, small towns, cold, hot—just about every climate and landscape imaginable.' I sighed dreamily.

'Maybe you and I can go someday?'

'Maybe.' I smiled.

We talked and talked for hours, completely unaware of anything going on around us. I felt so comfortable with him and we shared so many similar tastes and views. It was easy to relax into the conversation and, slowly, it dawned on me that I was actually enjoying his company, and not because it made me feel closer to Thane. 'Do you want to come back to my place?' he asked.

I shifted in my seat uncomfortably. 'Not for that,' he assured me hastily, his cheeks reddening. 'I just think you'd appreciate it. I'd like to show you around, then I can drive you home.'

'Um, yeah, I guess so.' I texted Myla to let her know where I was and what I was doing, then we set off.

Bastian's apartment was the coolest. It was situated on the third floor of an old, converted warehouse on the outskirts of the city centre. We had to take the stairs as the lift was out of order. I thanked the gods his flat wasn't on the top floor.

He opened his door and I was taken aback by the size of the place. It was a completely open plan space; his bedroom looked down on the main living and kitchen area from the top of a platform that could be accessed by a narrow set of wooden steps. There were only two doors in the whole place; the front door we'd just entered through and a door set into the bedroom wall, which I assumed led to the bathroom.

A battered, buttery-soft leather sofa sat in the middle of the floor, with a matching armchair beside it and a coffee table which was nothing more than a large, polished piece of driftwood. The walls were bare brick, covered here and there with art and movie posters. The place screamed *artist's studio* and I imagined I was in New York City with a young, budding photographer. My imagination began to wander to dangerous territory, so I caught myself before it went too far. 'This place is amazing!' I exclaimed.

'Thanks,' he replied, hanging his keys on a hook by the door. 'I'm glad you like it. I'm pretty proud of it.'

'You should be. You must be doing well for yourself to afford a place like this.'

'I have to admit, my parents helped me. They basically gave me my inheritance early; they said they'd prefer to see me put it to good use and use it for something I needed.'

'That's smart.'

'I do alright for myself, but I'd never be able to afford something like this if it wasn't for their forward thinking. It's my favourite place in the whole world. I'd probably never leave if I didn't have to.'

'I totally get that. I love my flat too. My writing's at its best when I'm in my room, surrounded by my books and stuff.'

'You write?'

'Yeah, didn't I mention that?'

'No! What do you write?'

'A little bit of everything. I write about real life, fantasy, science fiction, whatever's in here at that moment,' I said, tapping my head.

'Are you any good?'

'I think so. I enjoy it anyway,' I shrugged.

'Well, that's all that matters.'

'Yeah, I guess it is.'

'Do you want a drink or anything? A coffee?'

'I don't drink coffee.'

'Tea then?'

'I don't drink tea,' I mumbled sheepishly, knowing what his reaction would be.

'You don't drink tea!' he shouted. 'Call yourself a Yorkshire lass?' he teased.

'Yeah, yeah; I've heard it all before. But really, I'm fine, thank you.'

'You want me to take you home?'

'I think that'd be best.'

'Are you working tomorrow?'

'No, I'm just tired, that's all.'

'Well, can I see you tomorrow?'

I stiffened. 'Sorry, I have plans,' I lied.

'Are you free another time this week then?'

'Look, I—'

'Sorry, I'm coming on strong, aren't I?'

'A little. I thought guys were supposed to act aloof?'

'That's sexist,' he pointed out, smiling. 'I just feel like, we have a connection, you know? How we met…it was so weird, and then to find out that you're pretty much just a female version of me, it all seems so, well, fated. I mean, I don't believe in that stuff, but you have to admit it's all a bit out of the ordinary.' He took a deep breath, having not taken one throughout the entire speech.

I nodded, unsure what to say. 'Maybe it's just me then?'

'No, no, it isn't. It's not you. This is all a bit weird for me. It's hard to explain.'

'Try me.'

'Maybe some other time?'

'You're very mysterious, you know that?'

'Am I?'

'Yeah, I don't know what to make of you,' he admitted, taking a step closer to me.

I looked deep into his eyes and I could see Thane staring back at me. His blue eyes seared into me, just like Thane's had done, and I felt a tear roll down my cheek. 'Will you help me understand?' he whispered. His breath brushed my skin, his face now only inches away from mine.

'I don't know if I can.'

'Please,' he breathed. Our noses were almost touching.

I was acutely aware of his body, inches away from my own, radiating warmth. I wondered if he looked like Thane all over and my stomach flipped.

He kissed me then, breathlessly, his hands clasping my face fiercely. I kissed him back, melting into his touch, my body pressing up against his. I was kissing Thane; I felt his passion, his gentle warmth and I felt safe in his arms.

Then, I pulled away. I couldn't be thinking that. It wasn't right, it wasn't fair—not on him, not on me. This man wasn't Thane and, as much as I enjoyed his company, I didn't know if I could ever get past that. 'Can you take me home now?' I asked, looking away guiltily.

Bastian stood there dumbly, looking at me, frustrated and hurt. He paused, then answered, 'Sure.' He grabbed his keys, opened the door and gestured for me to leave first.

The ride home in his beat-up old car was awkward to say the least. We said our goodbyes bluntly—his more so than mine—then I watched as his car screeched away down the street, turned the corner and disappeared out of my sight.

*****

I spent the next week tormenting myself, to-ing and fro-ing in my head. I was utterly confused. Every choice I settled on seemed to be the wrong one and would lead to heartache for one or both of us.

The following weekend, I was sat in the communal garden feeling sorry for myself. Myla was sat beside me on the crisp, frozen lawn, reading a book. The winter sun shone down on us, warming our extremities and casting a fresh light over the garden. 'What is wrong with you?' she asked me suddenly, placing a bookmark on the page she was reading and placing it down in her lap.

'What do you mean?' I asked, startled out of my wallowing.

'I can feel your misery all the way over here. What are you moping about?'

Having told Myla about my feelings for Bastian and Thane and the current predicament I had found myself in, I was shocked at how cold she was being. 'You know why I'm miserable.'

'Well, actually, no I don't.'

'But, I—'

'Let me just stop you there, before you go giving me another sob story. I can't bear to see you like this; you're doing my head in. And, the worst part is, the only reason you feel this way is you! Nobody else would judge you for how you're feeling, you know that don't you? It's all in your head.'

'How can you say that? I—'

'You miss Thane, yes?'

'Yes!'

'And Bastian reminds you of him.'

'Yes.'

'And you can't be with Thane?'

'Well—'

'No, you can't! It was just a dream, Sara, a fantasy. You couldn't be together. It's over. Face it. I know it's hard to hear, but you'll likely never see him again.'

I felt like I'd been punched. 'But,' she continued, 'Bastian is here. He's real. You *can* be together.'

'I don't know if I really like him, or if I'm using him to play out some fantasy that Thane and I are still together.'

'If you ask me, you've got it made.'

'How'd you figure that?'

'You loved Thane, right? And you fancied him? This man looks exactly the same, so you obviously fancy him. He's also creative, intelligent, interesting and obviously cares for you. So, what's the problem?'

'I...' She had me there.

'I know what's stopping you, and it's not guilt or confusion; it's fear. You're scared because you don't want him to know the real you.'

'The real me?'

'Yeah. The you who can walk between worlds, who has visited another plane and who's been in love with a man who was, like, three-hundred years old or something. The you who sees things and knows things that nobody else does. You're scared that you'll have to reveal it all to him, when with Thane, it was already there. He already knew before you even opened your mouth. Even more so, you're scared that you won't be able to tell him and you'll have to hide it from him.'

She picked up her book and turned back to her page, apparently finished with putting me in my place, for now.

I sat there speechless. How did she do it? How did she know me so well? Even I hadn't thought of that, but hearing it out loud, it made so much sense.

At last, I said, 'well, really, how could I ever explain it all to him? He'd think I was nuts.'

'People are more adaptable than you think,' she replied, without looking up from the page she was reading.

Bastian had described himself using that very word—adaptable. But still, the thought of having *that* conversation filled me with so much negative emotion;

dread, panic, fear, worry, to name a few. 'Look, Sara,' Myla continued, putting her book down once more and turning to face me. 'If he thinks you're crazy then he's a wanker and he doesn't deserve you. You're amazing, an absolute wonder. Your gift doesn't make you a repulsive weirdo, it makes you unique. Don't you think he deserves the chance to see that? Don't you think you should at least take the risk? It could be the best thing you ever do.'

'Or the worst thing,' I mumbled.

'Well, that's the risk, but I think it's worth taking. Like I said earlier, as painful as it is, you're probably never going to see Thane again.'

I gasped. That hurt because I knew she was right. 'Which means that you either take a risk or you stay alone forever, never letting anyone in out of fear. You obviously can't do that.'

'Why not?'

'Because you have so much love to give, Sara. You have a huge heart; it would kill you to not be able to share it with anyone. Look, my point is, you can't be alone forever. You're going to have to open up to someone at some point, and the bottom line is, why not him?'

Since meeting Bastian, my thoughts had been jumbled, like I'd been trapped inside a maze, going around in circles, getting more and more lost, but Myla had gone straight in, reordered my entire way of thinking and cleared it all up in a matter of minutes. It all seemed so obvious and clear to me to now. 'What if he doesn't want me anymore? I was pretty abrupt the last time we spoke.'

'Well, that'll be your own damn fault, won't it?'

'That's helpful!'

'Stop distracting me from my book and go find out! Stop worrying about something that hasn't even happened yet!'

That afternoon, I called Bastian on the number he'd given me on our first date. He didn't answer so I disappointedly left him a voicemail. I said something along the lines of, 'Hey, it's me, Sara. I'm sorry for how we left things. I really want to see you again, if you want to see me that is. Give me a call, or not—it's up to you.' Both Myla and I visibly cringed afterwards. Dating is hard.

Only one (very long and nerve-wracking) hour later, he called me back. At first, he seemed standoffish and I was worried. He told me he was going up to Edinburgh for Christmas so I couldn't see him anytime soon. I assumed that this was just an excuse, until he arranged a date with me for when he got back.

Once I got off the phone, I gave Myla the hugest hug and thanked her over and over again for sorting me out. She just laughed and called me an idiot.

I spent the whole of the Christmas period feeling excited, nervous, but mostly happy, for the first time in a long while.

Chapter Thirty-Four

Bastian and I took things slow at my request. I realised how easily spooked I could be. My emotional state was obviously fragile as there were still so many issues weighing on me, some buried so deep that I wasn't consciously aware of them, so I didn't want any rash decisions to bring them all out of the woodwork. I wanted our love to be nurtured and left to blossom in its own time.

We took our time getting to know each other. Although I loved his apartment and felt comfortable there, I didn't want to spend all my time there and become too reliant on his company. We always met in public places and enjoyed long walks and drives together. It was like old-fashioned courting: arranging dates and spending quality time together.

I started to feel like I never got to see Lyanna or Myla, so I took the leap and introduced him to them both a few months into the relationship. Instead of making it into a formal occasion, we all went to a gig together and Bastian brought along some of his friends to even the playing field. The night was a complete success; everyone got along brilliantly and that night, we slept together for the first time. It was worth the wait. He was gentle and caring, but also passionate. Afterwards, we said we loved each other. It felt completely natural and right, and from then on, we made our relationship official.

I insisted that we were to still take things slowly. We took turns staying at each other's places on weekends and tried not to see each other during the week if we could help it. We wanted our time together to be special and enjoyable, not tainted with tiredness or distractions of the mundane kind. That way, our work time could remain focussed and productive, and we could look forward to the weekends when we could be together and be wholeheartedly present in each other's company.

I was focussing a lot of my energy on my writing and had managed to persuade Isaac to change my shift patterns to Monday to Friday only, leaving my weekday evenings free to write. Isaac understood my situation and, as most of the original crew had moved on to bigger and better things, he hired all new staff; mostly university students who could only work weekends, which worked in my favour.

It took a long time for me to open up to Bastian and truly trust him. For the first few months of our relationship, I was an absolute nightmare and I still, to this day, have no idea how or why he managed to stick it out. The demons I'd thought I'd put to rest resurfaced with a vengeance. I was paranoid, jealous, controlling and volatile. Every message he received, every call he took, I was convinced were from another woman. I demanded to see his phone and he handed it over without hesitation. I scrolled through his messages like an addict searching for my drug. He was so goddamned calm about it though! I could hear myself saying horrible, cruel, untrue words to him, accusing him of all the offenses under the sun, some unbelievably ludicrous, but I couldn't stop it. They tumbled out of my mouth like maggots from a festering wound.

Then, one day, it all changed. I got over it. I never found any scrap of evidence to support any of my accusations and so, as time passed and his actions proved to be as innocent as his plea, I stopped the worrying, the suspicion, the reading into every little thing he did. I let it all go. I let the layers of black, poisonous thoughts peel off me and beneath was revealed the real me; the loving, caring, happy me who was fun to be around. I never broke him down; he remained devotedly by my side and was rewarded for his perseverance and unerring loyalty with a carefree, affectionate, humble girlfriend.

I apologised to him for all that I'd put him through, and I thanked him for never giving up on me. He replied, 'I knew you were in there somewhere and it was worth the wait.'

Bastian and I grew closer and closer; we were best friends as well as lovers. We were compatible in every way and completely, utterly in love. We never spoke about our feelings in any great detail and we rarely discussed the future. I didn't want to plan everything out as I felt that things should be left to progress organically. I was terrified that if we stamped labels all over our relationship, I'd startle and ruin everything with my messy head.

Because of this relaxed approach to our relationship, all the pressures I'd originally felt, that Myla had so skilfully assuaged, were now buried deep in the back of my mind. Before, my mind had been a small boat getting battered on a tumultuous, stormy sea, now it was an elegant vessel, floating serenely beneath a swift, golden sunrise.

*****

Our one-year anniversary came around fast and I finally decided it was time to let him in—all the way in. I'd been considering it for a while—we were in love, we were at the one-year mark and I now completely trusted him. I prepared myself for all eventualities. If he couldn't handle it, I wouldn't force him to understand. I would have to accept his feelings and walk away with my head held high. If he accepted it easily then I would be glad I'd confided in him and all would be well—though, I'd have to question his sanity a little.

There was one scenario I would not be prepared to entertain however: if he labelled me insane and tried to find me "help". On this I would stand firm.

It was autumn and Bastian and I had just returned to his apartment from a brisk, woodland walk in the crisp fresh air.

Bastian had taken a shower and I was waiting for him on the sofa. He descended the steps leading from his bedroom and asked me what I wanted to eat. His hair was still wet and fluffy from the shower and his cheeks had a rosy glow. 'Before we decide that, I need to talk to you,' I replied.

'Ooh, that sounds ominous,' he said, half-joking.

'I'd tell you it's nothing to worry about but that's debatable. Sit down,' I urged gently, in as comforting a tone as I could muster.

'Okay.' He took a seat beside me, nervously.

'There's something you should know about me and I need you to listen and let me talk for a while. If you have any questions—and I can guarantee you will—I'll answer them when I'm finished.'

He nodded apprehensively. 'Right, well, this is very difficult for me to put into words and it'll probably be difficult for you to get your head around, but please, bear with me.'

'Sara, spit it out.'

I took the leap—it was now or never. 'There's another plane of existence, another world within our own that not many can see. I'm one of the few who can. It all started when I was a little girl. I used to have such vivid dreams. When I was near the end of primary school, I was taken by a faerie and she showed me the way to the Other Place, as I call it, but I chose not to follow her.

'I lied when I told you that both of my parents are dead. My mother was another gifted person who could see the other world and I found out later in life

239

that she had left me to be raised by my aunt so that she could escape to the Other Place.'

I paused, trying to read his reaction but his expression remained passive—neither shocked nor disinterested.

I continued, 'So, I chose to go to the Other Place to see it for myself. I went there in the hope of finding answers, but I didn't find any. I did, however, find my mum, but that wasn't the emotional reunion that you'd expect.

'I also fell in love there. I met a man called Thane—the man who bears a striking resemblance to you—and we fell in love. I always intended on going back; he even said he'd wait for me, but I didn't realise how dangerous it was to leave that place. The way back crosses through a place where you can become trapped between worlds, like purgatory. The other thing I learned once I returned home is that time passes much quicker there than it does here. I had been gone a year, or thereabouts, but when I returned, Lyanna told me it had only been a week. I realised then that even if I did go back there, I would likely never see Thane again.'

I sighed with relief, feeling like a huge weight had been lifted from my shoulders. 'So there, that's it. In a nutshell, anyway.'

Bastian didn't say anything for a long time. I knew he was probably processing everything I'd just told him and trying to work out which of his many questions he should ask first. So, I didn't press him, I just let the silence stretch on and gave him space and time to mull it over.

Eventually, he said, 'So that's why you were so shocked to see me the day we met and why you pushed me away at first?'

'Yes,' I answered. 'I was still in love with Thane at that point and I suppose you could say grieving. It wasn't just that you looked like my ex-boyfriend; you looked like my ex-boyfriend who lived in another world, a world he could never leave. And, you don't just look like him, you are him, only this world's version of him.'

Abruptly, he asked, 'Are you in love with him or me?'

'Well, I did wonder at that myself. I was so confused, I didn't know how to think or feel. But you have to believe that I one hundred per cent love you and only you. I know that now.'

He nodded but looked no less troubled. 'Do you believe me?' I asked, somewhat embarrassed. I felt naked.

'You'd have to have a pretty vivid imagination to make all that up. Plus, what would you have to gain from lying about it? There's only two possible explanations: it's real or you're crazy.'

I flinched. That was the exact response I was hoping not to hear. 'I mean, faeries, dead mothers living in another realm, purgatory. How am I supposed to understand all that?'

I looked away, determined not to let him see me upset. 'But,' he continued, moving closer to me on the sofa, 'I will, someday. I'm not going to pretend I can even begin to comprehend everything you've just told me, but I still love you, so I'll find a way to understand.' He held my face in his hands and looked into my eyes.

'It was very brave of you to tell me. Thank you for trusting me with this.'

I tried to look away, once again feeling totally bare but he forced me to look back at him. 'Don't be ashamed of what you are, Sara. You're amazing. If what you say is true, and I only say that because it's a tough thing to get my head around, then you are one special woman. You astound me more and more each day.'

'Really? Do you mean that?' I asked, my eyes brimming with tears.

'Yes, of course I do. I adore you, and you know what? I want to know everything. But right now, I'm starving. How about I cook us some chicken, then you can tell me the whole story, no details spared?'

'I'll tell you everything you want to know.' I was utterly overwhelmed by his reaction. I'd expected him to be sensitive and possibly understanding but I hadn't expected him to wholeheartedly go for it. Even if he didn't understand, he wanted to and that was enough to prove to me that I'd made the right decision; in choosing him and trusting him enough to let him in.

After we ate, I told him everything I could—about my family, my nightmares, my fears, my journey and everything I'd witnessed in the Other Place. It was therapeutic, going into all that detail, and I felt more connected to him then than anyone I'd ever met. Afterwards, he practically jumped on me and we made love savagely right there on the floor.

After that night, my world changed. I felt like a new person, reborn. Everything was out in the open now; no more secrets. I knew him and he knew me. I no longer felt the need to place boundaries on our relationship. We saw each other whenever we wanted, talked openly about our future and I felt content in myself and our relationship. The only thing that took a hit was my writing. It turns out that emotional turmoil fuelled creativity better than contentment, but I was so happy that I didn't care. Months turned into years and we continued to live blissfully. Like everything though, it couldn't last forever. Life will always deal you another blow. All good things must come to an end.

Chapter Thirty-Five

Myla met Ethan through work and they quickly fell head over heels in love. They were very similar people: both laid-back (horizontal, in fact) and creative, with a sickeningly positive outlook on life. I thought Ethan was great; both Bastian and I got on well with him, which meant we were able to hang out as a foursome. We went out for meals together, on camping trips and short holidays—all the fun things that young couples like to do. We all fit neatly together like a jigsaw puzzle.

However, you never know what goes on behind closed doors, and it seemed that their relationship wasn't as perfect as they'd had us believe.

It was a freezing cold November night. Bastian and I were snuggled up under a fluffy blanket on his sofa, watching the latest episode of *Stranger Things*, when my phone vibrated loudly on the glass coffee table, causing us both to jump.

It was an intense scene and the room was completely ensconced in darkness except for the eerie glowing light of the television screen. My phone screen shone out like a beacon, distracting me. It was only a text message, so I clicked off the screen without looking at the sender and continued to watch the action play out on the TV.

My phone vibrated again moments later, but I was so engrossed in the programme that I didn't even notice it this time. It buzzed twice more before Bastian paused the episode and asked me, 'Are you going to answer that?' He looked pissed off.

'What? Oh yeah.' I grabbed my phone and flicked through the messages. They were all from Myla:

Sorry to bother you, but would you mind coming home please? xxxx
Sara, please can you come home? X
Please reply.
Sara, I ned you. Pleas come home now.

I knew she must have been texting with some urgency by the typos in the last message. Just as I was about to hit call, she called me. 'Hey, Myla, I'm sorry. I didn't hear my phone.' I gave Bastian a guilty side-glance, knowing full well I was lying. I could hear heavy breathing on the line, but Myla didn't speak. I sat up straight. 'Myla, are you okay?'

'No,' she replied, her voice thick with tears. She was obviously crying.

'What's happened?'

'We broke up.' Her voice cracked and she began to sob uncontrollably. Her breathing quickened and she started to hyperventilate.

'Myla, calm down. Listen to me, listen to my voice. Focus on my voice.'

Bastian sat forward, picking up on the urgency of the situation.

Myla continued to heave and gasp through the phone speaker. 'I can't breathe,' she managed.

'Myla, I'm coming over. Stay on the line with me, okay?'

Bastian was out of his seat and grabbing his keys from the hook without me even having to ask. He drove me home and all the while I stayed on the phone with Myla, trying to calm her down. The drive only took five minutes but every second felt like an hour. I was beside myself with worry. Myla was verging on hysterical. Sure, break-ups were hard, but I'd never heard her so emotional—there was obviously more to this than I knew.

I hung up the phone as we pulled up in front of our place. I raced to our flat, praying the door was unlocked as, in our rush, I hadn't brought my keys. I sighed with relief as the door opened and I headed urgently inside, Bastian following quickly behind me. 'Myla?' I called out, walking briskly to the front room.

Bastian headed down the corridor to check the other rooms. 'Sara! She's in here!' he shouted after a moment.

I bounded down the corridor to find Myla on the floor of the bathroom with Bastian. Her hair was stood up at odd angles, frizzy and knotted, and her face was lobster red and drenched with tears. Bastian was rubbing her back soothingly. 'We're here now,' I told her calmly, kneeling down before her and looking into her sad eyes. She was distraught and it was heart-breaking to see. Myla was always so composed, never one for showing her emotions. To see her that way made me feel utterly helpless. I was never usually the one to comfort her, so I was at a loss at what to say. I tried my best nonetheless—she needed me.

I got her to breathe methodically with me and eventually, she mellowed. Once her breathing returned to normal, she slumped back against the bathtub, exhausted. Bastian disappeared into the kitchen to make her some green tea while I helped her into her bed.

I was sat on the side of the bed when Bastian reappeared, bringing with him a steaming hot mug of tea. 'Give it a while, it's hot,' he advised us, placing the mug down on the bedside table.

'Thank you,' Myla managed, her voice hoarse.

I followed Bastian out of the room and closed the door behind us. 'Thank you for this,' I told him.

'Of course; you know I love Myla. I'd do anything for you both.'

I hugged him in gratitude but also for my own comfort; it had been a scary, emotional hour. 'I'm going to stay here tonight,' I said, pulling away.

'Yeah, that goes without saying.'

'Well, thanks again and I'll call you tomorrow.'

'Sure, look after her. You know where I am if you need me.'

I kissed him goodbye. 'Don't finish *Stranger Things* without me.' I smiled.

'Ah, crap. We left it on a right cliff-hanger!'

I laughed. 'See you soon, babe.'

I crept back into Myla's room and found her sleeping. I looked down at her and for the first time in our entire friendship, I saw a vulnerable, innocent girl. Even when she was ten years old, I'd always looked up to her, idolised her even. She was so gutsy and fierce, never someone to dramatize a situation or openly display her emotions, but now, I could see every facet of her beautiful personality. It was finally my turn to help her.

The next morning, unusually, I awoke before Myla. I went into the living area, expecting to find her in the kitchen making breakfast or watching TV, but the place was deserted and strangely quiet. I made myself a bowl of porridge and waited for her to surface.

The wind howled outside and rain hammered the windows. I sat there for a good hour, listening to the tumult and wondering for how long I should let her sleep. Finally, I heard footsteps in the hallway and Myla appeared, bleary-eyed and puffy-faced, with her dressing gown tied haphazardly around her. 'Morning,' I said brightly.

'Hi,' she croaked in reply.

'Do you want something to eat? To drink?'

'Please, don't fuss.'

I was about to apologise but I shut my mouth quickly, sensing her need for quiet.

She pottered about the kitchen, looking lost and indecisive, before sitting down heavily on a chair facing the window.

I let the silence drag on as I figured she'd talk in her own time, but she continued to stare out at the dismal weather as though I wasn't even there.

I couldn't stand it any longer. 'Do you want to talk about it?'

She started. Maybe she really had forgotten I was there. 'Not really.'

'I think you should.'

Myla sighed heavily. 'You're probably right, but I don't want to.'

I couldn't force her to tell me if she didn't want to. She was a private person and found it difficult to articulate her feelings and reveal her thoughts to others, I knew that, but part of me couldn't help feeling hurt that, after all we'd been through together, she was still shutting me out.

I stayed quiet however, fighting all my natural instincts to press her for information. After a stretch of depressing, excruciating silence, she finally turned to me with tears in her eyes and said, 'Sara, I don't know what I'll do without him.'

All my bitterness was forgotten and I rushed to her side to hold her and comfort her. She cried in my arms for quite some time before she pulled herself together.

I made us some beans on toast—the only meal I could confidently throw together with my limited culinary skills—and put *Friends* on the TV while we munched our simple meal. I'd hoped her favourite sitcom might lighten her mood, but she couldn't even crack a smile at Ross Geller's terrible keyboard playing.

Once we'd finished eating, I cleared our plates away then sat back down beside her. Her eyes were focussed on the TV screen, but I could tell she wasn't really taking any of it in. Her mind was a million miles away, most likely with Ethan. 'Myla, what happened?' I asked her gently.

She broke her trance and looked down at her hands, picking at her fingernails nervously. 'It's complicated.'

'So? We've got all day and night. Tell me what happened.'

'It's so hard.'

'I know it is, sweetie, but it's me—you can tell me anything. I can't help you if you won't let me in.'

She sighed, defeated. 'We've been having problems for a while.'

'You have?' I asked, surprised.

She nodded sadly. 'We want different things.'

'Like what?'

'He wants a different future.'

'Is it not something you can compromise on? Surely, you can figure it out.'

She shook her head. 'No. I've decided I never want to have children.'

'Ah. And, he does?'

'So bad.' She sobbed a little, then composed herself. 'I feel so guilty. We can't be together because I won't give him the one thing he wants more than anything in the world. I'm so selfish. If it was the other way around, I know he'd agree to have them, just to make me happy.'

'Yes, but Myla, if it was the other way around, he wouldn't have to carry the child or give up his career, or have his body completely change for something he doesn't even want.'

She looked up at me, her eyes sparkling with anguish and yet, with potent clarity. 'I guess I never thought of it that way.'

'It's your body. If you don't want children, then you can't force yourself to have them. You'd end up resenting Ethan, or worse, the child, and that's not fair on anyone.'

'But it means we can't be together,' she choked, tears beginning to roll down her face in streams. 'I love him so, so much it hurts and yet, I'm the reason we can't be together. Why don't I want children? Is there something wrong with me? Why do I have to be different?'

'It's not your fault and it's more common than you think these days. People have choices now; we don't have to do what society dictates. It's not your fault you can't be together, it's just the circumstances,' I assured her. 'And there's no way you'll ever change your mind?'

'No. No chance. I've never wanted them. It's never even entered my wildest dreams. In fact, I never even thought of it as a choice to make until I met him.'

'When did he bring it up?'

'Well, he, er…'

I waited for her to continue. Whatever it was, she was obviously finding it difficult to say. 'He proposed to me a couple of months ago.'

I was flabbergasted. 'He did?' I gasped.

'Yes, and I'm sorry I didn't tell you, but things started to unravel quickly after that, and I didn't want to tell you when I didn't know if it was actually going to happen.'

'Wow,' I breathed, 'I had no idea.'

'Please don't take it personally.'

I felt suddenly defensive, hurt by her secrecy. 'How could I not? Really?'

'Please don't, not right now. It's just, after I accepted, we started talking about our future and that's when I realised we wanted such different things. We talked and talked and talked and talked,' she began to hyperventilate again, 'but there was just...no way around it,' she stammered.

'Ssh.' I put my arm around her shoulders. 'Well, that's it then, it's over. It's nobody's fault, it can't be helped. This is your life, Myla, you have to do what's right for you.'

Her breathing slowed and she wiped her tears away with her dressing gown sleeve. 'I know, I just miss him so fucking much.'

'Of course you do and you will do for a while, but it'll get easier, I promise.'

'Thanks, Sara. I don't know what I'd do without you.'

My heart filled with warmth at her words. It had really stung me to know that she had gotten engaged and not confided in me, so her sweet words assured me that our friendship remained the same. 'Please, don't be mad at me,' she appealed to me. 'I'm sorry I didn't tell you what was going on, I just didn't want to intrude on your happiness. Things are going so great with you and Bastian; it's the happiest I've seen you in so long. I didn't want to bring you down.'

'That's a shit excuse,' I scolded her. 'But I get it. Just know that no matter what's going on in my life, you can always come to me with anything.'

She nodded. 'Promise me,' I urged her.

'I promise. I'll never keep anything from you again.'

'You're right though, I haven't been around a lot lately. I've been so wrapped up in my own relationship.'

'Don't—it's not a problem. If none of this had come to light, I'd still be spending all my time with him.'

'I know, I know, but I want to have some *us* time. It's been too long since we did something just the two of us.'

'Really, Sara, you don't have to.'

'I know I don't; I want to. I miss you.'

'I miss you too,' she sniffed, the first glimpse of a smile forming on her lips.

'So, I think we should take a trip, just you and me. Where should we go? Anywhere you want.'

'Oh, erm, I'm not sure.'

'I think I know the perfect place.' I smiled mischievously.

'Where?'

'It's a surprise,' I replied. 'Now!' I stood up abruptly and clapped my hands together. 'I think it's time you got a shower and changed into some clean pyjamas, don't you?'

Myla laughed out loud. 'Do I smell that bad?'

I chuckled. 'No, I just think it'll make you feel better.'

'You're probably right. Thanks Sara, I feel a lot better.'

While Myla was showering, I googled some ideas for short trips and booked us a weekend away. I called Isaac and cleared some time off with him and called Bastian to let him know of my plans and how Myla was doing. Then, the very next weekend, we hopped on a train, and then a coach, to our destination.

*****

I didn't show Myla the tickets and managed to keep our terminus a complete secret until she saw the majestic view of Bamburgh Castle sat up on the hill.

Bamburgh is one of those places that is timeless. Walking down the main street leading up to the castle, you feel it could be any moment in history. Vikings could storm the beach, or the guns could fire from the battlements, or a couple dressed in Victorian clothing could stroll past at any moment. Ghosts whisper all around you, and yet, it feels so present. The brisk coastal breeze whips you and keeps you planted firmly in the now.

We stepped off the stuffy coach and retrieved our luggage then turned to look at what would be our home for the next few days. 'Thank you so much,' Myla whispered. 'I never tire of this place.' She inhaled the fresh air deeply. Bamburgh held more for Myla than just a pretty view; to her it was an echo of her childhood. Myla had once lived only a few miles away and had spent her summers and weekends building sandcastles on the beach there and charging down the sand dunes with a stick for a sword.

We checked into our B&B. From without, it was just another quaint seaside hotel but an imposing, rather grand interior greeted us when we entered. We were led up three floors of twisting staircases, finished with dark walnut woodwork, and on each landing, we were met with large, ornate-framed paintings depicting austere scenes of stern people and grim yet beautiful landscapes.

We followed our host—a friendly old man named Jim—all the way up to what appeared to be an attic room. When we reached the top floor, breathing heavily and in awe of the sixty-plus year-old guy who'd made it all the way up without breaking his stride, I felt a little uneasy. It felt like the kind of place that could be haunted. But when Jim took out a large, old key and opened the door to our room, I instantly felt at ease.

The room was spacious and bright. Two single beds sat neatly in the centre, freshly made up with crisp, white cotton sheets, and sunlight streamed in through the huge window, chasing away any shadowy thoughts.

The man handed me our key and left us to unpack. We laid out what little clothing we'd brought in the sturdy walnut chest of drawers and set our toiletries out in the small yet contemporary bathroom. We marvelled at the wonderful view of the castle and dunes from the window and were eager to get outside to start exploring.

Just as we were about to get ready to head out, there was a knock at the door. 'Hello-oo?' a charming, feminine voice called.

'Come in,' I invited.

A sweet old lady bustled into the room with a tray of tea and scones. 'I thought you might need feeding after your long journey,' she told us merrily.

We both thanked her and once again, like we had been with her husband, we were surprised at how spritely and able she was. She introduced herself as Enid and told us we were welcome to ask for anything we might need.

After she left, we sat and ate our scones and Myla drank the tea. It was precisely the pick-me-up we both needed after our long, cramped journey, and satisfyingly British.

We spent the afternoon and evening strolling along the beach and through the grassy dunes. It was a cool, windy evening so we wrapped up warm and stayed out until the stars started to peek out of the dusky sky.

After a day of travelling and walking, we turned in early, ready for the full day of sightseeing and seaside activities ahead.

We both slept soundly and woke up bright and early the following morning, ready for an adventure. We did it all: racing each other down the sand dunes, paddling in the sea, strolling along the coast down to the nearby Seahouses for a fish and chip dinner with ice-cream for dessert. We played on the two-penny slot machines and browsed in the many quaint stores selling trinkets and souvenirs, spent a couple of hours roaming the castle grounds back in Bamburgh and imagining ourselves in another period in time.

Once we'd done everything we could possibly think of, we went back to the B&B for a nap. Well, I napped, being the sloth that I am, while Myla laid on her bed and read a couple of chapters of a book. After my sleep, I showered, washing all the sand out of my hair and from between my toes, then changed into some clean clothes.

We ate our supper of a hearty cottage pie at the Castle Inn, just a stone's throw away from the path leading up alongside the castle walls. The night was oddly mild, so afterwards, we sat outside in the beer garden and rested our full bellies. 'I forgot how clear the skies are up here,' Myla observed, leaning back in her chair and admiring the stunning view. The Milky Way provided an awe-inspiring backdrop for the commanding castle towering high above us.

The castle lights had awoken and were glowing eerie hues of pinks and greens, illuminating the ancient stone and casting mysterious shadows. 'Yeah, I always feel closer to the universe up here,' I agreed. 'Do you ever want to move back?'

'Moraine is my home now and plus, it's not that far away. I can come here whenever I like.'

'I guess so.'

'What would I even have here? I don't know anybody. Why would I leave my best friend to come live in the middle of nowhere on my own?'

I laughed. 'I remember when I first met you; you hated Moraine and wanted to come back here more than anything!'

Myla smiled. 'Yeah, but I was just a kid who'd been uprooted from her home. I didn't know what the future was going to bring.'

'I know, I know. You were just so stubborn and strong-willed. It makes me laugh.'

'I wasn't, I was angry.' Myla sighed heavily, like a great burden weighed heavily on her.

'What is it?' I asked, sensing something was wrong.

'I was angry for most of my childhood, to be honest. I didn't show it, but I was raging at the world.'

'Really? But you were always so cool and calm.'

Myla shook her head. 'It's just a front I put on. I feel like my exterior is a hard wall of glass. Beneath the surface is a swirling, ferocious vortex of emotion.'

I was shocked at her confession. I'd had no idea, not ever, that she felt that way. 'What were you so angry about?'

Myla shrugged. 'My parents, my upbringing, the way I never managed to fit in anywhere. I still don't.'

'Why didn't you ever tell me any of this? I've shared every little thing with you and now I feel like I barely know you.'

Myla reached out and took my hand. 'You do know me, I promise. I don't have two personalities. The front I put on is still me, it's just how I process things and choose to deal with them. You know I'm not a sharer and you've never forced me into being someone I'm not.'

'Yes, but still; you've had all this going on inside and I had no idea! I'm supposed to be your best friend.' I tried hard not to sound like a sullen child, but I couldn't help it.

Myla shrugged again, nonchalantly. 'Like I said, that's the way I am. Every boyfriend I've ever had has ended up leaving because they've been unable to crack my hard shell, but you, all through the years, have never tried to force me into doing anything I'm not comfortable with. You've always given me time and space. Christ, you even know when to hug me and when it's best to leave me be. And I've never had to tell you, you just get it. You get me.'

I felt better, but still troubled by her sudden revelation. Why was she telling me all this now when she'd been hiding it all her life? 'Don't be shocked or sad. I never felt like I couldn't tell you these things; I didn't actively keep them from you. I trust you with my life. Just the comfort of knowing you'd be there if I needed you was enough. You've helped me so much in my life without even knowing it.'

'You mean that, don't you?' I asked.

'Of course I do!' Myla exclaimed.

'You know I'm always here for you, no matter what?'

'Of course.'

'Then that's enough.'

We took a break of silence and listened to the sounds of people chatting and the breeze whistling around the buildings. 'How are you feeling now?' I questioned, after a short period of silence.

'Truthfully, I feel better, but I still feel pretty crap.'

'I'm sorry. It'll get easier.'

'I know. I just feel like, maybe, I'm not cut out to be in a relationship. I keep failing, miserably.'

'Myla, everyone's cut out to be in a relationship. You just need to find the right person.'

'But I don't know if there is a right person for me.'

'Of course there is! You're still young; even if you don't find anyone any time soon, you're doing pretty good on your own. Just try to enjoy it, okay?'

'That's easy for you to say. You've never had to really BE on your own.'

'I suppose not, but what can a man give you that I can't?'

Myla sniggered. 'Apart from *that*!' I laughed.

'Well, you have your own life with Bastian now. Don't get me wrong, that's great, but where does that leave me? Alone most of the time, that's where.'

'You know you're always welcome to hang out with us.'

'It's not the same!' Myla suddenly erupted. She stood up, knocking the chair she was sat on backwards, causing the wooden legs to scrape across the flagstones. It was a jarring sound on such a quiet night, like nails running down a chalkboard.

'Woah! Calm down. I was just trying to help.'

'I know, I'm sorry. I think I just need a bit of time to myself.'

'Well, go ahead.'

'I'm going for a walk to clear my head. Shall I meet you back at the hotel?'

'Sure, be careful.'

I watched her walk away, down the path that led to the beach. I had no intention whatsoever of meeting her back at the hotel. After a few minutes, I followed her, keeping my distance, but always holding her within my line of sight.

Once Myla reached the beach, I sat down in the long grass at the top of the hill, the castle walls at my back, and watched her from there. I could see her shadowy figure against the sparkling, moonlit sea and the sound of crashing waves echoed all around, deafening me to everything else.

She paced up and down the same spot for a little while, dipping her toes in the water, her head bowed like she was thinking hard about something. Then, she stopped pacing and turned away from me, looking out to sea. She stood there a long time, just staring. I wondered what she was thinking about.

What had caused her sudden outburst? What had caused the apparent change in her personality? Why had she revealed so much to me that she had gone to such great pains all her life to hide? Even after all her reassurances, I felt like she was a different person, somebody I didn't know. The thought terrified me. Aside from Lyanna, Myla was my grounding force. Without her, I felt unsteady and frankly, terrified.

I took a moment to just breathe and calm myself down. I was being silly. She was still Myla, my best friend and the person who knew me better than anyone in the world, but the question remained; did I know her?

I was awoken from my reverie when I noticed Myla making a move, but not in the way I'd expected. She laid down on her back, letting the waves lap at her. Although it was a fairly mild night, I knew the waters of the North Sea must have been bitterly cold. What was she doing? Trying to give herself hypothermia?

I waited a good ten minutes to see if she was going to get back up and head back to the village, but she didn't move. I decided enough was enough and made my way down the winding path to the beach.

I stood over her peaceful form. 'Myla, what are you doing?' I asked.

She jumped and sat up, looking around disorientated. She finally noticed me standing over her. 'Sorry, I must have dozed off,' she admitted sleepily.

'Well, it's a good job I came looking for you then,' I said, eyeing up the creeping tide. 'That wasn't a great idea, was it?'

'I suppose not.' She shivered noticeably.

'Come on, let's get you—'

'Sara, I saw it.'

'Saw what?'

'The universe.' Her voice sounded dreamy, like she was high.

'What do you mean?' I asked, kneeling down beside her.

'While I was laying down, looking up at the sky, I felt like I was floating through space. It was amazing, like nothing else mattered anymore.'

I put my hand on her shoulder; she was icy cold. 'Come back to the room.'

'I've never felt like that before. I wanted to stay there forever and never come back.'

I was startled by her words. I knew she didn't mean them like they'd sounded but I couldn't help feeling disturbed. I looked up at the shimmering night sky and I relaxed a little. 'It is pretty amazing.' I smiled, tracing the Milky Way with my eyes. 'Let's go back now though, eh? You're freezing.'

'Yeah I am,' she agreed, and her voice sounded normal once again.

We walked the path back to the hotel briskly, trying to get the blood pumping through our chilled veins. We turned our conversation to brighter topics and soon, we were back at the top of the hill, making our way around the edge of the castle.

We reached the bowling green at the base of the castle wall and we were so deep in conversation that I failed to notice the wire fence in the dark. By a stroke of luck, Myla somehow managed to step clean over it, but I tripped on it and fell flat on my face, triggering hysterical laughter in us both.

Immediately, all the tension of the last couple of hours melted away and we were both children again: carefree and happy.

Once we controlled ourselves, we walked over to the floodlights illuminating the castle and made our giant shadows do obscene, silly things to one another. Beneath all of our issues, all our layers of adult affectations, this was us; two kindred spirits harnessing nothing but love and humour and our shared knowledge that we could never be parted. That night is one of my favourite memories of my entire life, and yet, it was such a simple experience.

We laughed until we cried; two girls, alone, enveloped in our joviality and blind to the deep, dark world around us. Our laughter echoed off the castle walls, so that everyone out that night could hear us, but we didn't care.

We left the following day. Sat on the coach heading out of the village, we noticed two dents in the wire fence that surrounded the bowling green. Once again, we broke into fits of laughter and didn't stop until we reached the motorway.

My plan had worked; Myla and I had had a chance to reclaim and strengthen our friendship, and I'd cheered her up in the process.

She never fully got over Ethan. For a while, she retreated inside herself, just like I had done so many times before. Sometimes, I worried for her mental state; she'd act erratic and put herself in danger. She took to wandering off, claiming she was clearing her head, when I had a suspicion that she was actually sneaking off to be with Ethan. I never confronted her about it, though now, sometimes I wish I had.

I finally understood what I'd put her through all those times I'd done the same. She came home though, acting as bright and chipper as always. Yet, I could tell she wasn't being genuine; her smile didn't quite reach her eyes.

I remained hopeful, convinced it was just a broken heart. She was strong, she would get through this, but as time passed by, I considered the possibility that there was more to her troubles than what she was revealing to me.

I wish more than anything that I'd asked her, that I'd gotten the truth from her, and maybe even helped her more than I did, but I never got the chance.

Chapter Thirty-Six

I will always remember my 28th birthday as the time when I lost a piece of myself. I still, to this day, have a gaping hole in my heart that can never be filled.

Bastian, Myla and I had rented a cosy lodge for the weekend, overlooking the tranquil Peake Lake. On the Friday evening, the temperature had been too cool to sit outside, so we'd curled up in front of the fireplace and began watching the full extended *Lord of the Rings* trilogy on Blu-ray, as was tradition on my birthday each year. The Saturday, however, was warm and the sun shone like a golden beacon, so we took full advantage of the weather. We sunbathed, swam in the lake and had a barbecue out on the decking. It was the best birthday I'd had in years.

The year before, Bastian had taken me to Rome on a surprise birthday trip, but although it had been amazing and romantic, without Myla my birthday just hadn't been the same. This time, it was perfect, just relaxing with my boyfriend and best friend, taking time away from our everyday lives.

At about nine-thirty in the evening, Bastian retreated inside the lodge to get some more drinks. Myla and I were sat by the edge of the lake, revelling in the peace and quiet. 'How are you doing?' I asked Myla. I picked up a pebble and skimmed it across the still water.

'Fine, thanks,' she answered vaguely.

'No, I mean *really*.' Myla didn't answer straight away. I watched the ripples on the surface of the lake, spreading gently outwards until eventually it was still once more.

'I'm okay, Sara, really,' she assured me. 'It's all in the past now.'

'Good, I'm glad. You do seem more yourself this weekend than you have in a while.'

'I'm having a great time. It's wonderful here.'

I nodded in agreement. 'I love the sound of the water and the breeze in the trees. It's so subtle; a comforting, calming background noise. No wonder people move to the country.'

'I could live somewhere like this.'

'Me too,' I agreed. 'Maybe, one day we will.'

'What, when we're old and batshit crazy?' Myla giggled. 'Maybe we can get a house with a porch, and sit out on our rocking chairs with a cigarette in one hand and a beer in the other and laugh at people walking by?'

'Yeah! And they'll say, *look, it's those mad old hags!*'

We both laughed. I wondered what we would actually be like when we were old and losing our marbles. My mind drifted for a short time and Myla's must have too as she remained silent. I was brought back to the present by the sound of clinking glasses coming from the cabin. I remembered Bastian was still inside, getting our drinks.

I suddenly realised I was cold. 'I'm chilly. I'm going to go grab my jacket. Do you need anything while I'm in there?' I asked her, standing up and brushing sand and dirt from my jeans.

'No,' she replied. 'I'm fine, thanks.' Before I turned to walk away, large ripples undulating on the surface of the water caught my eye. When I looked again, the surface was still. I figured my eyes had been deceived by the darkness.

I left her sat there and went into the house to retrieve my hoodie. Bastian and I were staying in the main bedroom, which was situated in the back of the house overlooking the lake. When I arrived in the bedroom, I looked out of the window to check on Myla.

Starlight reflected on the lake and I was reminded of the Pool of Infinity, somewhere I hadn't thought about for a long time. I realised it had been a long time since I'd thought about the Other Place at all. I'd been caught up in work, my relationship and generally just getting on with life. Since Bastian and I had started dating, I'd had no room in my life for the Other Place. Talking about it with Bastian had somehow slackened its power over me. Not for the first or the last time, I wondered if there was a connection between the Other Place and my state of mind.

Something caught my eye below and jolted me back into awareness. Myla was now standing ankle-deep in the water and she appeared to be reaching out to something. I looked further beyond her, out over the lake, but it was too dark to make anything out. There was a movement in the deep black, but I couldn't trust what my eyes were showing me.

Myla wholly immersed herself in the water. I thought it was strange as it was so cold outside. I grabbed a towel from the radiator, thinking she would need it to dry off when she got out, then, instinctively, I continued to watch her. Myla dipped her head below the surface so I could no longer see her at all; the darkness enveloped her completely. I waited for her to resurface, but she didn't.

All of a sudden, panic seized me and I realised something was terribly wrong. The water rippled and bubbled; the once still and peaceful depths now violent and disturbed. 'Bastian!' I screamed. 'Bastian!'

'What's up?' he shouted from the kitchen.

'Help her! She's drowning!' I yelled breathlessly, turning from the window and making a run for the door.

Bastian was ahead of me, sprinting down the lawn to the lake. He jumped in, thrashing wildly, searching for Myla. Just as I reached the edge of the lake, he reappeared, gasping for breath and hauling a limp body with him.

I stopped running and watched in horror as he laid Myla out on the rocky shore and attempted to resuscitate her. Not a single part of me, at any moment during the entire ordeal, thought she would die. Any minute now, she was going to cough and splutter back to life, and Bastian and I would wrap her up in blankets and carry her back to the house where we would warm her up and wait for an ambulance. It all played out inside my head and there were no doubts in my mind, but Bastian continued thumping away on her chest, breathing in her mouth and still, she showed no sign of life.

Eventually, he stopped. He slumped down beside her, his head resting on her stomach and I realised that he was sobbing uncontrollably. I marched over to him and looked down at them. 'Why have you stopped?' I demanded.

'Sara, she's gone,' he replied, through choking tears.

'Don't be stupid,' I snapped angrily, crouching down and pushing him out of the way. 'She's only been in there a few minutes.' I attempted CPR, pounding away on her chest with my palms.

I kept it up for a good few minutes, refusing to acknowledge what was happening. Then, I felt an arm around my shoulders. 'Sara, stop,' Bastian whispered, trying to pull me away.

'Get off me!' I shouted.

'Sara, she's gone.'

'She can't be—it's impossible.'

'I'm so sorry, angel. I'm so, so sorry.'

I felt it then, the grief falling down over my eyes like a curtain. I rested my head against Bastian's chest and wept.

The emergency services came and Lyanna followed soon after. The medics had taken Myla's body away shortly before and the police were now talking to me, though I couldn't hear what they were saying. I was staring at a chipped tile in the kitchen. The chip was in the shape of a ghostly face: two wonky eyes and a yawning mouth. I focussed on it like there was nothing else in the room, in the world, even. If I stared at it long enough, then everything else would go away.

'She can't talk; she's in shock,' Bastian told the police officer.

'I know this is difficult, but we must take a statement,' the officer replied.

'I didn't see her go in. I was in the kitchen getting some more beers when Sara shouted me, telling me that Myla was drowning and that I had to help her.'

'And where was Sara when she shouted you?'

'In our bedroom—she must have seen it happen from the window.'

'Was Myla okay? Does she have a record of any mental health issues?'

'Not that I—'

'No,' I interrupted, suddenly aware of my surroundings. 'She was the most positive, together person in the world. She did *not* kill herself,' I confirmed, knowing exactly what he was suggesting.

The officer wrote something down in his notepad with a half-chewed pencil. 'I know this must be very difficult for you, Miss Black,' he repeated, 'but would you be able to tell me what you saw?'

I swallowed nervously. I didn't want to relive it. 'She was standing by the edge of the lake and she seemed to be looking at something, but it was too dark for me to make out anything. Then, she walked out into the lake and went under. I thought it was strange because it's cold out, but then, she can be quite impulsive, so I figured she was just going for a swim. But she didn't come back up.' I started to cry, the memory a painful stab in my stomach. 'I should have gotten to her quicker, I should have realised something wasn't right.'

Bastian held me tight. 'You couldn't have known what was going to happen. None of this was your fault.'

'Please continue, Miss Black,' the officer prompted.

'Well, that's when I shouted to Bastian and we both ran out.'

'I got her out and tried to resuscitate her, but she was gone,' Bastian finished, his voice thick with emotion.

After the emergency services left, Lyanna, Bastian and I sat in the kitchen in a state of complete shock. Lyanna called the owner of the property for us to inform them of what had happened, and within the hour we had packed up our things and were on our way home.

*****

The coroner ruled Myla's death to be suicide by drowning. When I received the news, I screamed and cried and shattered into a million pieces. None of it made any sense; it didn't match up to the Myla I knew. I refused to believe it. 'It's not true,' I cried to Bastian.

'She wouldn't kill herself.'

'It's the only explanation.'

'No, it isn't! It can't be. She wouldn't have done that.'

'I know it's hard to process, but you never know what's really going inside a person's head.'

'But I did! I knew Myla inside out. She was happy!' I thought then of our trip to Northumberland and all that had transpired there. I thought about Myla's personality changes over the past few months. Did I really know her as well as I thought? Yes! I did! I knew *categorically* that if she had wanted to end her life, she would never have chosen to do it on my birthday weekend, in that beautiful place, where only moments prior, she had expressed her pleasure and discussed her future. She wouldn't have done that to me. 'No, I refuse to believe it. Something…'

'What?'

'Something lured her in there.'

'What do you mean?' Bastian asked, confused.

'I said, didn't I, that just before she went in, she was interacting with something, something I couldn't see because it was so dark. That's the only explanation.'

'What could have possibly persuaded her to go in the water?'

'I don't know! I know that she could see something and that she followed it in there. It all makes sense now.'

'Does it?'

261

'Yes, I… Oh no…'

'What is it?'

'Right before she went in, I was thinking about…' I couldn't say it.

'What?' Bastian was concerned.

'The Other Place,' I whispered.

'So, you believe that she was lured to her death by a faerie or something?' he asked incredulously.

'Not a faerie, a daemon,' I said with conviction. 'Don't you think it's a bit of a coincidence that on the same day I think about that place for the first time in years, that happened?'

'Sara, you're in shock. You're grieving. You're clutching at straws because you can't face the truth.' He gripped me firmly by the shoulders and forced me to look him in the eyes. 'Your best friend killed herself.'

'Don't do that. I'm not crazy,' I replied, pulling away from him.

'I know, I just think you need to get some rest.'

'I don't need to rest!' I yelled. 'I need support! I need someone who will listen to me and believe me.'

'I am listening to—'

'No, you're not; you're psychoanalysing me. I have to go!' I stood up, full of rage.

'Please, Sara, stay. I'm sorry,' he pleaded, following me to his front door. 'Where will you go?'

I hadn't been back to our flat since Myla's death as I hadn't been able to face it, and now was not the right time to go back. 'Lyanna's place—she'll understand,' I snapped, opening the door.

'Please, don't leave me like this,' he begged me, his eyes full of worry and anguish.

'I have to. Please, just leave me alone.'

I ran. I ran and ran and ran. I didn't, couldn't stop. Not when my legs felt like they were going to collapse beneath me, not when a searing, agonising stitch developed in my side, not when my pounding heart felt it was going to burst out of my rib cage or when my lungs could barely gasp any more air in. Not even when my head began to throb and my skin became sore, stung by the biting breeze that had begun to blow. Still, I kept on running, trying to escape my grief.

I knew the area like I knew my own body, as I had played, explored and wandered endlessly through Moraine as a child and walked every possible route as an adult, but now, none of it seemed familiar to me, not even slightly. I felt like I'd stepped through a portal into another dimension. There was no way I could be lost as I'd not gone far at all. One moment, I was in my hometown, the next, I was in the middle of nowhere.

I felt panic flooding my veins and fear, confusion, frenzy gripping my bones. A cry escaped my lips, building up and up and up until it transformed into an unearthly, piercing scream.

I was back at Moraine Manor, though this time I was before the house itself, with no recollection of how I'd gotten there. I begged the air, the house, the trees, the grass, the garden, the clouds, the sky, the world, the universe for answers, but all that greeted me in response was deathly silence. There were no birds twittering, no sounds of woodland creatures, not even a whispering breeze rustling the leaves. The universe was holding its breath.

My mind was fragmented, I was neither in this world or the other. Myla's death had ripped me in two.

*****

The funeral was pitiful. The day was overcast and I felt I would never see sun shine again. Some of Myla's university and work colleagues came to pay their respects but at the end, there was only me, Lyanna, Bastian and Myla's parents left standing by her grave.

I approached her parents after the service, determined to tell them that I didn't think she had killed herself. I wanted to ease their suffering, to comfort them, but they didn't give me the chance. All they said to me was, 'Why didn't you save her?' Then they turned their backs on me and walked out of my life. I crumbled into nothing, right there in the mud.

I fell into a deep well of despair for such a long time. Nothing and nobody could drag me out of it. Truth be told, I didn't want to be awoken. Myla was the light of my life, my soulmate, my equal, the only person in the world I truly trusted and knew I could tell anything to. The worst part was, she was the one person who would have been able to bring me back from the brink of the abyss, the only person who could reason with me and put my feet back on the ground. I felt there was no way out, no light in the endless pit of loss and misery I had found myself in. It was intolerable.

Grief is an unpredictable, nasty, all-consuming beast. Just when I would start to feel a little human again, it would creep back up and debilitate me all over again. My grief was particularly potent. I believe this was caused by the nature in which Myla had left this world. I detested that people believed she'd committed suicide, when I knew she hadn't. Her memory was defiled and tattered in the minds of everyone who knew her, except me. She was no longer Myla, the positive, smart young woman who was full of life and wisdom beyond her years, but Myla, the girl nobody really knew, the girl who had hidden issues, the girl who selfishly ended her own life while away for her best friend's birthday.

I no longer shared my thoughts with anyone else on the subject because they all looked at me with eyes full of pity and concern, like I was disturbed and in denial. It's something that has haunted me all my life since.

I never found out why Myla had drowned, what had really happened to her that night, and the not knowing paralysed me for so long. It swallowed up a huge part of my life, rendering me senseless, hounded by the thoughts and questions that would never be answered.

There was only one thing that I could do with any cognisance: write. I hadn't done any decent writing for years, but my melancholy had released my artistry. I had attempted to begin writing again not long before my birthday weekend, but I'd been cursed with writer's block. Staring at the blank page, unable to put pen to paper became torturous and I tired of trying. As I've said before, emotional turmoil breeds creativity. I holed myself up in Bastian's apartment day after day, writing, scribbling, immersed in the dark pool of my imagination, only hauling myself out to go to work.

Bastian could barely get two words out of me each day. It became, for him, like living with a lifeless machine. He would return home from work to find me with a wild look in my eyes and paper scattered all about the place. We no longer did anything together, even at weekends, and he took to going out alone, more than likely to get away from the oppressive atmosphere that shrouded the place. Our love was put on hold as my mind no longer had the capacity to think of anything else but the imaginary world I'd locked myself in. In truth, it was my way of escaping. When I was creating my characters and stories, I was no longer dwelling on my deep and overwhelming sadness. Instead of facing and dealing with it, I was hiding from it, and Bastian was a reminder of a world where Myla had existed and was now no more. More and more, I was yearning to return to the Other Place, to truly escape.

Lyanna and Bastian never gave up on me; they tried and tried again to coax me out of my melancholia. They would use all the clichés, all the textbook answers to give people who are grieving. They told me to celebrate her memory, her life, to live my own life for the both of us and remember that she hadn't died in vain. I could use her loss to guide me. It's the natural instinct of humans to find meaning in death, but I knew Myla's death had been needless and tragic and no amount of inspiring, corny speeches were going to relieve me of my overwhelming feeling of displacement. How could my life go on when Myla's had ended? Life and death go hand in hand, and both of them are cruel. How could I go on in such a merciless, unfair world?

Chapter Thirty-Seven

At the age of thirty, my first book was published, and I dedicated it to Myla. Though I was now accomplished in one area of my life, my mind and my relationship with Bastian were never the same again. I was changed. Any remains of my youth and spirit had completely deserted me. I was bitter and angry at the world, unable to move on. I had become reserved and moody, a shadow of my former self. So easily I had succumbed to darkness. Everyone experiences loss at some point in their life and most find a way out of that dark tunnel and back into the light, but I couldn't fight it, or didn't try.

Mine and Bastian's relationship fell apart like a fragile, dying flower. I was no longer the person he'd fallen in love with. All the joy and laughter had leaked out of our life and my depressive demeanour had a profound effect on his personality as well, like it was contagious. We were no longer lovers, or even friends; we were cohabiters. He only let our relationship drag on for as long as he did as he was so bereft at the knowledge that we were over and everything we'd had was lost. He held on to hope for as long as he could.

One day, he turned to me and said those immortal words. 'I can't do this anymore.'

I was in the middle of furiously scribbling down notes for my next book and I didn't comprehend what he was saying. 'Do what?' I answered distractedly.

'This. Living like this.'

I stopped writing, the weight of his words settling on me. 'We're not the same anymore. I've lost you.'

My shoulders slumped. Honestly, I'd been waiting for that conversation for a long time. I nodded, already resigned. 'I know.'

'Is that it? Won't you fight for us?'

'I don't have any fight left in me.'

'Do you care?'

'I do. I honestly do,' I said, reaching out to him. 'I'm heartbroken at what I've become, what *we've* become. What we've lost.'

'Won't you consider getting help?'

'I won't take pills, I won't feel fake happiness and remain numb to everything else. I won't do it.'

'I know how you feel about western medicine, but would you not even try it, for me?'

'I still wouldn't be me, my old self. Would you really want just a spaced-out, happier version of this robot you've ended up with?'

'No, I just want my Sara back.'

'I do too; only, I don't know where I've gone or how to even begin to find myself again.'

Bastian sighed, defeated. 'So, where do we go from here? I won't kick you out, but we can't stay living together.'

'Of course not. I'm not going to make this any more difficult for you than it already is. I'll go to Lyanna's and figure things out from there.'

'Thank you.'

'Despite everything, I still love you.'

'I love you too, so much.'

We made love for the last time then I packed up my things and walked away. Lyanna took me in without question and I found some comfort being back in my childhood home, but I was also miserable. I was degenerating.

I was surprised to find that I felt even more lost back at Lyanna's. I hadn't realised just how much I loved Bastian until he'd gone from my life. After we'd parted ways, I felt like a part of me had detached and stayed behind with him. Now, I was completely empty and adrift.

He had walked into my life and turned my world upside down. He'd made me a better version of myself and I had him. Now, he was gone, and it was all because of me. The light inside me had been extinguished, leaving me adrift in a dark sea of nothing without any sense of direction or purpose. I'd had everything I'd ever wanted; I'd reached the top of the mountain and left all my demons behind, only to slide back down again and lose it all.

I had finally experienced it—that fierce, immortal love that so many never get the chance to possess. The words I had read exchanged between my mother and father resonated within me and I understood. Even as the silence between us and the days since I'd last set eyes on him lengthened, I could still feel his gravity tugging at me, binding us together.

*****

'How long do you intend on staying here, Sara?' Lyanna asked me one wintry evening while we were sat at the dining table eating the hearty meal that she'd prepared for us. It was raining heavily outside and the sound of the raindrops pitter-pattering on the windows filled the entire room.

'Are you that eager to get rid of me?' I asked jokingly.

'No, of course not,' she smiled, 'but you can't intend on staying here forever.'

'I know, I know. I'm teasing. I've been thinking about it and I've come up with a kind of plan.'

'Kind of?'

'Well, with what I have left of my inheritance from Sef, the money I've saved from not paying any rent on Myla's place and the income I'm getting from my book sales, I think I'll go in search of somewhere quiet. Somewhere I can be alone and get away from bad memories.'

'Any ideas where that will be?'

'Don't worry, it'll be somewhere in Yorkshire, or further north. Nowhere too far. I just need to get away from here and get some peace.'

'That sounds perfect, just what you need. I'm so proud of you.'

'Proud of me? What for?'

'You're published and now you have choices in front of you, a chance to make a fresh start.'

'I don't feel that way—I feel like I'm running away. All the things I have are the remains of other people's lives. Serafina left me money and Myla's death gave me the ability to write my best work. I didn't do any of this myself.'

'Yes, you did. Don't you dare say that! If anything, those things are a positive. They're a part of your success.'

'No, I feel guilty, like I'm freeloading off their deaths.'

'No, no, you can't think that way. You're the one who's written your book, every word. It's all your skill and hard work that went into it and you're the one who's choosing to put Serafina's money to good use instead of squandering it.

You need to let all your guilt and negativity go. You can't carry it with you for the rest of your life.'

'Well, I suppose that's what I'm trying to do by getting away. I'm trying to move on.'

The property I chose was a small, cosy cabin nestled in a forest in Northumberland. Despite the awful memory of Myla's death, I also chose it for its view over a lake. In a weird, twisted way, the proximity to the water, and to where she had spent her childhood, helped me feel closer to her. I wanted to move on with my life, but I wasn't ready to let her go.

From the cabin, I could see no other properties through the dense trees, my nearest neighbour being a good quarter of a mile away. It truly was a slice of heaven.

The cabin was basic inside: a front room centred around a large, stone fireplace, a small, homely kitchen in the back of the house and leading off the front room, down a corridor, were two small bedrooms and a surprisingly bright and modern bathroom.

I decorated the whole place in warm, autumnal, earthy colours and hung-up photographs of wildlife and nature, some of which were gifted to me from Bastian.

I didn't like the idea of being completely alone in the middle of nowhere, so I bought a beautiful, chocolate-brown Cockapoo (hypoallergenic for my allergies) and named him Buddy as that was to be his role in my life.

I'd quit my job at Armchair Books and now, I was left alone to focus on my writing. It was a huge pressure taken off me: to no longer have the responsibility of anyone else's wellbeing resting on my shoulders. I didn't have to give anyone my attention, I didn't even have to talk, although I did find myself chatting to Buddy frequently, for my own sanity more than anything.

I wished Myla could have seen the cabin—she would have loved it—but then, I would never have ended up there if she hadn't died. A cruel irony. Life is bittersweet and paradoxical, full of coincidences, hypocrisy, fate, luck, circumstance, consequence and inconsistency. It's no wonder that a quiet place is hard to find.

*****

Lyanna helped me move in. By the evening, mere hours after we'd arrived at the cabin, all my boxes were unpacked, all my belongings had found a new home and we had a fire burning in the hearth. 'Why did you choose to move in the middle of winter?' Lyanna joked, warming her feet by the fire while Buddy curled up beside her.

'It's beautiful though, isn't it?' I observed, standing at the window and looking out into the night.

Darkness had fallen over my corner of the world. The pale light of the moon was the only light out there in the deep black, reflecting off the trees and, beyond that, the still lake.

I gazed up at the moon. Its lunar majesty was half-shadowed by windswept, smoky clouds, creating the appearance of dark ink swirling in pale water. The moon's outline was sharp and clear; a stark contrast between her ghostly face and the solid darkness of the night sky. So refined was her surface, that I could see the great craters with my naked eyes. Beyond the orb, bright, twinkling stars appeared, scattered behind the clouds. 'Sara?' Lyanna's voice broke me out of my trance.

'Sorry?' I asked, tearing my eyes away from the magical view.

'I was just asking if you want anything to eat yet.'

'Oh right, yes please. Soon.' I looked back out of the window—the night was calling me. 'I'm going out for a walk. Do you want to join me?'

'Urm, I've just warmed my feet up. How about I cook something up for when you get back?'

I smiled. That was just the answer I was hoping for. I was going to miss her cooking. 'If you don't mind?'

'Of course not. Don't be long though, I'm only making rice and soup.'

I grabbed my coat from the hook behind the door and stepped outside into the chill evening. I walked down to the lake and looked out. The moon's light was reflecting off its surface, almost blinding in its brightness. It highlighted the trees surrounding the lake on all sides. I felt like I was on the edge of the world, off the map. If it wasn't for the golden glow of the lights from my neighbour's houses peeking out from between the trees, I would have thought I was the only person in existence. I wished I was. Without love, without people, there could be no loss or heartache.

Moments like that, staring out at the glory of the universe, appreciating nature in its rawest form, made me feel like anything was possible. I knew that wherever I went, whatever I did, that same moon and those same stars would always be looking down on me. It was a comforting thought.

That night, after being unable to sleep, I went back out to the lake. I was drawn out by its alluring magnificence. Something about that place beckoned me and I felt like all my woes and worries could be forgotten there, drowned in its depths. I fell asleep, wrapped up in my coat and thick blanket, right by the lakeside.

I woke up early. Dawn had been and gone, the colour of the sky changing from dark crimson and violet to light blues and coral pinks while I had slept, untroubled. The sky was hazy, a white blur where the stars had shone, now erased by the morning sunlight.

I crept back into the house, hoping Lyanna wasn't yet awake. I dozed on the sofa for a little while until I heard her moving around in the back of the house. Ten minutes later, she appeared and warmed up some chocolate pastries for us.

'I best be getting off soon,' she told me after breakfast.

'Of course, yeah.'

'Are you sure you'll be okay here on your own?'

'Of course I will! I'm looking forward to the solitude, just my Buddy and me.' I smiled, stroking the dog's head beneath the table.

'I know, I know, I just worry about you out here, all alone. Will you not get creeped out?'

'No, Lyanna,' I chuckled. 'I'm a grown woman. You really don't have to worry about me.'

'I'll always worry about you. You'll always be my little gummy bear.'

'I'm glad.'

'Before I go, let's go for a walk. What do you say? A full lap of the lake, scout out the area?'

'You won't be able to sleep if we don't, will you?' I laughed.

Half an hour later, after a quick wash and a change of clothes, we headed out into the bright daylight. Standing on the threshold, I was transfixed by the sight that greeted me. The crisp, bitter air reached out to my bare face, rosing my cheeks and stinging my eyes. Frost layered the ground, glittering in the sunlight and the air was alive with the scent of pine and winter flowers. 'Come on then,' Lyanna urged, pushing me through the doorway. 'I can't wait around all day while you moon about.'

I felt something brush past my legs and Buddy bounded ahead into view, only stopping when the lead Lyanna was grasping pulled him back. I looked down at his eager, innocent face, ready for adventure, and I knew everything was going to be okay.

We walked briskly around the edge of the lake and, here and there, we spied a few cottages and cabins through the trees. We passed some fellow dog-walkers on our way around. Mostly they were retired folk, kind and welcoming people yet also unapologetically brusque in their chatter. They had obviously chosen to move to these parts for the same reason as me; for peace, quiet and solitude.

Satisfied that there were no murderers, rapists or devil-worshippers living nearby, Lyanna set off home just before noon, leaving me alone for the first time since my journey through the Other Place. This time, however, it all felt so right. I was where I was supposed to be.

I set about the one task I'd left myself to do: setting up my writing desk in the window overlooking the lake. It was a ceremony that I needed to do alone. Once it was in place, I sat down on my high, comfy chair and looked out at the view that would be accompanying me on my writing journey and I was suddenly overwhelmed. I couldn't believe this was mine. This was my dream come true, everything I could have ever wanted. Buddy nuzzled at my legs, looking up at me with eyes full of hope and contentment. I wondered why I hadn't done this sooner.

*****

I immersed myself in my writing pretty much non-stop for three years. In that time, I managed to push out two more novels. I credited my surroundings with my soaring creativity and keeping me motivated. I had nothing else on my mind or my agenda except my stories. I even managed to find time to write a few short stories, which went on to be published in magazines.

For Christmas each year, I returned home to Lyanna but by the end of each visit, I was yearning to get back to my quiet place, back in the world of my stories.

Buddy and I lived happily and simply. Having learnt to drive prior to moving into the middle of nowhere, we took weekly trips to the nearby village of Chillingham to stock up on food for us both and just, I think, to remind myself that I was part of the world.

Each morning, bright and early, we'd eat our breakfast (outside in summer, inside in winter) then I'd take him for a good, long walk to tire him out, before heading home to begin my writing for the day. I wrote and wrote until my eyes were so tired, I could no longer function, stopping only for toilet breaks and to give Buddy some attention.

Each night, when I'd finished my writing, we'd cosy up in front of the fire watching films or listening to music. Then, before bed, I'd take him for another walk to tire us both out. We'd both sleep deeply each night, ready for it all to start again the following day. When I sent my finished third book to my agent, I decided it was time for a break. I didn't know what a break could look like when I pretty much lived in paradise, but I knew I needed a change of scenery, something to interrupt my routine before I became a weird old hermit.

Recently, the Other Place had snuck back into my thoughts and it was coming through in my writing. Part of me yearned to go back, to see how it had changed. The following week, I found myself back in Moraine, dropping Buddy off at Lyanna's house, before heading back to the place that had haunted me my entire life.

This time, I found my own way, surprised to find that I remembered the way so clearly. It was like I'd never been away. I knew there was something wrong when I washed up on those dark and distant shores without so much as a glimpse of a fish in those weird waters.

I only walked for a couple of days before I reached my mother's village. The huts were still standing but there was no sign of life. Perturbed, but also slightly relieved, I pressed on, leaving the eerie, uninhabited village far behind.

Eventually, I reached where Thane's village had once stood. My stomach dropped when I saw there was nothing left. There was absolutely no sign that anybody had ever lived there: no huts, no tents, no remains of life whatsoever. I knew though that had been the place where I'd spent so much time, the place where I had lived and loved and learnt. The place was now ghostly, haunting.

I was brought to my knees with grief. Where had everyone gone? I had walked for days, even weeks, across the land and not encountered anybody or anything. The whole realm was deserted. Why had they all left? What had happened there?

I despaired, inconsolable, remaining there for another sunset, unable to let go. Thane was gone and I would never see him again. Though I hadn't thought about him much over the years, it still broke my heart. I wanted to know what had happened but there was no-one around to ask.

I did eventually leave that place behind, though it tore me in two, and set off for the Pool of Infinity. Yet again, I had gone there looking for answers and had instead found more questions.

I was approaching the Veil—I could tell by the changes in the atmosphere and the murky landscape—but first, barring my path, was the great black hole. I racked my brain, sure that we had reached it before Thane's village on my last journey, but then, I concluded, in that place it was not a stretch of the imagination for it to have moved. Anything was possible here.

The dark mass was bigger than I remembered it, a lot bigger. It dawned on me that not only had it moved, but it had grown. Part of me wondered if this was the answer to the mystery. Could the shadow have swallowed up all the life? It wasn't inconceivable but seemed unlikely. Maybe this was just another one of those things in life that would never be explained?

I stared into that great dark nothingness for what seemed like an eternity. There was no light, just an impenetrable black in place of the landscape. I could see nothing for miles in each direction, except back the way I'd come. I wondered how far it continued. I knew it must end somewhere, as I was stood on one edge of it, but I couldn't guess at its size. I had no choice but to continue however so I set off along its outer edge. I was tempted to try and walk through it, but my logical mind won out; I knew it was too dangerous to try. I didn't even want to get too close in fear of being sucked in, yet something about it sparked my curiosity.

I pressed on and tried to stifle my urges. I thought I would die trying, either from exertion or by giving into temptation and walking straight into the black hole. The sun beat down on me, making me delirious and exhausted. I stumbled and fell, my path slowly creeping closer to the monster. It would swallow me up and I wouldn't feel anything, ever again… No, I had to fight it. But I wanted it so bad: that numbness, that lack of anything. No fears, no worries, no sadness, no pain, no suffering—all of it gone, forever. All I had to do was walk into that black hole and never return. I dreamed of it with my waking mind. I imagined floating in the darkness, all memories, all feelings, gone.

Then I saw it—the end was in sight. It dawned on me that not only would I lose all the gut-wrenching, heart-breaking, horrible memories, but the joyous, heart-warming, wonderful memories as well. I had to keep fighting, I had to keep going. I staggered, like a deranged maniac, towards the finish line, intent on my goal, all the while being pulled towards my doom.

It took me hours, by my reckoning, but I finally cleared it. Once the mass was far behind me, I fell face-first onto the dry, solid ground and remained there for time out of mind.

When I awoke, I felt achy but refreshed. I had defeated it. I had fought and I had won. Ahead of me was a lovely, golden woodland, a welcome sight after the harsh, unforgiving wasteland. I washed myself in a nearby stream and ate some mushrooms and berries to restore my strength, then set off into forest. The trees towered overhead, as high as any ancient redwoods, and sundrops twinkled on the forest floor.

Some way along the path, I heard a voice from above. I had been deep in thought, so the voice startled me, causing me to stop in my tracks and look up, confused. I had been certain there was nobody left in this place. 'Escaped the shadow, did we?' a wise old voice called.

High above, resting in the branches of the nearest tree, stood a house made from wood. It was the finest treehouse I'd ever seen. 'Hi there!' I shouted up to the bodiless voice.

'Who are you?'

'Who am I? Who am I?' the voice called back incredulously.

'I should be asking you that, young lady.'

'Come down here then, so I can introduce myself.'

'Come down? A mortal telling me what to do,' the voice grumbled to itself. 'Here I come!'

I waited apprehensively for the stranger to appear. Who was this anomaly? What was going to come down that tree? At length, he emerged from behind the tree. He was an old man; his hair a white, fuzzy cloud crowning his aged, wrinkly head, yet his eyes gleamed with spirit and humour. 'How did you get down?' I asked, stepping closer to get a good look at my new acquaintance.

'A ladder, of course,' he replied, somewhat disgruntled, apparently at my stupidity. 'And who might you be?'

'I'm Sara, pleased to meet you. Who are you?' I walked forwards and extended my hand in greeting.

'I am Eavan, the tree-dweller.' He too stepped forwards and shook my hand. His skin felt papery and soft, but his grip was firm. 'What are you doing here again, Wanderer? I haven't seen a soul in many a sunset.'

That name curdled my stomach; all thoughts and memories of the time before flooded back to me unceremoniously.

I steadied myself and replied, 'I suppose I'm just wandering. I don't suppose you know where everyone went?'

'I could if I knew,' he responded heavily. 'There was a disturbance in the energy, then one day, I woke up and everybody was gone, even the animals. I wasn't so disturbed by the people disappearing—I've never much concerned myself with their comings and goings—but the disappearance of the animals has affected me greatly.'

'I'm sorry,' I told him, though my words seemed to fall short of the tragedy of the situation.

'But then, you walk by, as brazen as the mother sun. My, my, who'd have thought it?'

'I wonder why they've gone and you haven't?'

'Well, that's simple, if you have the answer.'

I waited, sure that he hadn't finished his train of thought, but he said no more. 'And the answer is?'

'I will live here forever. I cannot leave.'

Thane's words came back to me, echoing through time and space, bringing with them a tidal wave of emotion. *They are here from the beginning to the end and beyond.* 'Are you one of the protectors? An Elemental?'

'I suppose you could call us that, yes. I am one of those.'

I looked at the old man with a newfound awe. 'But you just look like an old man, and you can speak my language!'

'Ah, well, we come in many forms. We are not all fae and spooky and supernatural.' He laughed.

'Are there any more of you left?'

'Of course. They're all still here but many of them choose not to show themselves to mortals. They're here, all around us. Can't you feel them?'

'Well, no, actually.'

'That's because you're not really listening, not using your senses. You're wrapped up in your own world, blocking out anything that doesn't concern you, or what you believe doesn't concern you.'

'I suppose you're right,' I answered, feeling somewhat like a teenager being chided.

'No, I am right. I'm always right,' he chuckled mischievously. 'How do you think you made it here so fast?'

'I was told that the landscape changes, that it never stays the same.'

'And who do you think changes it?'

'I never really thought about it.'

'We do! My girl, your entire journey has been aided by my kin. They have moved the mountains, kept the storms at bay, changed the courses of the rivers, just to aid you in your passage through our lands.'

I stared at him in wonder. 'Why?'

'Because they want you out of here as quickly as possible!' He laughed, and not wholly kindly.

I suddenly felt on edge, like I was unwelcome, like I was being watched by unfriendly eyes.

Sensing my fear, he ceased laughing and added, 'Don't worry, my dear, we won't harm you. If we'd wanted to, we would have killed you the instant you arrived on our shores. No, no, it is not all that sinister.' He stepped closer, leaned into me and whispered conspiratorially, 'Between you and me, I think they're enjoying the peace and quiet without all those busybodies. You're a threat to their peace.'

I smiled and relaxed a little, though I had a sneaking suspicion that there was more to it than what he'd told me, if what he'd told me had been the truth at all. 'However,' he continued, 'I would suggest that you return home in haste.'

'Why?' I questioned, perturbed.

'Because you have unfinished business in your own world, young lady, and I have things to be getting on with. I can't just stand around chatting to you until the end of time, no, no!'

'I'm sorry for keeping you from your duties.'

'Don't apologise, child,' he insisted, comfortingly, kindness beaming out of those youthful eyes. 'Sometimes, curiosity gets the better of us, doesn't it?'

'Tell me, before you go, what's my unfinished business?'

'I think, if you search deep down, you will find all the answers you seek. I am not a fortune-teller.' He winked. And then, he disappeared.

I looked around, shocked and saddened at his departure. Something about his presence had comforted me greatly. 'Don't worry, young Wanderer! I've not gone! I am always here, like I said, yes, yes. Just as we all are, I suppose. Now go on! Be gone with you! Get back to your reality. Go find what you're looking for!' Eavan shouted from high above.

'Thank you!' I called, but he didn't reply.

I did not fear the Veil, or the Pool of Infinity. I had never wanted to be back in my home more than I did then. There was nothing for me in the Other Place: no life, no company. I bathed in the stars and I returned home.

Chapter Thirty-Eight

People hurt each other, people hate each other. People inflict pain, embarrassment, punishment, emotional and physical torture on each other, every single day. Humans endure such stress, such emotional strain on a daily basis. I don't know a single person who hasn't experienced trauma at the hands of another human being: heartbreak, betrayal, abuse of trust, bullying, domestic violence. How do people—just flesh and bone, small and insignificant on the face of the universe—get through these things?

The truth is, although it is us who commit these awful deeds, although we hurt one another and although there truly is evil in this world, it is also us who are beautiful and astounding. We start the wars, but we also endure them and fight them. We are not simple; we are complex, magnificent and strong.

Our greatest distinction? Not our accomplishments in science and technology and our greater understanding of the universe, not even the written word. No, love is the greatest of all.

I lived at the cabin for five years, all in all. I cut myself off from the world, hid myself away and got everything I ever thought I wanted: peace, quiet, time to reflect and write, beautiful views and most of all, solitude. I found a quiet place and yet, I still had an unquiet mind.

For a long while, I was content, at my most motivated and creative. My writing took centre stage in my life and it worked out well for me. I was published, I had an agent and, five novels and several smaller publications later, I had creative freedom. I felt like I'd finally achieved something, something I'd been yearning for and working towards my entire life. So, why did I feel so hollow?

The cabin was a retreat, a physical quiet place but, as the years scudded by, my mind became loud once more. I had all that I thought I needed. I racked my brain trying to work out what I was missing but I just couldn't solve the puzzle.

I was used to not seeing anybody, not speaking to anyone (except my Buddy of course) so it never occurred to me that it was the silence which was haunting me.

One day, I was knee-deep in my storytelling, writing a sweeping, romantic piece about two teenagers who had run away together. I realised I had been writing a lot about love lately, that my current story was pretty much a romance novel, a world away from the dark, twisted thrillers and fantasies I'd cut my teeth on.

Suddenly, the world closed in on me. I gasped for air, choking, as a panic attack gripped me. I was lonely. This restless, incomplete feeling I had was loneliness. It had only taken me five whole years, but I'd finally figured it out. I needed love in my life and although I loved Buddy, he wasn't enough. I needed physical and emotional interaction.

I put my book on hold and I left, almost immediately. I didn't sell the cabin; I still adored the place and couldn't bear to leave it behind for good, but I no longer required it. It had served its purpose. The place had brought me back down to earth, refocussed my mind, nursed me through my grief, quietened my demons, and for that I was forever grateful. But I wasn't sure who I was anymore. Who are you if you don't interact with other people? Who are you if you don't do things for other people? Who are you if you do the same things, day in, day out, never evolving or growing? I didn't know and the thought of that terrified me. Maybe I could go back to Moraine and find that I couldn't be around people anymore? That I'd forgotten how to act, how to communicate, how to be myself?

It was time to rediscover myself and reclaim my place in society. We're better people when we're around the ones we love and the ones who love us in return. I turned up at Lyanna's door unannounced, with a couple of holdalls. I'd left all my furniture and knick-knacks behind at the cabin, including the beginnings of my sixth novel, and taken only my clothes, toiletries and Buddy. 'Sara! What a surprise!' Lyanna beamed when she opened the door to find me standing there. She appraised my bags. 'Is everything okay?'

'Yes, actually. Everything's good, thanks,' I replied, dropping my bags down on the path. 'I'm sorry it's been so long.'

'It's fine. Come in, come in,' she urged, taking a bag and leading the way inside the house. Buddy whipped past me, eagerly following her.

'Is this a long stay or are you just passing through?' she asked me once we were seated in the kitchen. I could tell she was trying not to look too hopeful.

'Actually, I don't have any plans just yet. I just needed to get away.'

'You work too hard. How many times have I told you? You're burnt out, aren't you?'

'No, it's nothing like that, my writing's going fine. I just woke up one morning and realised that I can't stay there forever or I'll go mad.'

'You wanted some company?' she asked affectionately.

'So bad,' I confessed.

'I'm glad you're back. I've missed you.' She hugged me fiercely and I hugged her in return, glad to be back.

'So, you don't have any plans?' Lyanna questioned after a bite to eat.

'No, not really. My books are doing well, I'm still comfortable in my finances and I haven't got rid of the cabin. It's too beautiful to get rid of.'

'Plus, you'd like it there as a back-up.' She phrased it as a question, but I knew it was more of an assumption.

'Yes, I suppose so. I don't know; I was just thinking of keeping it as a get-away, a holiday-home or whatever.'

'That sounds like a good idea. It's always good to have a quiet place to retreat to. So, what else have you come up with?'

'I honestly haven't thought that far ahead. My plan was to come here; beyond that, I don't know.'

'So, once again, you're living with me.'

'I won't be staying here long if that's what you're worried about. I have enough money to get a new place,' I assured her hastily.

'No, I didn't mean I'm bothered about you staying here with me but, well, do you ever feel like you're going around in circles? And I mean that in the nicest possible way.'

'I've felt like that my whole life.'

'I'm sorry, I didn't mean it to sound like that, but I have to tell you, things have changed around here.'

'How?' I asked curiously.

'I have someone else living with me now.'

'Oh my God! Who?' I shrieked, my voice raising an octave in my excitement.

'His name's Chris and I've been seeing him for about six months now.'

'And you're already living together?' I blurted, realising too late how judgemental I sounded.

'He doesn't *live here* live here, but he stays over a lot.'

'I didn't mean to sound judge-y.' I laughed. 'It's just not like you to be so impulsive.'

'It's actually a lot like me to act impulsively. You've got to remember that Lyanna, Sara's auntie, and Lyanna, the single woman, are two different people.'

'You're not; you're the same person. You can have more than one side to your personality.' I sighed, feeling sad.

'What's wrong?'

'We used to be so close, you and I, and I didn't even know you'd met someone.'

'Aw, I know but that's life, Sara. Don't worry about it. You're here now.'

Lyanna told me the whole story: how she'd met Chris, where they'd gone on their first date, how he treated her. When she finished, the man himself walked through the front door.

'Lyanna?' he called.

'In here!' she shouted back.

Chris was handsome. He was well-dressed and well-groomed with silver hair and dark eyes. 'Oh,' he said, as he spotted me. 'Sorry, I didn't realise you had company.'

He marched over to Lyanna and kissed her on the head, before setting the bags of groceries he'd brought in down on the worktop. He turned to face me and fixed me with his genuine, warm gaze.

'I'm Sara,' I told him, shaking his hand.

'Ah, Sara, it's so great to finally meet you. I've heard so much about you.'

'Well, I've heard nothing about you until today,' I laughed, 'but I'm pleased to meet you too.' I went to the supermarket to pick myself up a few things then ate my tea in the dining room while Lyanna and Chris watched a movie in the front room.

While I was washing up my plate, Lyanna came in. 'You don't have to hide away, you know. Come join us. We're watching one of your favourites—the *Lost Boys*.'

'No, I'm fine, honestly, I'm just going to get an early night.'

I bade them both goodnight and climbed the wooden hill up to my old room. I unpacked a few things, changed into my pyjamas then brushed my teeth. I curled up in the window seat with Buddy and looked out at the night, listening to the sound of the television and happy voices drifting up from downstairs.

I was so happy for Lyanna. I realised that I'd always just assumed she would be just Lyanna, not Lyanna *and* [insert name here]. I don't know why I'd presumed that; I'd never *wanted* her to be alone, but it had been so long since there'd been a plus one. I realised, that was because of me. She'd always been so focussed on me and making a living. Or, maybe there had been others that I didn't know about? I hadn't exactly been present in her life, not since Serafina's death, really. Well, apart from when I needed a place to stay, a decent meal, or someone to talk through my problems with.

Wow, was I really that selfish? Had our relationship really been that one-sided? What had I ever done for her? What had I ever done for anyone? Everyone was always running around, trying to save me and comfort me and help me, but what had I ever given anyone else in return? I was crushed. I'd finally figured who I was and I didn't like me one bit.

I curled up in my old bed, feeling the weight and warmth of Buddy on my feet, and cried. They weren't all tears of guilt and sadness; part of me was relieved to finally be feeling human again, to be feeling anything again. I realised I hadn't properly laughed or cried in years (watching Bill Bailey live recordings and *The Notebook* excluded). Years! What even is that? How can a person go years without laughing or crying?

I thought about Lyanna and Chris downstairs, watching a film together (and hopefully nothing more) and enjoying each other's company. I wanted that: someone to share my life with, someone to laugh and cry with, someone to experience life with. One person immediately sprung to mind, one person I could have had all that with—Bastian.

Chapter Thirty-Nine

The next morning, I was woken up early by the sunlight streaming in through the undressed window. I left Buddy on my bed while I took a shower. I put some make-up on and tried to decide on something to wear. Being a recluse had had a negative effect on my wardrobe. All I owned now were band t-shirts and worn, fraying jeans. I settled on a *Motorhead* t-shirt, my blackest, least-worn jeans and the only pair of shoes I owned—shabby, fourteen-eye Doc Martens.

Downstairs, Chris was cooking breakfast for Lyanna and asked me if I'd like anything. My stomach grumbled hungrily, but I had no appetite. In fact, I felt positively sick as a dog, so I politely declined.

Buddy and I headed out, him trotting along beside me eagerly. It was twenty-five degrees Celsius out, with a nice, cool breeze. Even so, I was sweating profusely because I was so unspeakably nervous. I'd decided to pay Bastian a visit. After five and a half years, how was he going to react to me showing up on his doorstep? Why hadn't I called or texted him first? I suppose, I didn't know if he even had the same phone number. On that note, how could I be sure he even still lived in the same flat? I turned back more than once but Buddy, ever my guide and friend, kept pulling me onwards. I'd considered asking Lyanna and Chris to dog-sit for the morning, but one; I didn't want to put them in awkward position if they had plans, and two; I thought that the sight of Buddy's cute face might soften Bastian's reaction to my sudden appearance. 'We can do this, Bud,' I said to him. He looked up at me with those huge, dark eyes, his pink tongue lolling out of his happy mouth and I actually felt a little more confident.

I arrived at the entrance to the building and instantly felt like I was going to vomit. What was I going to say when he answered the intercom? What if he wouldn't let me in? I was being stupid; the last time I'd seen him, he'd been perfectly friendly and had gifted me his prints, which were still hanging up in the cabin.

As if in answer to my prayers, someone exited the building, saw me standing there looking sickly and held the door open for me. I thanked them and entered. I climbed three flights of stairs to his apartment and loitered outside anxiously.

What if he didn't live there anymore? What if he was out? What if he had a girlfriend and *she* answered the door? Buddy looked up at me expectantly and I could hear him saying to me, *Come on! What are we waiting for?*

I took a deep breath and knocked on the door. I heard movement inside, which was a good sign. Thirty long seconds later, the door opened.

Bastian looked good, really good. He'd shaved his head, which I never would have imagined being a good look for him, but it surprisingly suited him. He'd grown a beard and gotten a few new tattoos. I laughed, partly through nerves, partly because he was wearing the same t-shirt as me. 'Sara? Hi!' He beamed, looking genuinely pleased to see me.

'I'm sorry, hi! I was just laughing at our matching shirts,' I confessed, pointing at his chest.

He looked down. 'Oh right, yeah! What are you doing here? And, who is this?' he asked. His voice turning all gooey when he spotted Buddy wagging his tail by my feet.

'This is Buddy,' I told him proudly.

'Is he yours?'

'No, I just picked him up off the street,' I replied sarcastically.

He laughed. 'Come in, both of you.'

Buddy nosy-ed around the apartment while I took a seat on the sofa. I noted it was the same sofa he'd had all those years ago. In fact, the entire apartment looked pretty much the same as the day I left.

'You don't mind him wandering around, do you? He's a good dog.'

'No, not at all—he's fine,' Bastian answered, stroking Buddy's head. 'Can I get you a drink?'

My mouth was dry as a bone. 'Yes, please. Just some water'll do.'

Bastian passed me a glass of water and put a bowl down for Buddy. 'So, how are you doing?' he asked me, taking a seat at the other end of the sofa.

'I'm good, thanks. How are you?'

'Yeah, alright. What are you doing back in Moraine?'

'Actually,' I decided to get straight to the point, 'I'm here to see you.'

'Aren't I lucky? You came all this way just to see me?'

'Yeah,' I confirmed shyly.

'It's actually quite bad timing. I'm really busy with work at the moment. How long are you staying for?'

'No, I think you've misunderstood me. I've moved back.'

'Oh, really? Where are you living now then?'

'I only got back yesterday so I'm technically 'living' out of a bag in my old room at Lyanna's.'

'Right.' He seemed confused. 'How come you decided to move back?'

'That's what I was *trying* to tell you. You're the reason.'

Bastian looked both flattered and concerned. 'What do you mean?'

'As you can imagine, I've had a lot of time to think up there and last week, I decided I wanted to come home.'

'Just like that?'

'Just like that. I was so lonely up there, but it took me a long time to realise it.'

'So, you realised you were lonely and you thought, hey, Bastian will keep me company.'

'Wait, no. No! What? How did you get that from what I said?'

'How could I *not* get that from what you said?'

'It's not what I meant, not at all.'

'Then, what *did* you mean?'

'I love you.'

There was an awkward silence. Buddy's collar jingled next to me. I could never ignore him so, despite the tension of the moment, I turned to ruffle his fur. I couldn't handle the awkwardness any longer. My face was turning redder and redder by the second.

'So, have you been seeing anyone? I asked, as nonchalantly as I could.

'Yeah.'

I froze. A feeling of cold spread up my back and heat burned through my front, meeting in the middle to create a thunderstorm of embarrassment and disappointment. I realised I should have started with that question. 'What's her name?' was all I could stomach to ask.

'Jane.'

'Are things serious?'

'They were.'

'Were?'

'Yeah, we broke up.'

'I'm sorry,' I said, feeling not sorry at all. Bastian was smiling. 'You did that on purpose, didn't you?'

'Yes. I'm sorry. That was low, but fun.'

'Sadist.'

He shrugged. 'You love me?'

'Yes,' I admitted, unable to look him in the eyes. 'I never stopped.'

Bastian ran his hands through his imaginary hair, a new tick I imagined he'd picked up since shaving it off. 'Well, I wasn't expecting this when I woke up this morning.'

'I'm not expecting you to say it back, you know. I didn't come here to back you into a corner. I came here to be honest, to get things off my chest, just to see you again, really. I've been alone for so long.'

'Do you know how selfish that sounds? You might not have intended any of that, but that's exactly what you've done. You just waltz in here and say all this stuff and what? What did you think would happen? I've been alone too, Sara, you know? You don't just get to walk back into my life and pick up where we left off.'

I didn't know what to say. He was right. I'd handled it in completely the wrong way. I'd put too much on him, with no warning. I *was* selfish. He'd confirmed all my worst fears about myself. I wanted to cry, but I didn't want to appear weak, or like I was trying to manipulate him, so I bit my bottom lip and kept schtum.

Bastian stood up, obviously frustrated. 'I'm sorry, I shouldn't have said all that. I'm just shocked, that's all. I never thought in a million years that you'd walk back into my life, let alone that you still love me.'

'I get that. What I really want to say is, I'm sorry. I'm sorry for everything that's happened, for how it ended.'

He sat back down, right beside me, and took my hand. 'Sara, you don't have to apologise for how you acted after Myla died. It's in the past. We smoothed everything over. You know I'll always care for you—none of that matters anymore.'

I couldn't stop the waterworks this time. I let it all flow. Being back there was bringing back so many painful memories. I was suddenly terrified that I'd made a huge mistake returning. 'I miss her so much.'

He put his arm around me. 'I know you do.'

He held me for a while, while Buddy nuzzled my legs, sensing there was something wrong.

While he held me, I thought about my feelings and this time, I confronted them instead of willing them to go away.

I missed Myla. Fine. That was normal. She had been a huge part of my life— my best friend—and I'd lost her in such a tragic way. I would always miss her, I would always think of her and I would always imagine her being there next to me, sharing every moment of my life.

I missed Serafina. I still carried the guilt of our final moments together and that was something I would never quite shake off. I would think of her whenever I read *Lord of the Rings* or saw someone with bird's nest hair, and I would always remember all the life-skills she'd taught me. I would carry them both with me wherever I went, and that's how they would live on.

I'd wasted five years of my life, living in solitude, missing out on so much; time with Lyanna, time with Bastian, but time is irrecuperable. It would do me no good to dwell on things that I couldn't change. The fact was, all that time away from society had allowed me time to write and live what I thought was my dream, to reflect and order my chaotic mind, and now what? I was in Bastian's arms. Sure, I didn't know for how long, but I was there, right then.

Once I got my emotions back under control, I left him to his work and returned to Lyanna's. The happy couple were out for the day, so I curled up on the sofa with Buddy and watched a film. When they arrived back in the afternoon, we ate together, watched another movie and had a proper catch-up. The day before, I'd felt out of place, like I was trespassing on their lives, but now it felt like I'd never been away.

*****

Bastian and I had made no more plans to see each other; I was leaving the ball in his court. If he wanted to see me, he knew where I was. So, I spent the next week or so house-hunting. I didn't have a clue what I wanted to do next, so I rented instead of buying to prevent getting tied down to another property.

I signed an agreement for a place right in the centre, above the stores on the main street. After so long spent in silence, I was desperate for some noise, some activity. At first, I felt like it was too much to handle, a world away from the peace and quiet of my cabin, but before long, the sound of traffic and people's chatter as they went about their business drifting up from the street below soothed me.

A few weeks went by and I still hadn't heard anything from Bastian. I tried to tell myself that it was okay, that I'd told him everything I'd wanted him to hear and he just didn't feel the same way, but of course I was heartbroken. I hadn't expected anything from him but part of me had truly hoped we'd get back together.

My agent started pressing me for some new chapters, so I threw something together to keep her happy but deep down, I just wasn't feeling it. My heart wasn't in it. I needed to consider my next steps and where I wanted to go from there. I wondered whether I should completely scrap my latest novel and start something entirely new, when my attention was drawn away from my work altogether.

I was munching my way through a microwave meal for one, enjoying a quiet night in with Buddy, when my phone started vibrating. 'Hello?' I didn't recognise the number but assumed it would be my agent, one of the two people who ever called me.

'Hey, Sara. It's Bastian.'

I spat my half-chewed pasta out and stood up. 'Hey! How are you doing?' I asked, trying to sound casual and failing miserably.

'Not bad, you?'

'Yeah, I'm fine, thanks. What's up?'

'Are you free sometime soon?'

'I'm free any time,' I replied, then silently berated myself for sounding so eager.

'Great. Well, can I see you tomorrow?'

'Tomorrow's fine.'

'You wanna come to mine for, say, eleven?'

'Sounds good.'

'Great. See you then.'

'See you.'

When I hung up, I realised I was pacing up and down my small flat like a caged tiger, while Buddy confusedly darted around my feet. I'd walked into the bedroom, bathroom and done four lengths of the living room and kitchen without even noticing.

I couldn't finish my meal-for-one and instead, spent the rest of my evening nervously wondering why the hell he wanted to see me. I tried not to get my hopes up, but I just couldn't help myself.

The next day, I turned up to Bastian's place at precisely 11 am as we'd arranged, this time without Buddy. Lyanna was going to the seaside with Chris for the day so had offered to take him with her.

Once again, I found myself nervously waiting outside his door, but when he greeted me with a huge, welcoming embrace, all my anxiety melted away.

We talked, for what seemed like days, about everything we'd been doing since we'd broken up. Everything was laid out on the table and by the end of the conversation, I felt like I was meeting him again for the first time. It was a clean slate.

Bastian looked out of the floor-to-ceiling windows at the bright, sunny day passing us by. 'Do you want to get out of here?'

'Sure, where do you want to go?'

'Just for a walk or something?'

We headed out in Bastian's car. I was pleased to find that he'd finally upgraded his old piece of junk.

We drove for a little while, still talking and laughing. I was so absorbed in the conversation that I hadn't noticed where he was taking me. When we pulled up in a layby off a winding country road, I still hadn't taken in my surroundings.

We headed into the woods, still relaxed and chatty. Eventually, the conversation lulled and I realised the scenery was familiar. 'Where are we?' I asked. But then, I saw it up ahead and I no longer required an answer. Moraine Manor. I stopped and demanded, 'Why have you brought me here?'

'Now, don't freak out, Sara. Just listen to me.'

'Is this some kind of test? A joke?'

'No, you know I'd never do anything like that.'

'Did you plan this?'

'Only while we were sat talking. I promise you, it's nothing sinister.'

'Then what is it?' I questioned, close to tears.

He put his hands on my shoulders and looked right into eyes. 'You know me, yeah?'

I nodded apprehensively. 'If I'd have told you, you wouldn't have got into the car, would you?'

'No.'

'I want to get to know you again. I want to start over. I want to be a part of everything, and that means the Other Place too.'

'Right,' I responded dubiously.

'Will you show me the way?'

I thought about what he was asking me. I'd never been there with anyone except Myla and I'd trusted her unquestionably. Did I really want to let him in to that part of my life? I thought about what he was to me, what I wanted him to be and what I wanted to be to him, and I realised, if I wanted him in my life for good, I was going to have to unlock this other, hidden part of myself.

I led the way to the Manor, feeling nervous and a little frightened. We both stood at its front, looking up at its poetic dereliction. The paint had once been a pale pastel colour but was now faded and cracked. The wooden shutters over the windows were broken, hanging loosely on their hinges like tired eyelids. Nature had reclaimed it; ivy and creepers, plants and flowers, were all snaking their way up the building, weaving in and out of the empty windows and up into the gaping hole in the roof where the chimney had once stood.

It was unnerving yet peaceful. The house was surrounded on all sides by dense greenery; all sounds were muffled and the sunlight peeking through dappled the house and grounds with golden flecks. The whole place felt magical, like we'd stumbled upon a secret, hidden from the rest of the world. 'I've never actually been up to the manor before,' I admitted.

'You haven't?'

'No. The portal is further into the woods.'

'Well, I'm glad you came here for the first time with me. It's amazing.'

'It is, isn't it?'

'Why haven't you ventured over here? Weren't you a little curious?'

'I was, but I was too scared on my own.'

'Scared? You? You wandered off into another realm, all alone, but you were too scared to look in an abandoned house?'

'You don't understand. You can't feel it.'

'Feel what?'

'The Other Place. I can feel it here, but not in a good way. It's hard to explain, but something about this place has warned me to stay away.'

'Well, now I'm creeped out.' He laughed uneasily.

I laughed too. 'I'm sorry. I'm sure there's nothing to worry about. I feel safe with you.'

'I'm glad to hear it. Do you want to go in?'

'Go in? Are you out of your mind?'

'I thought you said you feel safe?'

'I feel safe from like, attackers or something, but wouldn't it be dangerous? We don't know how safe the structure is.'

'We could at least peek through a window, couldn't we?' he suggested mischievously.

'I guess that wouldn't hurt,' I said, though I was on edge.

We crept over quietly, though I don't know why—there was obviously nobody living there. A twig snapped loudly beneath my feet, causing me to jump and scream dramatically. We both sniggered at my overreaction.

Bastian pulled open the shutter on the nearest window. It creaked reluctantly against his force, before breaking away from the frame and falling to the ground with a loud *thump*.

We both visibly cringed. 'I suppose if there is anything in there, it knows we're here now.'

'Why would you say that?' I asked, my heart beating violently.

'Come on, you were thinking it too.' He smiled.

'It's not funny,' I whinged.

We looked into the house through the glassless window. A breeze blew through, bringing with it a stench of musk and decay. The interior was breath-taking. We were looking into what appeared to have once been a library or study. The walls were lined with mahogany shelves and here and there, forgotten, wrinkly, old books were strewn, tattered paper quivering in the breeze. The floor was littered with debris and remains of heavy old furniture—a large bureau and writing desk with a few shabby armchairs sat stranded amongst the filth. 'Wow! Can you imagine what this used to look like?' I gasped.

'I know, it's awesome,' Bastian agreed, trying to get a closer look at the cracked ceiling and rotting floorboards.

'What are you planning?' I questioned him suspiciously.

'Come on, Sara, we have to go in.'

'Why? We can view every room from out here, through the windows.'

'I want to see upstairs.'

'You want to go upstairs?' I repeated incredulously.

'Yeah, don't you?'

'Not really.'

'Why? Aren't you curious?'

'Not enough to risk my life.'

'Don't be so dramatic! We'll be super careful.'

I held back; it was a terrible idea. I could feel it in my bones. 'I promise I'll look after you. If it looks unsafe, we'll turn back, I swear.'

'Fine,' I agreed resignedly. 'Go on then.'

Bastian grasped the tarnished doorknob on the great double doors and pulled, hard, but they wouldn't budge. 'Be careful,' I whispered, an image of them falling down and crushing him flashing through my mind. He pulled and pulled but they wouldn't budge.

I pushed him out of the way, grabbed the handles myself and gave them a huge shove, and the doors opened inwards. 'When have you ever known a front door to open outwards?' I chuckled.

'Oh yeah.' He looked embarrassed, but then his expression turned to one of wonder. 'Sara, look.'

I turned to find myself standing in a cavernous entrance hall. The ceiling was high above the second floor and, beneath the grime, I could tell that the floor was tiled black and white like a grand chessboard. Busts and statues lined up on either side, watching us, and at the far end, an imposing staircase wound its way up to the balcony above. 'Oh my God,' I breathed.

'I wish I'd brought my camera,' Bastian mused.

'Why didn't you? You usually take that thing everywhere with you.'

'I wanted all my focus to be on you today. I keep trying to switch my work brain off. But this…' he trailed off. 'I could get some really amazing pictures.'

'We can come back another time, don't worry about it. Let's just explore, lens-free.'

He agreed, following me into the hall.

Some of the floor tiles were chipped or broken, yet still welded solidly together. Before long, we were treading less cautiously; nosing in each room, gasping at the high ceilings, touching the moth-eaten drapes hanging around the empty window frames and studying the remains of chandeliers, china and books that littered the floor.

We came to the bottom of the staircase. I felt anxious for our safety, but Bastian reassured me the steps were solid marble and still in decent condition. He walked ahead, stepping carefully and pointing out any places where I might slip or trip. I followed closely behind.

We made it to the top and it was so worth the climb. The balcony ran around all four edges of the stairway, bordered by a golden balustrade. Doors led off in every direction, all of them shut, which I found rather odd. On the facing wall at the top of the stairs, was a gigantic oil painting of a glamourous, attractive woman dressed in 18th century finery. At first glance, her face was handsome and proud, but as I stared up into her dark eyes, I suddenly became terrified. Her irises were a piercing violet and I was violently transported back in time to when I'd looked into those eyes before. Her expression told me there was definitely more to this woman than she'd wanted her painting to suggest, whoever she was. I could almost feel her presence; a foreboding within the confines of the house, as though it was fearfully awaiting her return. I shuddered, shaking off the memory. 'Sara?'

I snapped out of my trance. 'Sorry, what?'

'Are you okay?' Bastian appeared beside me to inspect the cause of my hypnosis.

'Yeah, there's just something about this painting that doesn't sit easy with me.'

'I know what you mean. Come on, I don't want to look at it.'

We tried every door on the top floor; some appeared to be locked and wouldn't open no matter how hard we tried, some led into rooms with no floors and some into rooms with no ceilings. One room appeared to have been a child's playroom; broken, discarded, old-fashioned toys stared back at us. We shut that door fast. Only one room invited us in: the master suite.

The floorboards were in poor condition near the doorway, so we crept around the edges of the room as carefully as we were able. Once in the middle of the room, the boards seemed to be much safer.

A gigantic four-poster bed filled the far corner, sheer shabby drapes hanging down limply on all sides. The sunlight shone in, creating an ethereal glow and dead, blackening ivy vines crept in through the window, across the ceiling and down the walls, suffocating all it came into contact with. 'Wow, this is beautiful. I don't know where the outside ends and the inside begins,' Bastian murmured.

'I know,' I breathed, and for some reason, I found myself filled with lust. There was something about that house which had filled me with all kinds of emotions, changing from room to room.

Out on the landing, I had felt an awful sense of dread, like I was unwelcome or being watched. At the children's room, I'd felt utterly bereft and had had to shut the door before I broke down in tears. But in here, I felt exhilarated, confident and ravenous with lust. I eyed Bastian, wondering if he could feel it too. He glanced at me and I knew that he did.

We grabbed hold of each other; his hands were in my hair, on my neck, forcing their way beneath my clothes. We clawed at each other, desperately trying to unclothe each other, like starving predators eating their prey. We succeeded and stood before each other naked.

All around us, the sun seemed to glow ever more brightly, the dust motes dancing and twinkling in the beams. I don't know if it was a trick of the light, but the dead plants and vines suddenly came to life in a vibrancy of colour. I felt that we were no longer alone, but I didn't feel perturbed by this; I was overcome with love and desire and a deep need for his flesh. I felt like the entire world could have been watching at that moment and it wouldn't have held me back.

We took our time, feeling and caressing every part of each other, letting the sunlight play across our skin, our bodies entwining in every possible way, our thirst unquenchable. We enjoyed each other for hours and hours, neither of us able to stop, until finally, exhausted, our skin red with exertion and heat, our bodies ready to give in, we both climaxed in an explosion of colour. We laid, side by side, breathless, emotional and in quite a lot of pain, wondering what the fuck had just happened.

Once we'd recovered, we dressed in haste and left, our footsteps echoing around the empty house. Outside, we felt an even greater sense of urgency, like we were being compelled by a sinister force. We didn't stop until we were back in the car. 'What *was* that?' I asked breathlessly.

'I don't know,' Bastian panted. 'It feels like it was some sort of dream.'

'Like we weren't us?'

'Yeah. I mean, I was present, and at first, I loved what we were doing, but then, I don't know. I felt like a puppet on strings or something, like I was unable to control myself.'

'Me too.'

'I don't think I'll be going back to get any pictures.'

I felt vulnerable, bare; I was suddenly extremely aware of what we'd just done to each other. 'This hasn't made things weird, has it?' Bastian asked.

'No,' I replied reassuringly. 'I'm just glad that I was with you and nobody else.'

'Do you really think that it was that room? Would the effect have been the same whoever we were with?'

'I honestly don't know. I think yes, but I hope not.'

'I know what you mean.'

We both shuddered. 'I've always wondered what the manor's connection with the Other Place is; why the portal is in these grounds and why strange things always happen to me here.'

'Did you get any clues?'

'I don't think so, but I definitely felt something when I saw the painting of that woman. Somehow, I felt like she was the root of it all.'

'I felt something too, it was in her eyes.'

'Yes,' I agreed, glad I wasn't totally insane. 'The Other Place isn't bad, but I suppose the lure of it can be. I feel like she was at the heart of it. It's a little terrifying.'

'I'm sorry for bringing you here,' Bastian admitted.

'Why? Nothing happened to us, we weren't hurt. I'm glad we came.'

'You are?'

'Yes, because now I think you get it.'

'Well, I don't know about that.'

'No, well, I mean you get it as much as anyone could. It's unexplainable, a total mystery, but you can finally understand the way a place can *feel*, like it has emotions, how it can draw you in. That's what the Other Place feels like; a constant tug inside my head and you never know what's real and what's not. It's a suspension between reality and fantasy. I've never been able to explain it but now, I think you understand. I don't need to explain myself anymore.'

'You're right, I do understand, and I suppose that's exactly why I wanted us to come here.'

'Exactly.'

We both fell silent, a million questions racing through our minds.

At length, Bastian said, 'I don't know about you, but I'm starving after that.' So we drove off in search of sustenance, leaving that strange place in the rear-view mirror.

Chapter Forty

It was mid-winter; the sound of rain thrashing against the window and the wind howling across the roof woke me up. It was still dark outside but in winter, that was no indication of the time. I groaned and stretched, reaching out beside me, feeling for Bastian beneath the warm, soft covers.

Bastian and I were living together and it was the happiest I had ever been. Things had developed between us quickly after that day at Moraine Manor. We became inseparable, only spending time apart to work. We had spent so much time at each other's places that it hadn't been long before I'd moved in with him. We never even discussed it; one day, I just didn't return home.

Buddy loved our new home and he loved Bastian even more. I actually felt pushed out, like they had a special male bond that I couldn't be a part of and yet, seeing them together melted my heart. Everything was right with the world. 'Babe?' I asked the empty room. Bastian wasn't beside me. I opened my eyes, blinking away the haze, and looked around the room for a sign of him. His side of the bed was cold; he must have been up a while. I checked the time on my phone—it was 7 am. 'Urgh!' I rested my head back down on my pillow. *What is he doing up so early?* I thought.

I flicked on the television and let the soft voices of the news presenters lull me back into a doze.

I awoke a short time later to Bastian "sneaking" along the edge of the bed as quietly as a bulldozer. I heard an 'ah!' as he stubbed his toe on the bed frame. I groaned blearily. 'Sorry, sorry,' he whispered. 'Ssh! You just go back to sleep.'

'It's okay, I'm awake now.' I laughed lazily. 'Why did you get up so early, anyway?'

'I couldn't sleep,' he replied, slumping down on the bed beside me. I nuzzled my head into his lap and he stroked my hair. Usually, I could lay that way for hours but that morning, Bastian was fidgety and trying my patience as my head bounced up and down on his legs.

I sat up and looked him in the eye. 'What's going on with you today?'

'What do you mean?' He looked genuinely surprised.

'You were up way too early and I *know* you have nothing on today, and you're being all annoying and twitchy. What's on your mind?'

'Nothing,' he promised me unconvincingly.

'Fine then, if you don't want to tell me...' I made to get out of bed, but he grabbed me by the arm and pulled me back.

'Honestly, it's nothing. Don't worry about it.' He kissed me on the head.

We sat in bed and flicked through channels for a while longer. I felt Bastian moving about behind me and then, he tapped me on the shoulder. I turned around and found him sat cross-legged on the bed, holding out a ring-box with the most terrified, hopeful, excited expression I had ever seen on a man's face before. I clapped my hand to my mouth and bounced up and down where I sat. I think I squealed like a pig, but my memory is hazy.

Buddy bounded up onto the bed, wanting to be a part of the excitement. 'Will you marry me?' he asked while Buddy licked my face.

I said yes, instantly.

The ring was simple and feminine: an emerald-cut one-carat diamond set in a vintage-inspired, white gold band. He knew flashy wasn't my style. It was perfect.

After I slipped it on my finger and assured him for the millionth time how much I loved it and that it fit, he said, 'You don't mind, do you?'

'Mind what?'

'How I proposed?'

'What? It was perfect! It was totally unexpected, *and* I got to stay in my pyjamas!'

'You didn't want me to write it in the sky or propose in a helicopter over Manhattan while streaming it live to all our friends and family?' he smirked.

I laughed. 'You know the answer to that. While those things are amazing, I'm sure, I can't imagine it any other way.'

We spent the rest of the day in bed: me and my two favourite boys. That evening, we paid Lyanna a visit and told her the good news, then we all went out to eat and celebrate. I was ecstatic—really, truly over the moon—but as the night wore on, I became keenly aware that there were two people who I was dying to tell but never could: Serafina and Myla.

*****

The day Lyanna and I went shopping for my wedding dress was nothing like what I'd dreamed of. I woke up that morning and knew it wasn't going to go well, I had a gut feeling. Instead of feeling anticipation and excitement, I felt drained, like it wasn't worth the effort.

The store we visited was fine, the staff was nice enough, the dresses were *fine* but none of it, absolutely none of it, was *right*. I had one person with me: my aunt. No mother, no Serafina, no best friend. What kind of bride goes wedding dress shopping without her mother or her bridesmaid?

Lyanna sensed my negativity and tried really hard to make it feel special for me, but I just couldn't summon the right emotions. I tried on the fifth dress I'd picked out—a sprawling princess dress trimmed with lace—and looked in the mirror, but all I saw staring back at me was a hideous monster. A lonely, sad, hideous monster. I burst into tears. 'What is it?' Lyanna asked, rushing over to me, while the assistants tried to look busy. 'Is it the dress?'

'Yes, it's the fucking dress!' I yelled. 'My face! My body! My head! All of it—the whole thing.'

Lyanna held me. 'It's not the dress, is it?'

'No, the dress is fine,' I sighed. 'It's this wedding. There's going to be nobody there; you, me, Bastian, Chris and maybe a couple of Bastian's friends. I have no mother, no bridesmaids, nothing!' I cried, hard.

'I know, I know. I'm sorry, honey. This must be so hard for you.'

'Myla should be here, you know?'

'I know.'

'I'm being a huge baby, aren't I?'

'No, I think we should just come back another day.'

'Why? Will I feel better about myself and my wedding another day?'

'Maybe, maybe not, but today is not the day, clearly.'

The assistants helped me out of the dress. I apologised profusely for wasting their time and thanked them for their help before getting the hell out of there, hanging my head in shame.

Back at Lyanna's, over a mug of hot chocolate piled high with whipped cream, marshmallows and chocolate sprinkles, she asked me how I was feeling.

'Better now I'm out of that dress.'

'Don't worry about it. You'll find something.'

'I know. I don't even care, to be honest. I just feel deflated, like there's no point in the wedding.'

'Sara! Don't say that. Regardless of who's there, you deserve your dream wedding; you both do.'

'I feel like they've died...all over again. It's so fresh.'

'That'll happen a lot in your life. Every now and again, it hits you like a ton of bricks but eventually, it'll subside and go back to that dull ache in the back of your head again.'

'I want them here, so bad. It's not fair.'

'Me too.'

We sat in silence, sipping our hot drinks and trying to swallow our tears.

'Lyanna,' I said, 'I don't know what I'd do without you.'

She placed her hand on mine. 'You'd be okay. You're stronger than you think.'

'No, I mean it. You and Bastian are the only people I have left. And Buddy, of course.'

'And is there anything wrong with that?'

'No, I'm sorry, I didn't mean it like that...'

'I know, I know. I'm not offended—that's not what I meant. I meant, as you get older, you realise that it's not the quantity of the people in your life that give it meaning, but the connections you have with the people you do have.'

'I know that and I'm so grateful to have you guys. It's just this wedding; it's dragging up so many...bad emotions...'

'It will do but sometimes it's important to act strong even if you don't feel it.'

'You mean, fake it?'

'Sort of. You just have to take each day at a time. Put on a bold front, hold your head up high and muddle through. I promise you it'll get easier. Remember the reasons you're marrying Bastian. It's not about the wedding or the guests or the party, it's about your future together. That's all that matters.'

I thought on Lyanna's words of support; I clung to them for weeks and weeks. I was desperate for her to be right. I mean, I knew she was, of course— all that mattered was our future together—but no matter how hard I tried to tell myself that, I could still feel the stinging pain of loss.

I was desperately lonely. I wanted nothing more than to sit down with Lyanna, Sef and Myla and plan our wedding, have a bridal shower, throw a hen party—all the fun girly stuff that most brides get to do—but I couldn't. I couldn't do all those things with just one person. I didn't want to tell Lyanna how I felt in case I offended her, and I certainly didn't want to tell Bastian. The last thing he'd want was our wedding to be the cause of so much anxiety.

These were the kind of feelings I would have confided in Myla, but she wasn't there. Of course, if she had been there, I wouldn't have been feeling that way. That thought made me feel no better.

I hoped that it would pass over like a fleeting summer storm, but it didn't. If anything, it got worse, and from morning until night, I had a tight pain in my chest and an empty pit in my stomach. What if I was heading for another breakdown? What if it all became too much and I did something stupid? What if I hurt Bastian and ruined his life, again? Why were we getting married? Why did he love me? I was broken, unfixable. I thought, maybe, things would be different now—it had been so long since I'd felt any of that—but I was sorely mistaken. I mean, I was a fully grown adult, so why was I still acting like a moody, emotional teenager?

Of course, my age was irrelevant—I know that now. An illness in your mind doesn't just go away; you can't just ignore it or push it down into small spaces. It would always be there. No matter how good things got, it would always come back. I was cursed. I was never going to be happy and I couldn't let myself drag Bastian down.

*****

A few weeks after my talk with Lyanna, I came dangerously close to taking my own life. I was alone in the apartment one overcast afternoon while Bastian was out on a shoot. I was attempting to find some wedding venues that were both classy and cheap and failing miserably. I wasn't even trying, truth be told. We could have gotten married in a farmer's field freshly sprayed with manure for all I cared at that point.

I heard a noise up in the bedroom—a strange, scraping noise. 'Buddy?' I whistled. 'What are you doing up there?'

I climbed up the steps and looked around for him. 'Buddy?'

I heard a whimper coming from underneath the bed, so I crouched down and peered below. Buddy was cowering in the corner. 'What are you doing under there?' He growled angrily. 'Woah! What's going on, Bud?'

Again, he growled then began to bark aggressively. I'd never seen him act that way before, he was normally such an affectionate, good-natured dog. I started to panic.

I stood up to walk around the other side of the bed with the intention of pulling him out, when I felt a hot breeze on my back.

Assuming it was Bastian home early, I swung around, only to find nothing. I shivered. No windows were open—it was still spring and not yet warm enough—yet it wasn't cold enough to have the heating on so it couldn't have come from a radiator either. Still, I was sure I'd felt a warm breeze.

Then, I felt it again, closer, harder, so strong that it blew my hair in front of my face. I jumped, terrified. Buddy clambered out from below the bed and barked madly. He was fixated on a point right beside me, angrily growling and barking like he was possessed. 'What is it, Bud? What do you see?' I dared not move but then I felt it again, right in my ear and I freaked out. I ducked away and tried to scramble across the bed and into the bathroom, but something grabbed my ankle and yanked me backwards. I hit the floor with an almighty *thwack!* and yelped in pain. Buddy yelped too, in fear and, I believe, in sympathy. I remember being dragged across the floor and feeling the burn of the carpet against my arms and stomach. I tried to clutch onto something, anything, but nothing fixed was within reach. Then, the ground disappeared beneath me as I was pulled to the top of the stairs and left dangling in mid-air. I remember no more.

I woke up to Buddy licking my face. I tried to move but everything hurt. I wriggled my toes and fingers and turned my head side to side to check there was no serious damage. I suddenly remembered what had happened and sat up straight, looking around, searching for a sign of danger.

Buddy nuzzled my armpit and calmed me down. I cuddled him and made a fuss. 'I'm sorry, boy. That must have been super scary for you.' He licked me excitedly, glad I was awake and showering him with affection. 'I'm okay, don't worry, Bud. Thank you for protecting me.' I kissed him on the head then stood up, stiffly, groaning with the effort. I was going to look battered and bruised in a few hours.

Not this again, I thought. How could I have let it get *this* bad again? How could I have let them back in and put my family in danger? I couldn't let Bastian see me in that state. I couldn't risk Buddy getting hurt. I had to get out.

I found myself back at Moraine Manor. I don't remember driving there, which worried me greatly, and I had no awareness of what I was doing or where I was going until I was stepping out of my car and staring at the path ahead, knowing where it would lead. Something was drawing me in.

I locked the car and trudged on. I felt high, like I wasn't really there, like I was walking through a dream, or a nightmare.

I arrived at the house and became acutely aware that I was alone. The place gave me the creeps, but I was compelled to enter. The door was still ajar from when Bastian and I had broken in (and then rushed out) on our previous visit. A wind picked up, chilling me to the core. I realised I hadn't brought a coat, despite the chilly spring air. I entered, against my will.

I made my way up the staircase, taking care on the uneven, broken steps. I merely glanced at the painting of the austere woman at the top, not wanting to get seduced by her gaze again. I turned around and found that all the doors leading off into the other rooms were wide open. When we were there previously, all the doors had been closed, and some not just closed but locked. I felt sick with fear.

I walked along the landing, keeping the stairs on my left, and peered in every room. I felt like I was searching for something, but I had no clue what for. I reached the room at the far end of the hall and instantly found what I had apparently been searching for.

The room was stark and empty; bare peeling walls and bald, uneven floorboards exposed by the harsh daylight streaming in through the single grubby window. There was no furniture or fittings, except for one three-legged wooden stool placed directly in the centre of the floor beneath a length of rope tied into a noose that hung limply from the ceiling.

It was grim, possibly one of the bleakest sights I'd ever seen. It was there for me and I should have been grateful, I told myself. That was it, what it all amounted to. It was my way out of this living hell. The constant fear and uncertainty, the misery and the disappointment, the pain and sadness. This was my way of saving Bastian from a lifetime of having to put up with me and all my problems. This was my wedding gift to him.

Twisted, I know, but that's what I truly believed. I climbed up onto the stool and placed the rope gently around my neck. It grated on my skin, but it felt right. I was doing the right thing.

I took in what was going to be my last view of the world; a forbidding, stern, gloomy house, deserted of all life. From my position in the room, I had a clear view of the painting at the far end of the hall above the stairs. The witch was watching me with those cold, dead eyes. I swear I saw her smile.

The rope suddenly tightened around my neck without me touching it. And then it hit me: I didn't want to die. *What the fuck am I doing?* The rope tightened further so I grasped it, struggling to break free of its choking hold. I panicked and gasped for air as my chest and throat began to burn. *Please, I don't want to die.*

I managed to struggle free and collapsed onto the floor, taking a deep lungful of air. I stumbled to my feet and ran like the wind. I didn't dare look up at the painting as I sped past it and down the stairs. I felt her eyes bore into my back, nonetheless.

Somehow, I made it home without crashing my car, despite shaking violently and not being able to think straight. I burst through the door, grateful that Bastian wasn't yet home.

Buddy greeted me, jumping up and begging for my attention like he could sense something awful had happened. I headed straight up the steps into the bedroom, Buddy following eagerly at my heels, and sat down heavily on the bed. I took off my boots and kicked them away.

Buddy jumped up and demanded my attention. 'I am so sorry, Bud. I shouldn't have left you. I shouldn't have gone there. I promise I'll never leave you again.'

I went to take a shower, in an effort to wash away the past couple of hours of my life. I cracked open the window, turned the shower on and while I was waiting for the water to reach the right temperature, I undressed. Standing there, stark-naked, I felt extremely exposed. There was nobody in the apartment, except Buddy, but I felt uneasy. The events of the day had made me a nervous wreck.

I dashed inside the shower cubicle and slid the doors shut, breathing a sigh of relief as though I'd narrowly escaped something. The feeling was entirely irrational but authentic, nonetheless.

Rammstein was playing through a portable speaker, the heavy booming riffs and deep drumbeat echoing around the small space. I'd chosen their music to drown out my thoughts. Over the music, I heard a growl of thunder drifting through the open window. A flash of lightning followed seconds later, then the rain began to fall.

I let the water from the shower pour over me and I listened to the music thudding away, almost in time with the natural melody of the storm.

Once washed, I turned the tap off and squeezed the excess water from my hair, before taking a squeegee to the steamy cubicle panels. The water wiped away and through the misty glass, I could see eyes watching me. My first thought was Buddy, but they weren't his eyes. I jumped back and banged my head against the tiled wall. My lower back impacted with the shower tap, causing me to yelp in pain. I was aware of Buddy barking somewhere nearby. I dropped the squeegee and almost fell but managed to steady myself.

I looked again to the doorway where I'd seen the eyes and clearly, through the crack in the open door, I could see the outline of a strange, hunched figure. I screamed in fear and shouted, 'Get away from me!' But the thing remained, watching me intently with its yellow demonic eyes.

The lights went out. The storm was overhead, raging violently. I whimpered in fear and wrapped my arms around my cold, wet body. I wished I'd never put any music on so that I could hear what was going on. I was blind and deafened; the roar of the storm and the music together had created a cacophony of noise. With each flash of lightning, I caught a glimpse of the creature and each time, it appeared closer and closer, until eventually, it was right outside the cubicle.

The lightning stopped, the thunder ceased, the song finished; all that could now be heard was the soft pitter-patter of the ebbing rain. Fear gripped my heart—I still couldn't see a thing. Then, a scraping noise. The sound of the shower door sliding open. I curled up in the corner, as far back as I could press myself, mewling like a wounded animal. What was going to happen to me? What could I possibly do? Nothing. I had no weapon, I couldn't see, I could only sit there and await my fate. I could sense its maleficent presence.

The lights came back on and the creature was nowhere to be seen. 'Sara?' It was Bastian calling my name. I could hear his footsteps coming up the steps to the bedroom. 'Sara?'

The bathroom door opened fully with a creak. Bastian's face was contorted into a mask of horror and concern at the sight of me. What a sight I must have been, curled up in that corner like that, the wet tendrils of my hair snaking over my shoulders and my face, my skin ghostly as though all the blood had drained out of me. 'Sara!' He rushed to my side and hauled me out of the shower. 'What the hell happened? What's wrong?'

He dropped me onto the fluffy mat on the floor and hurriedly wrapped me in a towel. I was shaking with the cold. He shut the window swiftly then proceeded to rub me dry to try and warm me up. 'What happened?' he questioned urgently, eyeing up my bruises.

I shook my head. I was in such a deep state of shock from the horror in the bathroom that I couldn't speak. I winced as I tried to stand, aching all over. He helped me into the bedroom and onto the bed where Buddy was waiting for me. I curled up beside Buddy and drifted into unconsciousness, utterly drained.

Sometime later, Bastian woke me up, worriedly calling my name. He was sat on the edge of the bed, apparently having not moved an inch since I'd fallen asleep. 'Sara, I'm worried about you. What's happened? What's going on?'

'I'm fine, honestly,' I lied, turning to face him.

'I'd believe you if you weren't wincing in pain as you said it. Did someone do this to you?' His voice was deep and booming; he sounded like he wanted to kick the shit out of someone.

'I think I need time to explain.' I didn't want to talk about it right then, but I supposed I owed him an explanation. He must have been going insane with worry.

'You have time, now. Tell me, Sara. What happened?'

'Well, to explain what happened today, I'd have to explain what's been going on over the past few months,' I told him.

'You're really scaring me.'

'I'm sorry.' I didn't want to drag it out, so I told him as bluntly as I could. 'Since you asked me to marry you, I've been having doubts and...' I paused. 'I've been really fucking sad.'

Bastian looked hurt and confused. 'What? I—'

I held up my hand to stop him. 'Not because of you,' I continued. 'It's brought up a lot of really horrible memories and emotions because Sef and Myla aren't here to share it with me.'

Bastian nodded in understanding, looking relieved and sad and still perplexed, all at once. 'I'm sorry, I should have known.'

'It's okay. Basically, all that has sent me into a downward spiral. I started having nightmares and visions again. My thoughts got dark, really dark, and instead of talking about it, I decided I needed to shield you from it. I decided you deserved a better wife; I still think that, in fact.'

'You really think that?' Bastian's eyes brimmed with tears and my heart broke at the thought of what it would have done to him had I actually taken my own life. I suddenly felt sick, as an image of myself hanging from the ceiling in that dark, dusty old room in that horrible house, sprang into my head. I blinked, trying to rid myself of the thought.

'Today, my demons came back. I felt like there was something in the house with us. And then…' I couldn't bring myself to say it, so I didn't. 'I fell down the stairs trying to get away from it. In the shower just now, I thought I saw something again and I fell again.'

'Aww, my poor angel.' He reached out to stroke my face.

'That's not all—I went back to Moraine Manor.'

'Why?' He flinched as though my words had burned him.

'I don't know. I needed to get away and I just found myself there. It was even creepier than last time. There's something really wrong with that place.'

'I know! That's why we said we wouldn't go back!'

'I know, but I found myself there anyway and all the doors were open upstairs. I went into this empty room and…'

'What is it?'

Tears rolled down my cheeks. 'There was a noose hanging in there and a stool, and I got on the stool and…'

'You didn't?'

I nodded then lifted my chin.

His eyes widened at the sight of the bruising on my neck. 'You tried to kill yourself?' he whispered in disbelief.

'No! You have to believe me! As soon as I put it around my neck, I realised I didn't want to!'

'But you still thought about it!'

'I wasn't thinking straight. Everything got too much, I wasn't myself. I don't want to die, I promise!'

'You were going to leave me.'

'No Bastian, please. Please believe me.' I reached out to him, desperate.

He pulled away from me and my heart shattered into pieces. 'I can't deal with this. I have to go.'

'No, don't go,' I begged.

'I'm sorry, I need some air. I'll be back.' And with that, he descended the stairs and stalked out of the house, slamming the door behind him. What had I done?

I laid back down on the bed, unable to summon the energy to do anything more.

I had drifted back into an uneasy sleep and was awoken by the sound of the front door clicking shut. I pulled myself upright and shook my head in a meagre effort to wake myself up. Buddy jumped down from the bed and disappeared down the stairs.

'Hey, boy,' I heard Bastian greet him.

I stood up and the world instantly shifted on its axis. My legs turned to jelly and gave way beneath me, as hot stars exploded in my vision. I heard the sound of quick footsteps and I felt strong arms lift me up and lay me back down on the bed.

'Sara? Can you hear me?'

The feeling subsided and I opened my eyes. 'Yeah,' I replied. 'I'm just tired.'

Bastian ran his hands across his bristly head. He appeared on edge.

'I'm sorry,' I croaked.

He stood up, agitated, and made towards the stairs. He stopped and turned, apparently changing his mind. He seemed torn: wanting to leave but not able to.

'Let it out,' I urged him, bracing myself for a torrent of anger.

'I don't know how to process this, Sara, I really don't.'

I nodded and let him continue.

'Why didn't you talk to me? Why do you always bottle it up until you explode?'

I sat there silently and let him rant. I began to cry, but still stayed deathly quiet. He was right, about all of it. I felt so low for what I'd done, or what I'd almost done.

His rant continued for some time, then finally, he stopped and turned to look at me. His expression morphed from anger and pain to that of total and utter compassion. 'I'm so sorry, Sara.' He embraced me, encircling me in his huge, protective arms.

'Why are you sorry?' I sniffed.

'For not seeing this coming, for not realising what you're going through.'

'You're not a mind-reader, and things have been good for a long time. You weren't to know.'

'No, but I am going be your husband. I *should* have known.'

I shook my head vehemently. 'No, I'm sorry for putting you through this. This was what I was trying to protect you from, and I've just made everything worse.'

'You've got to stop doing this! It's not you and me; it's us. We're in this together, good times and bad. You have to let me in. After all we've been through, I can't believe that you still don't feel like you can open up that part of yourself to me. It's not a weakness, letting someone in.'

I took in everything he said and stayed quiet, processing it all.

'You're not alone,' he added.

He was right; I wasn't alone, or at least, I didn't have to be. I could let him in. I mentally berated myself for not doing it sooner. I'd told myself that the only person I could truly be myself around was Myla and after she'd died, I'd never let go of that notion, like I had died with her and I could never let anyone in ever again, but I was wrong. I was marrying Bastian. I was promising to spend the rest of my life with him. I had two choices: let him in or call off the wedding.

'Are you hearing me?' he asked genuinely.

'Yeah, sorry. I have a lot to process.'

'I can't sit and wait for you to process. The more you think on it, the more likely you are to talk yourself out of it.'

'No, you're right. Everything you've said is right.'

He looked relieved. 'You have to promise me you'll never let it get to that point again. Promise me you'll never even think about suicide.' We both visibly cringed at the word. His voice became deeper and gruffer, like the word itself had sent him into a rage. 'And if you even have the slightest inkling of a thought about anything like that, you'll talk to me, won't you?'

I nodded, scared to open my mouth. 'Promise me, Sara!'

'I promise, I really do.'

His shoulders relaxed and the creases on his forehead and around his eyes melted as his expression softened. He looked drained and sad. 'Come here,' he whispered and pulled me close. 'I don't know what I'd do without you.'

'I don't know what I'd do without you either,' I replied and felt hot tears swelling in my eyes again. I meant it.

He held me for a while then ran me a hot bubble bath to soothe my aching bones and bruised skin.

I emerged downstairs an hour or so later, to find Bastian and Buddy curled up on the sofa watching *The Empire Strikes Back*, Bastian's go-to feel-good film. Upon my entrance, Bastian paused the film and Buddy stood up, wagging his tail. Bastian extended his arm, gesturing for me to join them. I sat myself down and nestled into the curve of his body. 'How are you feeling?' he asked, kissing the top of my head.

'Like I've been hit by a truck.'

'You're in a mess, babe. I'm surprised you didn't break a bone falling down those steps.'

'Me too,' I agreed, glancing over to the steps and pushing the memory out of my mind.

'You're safe now.'

'I am.' I smiled, pushing myself even closer to him.

'You know, I've been thinking…'

'About what?'

He pulled away and turned his body to face me. 'We should elope.'

'Elope?'

'Yeah, let's just go to Vegas. It relieves all the stress you've been feeling and plus, we've always wanted to go there.'

I mulled it over. It did sound like a good plan: less stress and more fun. 'We could have our honeymoon over there and do that road trip we've always talked about.'

My stomach lurched at the thought of living out the trip of a lifetime in the west of America; somewhere I'd dreamed of going since watching cowboy movies as a kid and listening to Motley Crue sing about the Sunset Strip. It felt right and for the first time since I'd started planning the wedding, I actually felt enthusiastic at the thought of our wedding, instead of filled with dread. 'Let's do it!' I shrieked and threw my arms around him.

Chapter Forty-One

After that day, and our decision to elope in Vegas, the pressure evaporated off me. Lyanna and I sat down, booked the flights and hotel and researched wedding venues. There were so many to choose from that I lost interest and we decided we'd wing it when we got there.

One thing we did decide on was my wedding dress. It was off-white, loose, long and dreamily romantic: layers of lace and tulle with flared, off-the-shoulder half-sleeves. We ordered it online from Europe and the day it arrived, I rushed around to Lyanna's to try it on in front of her floor-to-ceiling mirror. I felt like a bohemian princess and couldn't wait to wear it in the middle of the desert, with the hot desert wind blowing through my hair and the sun beating down on my naked, sun-kissed shoulders. Most importantly, I would have the coolest, hottest, best guy on the planet by my side.

I spent the months running up to the wedding planning our honeymoon. I googled the time it would take to drive between each place and measured it against how much driving we would want to undertake in one day and the length of time we wanted to spend in each place. Overall, we would be over there a month. A month! Planning the trip was like a science. I loved every moment; it gave me focus and something to hang my hopes on.

I booked a rental van and the accommodation accordingly, mainly keeping to motels and hostels to keep the cost down. Cost wasn't necessarily an issue, but even though we made enough money to live well, really well, I still didn't like overspending for the sake of it. The richest experiences I'd ever had in life were the ones I'd experienced with empty pockets. What mattered was the person I would be experiencing it all with.

The evening before we were due to fly out, we dropped Buddy off at a kennel. It absolutely broke my heart to hear him whimpering and I wondered if he thought we were never coming back. I wanted to reassure him that we weren't leaving him for good, that we'd be back, that we loved him, but that's the curse of being a dog owner. Lyanna promised me she would collect him as soon as she got back from Vegas. Even so, I very nearly called the whole thing off at the sight of his huge, dark, sad eyes. I wanted to take him with us and let him share in our adventure, but I couldn't and had to say goodbye.

I couldn't sleep that night; I missed Buddy immensely, but I was also unbelievably excited about our trip. This was going to be my first holiday abroad since I was a teenager and we weren't doing it by half. It was a huge undertaking. I suddenly felt nauseous with apprehension. What were we doing? Were we mad? I flicked between these emotions, up and down, up and down, for some time, until finally I drifted off.

*****

I ended up enjoying the entire experience—I'd forgotten how much I love travelling. We got up at 4 am and jumped in the taxi to the airport an hour later, picking up Lyanna and Chris on the way. The others were quiet, even a little grumpy, whereas I was bouncing off the roof of the taxi.

We checked in and went straight for the breakfast buffet in the lounge, then, after getting our fill of bacon, sausage and hash browns, we sat and watched the planes taking off and landing and the other passengers dashing to their terminals, ready for their journeys to various destinations. The others came around after coffee and food and by the time we boarded the plane, we were all in high spirits.

I'd forgotten how nervous I could get when flying. When the plane set off down the runway and started climbing up into the air, my ears popped and my skin stretched white across my knuckles as I gripped the armrests, but once we were at cruising altitude, I relaxed and listened to some music, staring out at the glowing mountainous clouds undulating all the way out to the horizon.

My first impression of JFK airport was 'fuck!'. I'd never seen anywhere like it in my life. Bastian and I instantly went for pizza and fries in the food court then spent hours rifling through racks of American publications, boxes of sweets and snacks we'd never heard of and NYPD memorabilia.

The gap between our connecting flights was six hours long but somehow, we filled it flicking through doorstop magazines and observing people from all backgrounds and places as they went about their business. We were already in awe of America and we hadn't even left the airport.

The internal flight to Vegas was much less comfortable and I started to get achy, irritable and itching to be at our destination.

When we finally stepped out of McCarran International airport, some twenty-two hours after we'd walked out of our front door back home, the sun was going down and the sky was lit in a thousand shades of violet and pink and flaming orange. The heat, dry and intoxicating, hit us square in the face.

The cab drove us to the Strip, which dazzled us and overheated our senses after our exhausting travels. My eyes couldn't take in what they were seeing.

We checked into our hotel, went straight up to our room and closed the door on the world. I showered, turned the air con on full then climbed naked into bed and slept like a baby all the way through to sunrise. Bastian and I awoke at 7am the following morning, after quite possibly the best sleep I'd ever had, to sunlight streaming in through the thin, pale curtains. I padded across the room, my bare feet tacking on the tiled floor and threw open the curtains. The sun dazzled my eyes and the heat, even through the closed window, enveloped me, but the view was what really took my breath away. There it was: the Las Vegas Strip, right below us. Despite it being so early in the morning, I could still see plenty of people milling around on the streets below, like tiny ants. The pinks and yellows and oranges of sunrise sparkled and reflected off every building; it was like a dream or fantasy, unreal in its placement and structure.

Bastian joined me. 'That's something, isn't it?' he observed.

We spent the morning finalising all the details for the wedding—which would take place the following day—then we whiled away the afternoon cooling off in the hotel pool. After a swim, we headed up to the room for a nap. Nevada heat was suffocating and exhausting.

The night-time view was just as spectacular as the day. As the sun was setting in a field of burning crimson, the city came to life in flashes of gold and neon, like a crude mirage shimmering amid the desert wasteland.

I dressed up in a sequinned mini-dress and studded Doc Marten boots and joined Bastian, Lyanna and Chris in the lobby. Bastian's best man, Max, had arrived and greeted me with a hug. He looked run-down from his travels so headed straight to his room to rest, as we had done the night before.

We were staying at the Flamingo hotel, not the most awe-inspiring or glamorous of all the Strip hotels, but it felt like the beating heart of Vegas. The Flamingo is the oldest resort on the Strip and everywhere we looked were reminders of a time past, when mobsters ran the city and the men and women were glamourous and elegant. Aside from the modern facilities and giant television screens, the décor and the atmosphere made us feel like we could have been sitting alongside old Hollywood celebrities in the glittering post-war 1950s, sipping martinis and smoking cigarettes in the long, black holders.

The four of us weren't much for gambling and we didn't want to be hungover for the next day, so we simply strolled up and down the Strip, sightseeing and people-watching. Despite the city's seedy reputation, I found the place fascinating.

As the night deepened and the lights brightened, my mind awoke. I suddenly couldn't contain my excitement any longer. I was getting married the very next day, to the man I wanted to share all these experiences with.

Bastian and Chris stayed together in Chris' room and Lyanna joined me in our wedding suite. I kissed goodbye to Bastian at the door with butterflies in my stomach, knowing the next time I'd be seeing him, I'd be walking down the aisle. I'd never felt more alive.

*****

The sun rose on the morning of our wedding. Outside, starry-eyed youths lounged by the pool in the baking heat, golden-skinned millionaires drove their shiny, classic cars up and down the Strip and tourists flip-flopped along the sidewalks, all oblivious to the butterflies racing around my stomach on the most important day of my life.

Lyanna and I were sat in the hotel suite, picking at our room-service breakfast and chattering excitedly. 'I can't believe my little gummy bear is getting married today,' she sighed emotionally.

'Don't cry already!' I laughed.

'I know, I'm sorry. I'm so happy for you. There was a time when I never thought I'd see this day.'

'Me too. I really am so happy but…'

'What is it?'

'I wish Myla and Sef were here to share it with us.'

'I know, I've been thinking about them, too.'

'Sef, of course, would be practical: organising everything and making sure everyone's doing their jobs. Myla would obviously be my bridesmaid, helping me get ready.' I smiled, imagining another life where these dreams would have been reality. 'It breaks my heart that they're not here. Somehow, the entire thing just feels sad and pointless without them.'

'It does now, but I promise you, once the ceremony is over and we're celebrating, it will really feel like your wedding day. I'm here for you: me *and* Chris.'

'I'm so glad.' I battled against the sombre atmosphere and the aching in my heart. I poured us some champagne. 'To Bastian and me, and to you and Chris,' I toasted.

'To us.' We took a deep drink. 'Now come on, let's get you ready.'

Two hours later, my hair freshly washed and hanging naturally all the way down my back, my make-up done, my lacy, loose bohemian-style dress and cowboy boots on, I was standing before the Little Neon Chapel with clammy hands and stomach ache.

Lyanna grasped my hand. 'You look gorgeous,' she beamed. 'Are you ready?'

I nodded, took a deep breath and we walked in, side by side.

Bastian stood at the end of the aisle, waiting nervously for me, dressed head-to-toe in black, Johnny Cash-style. Max and Chris stood to his left. Bastian's face glowed when he saw me and I thought he was the most handsome man I had ever seen.

The ceremony was short and sweet. Being atheists, we'd prepared our own vows and skipped all the religious rambling. After our vows, we exchanged rings, were declared husband and wife and signed the register with our witnesses. It was all a blur, really. I barely remember the details; it happened so fast, like a dream you're only aware of once you wake up.

We exited the chapel into the burning Vegas noon, while Lyanna, Chris and Max threw confetti into the air. We stood side by side and held hands, staring out at the white desert as it stretched all the way out to the distant mountains, bleached and shimmering like a mirage. It was breath-taking.

We held the wedding breakfast at a retro diner and stuffed our faces with burgers, fries, pizza and ice-cream. I was glad I'd chosen a loose-fitting gown.

In the lull between our main courses and dessert, I took myself off to the restroom to cry. I knew just how much Myla would have loved that place. I missed her desperately. I pulled myself together; Myla would not have wanted me crying in the toilets on my wedding day. So, I touched up my make-up, held my head up high and made my way back out into the bright, bustling diner.

That night, we drove out into the desert to a bar I'd googled a few weeks before. It was, quite literally, in the middle of nowhere, stood between a motel and a brothel. Some might think that would be the last place a bride would want to celebrate her wedding day, but to us it was perfect: informal, fun, unique and real tongue-in-cheek American-style.

We all got absolutely shit-faced drunk, danced, laughed and sang along to country music until 3 am. The next day, severely hungover and exhausted, we drove back to our hotel on the Strip and spent the day relaxing by the pool and sleeping it off.

*****

It was time for our adventure. We said goodbye to Lyanna, Max and Chris at the airport then set off on the first leg of our trip. First stop: Monument Valley.

As our road took us north, the scenery changed from bleached and dry to vibrant and colourful. We drove through a savage rainstorm and, though it was still warm, the rain dampened the air and relaxed us. I watched from the passenger seat, my feet up on the dash, as we passed giant cacti, desert roadkill and stunning views of mountains and red rock.

Monument Valley, especially after leaving the noise and bright lights of Vegas, was heaven on earth. During the day, we drove around the dirt tracks and explored the Mesas and Buttes. The place was like nothing I'd ever seen.

On the first night, we were treated to a majestic view of a thunderstorm over the distant mountains. We sat in our campervan with the side door open, listening to the rain pattering on the roof and watching the colourful, intense display of lightning and dark, swirling clouds in the distance. All our belongings got soaked through, but it was worth it.

The next morning, after a breakfast of pancakes, fresh fruit and pastries up at the hotel diner, we sat and looked out at the three Mittens—the most famous Monument Valley viewpoint, bar John Wayne's point. The Navajo were chanting up on the hill, the air was fresh after the storm and the colour of the red rock and green shrubbery were dazzling in the bright sunlight. I wanted to stay there forever and ever.

On our last morning there, we sat and looked out, taking in our last view of quite possibly our favourite place on this planet. It was so quiet and peaceful. I felt like we were the only two people in existence, and I realised if I had to choose

316

one person to be left alone on the earth with, it would be Bastian. He was not only my lover, my partner and now, my husband, but he was my best friend.

We had to move on—our road to Los Angeles lay ahead. On our journey to the City of Angels, we ate dinner with the Hualapai tribe overlooking the Grand Canyon, unwittingly ate our breakfast alongside a pair of wild tarantulas the size of bricks and got chased by a dust devil somewhere along the Veteran's Highway. We witnessed a re-enactment of the OK Corral gunfight and drank in Big Nose Kate's Saloon in Tombstone and, somewhere near the border of Arizona and California, we laid beneath the stars and glimpsed the ISS cross the sky as the Milky Way glittered silently beyond.

We spent two weeks in LA and we did *everything*: star-spotting on the Walk of Fame, the celebrity homes tour of Beverley Hills, drinking in the Rainbow Bar & Grill, shopping on Melrose Avenue, drinking shakes in Mel's Diner on Sunset Strip, swimming in the Pacific Ocean, strolling along the Venice boardwalk, touring Paramount Studios, visiting Johnny Ramone's grave in the Hollywood Forever cemetery, hiking up to the Griffith Observatory to take in the view of the whole of the city, visiting Jim Morrison's house in Venice and, on our final night, sunburnt and shattered, we had an impromptu sing-along with one of our favourite singers back at the Rainbow.

Los Angeles is an alien city. It's a million miles away from anywhere in the world; there's nowhere quite like it. None of it is real. There's a glossy, glamorous veil masking the dirt and the sleaze, and what at first you think is natural and soft is actually nothing more than cold, hard plastic: the lights, the buildings, the people. But it was everything I imagined and wanted it to be.

It was the trip of a lifetime and I'd had the fortune of seeing it with my best friend and new husband. The morning we flew back to the UK, we had major holiday blues, but I was ready to leave. I missed Buddy, I missed the rain, I missed my dressing gown and my teddies. I had gone there with my eyes wide open, well aware it was a fantasy land, an adult playground, but now, I was ready for a large dose of reality.

*****

Back home, Bastian and I moved out of his apartment and bought a place together: our very own home. After all we'd been through, it felt like a dream come true to finally be settled and happy in our own space.

It was a detached, double-fronted house with an enormous master suite, decorated with baroque-style furniture and sultry, gothic details, a photography studio and dark room for Bastian, a homey, comfortable writing study for me, an open-plan kitchen and living space decorated with bits and bobs we'd collected on our travels, graphic art and photographs, and movie and music memorabilia, and our favourite part—a wrap-around porch where we could sit and look out over our land. We were surrounded by nothing but trees and wildlife. Our house had everything—Buddy even had his very own room.

I kept the cabin, which we used to holiday in twice a year. We were truly content and felt like life was finally how it was supposed to be. Both of us were generating a decent income and prospering in our respective fields, and we managed to fit much more travelling in too. A perk of our professions was being able to work anywhere in the world. For a long time, we remained that way, thriving in our new life together and completely, unashamedly, in love.

Chapter Forty-Two

Soft, yellow lights hung from the eaves of the cabin. They twisted and coiled their way around the nearest trees like a string of fireflies. A bushy holly wreath, trimmed with pinecones and red berries, sat slightly off-centre on the front door. Inside, festive bunting, red and green ribbons, and twinkling fairy lights decked the walls, and a seven-foot, lush Christmas tree nestled in the corner of the room by the wide, front window, adorned with baubles and trinkets of all values, shapes and sizes, and as many lights as I could possibly fit on there. Our tree could be seen all the way through the woods from the lake, like a shining beacon of Christmas spirit.

We loved Christmas, both of us. Well, maybe I did slightly more, but we both enjoyed it. It was a time to relax, pig out, wrap up all cosy and see family. It was our first Christmas as a married couple and we were determined to make it as special as we possibly could.

It was Christmas Eve and we were busy decorating the cabin ready for Lyanna and Chris to join us. We had arrived the evening before and had been too lazy and tired to start dressing the place up.

I was balancing precariously atop a stool, trying—and failing—to stick the huge, gold, glittering star on the top branch of the tree. 'Need any help?' Bastian chuckled, noticing my struggle.

'No…I've…almost got it…' I grunted, straining to reach up.

I leant back to assess my handiwork. *Perfect!* I thought, until it drooped limply to one side.

'It looks so sad!' I exclaimed hopelessly.

'Come here, let me have a go.' Bastian picked me up by the waist and set me down heavily on the floor.

He faffed and rustled around for a few moments then heaved a grunt of satisfaction. 'Move your big head! Let me see!' I demanded.

He stepped down from the stool, allowing me to view his masterpiece. It remained droopy and lifeless, exactly the same. We both laughed and decided to give up the fight. *It gave the tree character*, I told myself, though I spent the next few days looking up at that star and wanting to tear it down.

I still had a small box of baubles to give a home to and I was determined to use every last one. I picked the first few from the top of the box and began arranging them methodically on the few bare branches that remained. 'Hot chocolate?' Bastian asked.

'Mmm, yes please.'

I could hear him shuffling around in the kitchen and clinking mugs together as he took them out of the cupboard, then I heard the *click* as he switched the kettle on. 'When will they get here, do you think?' he asked of Lyanna and Chris.

'Chris checked in about half an hour ago, they're probably not far off now.'

Bastian asked me another question, but I couldn't hear him over the sound of the water coming to boil.

Something reached out through the branches of the tree and grabbed me by the wrist. I leapt back, alarmed and tripped backwards over the box of baubles.

The kettle clicked off and the cabin fell silent. Then, I heard the sound of laughter coming from multiple directions. I was laid, sprawled out on the flat of my back, confused, startled and unsure whether to laugh or cry. Three faces appeared above, peering down at me with humorous grins. Lyanna and Chris had arrived. 'Need a hand?' Chris asked, pulling me to my feet.

I brushed myself off and tried to keep my voice level. 'Hey!'

I gave Chris and Lyanna a welcome hug while Bastian topped off the hot chocolates with whipped cream.

We drank our beverages and caught up, before Lyanna and Chris disappeared into the guest bedroom to unpack their things. I took the opportunity to disappear myself. I found Buddy in our bedroom taking a nap. I sat down beside him and gave him some much-appreciated attention in an effort to settle my own nerves.

What *was* that? Had I imagined it? I didn't know, but I sure as hell hoped so.

That night, we drank and ate festive treats and played Monopoly (Lord of the Rings-themed, of course) while the soothing tones of *A Muppet's Christmas Carol* played in the background. There was no snow outside—surprise, surprise—but we were cosy and warm and happy, nonetheless.

We had been playing Monopoly for three hours; we'd lost Lyanna and Chris and Bastian were holding on by a thread. I, on the other hand, was sitting atop a great fortune. Bastian just needed to roll a five and he would land on my Mount Doom, complete with a fortress. He rolled, the dice hit the board with a *thunk* and…a two and a three! I won!

I jumped up and down in my seat excitedly. He gave me a congratulatory kiss on the head before standing up to stretch his stiff legs. 'Finally,' Lyanna sighed. 'That game is no fun to watch.'

'Well, you should have had a better strategy and you wouldn't have gotten kicked out so soon,' I scorned, sticking my tongue out at her playfully.

We cleared the board away and settled on the shabby, spongy sofas to watch the end of the film. Michael Caine's Scrooge was singing his song with the villagers and was on his way to Bob Cratchett's house to surprise him—my favourite scene of the film.

A strange noise caught my attention: the sound of a marble rolling along a wooden floor. I turned to see where the noise was coming from and a small, plastic ball rolled into view out of the darkness of the hallway. It came to a standstill in the middle of the room, where it hit the rug.

I looked around at the others. Nobody else seemed to have noticed. 'Guys?'

They all looked at me. 'What's up?' Lyanna asked.

'Where did that come from?' I questioned, pointing down at the ball.

'I don't know,' Bastian admitted, looking perplexed. 'I've never seen it before, have you?'

I shook my head. 'Buddy was probably playing with it,' Chris offered.

'No, I swear it just came from the hall,' I told them, eyeing up Buddy, who was asleep before the fire at the opposite side of the room to the hallway, where he had been resting for the past few hours. 'I've never seen that ball before in my life.

'I'm sure it's nothing, Sara. The wind probably just blew it out from under one of the sofas,' Lyanna assured me.

'No, it came—'

I was cut off by Chris as he stood up. 'Whisky anyone?'

I shut my mouth with a *clack* as my teeth clashed. 'Sorry, Sara. Were you saying something?'

'No, it's fine. No whisky for me, thank you.'

They busied themselves in the kitchen, putting yet more snacks into bowls and pouring out tumblers of whisky for their nightcaps while I stared at the deep, dark hallway. It now appeared threatening, malevolent even. I pictured something lurking there, just out of sight, watching us and ready to jump out on anyone who strayed too close.

I was unsettled and creeped out for the rest of the night. Part of me wanted to march over and take a look. I was a grown woman; I shouldn't have felt scared in my own house. I wanted to prove to myself that I was being irrational, silly even, but I knew I wasn't. After all I'd seen and done in my life, I knew that it could be anything I imagined it to be, or worse.

When it finally came time for bed, I walked apprehensively towards the hall. I had to be the first one to enter; I couldn't reveal my nerves to them. I didn't want them to know anything was bothering me.

The darkness crept closer and closer until I was stood before it, looking right into it. It was impenetrable as all the doors were shut along either side of the hall and there were no windows in the narrow space. I refused to walk into it, no matter how brave I wished to appear, so I felt for the light switch which I knew was only a foot or so away. I felt around, panic rising inside me when it didn't immediately make itself known to me, imagining something grabbing my wrist again. Then, I found it. The light flickered to life, illuminating every corner and shadowy nook. Nothing. It was just my old, dingy hallway. I sighed with relief, kissed Lyanna and Chris goodnight and headed into our bedroom, Buddy and Bastian following close behind.

In bed, Bastian said, out of the blue, 'That ball really got you spooked, didn't it?'

I didn't respond at first, surprised that he had picked up on my anxiousness. 'You noticed that, huh?'

'Of course I did.'

'Well, yeah. You guys didn't see it, but I'm telling you, that ball rolled down the hallway and into the front room on its own.'

'You don't have to tell me twice. I've learnt by now when you're just being a drama queen and when you're being honest.'

'What could it have been?'

'I don't know, a ghost maybe?'

I shuddered. 'I actually wish it was.' I imagined a host of demons hiding in my house and felt sick to my stomach.

'I knew you'd assume it was that,' Bastian sighed, as though reading my mind. He snuggled up close to me and put his arm around my shoulders. 'Don't worry about it. I promise you're safe with me.'

I nodded. 'I know,' I replied, though I still felt uneasy.

'You know what? I've figured it out!' Bastian exclaimed.

My hopes lifted, dying to hear a logical explanation to settle my disturbed mind. 'You have?'

'It's Santa Claus!'

I punched him in the ribs. 'Not funny,' I told him, smiling.

He brushed my lips with his fingers. 'Made you smile though, didn't I?'

'I suppose.' I found that I did feel less tense.

Bastian pulled the covers up over our heads and we both burrowed under, facing each other. 'It's Christmas tomorrow,' he whispered.

'I know,' I replied, feeling excited all of a sudden, as though I'd only just been made aware of it.

'Our first Christmas married.'

I grinned. Hidden away under the covers, in his arms, I felt like nothing could touch me. I filled my mind with images of Christmas morning and all the joyful things it would bring and banished the darkness from my thoughts. This was going to be a special Christmas and I wasn't going to let anything ruin it. Christmas morning greeted us bright and crisp. I'd like to tell you that it was postcard perfect, with a layer of glittering snow layering the ground and tree branches, as I poked my head around the curtains, but it was the same old view; beautiful, but nothing new or miraculous.

It had, in fact, rained heavily in the night and the ground was a sloppy mush. Nonetheless, we threw on our large, fleece-lined parkas and old, sturdy boots and headed out into the biting cold morning air with Buddy, leaving Lyanna and Chris dozing in the guest room. The air was pungent with the smell of earth and it woke me up instantly.

Buddy pulled us all the way around the lake; it was like he knew he would be receiving presents once we got back to the cabin. On more than a few occasions, I nearly slipped and fell into the mud. 'Buddy! Slow down!' I laughed, as we neared the front door. Bastian opened the door and we took our boots off on the step, leaving them outside to dry off. Before we'd left, I'd lit the fire so the room was nice and toasty. We hung up our coats by the door and closed it behind us, locking out the cold, while Buddy watched on expectantly.

Buddy unwrapped his clumsily wrapped gifts of doggy treats and chew toys then proceeded to run around with the wrapping paper, leaving shredded, red pieces all over the floor and completely ignoring his actual gifts. We wrestled with him for a little while, playing along with his game, then I opened his treats and fed him a few, leaving him to calm down in front of the fire. 'Shall we wait for them to get up before we do presents?' I asked.

'There's just one I'd like to give you alone,' he grinned.

Visions of sex toys and revealing underwear passed through my mind and I sniggered like a schoolgirl.

Bastian pulled out a large box from the back of the tree and slid it over to where I was sat cross-legged on the shaggy rug. 'It doesn't look like anything naughty,' I mused.

'It's better!' he proclaimed, looking like he was going to burst with anticipation.

I peeled back the Sellotape, slowly and carefully, feeling Bastian's eyes on me, urging me to speed up. 'Come on!' he demanded impatiently.

I laughed and ripped the rest of the paper off, throwing it to Buddy to add to his pile.

In case you haven't already surmised, I am a geek. A grade A, true and honest nerd. My love of Tolkien knows no bounds therefore the present I received that day was the best gift I have ever received in my entire life.

Encased in a plastic display case, sat a replica of Aragorn's crown, atop a blue velvet plinth, gleaming silver in the morning light. I actually cried tears of joy, then proceeded to scream like a fangirl at a gig. 'Thank you! Thank you!' I shrieked, unable to contain my emotion or my gratitude.

Lyanna and Chris came running in to see what all the noise was about and burst out laughing when they saw me stood there, tears streaming down my face and a giant crown perched on my head.

I showed them my new "toy", which, of course, was not a toy but something to be revered and not touched from that day onwards, and would sit in pride of place on our mantelpiece back home.

After breaking into a selection box for breakfast—hey, I'm an adult, I can do things like that—we all exchanged gifts while cheesy Christmas tunes played on the radio.

The day was simple and perfect; Chris and Bastian cooked Christmas dinner together, while Lyanna and I watched *Home Alone* 1 and 2 and played Trivial Pursuit. We sat down to eat at the large, oak table we'd bought especially for the occasion. We'd positioned it in the back of the house, overlooking the depths of the forest through the wide patio doors leading out to the back porch.

We'd decorated the table with ivy and holly and a festive gold and red tablecloth. Plates were piled high with meats (gammon, turkey, beef), golden potatoes roasted in turkey fat, balls of stuffing, pigs in blankets, cranberry sauce, colourful, gleaming vegetables, to name just a few. We all dug into the feast until we could no longer move or speak.

Afterwards, we laid out on the sofas to rest our bursting bellies and watched back-to-back cheery films with flimsy storylines and poor acting, but that entertained us, nonetheless. Later on, we played some games—charades, Pictionary, Cluedo—and drank creamy, core-warming liqueurs. On Christmas night, we stuck to our tradition and watched *Gremlins*, as we had done every year we'd spent together since I was a kid.

The last Christmas I'd spent at the cabin, I had been alone with Buddy. I had eaten a questionable frozen pizza, exchanged no gifts with anyone and had spent the entire day and evening writing, unable to tear myself away from whatever I'd been working on at that time. Worst of all, I'd lost all sense of what life was about: people. Family and friends. When you're alone, all special occasions, all great life events lose meaning. What is the significance of a birthday or a holiday when you have no-one to share it with?

Right there, right then, I had everything I could ever want with me. The leftover smell of dinner lingered in the air, remnants of wrapping paper and chocolate wrappers littered the floor, opened presents were stacked up in every corner and, most importantly, the faces of the people I loved glowed with the light of the fire as they laughed at Gizmo's antics.

I felt the familiar twinge in my chest, as I always did during those truly happy moments in life; a mental nudge to remind me that Myla and Sef weren't there. I could call it guilt—I genuinely did feel guilty for enjoying myself without them—but it was also love. That feeling meant that I thought of them, and if I thought of them, then they were still with me and a part of my life.

There were no more strange happenings that day. I didn't realise until I climbed into bed in the early hours of Boxing Day, but I hadn't even thought of the odd occurrences of the night before. I felt relieved and glad that nothing had ruined our day. Our first married Christmas had been a success and I was looking forward to many more.

The next morning, we waved Lyanna and Chris off at the door then stayed in our pyjamas all day, picking at leftover food and binge-watching Clint Eastwood westerns. This was us: best friends who shared everything, including our awesome taste in films and music. I felt safe and at ease, like no matter what happened in the future, as long as I had Bastian at my side, I could face anything.

Chapter Forty-Three

I've always had a restless mind and I'm sure that it loves to sabotage me. No matter how happy I am, whether I've got everything I think I've ever wanted, my demons always resurface. I thought this time would be different, that they'd gone for good and had been left behind with my twenties, as it had been so long since I'd had an "episode". I was wrong. The nightmares began to plague my sleep once more and the darkness within me crept back into the daylight of my mind.

It was an in-between moment in our marriage. Bastian and I were knee-deep in work, unable to spend much time together and we had no trips planned to break up the day-to-day grind. I knew *it* was rearing its ugly head again and so, to alleviate any stress I might have felt at home and subsequently taken out on Bastian, I took to writing in a café in York. I figured fresh air and a change of scenery would lift me out of my slump.

Every morning, I rose early, kissed Bastian goodbye and headed off on the train to York. In the café, I sat and wrote and watched the world go by, until the evening when I would join the other commuters on the train home. It allowed me to separate my work from my home life. For a while, I felt like it was working. I'd go home feeling accomplished and able to give Bastian my full attention. The nightmares receded for a short while, but soon resumed with a vengeance.

I kept my word and confided in Bastian all that was going on inside my head, and he kept his word and promised me that he'd support me and give me anything I needed: comfort or space, whatever would help. I knew then that he was truly the most magnificent man in the whole world. So, why did I have an affair?

Once again, my deep-rooted issues resurfaced. They had been buried so deep and for so long, I'd forgotten they even existed, but they did, and it was Bastian who suffered because of them.

I don't know where my restlessness comes from or why I have so many issues with intimacy. I don't think I can pin-point an exact event in my life that caused it, rather, it's an amalgamation of a whole load of shitty things that have happened to me and how my mind has wired itself to cope.

I find it easier to have sex with people I don't know. One-night stands, new relationships, flings, they make me promiscuous and sexually adventurous. I have no inhibitions, no nervousness when showing off my body, just a desire to be wanted and lusted after. Then, once I trust somebody and love them, once there is an emotional connection, my sex drive evaporates. I feel ugly and self-conscious, and the thought of being naked in front of that person becomes repulsive. Don't get me wrong, I still thought Bastian was one of the sexiest, most handsome men on the planet, but I just couldn't bring myself to WANT him. We still had sex, but that was mostly because I knew we had to, rather than out of any desire. It was wholly crushing. I would look at other men and imagine them naked, imagine them wanting to see me naked, imagine us together, but I couldn't do the same with the man I loved: the man I wanted to feel those things for. What was *wrong* with me?

I never wanted to cheat; the thought of actually going through with any of these fleeting fantasies made me feel physically sick. Nonetheless, I couldn't get rid of the unwanted thoughts that plagued me.

*****

It was a Wednesday afternoon and I was sat in the café, typing away furiously on my laptop, when I noticed a man across the room. He looked to be quite a bit older than me; dark eyes, dark hair speckled with silver and creases etched around his eyes. He was watching me intently. I blushed, feeling flustered, and returned hastily to my typing. When I looked back up, he was gone. I smiled to myself, flattered.

Over the following weeks, I saw him again and again. Not every day, but a few times a week. I would be sat in my usual spot and he would appear in the corner. We'd make eye contact, nothing more. I saw it as a harmless flirtation, just a little bit of light fun to break up the monotony of my day. I never intended to speak to him.

One evening, I was packing away my laptop when he appeared beside me. 'Would you mind if I joined you?' he asked me in his heavy Southern Irish accent.

I looked up and my heart leaped into my mouth. 'Sure,' I replied, trying to sound casual.

He pulled up a chair opposite me and every hair on my body stood on end. 'I'm Tom, nice to meet you.'

'I'm Sara.' I didn't feel like myself at all; it was like an out of body experience. Everything about it felt wrong yet also exciting.

'Are you leaving?' he asked, studying me intensely.

'I was, yes.'

'Sorry, I just didn't want to disturb you before. You looked so deeply involved in your work.'

'I usually am.'

'I noticed. What are you writing?'

'A novel.'

'Your first?'

'Seventh.'

'Seventh, woah. Anything I might know?'

I shrugged. 'I write science fiction and fantasy, mostly.'

'No, probably not then.'

I smiled. 'I'm glad.'

'Why?'

'Sci-fi and fantasy fans are very, um, passionate about their genre. Conversations can get quite heated.'

'Ah, I see. Don't worry, I won't chew your ear off.'

I looked at the clock. I was going to miss my train if I didn't hurry up. 'Sorry, I'm keeping you.'

'It's okay but I better get going,' I told him, standing up, feeling flustered under his intense gaze. I noticed the way he appraised my body as I stood over him.

'Will I see you again?'

'I'm sorry—I really have to go.'

'Okay.' He nodded, though he showed no sign of defeat. 'Well, I'll be back on Monday, about 2 pm. I might see you then.'

'Maybe,' I shouted over my shoulder and fled.

That weekend, I tried desperately to put this sexy stranger out of my mind, but I couldn't. Every time I looked at Bastian, I was riddled with guilt, even though I technically hadn't done anything wrong, yet. He was showing interest in me, not the other way around. Although, I had flirted with my eyes, just a little. Was that enough to damn me to hell? I told myself, if he tried anything, I would make it clear that I'm married and not interested.

I realised that I always wore my wedding ring; he had noticed that, surely? But then, had I noticed a wedding ring on his finger? No. I was sure that was because he didn't wear one, though. If he knew I was married, what kind of man did that make him?

Round and round and round the thoughts went. Despite all the guilt and confusion that I felt, it was utterly thrilling.

On the Monday at 2pm, I found myself watching the clock, so distracted I was unable to type. By 2:30 I realised he wasn't coming and cursed myself for letting it affect me so. He was just a man I'd met once for five minutes; I was acting like a selfish, stupid teenager. I figured I wasn't going to get any more writing done that day, so I began packing my laptop away when Tom sat down across from me. 'Sorry I'm late,' he apologised.

'Late for what?' I shrugged. 'We didn't arrange anything.'

He fixed me with an inscrutable, intense stare and right then I knew, without a doubt, something was going to happen between us.

Nothing did for a while, though we sat together for half an hour or so a few days a week. We didn't talk about our interests, our families, our pasts or our home-lives; no, all we talked about was sex.

I can't remember how it began or where I got the guts from (and lost my morals), but that's how it was. It pains me to talk about. It still kills me to think I did that, but I felt detached, like it wasn't really happening to me. I felt like two people: Jekyll and Hyde.

I believe it began by discussing other people in our immediate surroundings; he made a smutty comment about an attractive woman and we began to judge passers-by and discussing what we thought their sex lives were like. It started as a joke, but soon, we were describing the things that *we* liked to do and what *we* dreamed of doing, though we never outright said we wanted to do them with each other, as if that makes it any better. We never touched, not once, and we spoke quietly, almost in whispers. Any nosy onlookers may have just thought we were having a very serious, private discussion. I was so careful, unable to confront the thought of what would happen if Bastian ever found out.

The final time I saw Tom, our conversation was weaving its usual twisted, sordid web, when he whispered, 'Will you follow me?'

330

'Where?' I was suddenly terrified, but also excited. I was in turmoil, my insides twisting and turning like a tangled mess of fear and anticipation.

'I know a place.' I should have stopped and thought then. If he had a place, a place he had prepared for this very thing, how many times had he prepared before with other women? But I was stupid and impulsive, swept up in the heat of the moment and the fantasy.

'Your place?'

He shook his head.

Good. Somehow, I thought, if we never knew anything about each other's real lives then this thing between us wasn't really happening, like it existed outside of reality, like the Other Place.

I nodded, picking up my laptop case and slinging my bag over my shoulder. I followed him out of the café; neither of us looked at the other and I stayed a few feet behind him so that nobody would know that we were together.

I followed him all the way to a little park on the outskirts of the city wall. We weaved between the trees and came to what appeared to be a shed. Still, I didn't see the warning signs, I refused to listen to my own conscience screaming at me; I was an actress in a film and none of this was real. It was all going to be exactly as I'd pictured it.

I stood away from him and watched as he pulled out an old key, unlocked the door and stepped inside. I looked around to check there was nobody nearby, then slipped in after him.

That night, lying beside Bastian in our bed, I cried myself to sleep. What had I done?

Fantasies are fantasies for a reason—they don't exist in reality. They don't match up with the real world. You can't lead a double life and be happy in both. There can be many different facets to a person, but you can't be two people at the same time. Eventually, something's got to give.

Tom, as soon as he'd gotten what he wanted, was cold and cruel. He pulled up his trousers, straightened his shirt and left without a word, leaving me sitting there in that dark tool shed with nothing but the spiders and moths for company. I never went back to that café and I never saw Tom again. The thought of him now makes my skin crawl.

I'd thought I was a grown adult: a woman who was successful in all areas of my life. I had a career, a husband and a life in which I was confident, adventurous and in control. Not anymore. I was a silly little girl: naïve, gullible and reckless. I was everything I'd always been terrified I was—worthless and broken.

Bastian was my heart, my soulmate, my friend and companion in life. He adored me, doted on me and with him, I felt like I could rule the world. I was safe, protected, loved and the sun shone that much brighter with him. We had our routines, our alone time, our world which existed inside a bubble where nothing could harm us. But now, it had imploded. Why? Why had I done it? What had I gotten from it?

Nothing. I had gone to that café to get out of my head, escape the four walls of home, to try and get the monster off my back but instead, I'd let it in. Things were so much worse now and the worst thing of all was the shame and the guilt, and the fear I now felt could not be relieved by confiding in my best friend. My true best friend was dead and the person who had effectively taken her place, was the very person I had betrayed. I had nobody to turn to, nowhere to go. I had hit rock bottom.

That day, I went straight home and jumped in the shower to scrub my body. I scrubbed so hard I bled. I wasn't only scrubbing any remains of another man away, I was scrubbing off my own shame, my own betrayal.

I became reclusive, incommunicative and I could barely bring myself to look at him. Of course, he sensed something was wrong straight away. He repeatedly asked me if I was okay, assuming it was just my mental health causing my mood shift. He went out of his way to try and make me happy but any show of affection or love just made me feel worse. I built a wall between us and reacted to his affection with aggression and hostility, pushing him as far away as I possibly could.

He was everything I'd ever wanted in a man and I had trodden all over him like a worthless piece of rubbish. I told myself I would never forgive myself for what I'd done to him, and I never did.

One Sunday, Bastian confronted me, finally unable to take any more of my coldness. We had a huge, blazing row, which ended in me confessing everything. I can't bring myself to write down the details of my confession. It was the most shameful, dirty, lowest point in my life. To look the person you love in the eye and tell them that you have betrayed them, in the worst possible way, to break their heart, is one of the most painful experiences I've ever been through. I'm not feeling sorry for myself; if anything, this is the exact opposite, but I have been both the heart-breaker and the heart-broken and truly, I believe to be the heart-breaker is the hardest. You feel all your own pain, but you can also feel all of theirs. Every last ounce. It's unbearable and there's absolutely nothing you can do or say to take it away from either of you. Not that I deserved to have my pain eased. I deserved to feel every part of it.

He left me. He walked straight out of our front door, slamming it behind him with tears streaming down his face. I was the lowest of the low and that first night alone, I once again contemplated ending my life. Who was I? Nobody. No-one would miss me. Once Lyanna found out what I'd done, she'd disown me. I was scum, filth. I thought back to that day at Moraine Manor, the feel of the noose around my neck. I should have done Bastian a favour and seen it through, saved him all this heartache. He, and the world, would be better off without me. Four days later, Bastian returned home to find me on the floor in a dreadful state, with Buddy whining at my side. I had not tried to kill myself and instead, I had drunk myself into oblivion and stayed in that same spot on the floor for three days, not eating, sleeping or washing; apparently only moving to feed Buddy and top up my glass. I don't remember any of it.

And, do you know what he did? After everything I'd done to him, he picked me up off the floor, put me in the bath, washed my hair then put me to bed to sleep it off. When I came around a day or so later, I found him sat on the edge of the bed, watching me. He told me to come downstairs where he'd prepared me some food. He sat and watched me as I ate, making sure I swallowed every mouthful. 'How are you feeling?' he asked, as I finished my last mouthful.

'What does it matter?' I mumbled.

'It matters a lot. What were you doing? Trying to kill yourself?'

'I don't know. Trying to block the world out, I guess.'

'What am I going to do with you?' he said with genuine affection and I fought the urge to retch. This was the hangover from hell. Why did he care about me? I didn't deserve it.

'I thought you'd gone. I thought we were over.'

'I came back for Buddy.'

His words hurt, but I deserved them. I looked down at the cute ball of fluff beside me. He looked terrified. I then felt even more guilty. How could I have neglected and scared him like that? He won't have understood what was going on. I sat down on the floor beside him and cried into his fur. 'I'm sorry, Bud. Please forgive me.'

Bastian joined us on the floor. 'How could we be over?' he asked, looking at us both. 'We tried that—it doesn't work.'

'I betrayed you!'

'Yes, you did.' He was suddenly stern. 'Don't think I've gotten over it, not by any stretch of the imagination. I'm fuming, frankly, but the truth is, I know you. I know your mind. I know that darkness inside you takes over and you can't help yourself sometimes.'

'Don't make excuses for me.'

'I'm not, Sara, it's true. Somewhere inside you is a lost little girl who has no idea who she is or what she wants or what she's doing.'

'Stop it! I need punishing, not mollycoddling! Why are you being so understanding?' I yelled. Buddy nudged my knee with his nose. I looked down into his deep, brown eyes and my chest tightened with grief.

Bastian sighed. 'Because I love you, you arsehole! I'd do anything for you. I won't let you ruin your life, or mine. I won't let you tear apart our marriage. That's not your choice to make. I meant it, you know, in sickness and in health, and this is your sickness. It may not be something we can see, but it's there alright.' He paused. 'How did you feel, afterwards?'

My eyes widened. I didn't want to talk about it, especially with him. I couldn't bear it. Bugs crawled all over my skin and wriggled inside my brain. 'Tell me,' he insisted.

'Disgusted with myself. Guilty, sorry, heartbroken, angry, dirty; you name it, I felt it.'

'And, after I left, you drank your bodyweight in vodka and sat there like a pitiful, lifeless creature on the floor.'

I nodded, thoroughly ashamed. 'And, before that, all your life, you've struggled with intimacy, with relationships, with being close to someone. You've struggled with your family, with your mind, with the death of two of the most important people in your life and most of all, with yourself. I think that's enough punishment. I don't want to inflict any more pain on you. I just want you to be happy.'

I sobbed then. He truly was my guardian angel. How could he see all that? How could he love me, darkness and all?

'The first time we broke up, it wasn't your fault. Your best friend died; you were grieving. This time, you hurt me, really fucking hurt me. There are no second chances. I've forgiven you. It took a great deal of courage and a lot of ranting at Max and, admittedly, a lot of whisky, but I've forgiven you. I want to make this work. But,' he repeated, 'there are no second chances, do you understand me, Sara?'

'Yes! Yes. Of course I do. I am so, so sorry. I will never, ever hurt you again. Losing you nearly killed me. I will never risk losing what we have for anything. Nothing is worth that.'

'I need to ask you one thing before we move on.'

'Anything.'

'Do you have feelings for him?'

'No. None. I never did. In fact, I hate him. I hate him so much. I'm so sorry,' I said, over and over again.

Bastian slid over to me and put his arm around me. 'Ssh, I don't want to hear any more about it. I want to forget this whole horrific part of our life. I want to pretend it never happened. Stop apologising now, wipe your tears and go get dressed.'

*****

I expected things to be weird between us, for him to be stand-offish, untrusting, but he wasn't, not ever. It took some time but eventually, things went back to exactly how they were before.

The thing is with Bastian, he is resilient and strong and pragmatic. Some people might think that he was too easy on me, maybe even that he was cowardly for forgiving me so easily, but what he did was unbelievably strong and brave. To forgive someone when they've hurt you takes a remarkable amount of courage and I truly respected him for that. He was steadfast in his loyalty and his beliefs; he let them guide him through life and never allowed his judgment to be swayed. He made his own decisions and he stuck to them ardently.

I don't think I could have done that; I don't think I'm comfortable enough in myself to be able to. To look at a situation objectively when you're so emotionally involved is difficult. To have the ability to do that is almost a superpower. But then, he was a self-assured, confident person and I loved every bone in his body. I knew that I would never jeopardise our love ever again. If anything, that awful period made us stronger. Our spark reignited, not that it had ever dwindled for him, and we were tighter than ever. We lived happily ever after. Sort of.

Chapter Forty-Four

The little worm was wriggling around inside my brain, again. For some reason, every part of me was screaming to go back. The Other Place was calling me once again.

Over our meal one evening, I broached the subject with Bastian. 'I think I might have to go back to the Other Place,' I told him out of the blue.

He almost choked on his salmon. 'Where did that come from?'

'It's been playing on my mind for a while,' I admitted.

'Do you know why?'

'No. I really don't.'

'Then you have to go.'

We didn't discuss it any further that night, or the next, but the day after that, I decided that it was time. It was an emotional goodbye, with both him and Buddy. I left them in his studio, the daylight pouring in, leaving a lasting impression of his handsome face on my sight.

While I'd been away, the Other Place had sprung back to life. From the moment I set foot on dry land, I saw all kinds of peoples and beings and creatures, like it was the spring of life following the dead of winter. Desolate lands had given birth to rich, vibrant wildlife. The waterfalls and rivers flowed once more and a fresh breeze blew through the land, awakening all it touched.

The landscape no longer felt confusing or arduous; I knew all that it contained. I felt as though I'd touched every rock, trodden every path, climbed every mountain. It was another home, greeting me like an old friend and letting me pass through with courage and ease.

I met my mother again and this time, she welcomed me with open arms. I spent time with her and her people, though this time, we bonded, and I enjoyed their company. My mother would never be to me what Lyanna was, but I finally felt like I could move on, forgive her, even understand her.

I asked her what had happened to them the last time I had visited but none of them had any recollection of that period. It was an empty void in their memories where all things had ceased to exist. All they knew was they were alive and they were all the more grateful for it.

I was full of energy, hope and renewed vigour as I left them and passed on through the land. My departure didn't weigh so heavily on us the second time around; I felt certain that we had closed that chapter, that we had said all we needed to say and that it was time to look forward, not behind.

Not everywhere was thriving. Here and there, I saw forests still half-dead, burnt out cottages and frozen lakes that were yet to thaw after the cold, hard winter of nothingness, all waiting for life to be breathed back into them.

As I passed through villages and communities, I also heard many stories of the witch. I had encountered her on my first venture into the Other Place, though I hadn't heard or seen anything more of her. For that, I was glad but now, hearing of her comings and goings, her seemingly needless acts of violence, I felt uneasy. Alone, travelling through the realm, I was a vulnerable, easy target. There was no-one willing to be my guide or protector this time, so I had no choice but to continue on alone. I made sure I kept my wits about me and a knife within easy reach, though I wasn't sure if such a thing would be of any use against a supernatural being. Nonetheless, it comforted me.

I arrived at Thane's village, or where it had once stood, yet still none were to be found there. It seemed they had been erased from the Other Place entirely. I wondered why; had it anything to do with Thane's doppelganger living in the real world? While Bastian was in my life back home, was Thane unable to exist here? But then, the last time I had been in the Other Place, Bastian and I were no longer together. It seemed some mysteries would never be solved.

Once again, I came to the great, black hole. It didn't appear to have grown any larger but it hadn't shrunk either. It remained there, ever dense, ever dark and ever magnetic. Part of me wanted to take a closer look, to try and understand what it was, to touch it, but the thought of never returning from that place and never seeing Bastian again was more than I could bear.

I missed Bastian terribly. I longed for his comforting touch and interesting conversation. I wished, more than anything, for him to be there with me and I realised, I wanted to go home.

I had no more need of that place. It didn't offer me anything and there was nothing that I wanted from it. I wondered why it had called to me so powerfully, when all it had shown me was life continuing as it had before. There were no revelations, no answers to be found. I worried it had been a huge waste of time going there, but maybe it was just something I needed to get out of my system? Some kind of closure.

I came to the forest where I had met Eavan and part of me hoped I would see him again; the memory of his presence heartened me.

It was quiet within the walls of the forest, spookily quiet. Every snapping twig and creaking tree trunk jarred me. My eyes scanned my surroundings tensely, my body rigid and ready to react. Then I felt it: her presence. I could feel sinister eyes surveying me and my step quickened. I heard her voice inside my head, willing me to follow it, luring me into her trap. My body responded as though under a spell and my feet took me from my path. I urged them to stop, to turn back, but she was too powerful. Where would I be taken? What was going to happen to me?

I heard voices behind me, but my head wouldn't turn to see who was speaking. Then, the spell appeared to break and my limbs were back under my control. I stopped, terrified, unsure whether to turn back or stay where I was.

From behind me, a familiar voice. 'Don't worry; she's gone,' Eavan assured me.

I turned, never before so glad to see a friendly face. 'Eavan?'

'Hello, Sara,' he chuckled. 'We meet again.'

'What happened?'

'The witch was trying to lure you into her lair, and I doubt her motives were innocent.'

'Is she gone?'

'No, not by a long shot, but she has let us be, for now.'

'Thank you,' I gasped. I took a moment to steady myself while Eavan gazed on patiently. 'What does she want?' I huffed.

'Nobody knows.'

'Where did she come from?'

'Nobody knows. Where does anybody come from? Why do any of us do the things we do?'

'Do you mind if I sit?' I enquired, my legs buckling. It had only been a few moments of terror, but I had truly feared for my life.

'Be my guest.' Eavan took a seat beside me, crossing his legs beneath him. He seemed incredibly flexible for one so ancient.

338

Through the trees, I saw two pale figures. I froze. 'Don't worry. They're your friends.' He smiled.

I looked closer and recognised the first to be the faerie who had guided me on my very first journey to the Other Place. My shoulders relaxed. The figure faded then vanished, leaving only the other. I squinted, trying to work out who the second figure was. 'What are you searching for, Wanderer?' Eavan asked softly.

'What do you mean?'

'Why do you keep coming back?'

'It calls to me. I can't explain it.'

'Do you know why?'

I shook my head. 'Could it be that you're trying to understand it?'

'Well, yeah, of course I am. I've been plagued by this place all my life and I still don't know what it is or why I have the ability to see it.'

'You don't?'

My stomach clenched. His tone suggested that he did. Could he give me the answers I'd been searching for? 'No,' I responded.

'One can never know the whole story. No matter how much you read, listen, learn, you'll never have all the answers. Every life, every action, impacts another, in an endless chain of events. We are all connected to each other, each a small chapter in one never-ending story. You may never find all the answers to your questions, or to any questions in life, no matter how big or small. The real challenge is coming to terms with that. Searching for answers to questions that cannot be answered is the road to madness. Can you accept that you may never know?'

I meditated on this a while and when I looked up to answer him, he was gone.

I sat and contemplated all that Eavan had said. Lost in my thoughts, I didn't see the figure approaching. When I looked up, she was standing over me, her dark form in stark contrast to the ghostly, pale mist that shrouded the forest. She held her hand out to me and I took it. The light grew brighter and the trees sparser. The trees ended abruptly and we exited the forest into the harsh light of the day. We were stood upon the top of a great, white cliff, looking out over a field dashed red with poppies. Beyond, I could see the Veil, cloaked in a fog too dark to penetrate and further still, as far as my eyes would allow me to see, lay the Pool of Infinity, like a shard of mirror-glass laying between the cracks of the earth.

The mist inside my head cleared and I turned to view the woman who had led me there. It was the witch. Her violet eyes bore into me and pierced my heart, but her face was familiar. First, it was the face of the woman from the painting at the Manor, then it was my face, my own eyes looking back at me, my own mouth smiling at me. It wasn't just my face, it was also the faerie who had no name, my mother, Myla, Serafina—they all stared back at me.

When she spoke, I heard all their voices simultaneously, like an angelic chorus of familiarity. 'Don't you understand it yet?' they asked me.

'Understand what?'

'This, the Other Place, all of it.'

I shook my head. 'Should I?'

'This is death.'

I looked on dumbly. 'This is not heaven or an afterlife; this is death. It's not where the body goes, or even the mind, but where the spirit goes.'

Still, I didn't know what to say. 'Do you remember what I said to you, the first time I saw you here?' It was my mother now, only my mother.

I shook my head. 'I told you that just because it exists in your mind, it doesn't mean that it's not real, as it's real to you.'

'Are you telling me that this is all in my head?' I felt sick, displaced, like I was having an out-of-body experience. I had spent so many years telling myself it was real, telling everybody else it was real, I'd stopped doubting that it was. But did I have any proof? Besides the strange things that had happened to Bastian and me at Moraine Manor, nobody I knew had ever seen anything with their own eyes. A booming sound echoed across the land and the ground shook beneath my feet as a huge piece of the cliff broke away and fell down to the ground far below. 'You're not listening to what I'm saying. If it exists in your mind, then it still exists.'

'But it's not real,' I wept. The ground continued to shake.

'Death is real and the experience of it is personal to everyone. Some people believe in reincarnation, some in heaven. This is just your version.'

'But I'm not dead! Why can I see this place when I'm alive?'

'Some people are closer to death than others.'

'What does that even mean?'

'We're special, our family, especially you and me. Our minds are wired differently. We see the world differently, we see it how it really is. We see beneath the Veil. We know what matters and what doesn't, we know our place

340

in the universe, we feel things deeper than others. That opens us up to things that other people couldn't even imagine.'

'Why?'

My mother sighed and more of the cliff wall crumbled, the edge slowly creeping closer to us. 'I think, deep down, you know why. Search inside and you'll find all the answers you've been looking for. You know why you've been visiting the Other Place, you know why you have this connection to it and, most importantly, you know why Moraine Manor is at the centre of it all.'

'Do I?' I wracked my brain, but I could no more think of an answer to it all than I could solve the most complex mathematical equations.

My mother merely nodded and explained no more. 'You have a gift,' she said.

'A curse, you mean.'

She frowned. 'I'm not a scientist, or a spiritualist or even a priest. I'm only telling you what I do know; you don't have the ability to walk between worlds, you have the ability to walk between life and death. Why do you think these places can't exist alongside each other? Because it's impossible to be both. I didn't stay here because I was afraid to return, I stayed here because I had to. Because I'm no longer one of the living.'

'Why didn't you tell me all of this?'

'Because I couldn't, not until you were ready.'

None of this made any sense to me. I didn't know what to believe. 'Are you really my mother?'

'Yes and no. If you try to touch me, your hand will only meet air. I am a projection.' Her face shimmered and I saw them all again. Serafina and Myla now stood before me. A tear escaped and rolled silently down my cheek. The earth was violently quaking beneath my feet, the noise deafening.

'Don't cry,' Myla spoke in her calm, soothing voice, drowning out all the noise. 'I miss you too.' She reached out and took my hand. The ground collapsed beneath our feet, turning into nothing but broken trees, churned earth and dust far below, but we stayed high up above.

My stomach lurched as my feet felt nothing but air below them, yet I found that I wasn't scared: I trusted Myla completely. The world opened up and I felt the breeze in my hair and on my skin, caressing me and comforting me. Down, down, down we flew, until our feet touched the earth once more. 'It's time for you to go home,' she told me and was gone.

On my journey to the Pool, the feeling of elation I'd felt flying through the air evaporated rapidly and I felt muddled and tired. I didn't know what to think. I'd returned to the Other Place for closure but had, in fact, ended up with more questions. Would this vicious cycle ever end?

What had my mother meant? Did I hold all the answers? I tried to search for clues in all that I'd seen and experienced but still nothing occurred to me. Why couldn't she have just told me? Put me out of my misery? But then, if she truly was just my mind's projection, surely she could give me no more answers than my own mind could? The answers were hidden within me, deep inside me somewhere; the question was, how could I unlock them?

It wasn't until I arrived back in Moraine that I finally understood. The realisation hit me full force, so hard that I almost passed out. How could I not have seen it sooner? It all washed over me like a wave of truth and clarity; who the faerie was, why she had led me to the Other Place, why I saw the woman in the painting from the Manor as an evil witch, why I was drawn to the Manor itself and why it seemed to hold so many ghosts. My mother—it all stemmed from my mother and her disappearance. Not her disappearance, but how she'd died.

Death had followed me all my life. Now it was time for me to live.

The Other Place was neither good nor bad but a mixture of both, like there is in everything. Humans, and the world we occupy, are a balance of dark and light. There are no clear-cut, defined answers to anything, there are only the choices we make and the way we deal with the consequences of our actions.

I felt calm back in my home with my feet planted firmly on the ground, my head no longer in the clouds. It would take time to come to terms with all that I had learnt, but that was okay. I would get there in my own time and on my own terms.

*****

I arrived home on a Tuesday afternoon. Bastian was precisely where I had last seen him: in his studio, bent over his prints and studying them intently, with Buddy by his side. 'Hey, gorgeous,' I said from the doorway.

'Hey!' he exclaimed, jumping up and rushing over to embrace me.

We held each other for a while, breathing in each other's scent and finding comfort in the familiar shape our bodies made when interlocked. 'How long was I gone?'

'Ten days, and I missed you every second.'

'It was so hard without you. I've missed you so much.' I kissed him gently.

'Did you at least find what you were looking for?'

'I think I did.' I smiled. 'I think I might never have to go back.'

'Really?' he questioned, looking relieved and hopeful.

I nodded. 'That's amazing. I hope this can be a fresh start for you.'

'Me too, for both of us.'

Everything I'd ever wanted was right there: a man who loved me truly, a strong, unbreakable marriage, a job I loved that allowed me creative and financial freedom, and the ability to travel and learn and explore. Our life together was perfect, well, as perfect as any relationship can be. Nobody's truly perfect. We still got on each other's nerves sometimes, fought on occasion and disagreed, but that was all part of the beauty of it. To love someone because of their flaws, rather than in spite of them, is the truest love of all.

I'd had all these things for a long time, but it was only now that I was truly grateful for them, able to let my demons sleep and allow myself to revel in my own happiness.

Sometimes, it's okay to feel, but not act upon, human emotion. To just accept that that is the way you feel. Anger, sadness, agitation, jealousy, all the 'negative' emotions; they're natural. You're supposed to feel that way, as much as you're supposed to feel happy. Emotion is what makes us human. Once you accept that and reach a state of self-awareness, life becomes so much easier to live. If there's one thing I've learned in this life, is to stop beating yourself up about things that are out of your control; feel them, deeply, dwell on them even, then let them out, take a deep breath and move on.

There are some emotions that are fleeting, that feel utterly devastating for a small period of time, then disappear into the ether like they never existed, and there are some that you will carry with you every moment of your life, like a dull ache in the back of your head, but any emotion can become easier to deal with once you accept that they just are. Don't suppress them or try to change them, just learn to live with them like a scar.

One day, you'll have lots of scars—some faded, some deep, some you'll remember how you got them like it was yesterday and some you won't have a clue about—but all of them make up you and your life story—your history. Remember, you're a deeply complex, emotional human being and you're not alone. There are billions of us, and we all think and feel and make mistakes and hurt each other and love each other. In an age of connection, we're all so incredibly disconnected, but we need to remember that we're all navigating the wilderness of life, trying to find a quiet place.

I don't regret anything that happened in my life; anything awful that happened to me, or that I'd done to others, shaped me as a person and helped me grow.

We all must face pain and grief and difficult decisions. It's easy to give up and stop trying, but it takes great strength of character to use your experience, no matter how traumatic and let it shape you into a better version of yourself.

All the trials I faced and all my forays into the Other Place had, if nothing else, given me a greater understanding of myself and the universe I inhabited. Self-awareness is a beautiful thing. It doesn't always make you a 'good' person, but once you understand your flaws and knowledge gaps, you can make better choices and accept that things are sometimes out of your control.

I finally found my quiet place. It's the place of acceptance; of myself, the world and everyone around me. I am what I am, you are what you are and the world is what the world is.

Comfort and happiness in my life allowed me to come to terms with who I am—the good and the bad—and everything else then fell into place. I no longer dwelled on the things I couldn't change, in myself and in others, or laid awake worrying about things that had already happened or may happen. The world is full of peril and sometimes, it's better to just let things go than get dragged down with it.

I realised I'd spent most of my life in pursuit of a fantasy instead of living the life I already had. Now, I wanted to focus on my future with Bastian.

Chapter Forty-Five

My twenties had been a time of uncertainty, a time when I was unsure who I was, where I was going or who I wanted to be. My body no longer loved me the way it used to; I had to be more aware of what I was putting in my body and none of my clothes ever seemed to fit right. I was constantly trying to mould myself to the views of others—acting how I thought I should rather than how I wanted to be. My work took the hardest knock because of this. Some of my worst ever work was created in my twenties because I wasn't writing what I wanted to write, but what I thought others would want to read. It all sounded so forced and confused, lacking in truth and substance.

My thirties were mildly better; I felt sure of myself mostly, yet I still had crippling moments of self-doubt, especially in my work. Even as an accomplished writer, I still felt like a fraud. Who was I—weird, screwed-up, confused me—to tell people what they should be reading and discuss big life themes when my own life was so messy? I expected, at any moment, for someone to pull me up on it: my agent, a reader, a critic. *I can see right through you,* they'd say. *You don't know what you're doing and you're not fooling anyone.*

My forties are when I really came into my own. This was the decade when I came to terms with how I looked, what I liked and what I wanted. I wasn't afraid to ask for it, to challenge what I was told and form my own opinions. The world had changed so much since I had been born and I had been forced to grow and change with it, only I didn't. I didn't want to conform to society, I didn't want a social media account, I didn't want to take pictures of myself or broadcast my troubles on a public platform. I didn't want to be fluent with technology or be a part of that world, and I was steadfast in my beliefs. I didn't want to become a self-absorbed zombie who was shovel-fed fake news. I wanted my life to be rich, not in material goods or money, but in experience and knowledge. So, I continued to read my books in paper-form and listen to music on vinyl and view the world through my own eyes instead of through a screen or a projection of what I thought other people's eyes would see.

My fifties, well, I never lived to see them. I died at the young age of forty-nine, still with so many things I wanted to do, so much more time I wanted to spend with Bastian and my aunt, so many places I wanted to see and so many stories I wanted to tell.

I was walking across the hill on the outskirts of town with Buddy, looking down on the moonlit valley below. Nestled amongst the trees at the bottom of the bowl, I could see Moraine Manor, a ghostly, pale square among the dark wilderness, and further away, I could see the village—my village, my home. It was deep dusk; I could see lights twinkling, slowly igniting in the face of the approaching darkness.

As I walked, the autumnal wind blew. It whistled through the branches of the trees and soared overhead. On the wind carried the sound of a billion voices, the vibration of a billion heartbeats and the memory of all, dead and alive.

The wind can't be seen or held or kept but it was both mine and everyone else's. It swept over the land, person to person, place to place, far and wide, but here it rested long enough for me to hear the whispers of lives lived and lost and the echoes of past and present.

I often went for long walks with Buddy, sometimes just the two of us if Bastian's attention was captured by a project. This was one of those times. I liked to be surrounded by nature, with time to reflect and ponder. It was a tool I used to keep my mind quiet. Despite the revelations of my last visit to the Other Place, I had come to terms with the fact that that darkness would always be a part of me and it would never be entirely vanquished. The only thing I could do was take small steps to keep it at bay, like taking time for myself and being amongst nature. As Myla had once told me, in slightly different words, it's these seemingly small acts that bring us joy and peace.

Headlights shone around the bend in the road ahead, so I stepped as far off the road as possible without tumbling over the side of the hill. I pulled Buddy gently behind me by his lead. I remember the screech of brakes and seeing swerving lights in the creeping dark. I decided to jump down the embankment to get out of the way of the out-of-control vehicle, but I was too late. The car hit me and I was thrown several metres, where I hit a tree and thumped heavily to the ground, my body broken.

I felt a warm form shaking beside me and I realised it was Buddy. He was dying too. I was glad he was there by my side, in it together until the bitter end, though my heart ached to know that he was suffering and I couldn't comfort him. I hoped he could hear my thoughts and feel glad, as I did, that we were departing this world side by side.

In my final moments, I thought of Bastian. I wanted him there next to me, more than anything. I missed him and I grieved to know I would never lay eyes on him again, never hear his voice, smell his scent or feel his skin on mine. I was sorry that he would have to mourn my passing alone. I wished that I could comfort him and yet, I hoped that he would, eventually, continue living and enjoying his life without me and in that way, he would keep me alive.

I was glad in the knowledge that Lyanna had found peace and love with Chris. I missed her incredibly and I hoped that Chris would look after her and help her through her sadness. I knew that he would; he loved the bones of her, just as she deserved.

I remembered all the beautiful things we'd all done together, the amazing places I'd been and the moments I'd shared with Bastian, Lyanna, Myla and Sef. All the memories that passed through my mind were those that I'd created with others. In life, the only experiences that matter are the ones we share with other people.

Life is a gift. Sometimes, it can feel like a curse, but it is a gift and I truly believe that. The best way to celebrate that gift is with those who inspire us, who love us and with whom we have a connection.

I should have seen life as a journey, not a destination. Instead of focussing on where I wanted to go, who I wanted to be, I should have paused to think: *What am I doing right now? What do I like about this moment?*

I grieved everything I would miss, the memories that I wouldn't make. All this passed through my mind in mere seconds as the life leaked out of me.

There was no feeling of calm or acceptance as I died. I didn't have an epiphany, no realisation that this was how it was meant to be. It shouldn't have been my time to go and I tried to fight for my right to live. I didn't want to die; not many people do, especially so young. I was heartbroken that this was the end for me—the final curtain. Gone, like that, in mere minutes. All my hopes and goals extinguished. My final thought was, S*hit, this is it*, and I breathed my last breath.

Life has a gap that you don't always need to fill. Sometimes, you will feel depressed or anxious or empty or restless for no apparent reason. Don't try to fill it up, just learn to accept it and it will pass.

No story really has an end. As Eavan once told me, we are all a small part of one never-ending story. Everything is connected to everything else. Our lives are just a series of moments leading up to one big one. Make every second count.

*****

I looked out over the field. The meadow was glowing golden, the sunlight reflecting off the grass as it rippled in the breeze. The black hole lay before me, overbearing, oversized and ominous, as it always had been. That was my path.

As I walked towards it, the darkness within it faded, lightening ever so slowly. When I finally reached it, it was no longer a black mass but a white orb, dazzlingly bright and beautiful. The faerie with no name, whom I had met so many years ago when I was a child, appeared before me and took my hand. She smiled warmly at me and I followed her into the light.